OXFORD WORLD'S

THE VAMPYRE
AND OTHER TALES OF
THE MACABRE

JOHN WILLIAM POLIDORI (1795–1821) was the oldest son of a distinguished Italian scholar and translator. He was educated at Ampleforth, a Catholic college near York, and later at the University of Edinburgh, where he wrote a thesis on somnambulism and received his medical degree at the unusually early age of 19. In April 1816 Polidori became Lord Byron's personal physician and travelling companion, and was commissioned by Byron's publisher John Murray to keep a journal of his time with Byron that was later published as his *Diary* (1911). Polidori was present at the famous ghost story competition at the Villa Diodati on Lake Geneva that was the genesis of Mary Shelley's *Frankenstein* (1818), Byron's prose fragment 'Augustus Darvell' (1819), and his own tale, *The Vampyre*, which he based on Byron's fragment, and which he completed in late summer 1816, just before he and Byron parted company. Polidori travelled extensively in Italy before returning to England in spring 1817, where he settled in Norwich and established a medical practice. *The Vampyre* was first published in the *New Monthly Magazine* in April 1819, and later that same year Polidori published his only full-length novel, *Ernestus Berchtold; or, The Modern Oedipus. The Fall of the Angels: A Sacred Poem* appeared two years later, but by this time Polidori was in debt and deeply disappointed in his career as physician and writer. He committed suicide in his father's house in August 1821.

Thirteen other authors are represented in this volume as contributors to macabre magazine fiction in the period 1819–38. These include Edward Bulwer, James Hogg, Letitia Landon, and J. Sheridan Le Fanu. Details of their lives appear in the Biographical Notes.

ROBERT MORRISON is Professor of English Literature at Queen's University, Kingston, Ontario. He has edited De Quincey's *On Murder* and co-edited, with Chris Baldick, *Tales of Terror from Blackwood's Magazine* for Oxford World's Classics.

CHRIS BALDICK is Professor of English at Goldsmiths' College, University of London. He has edited *The Oxford Book of Gothic Tales* (1992), and is the author of *In Frankenstein's Shadow* (1987), *Criticism and Literary Theory 1890 to the Present* (1996), and other works of literary history.

OXFORD WORLD'S CLASSICS

*For over 100 years Oxford World's Classics have brought
readers closer to the world's great literature. Now with over 700
titles—from the 4,000-year-old myths of Mesopotamia to the
twentieth century's greatest novels—the series makes available
lesser-known as well as celebrated writing.*

*The pocket-sized hardbacks of the early years contained
introductions by Virginia Woolf, T. S. Eliot, Graham Greene,
and other literary figures which enriched the experience of reading.
Today the series is recognized for its fine scholarship and
reliability in texts that span world literature, drama and poetry,
religion, philosophy and politics. Each edition includes perceptive
commentary and essential background information to meet the
changing needs of readers.*

OXFORD WORLD'S CLASSICS

▬▬

JOHN POLIDORI

The Vampyre
and Other Tales of the Macabre

▬▬

Edited with an Introduction and Notes by
ROBERT MORRISON
and
CHRIS BALDICK

OXFORD
UNIVERSITY PRESS

OXFORD
UNIVERSITY PRESS

Great Clarendon Street, Oxford OX2 6DP

Oxford University Press is a department of the University of Oxford.
It furthers the University's objective of excellence in research, scholarship,
and education by publishing worldwide in

Oxford New York

Auckland Cape Town Dar es Salaam Hong Kong Karachi
Kuala Lumpur Madrid Melbourne Mexico City Nairobi
New Delhi Shanghai Taipei Toronto

With offices in

Argentina Austria Brazil Chile Czech Republic France Greece
Guatemala Hungary Italy Japan Poland Portugal Singapore
South Korea Switzerland Thailand Turkey Ukraine Vietnam

Oxford is a registered trade mark of Oxford University Press
in the UK and in certain other countries

Published in the United States
by Oxford University Press Inc., New York

Editorial matter © Robert Morrison and Chris Baldick 1997

First published as a World's Classics paperback 1997
Reissued as an Oxford World's Classics paperback 1998
Reissued 2008

British Library Cataloguing in Publication Data

Data available

Library of Congress Cataloging in Publication Data

The vampyre and other tales of the macabre / edited with an
introduction by Robert Morrison and Chris Baldick.
(Oxford world's classics)
Includes bibliographical references.
1. Horror tales, English. 2. Vampires—Fiction. I. Morrison,
Robert, 1961– . II. Baldick, Chris. III. Series.
PR1309.H6V36 1997 823'.0873808375–dc21 97–915

ISBN 978–0–19–955241–2

3

Printed in Great Britain by
Clays Ltd, St Ives plc

CONTENTS

ACKNOWLEDGEMENTS

WE would like to thank the following people for their help with the production of this book: Lindsay Bell, Peter Bell, Gerard Collins, Giselle Corbeil, Jane Desmarais, Maud Ellmann, Michael Fitzgerald, Ann Hennigar, Gillis Harp, Barbara Harp, Graham Hogg, Colin Jones, Larry Krupp, D. L. Macdonald, Andrew MacRae, Bill McCormack, Murdina McRae, Dale Miller, Carole Morrison, Sue Rauth, Ruth Richardson, Debbie Seary, Ralph Stewart, Darlene Sweet, Jennifer Taylor, and Beert Verstraete. We would also like to thank the staffs of the Acadia University Library, the Cambridge University Library, the Widener Library, Harvard, as well as the Social Sciences and Humanities Research Council of Canada for their generous research grant.

INTRODUCTION

In the autumn of 1818 the London *New Monthly Magazine* came into possession of a package of documents that was certain to cause a literary sensation. It contained not just a letter retailing a few precious nuggets of gossip about the exploits of Byron and Shelley during their sojourn by Lake Geneva in the summer of 1816, but also what appeared to be an original prose story composed by Lord Byron himself, at this time the most famous living writer in the world. Better still, this prose tale, entitled *The Vampyre*, seemed to follow the pattern of Byron's best-known poetical productions—*Childe Harold's Pilgrimage* (1812–18) and *Manfred* (1817)—by incorporating a strong element of confessional self-portraiture, but this time treating the familiar figure of the accursed outlaw in even more lurid terms as a bloodsucking demon or 'vampyre' with the tell-tale name of Lord Ruthven—clearly an echo of another recent fictional portrayal of Byron as Clarence de Ruthven, Lord Glenarvon in the novel *Glenarvon* (1816) by Lady Caroline Lamb, Byron's cast-off mistress. The story seemed, then, to have Byron written all over it, lacking only the authentication of his signature.

To the *New Monthly*'s proprietor, Henry Colburn, disappointed by sluggish sales of his magazine, and alarmed at the great success of its new Scottish rival, *Blackwood's Magazine*, the package from Geneva came as a godsend. He set his staff to work in preparation for the coming literary coup, commissioning an explanatory introduction that could illuminate for a readership still largely unfamiliar with vampire-lore the nature and literary lineage of the curious body of East European folk beliefs embodied in *The Vampyre*. The prefatory account of 'this singularly horrible superstition' was probably written by Colburn's sub-editor Alaric Watts, who also prepared an editorial statement to appear above the 'Letter from Geneva' and the other preliminary materials, noting cautiously that

The tale which accompanied the letter we also present to our readers, without pledging ourselves positively for its authenticity, as the production of Lord Byron. We may, however, observe, that it bears strong internal evidence of having been conceived by him; though from the occasional inaccuracies, probably the result of haste, which occur throughout the whole, we should suppose it to have been committed to paper rather from the recital of a third person, than under the immediate direction of its noble author.[1]

Watts hereby discharged his journalistic duty with honour; but the less scrupulous Colburn, eager to seize the opportunity for greatly enlarged sales, was having none of this hesitation. He struck out the above passage, and saw to it that *The Vampyre* was announced forthrightly as 'A TALE BY LORD BYRON' when it appeared, appropriately, on April Fool's Day, 1819.

Colburn's commercial instincts were fully justified: *The Vampyre*, widely credited as Byron's latest masterpiece, not only launched a vampire craze that still shows no sign of subsiding, but also helped to put the *New Monthly* itself back on the road to success, making it the natural repository of macabre short stories for the next twenty years. Alaric Watts, however, who resigned in protest at his employer's unprincipled interference, was proved right in his hunch that Byron had 'conceived' the story but not himself written it. Byron quickly let it be known that he was the author not of *The Vampyre* but of an unfinished tale called 'Augustus Darvell', which his publisher subsequently printed as an appendix to the poet's *Mazeppa* (1819) in order to illustrate the difference between his prose fragment and the piece published falsely under his name in the *New Monthly*. Meanwhile, the true author declared himself: it was John William Polidori, a young doctor who had, against his parents' advice, accompanied Byron in 1816 to Switzerland as his paid travelling companion, personal physician, and amanuensis, staying with him at the Villa Diodati at Cologny, near Geneva, before being dismissed from his lordship's service later in the year.

[1] Cited in D. L. Macdonald, *Poor Polidori: A Critical Biography of the Author of The Vampyre* (Toronto, 1991), 178.

While Byron and Polidori were at the Villa Diodati, they were joined in June 1816 by a new party of sexual and literary outlaws, comprising Byron's most recent mistress, the 18-year-old Jane 'Claire' Clairmont, who had conceived a child by the poet (a daughter, Allegra, was born in January 1817); her step-sister, Mary Wollstonecraft Godwin, also 18 years of age; the poet Percy Bysshe Shelley, who had abandoned his wife and child to elope with Mary two years earlier; and their illegitimate infant son William. The Shelley entourage took up residence at the nearby Maison Chappuis, but regularly interrupted Byron's composition of the third Canto of *Childe Harold's Pilgrimage* by walking up to the Villa for literary, philosophical, and other entertainments, which other English tourists in the neighbourhood assumed to be diabolical orgies. As the *New Monthly*'s 'Letter from Geneva' later disclosed—and it was the first public document to identify the persons involved—the five English tourists had amused themselves rather less strenuously by reading some German ghost stories and had then challenged each other to compose similar tales of supernatural terror. This legendary competition elicited from Byron himself the 'Augustus Darvell' fragment, in which a mysterious gentleman touring the ruins of Ephesus arranges for the fact of his impending death to be concealed by his travelling companion. Of the other competitors, Claire Clairmont and Percy Shelley defaulted, while Polidori began his only novel, *Ernestus Berchtold; or, The Modern Oedipus* (1819), and Mary Godwin—soon to become the second Mrs Shelley after the suicide of the poet's first wife, Harriet, later in 1816—embarked upon the composition of *Frankenstein; or, The Modern Prometheus*, which was published anonymously, and with only the vaguest reference to the ghost-story contest, in 1818. Mary Shelley's own fuller account of this competition did not appear until the third edition of *Frankenstein* was published in 1831, by which time Byron, Percy Shelley, and 'Poor Polidori', as she called him in the new Introduction to her novel, were all dead. As for *The Vampyre* itself, it was, as Polidori explained in a note attached to the Introduction of his *Ernestus Berchtold*, composed by him with some knowledge of Byron's intended conclusion of 'Augustus Darvell', and in response to a challenge from an unnamed lady who doubted that the fragment could be developed into a plausible story at all. Polidori seems to have left the manuscript of *The Vampyre* behind him when he left Switzerland in the autumn of 1816, and how it reached the offices of the *New Monthly* in London two years later remains a mystery. Behind it lies some unknown scavenger of Byroniana, whose unwholesome curiosity led him or her to interrogate the servants in and around the Villa Diodati, with momentous results.

The principal documents in this tangled case—the 'Letter from Geneva' with its accompanying editorial notes, Byron's 'Augustus Darvell' fragment, and Polidori's explanatory note from the Introduction to his novel—are provided here as appendices to the present volume.

Colburn's conveniently misleading attribution of *The Vampyre* to Byron was corrected, then, both by the imputed and by the true author; but by this time few readers were willing to bother about the exact details of the tale's composition. Whether or not the celebrated poet was willing to put his name to the piece, it was clearly 'Byronic' in conception, and could thus be greeted as a product of his genius, even as the greatest of his works—a critical view held by Goethe among others. After its magazine début, the story was published in book form, running through seven English printings in 1819 alone. It was quickly adapted for the stage, in J. R. Planché's *The Vampyre* (1820) and other versions; in France it was expanded into a two-volume novel by Cyprien Bérard as *Lord Ruthwen ou les vampires* (1820); and by 1830 it had been translated into German, Italian, Spanish, and Swedish. The story had made an indelible impression on the imagination of Europe, and Polidori had succeeded, however inadvertently, in founding the entire modern tradition of vampire fiction. Not only was his tale the first sustained fictional treatment of vampirism in English, it also completely recast the mythology upon which it drew.

There had indeed been earlier appearances of vampires in English literature, as the editorial commentary of the *New*

Monthly helpfully acknowledged: Robert Southey's poem *Thalaba the Destroyer* (1801), Byron's own poem *The Giaour* (1813), and Samuel Taylor Coleridge's more celebrated *Christabel* (1816) had all fleetingly introduced vampiric figures or direct references to vampiric folklore. These three poets, all of them champions of the new Romantic movement, were engaged, along with many other writers of their generation, in the imaginative exploitation of folk beliefs, rescuing them from the degraded category of 'vulgar superstitions' and finding in them depths of moral and psychological significance that lay beyond the grasp of conventional rationality. In their rediscovery of the popular imagination and its symbolic resources, the Romantic authors of the early nineteenth century often relied upon the humbler efforts of the previous century's antiquarians, bibliophiles, and folklorists—those numerous collectors of mythological curiosities, travellers' tales, medieval romances, popular ballads, forgotten legends, and unusual local customs. The figure of the vampire found its way into the repertoire of English Romanticism by a similar route. Following a series of vampire scares in remote villages of Serbia, Hungary, and Silesia in the early part of the eighteenth century, a respected French biblical scholar, Dom Augustin Calmet, had gathered an extensive anthology of reported vampire sightings and exhumations with related anecdotes and discussions of these phenomena, as *Dissertations sur les apparitions des anges, des démons & des esprits, et sur les revenans et vampires de Hongrie, de Boheme, de Moravie & de Silesie* (1746). The significance of Calmet's materials was in turn widely debated among some of the leading minds of the Enlightenment, usually as evidence of the limitless credulity of priest-ridden peasants. At the same time, the image of the vampire passed into the vocabulary of French and English satire as a vivid metaphor for such commonplace 'bloodsuckers' as landlords and governments. Eventually, Robert Southey at the turn of the century included a sample of Calmet's vampirology in the notes to his *Thalaba*, along with an earlier French account of vampire-hysteria on the Greek island of Myconos; and English readers at last had more than a snippet of this folklore to bite on.

As the basis of imaginative literature rather than of sick jokes, however, the folklore of vampires as represented in Calmet's accounts had some serious deficiencies: it was obscure, confused, and above all comically disgusting. According to the villagers of Serbia and Hungary, their vampires were bloated, shaggy, foul-smelling corpses who preyed on their immediate neighbours and relatives, or on nearby cattle (so that vampirism could be acquired by eating contaminated meat). Popular remedies against vampires involved digging them up and smearing oneself with their blood, or pulling out their teeth and sucking their gums, as well as the more conclusive precautions of staking, decapitation, and incineration. Still more unappealing was the fact that the legions of the undead were composed entirely of peasants. Some readers of Calmet's anthology pointed out that there seemed, oddly, never to have been an urban vampire, nor an educated bourgeois vampire, let alone one of noble birth. The historical and mythological importance of Polidori's *The Vampyre* lies in its drastic correction of the folklore's shortcomings, and especially in his elevation of the *nosferatu* (undead) to the dignity of high social rank. By removing the bloodsucker from the village cowshed to the salons of high society and the resorts of international tourism, he set in motion the glorious career of the *aristocratic* vampire, a figure later incarnated as Sir Francis Varney, in J. M. Rymer's interminable *Varney the Vampire* (1847), as Countess Mircalla Karnstein in J. Sheridan Le Fanu's *Carmilla* (1872), and of course as Count Dracula in Bram Stoker's *Dracula* (1897), the novel that has defined our conceptions of lordly vampirism for the last century and more. Polidori's tale has commonly been treated as a fairly simple projection of its author's passive subjection to Byron's dominating genius, in the form of Aubrey's hypnotic obedience to Ruthven. But, as Ken Gelder has pointed out, *The Vampyre* in fact takes a more actively ironic attitude to its Byronic villain, turning some of Byron's self-dramatizations against their originator.[2] Like Lady Caroline Lamb before him, Polidori knew himself to be an expendable amusement, and so inscribed the

---

[2] Ken Gelder, *Reading the Vampire* (London, 1994), 30–4.

inevitable resentments of this position into his fictionalized Byron. And it is above all middle-class resentment against the sexual allure of the noble *roué* that sustains the modern vampire myth, at the same time absorbing it effortlessly into the conventions of melodrama.

Another volume in this series, *Tales of Terror from Blackwood's Magazine* (Oxford, 1995), gathers some of the best short fiction from the early years of that pioneering magazine, including works by Samuel Warren, William Mudford, John Galt, William Maginn, and James Hogg. The aim of the present collection, however, is to exhibit the variety and vitality of the terror-tales and similarly macabre fiction published in the rival magazines of London and Dublin, in the two decades following the appearance of Polidori's tale; that is, the 1820s and 1830s. Most of the stories selected come from the *New Monthly* itself, but there are two stories from the *Dublin University Magazine*, with one apiece from *Fraser's*, the *Metropolitan*, and the *Dublin Literary Gazette*. More than any other single story, *The Vampyre* heralded a new phase of modern British fiction in which the opportunist sensationalism of the monthly magazines assumed an unprecedented importance. When *The Vampyre* appeared in 1819, there were three major divisions of the periodical press: newspapers, magazines, and reviews. Daily newspapers like *The Times*, and weekly newspapers such as William Cobbett's *Political Register* and Leigh Hunt's *Examiner*, were devoted largely to politics. Magazines such as *Blackwood's* and the *New Monthly* appeared monthly and prided themselves on variety, instruction, and amusement, as well as on the regular publication of original fiction. Reviews like the *Edinburgh* and the *Quarterly* were published every three months, and were sombre, substantial, and highly respectable: in 1818 William Hazlitt commented that 'to be an Edinburgh Reviewer is, I suspect, the highest rank in modern literary society'.[3] But for many, including Thomas De Quincey, magazines were 'entitled to . . . precedency' over reviews because they were more intimately

---

[3] *The Complete Works of William Hazlitt*, ed. P. P. Howe (21 vols.; London, 1930–4), xii. 365.

connected 'with the shifting passions of the day' and naturally became 'a general *depôt* . . . both for life and literature'.[4] The magazines offered a broader and more sophisticated consideration of political events than the newspapers, and they possessed an immediacy and variety that the reviews could not match. They were the most exuberant and original of the periodicals, while their preoccupation with violence, scandal, and hysteria made them a natural outlet for terror fiction.

Magazines at this time were also one of the most dependably profitable commodities for publishers such as Henry Colburn, William Blackwood, and John Murray. Technological advances in papermaking and printing meant that more copy could be produced faster and at a cheaper rate, and a growing middle class combined increased wealth and leisure with a voracious appetite for the kind of information and amusement the magazines provided. 'WE ARE ABSOLUTELY COINING MONEY', cried John Wilson in *Blackwood's* in 1820, and two years later in the *London Magazine* P. G. Patmore wrote that magazines were 'emerging from the shell with which they were encrusted' and 'soaring aloft into higher spheres', chiefly because 'the very highest names in English literature' had become contributors.[5] The days of Grub Street gave way to the patronage of the reading public, and magazines became powerful, lucrative enterprises, for both writers and publishers. In 1823 Mary Shelley was amazed to discover that Horace Smith was making '200 per ann . . . clear, regularly, for writing . . . for the New Monthly'.[6]

The rise of the magazines began with the founding of the *Monthly Magazine* in 1796, and was consolidated with the unprecedented success of *Blackwood's Magazine* in 1817 which, along with the *New Monthly* (1814), dominated the magazine scene for over a decade, before being challenged in the early 1830s by powerful rivals such as *Fraser's*, the *Metropolitan*, and the *Dublin University*. In the 1820s and 1830s all the

---

[4] *New Essays by De Quincey*, ed. Stuart M. Tave (Princeton, NJ, 1966), 213.

[5] *Blackwood's Magazine*, 8 (1820), 80; *London Magazine*, 6 (1822), 22.

[6] *The Letters of Mary Wollstonecraft Shelley*, ed. Betty T. Bennett (3 vols.; Baltimore, 1980–7), i. 374.

leading magazines published large amounts of fiction, partly in response to the enormous public demand for novels generated by recent publishing successes like the 'silver-fork novels' of high society made popular by Edward Bulwer and Catherine Gore, and cheap reprints such as Colburn and Bentley's Standard Novels series, founded in 1831. But there was a long tradition of serializing fiction in the magazines—Tobias Smollett's *The Life and Adventures of Sir Launcelot Greaves* had appeared in the *British Magazine* in 1760–1—and the idea received new life as early as 1820–1 when *Blackwood's* serialized John Galt's *Ayrshire Legatees*, and then followed up this success with David Macbeth Moir's *The Autobiography of Mansie Wauch*, Michael Scott's *Tom Cringle's Log*, and Samuel Warren's *Passages from the Diary of a Late Physician*. Other magazines soon followed suit, and in the 1830s the *New Monthly* serialized Benjamin Disraeli's *The Infernal Marriage*, *Fraser's* ran Thomas Carlyle's *Sartor Resartus* and William Thackeray's *The Yellowplush Correspondence*, the *Dublin University* published William Carleton's *Fardorougha the Miser* and Charles Lever's immensely successful *The Confessions of Harry Lorrequer*, and the *Metropolitan*'s great popularity was based almost exclusively on its serialization of the sea adventure novels of Frederick Marryat and Edward Howard.

Short fiction, too, was a long-established tradition in the magazines, dating back to the late seventeenth century, thriving in the eighteenth, and increasing in sophistication and influence in the nineteenth, when the leading magazines featured hundreds of tales of sentiment, humour, folklore, fantasy, burlesque, and much else. Gothic tales and fragments began appearing in the magazines shortly after the publication of Horace Walpole's *The Castle of Otranto* in 1764, and were common after 1790, when the craze for the Gothic in Britain reached its height. Many of the Gothic tales that appeared in magazines between 1770 and 1820 were written by readers themselves, and were most often simply crude abbreviations or redactions of the novels of Walpole, Clara Reeve, Ann Radcliffe, Matthew Lewis, and Charles Brockden Brown. What Robert Mayo has described as 'Gothic fragments', on the other hand, took as their model Anna Laetitia Aikin's 'Sir

Bertrand' (1773), and while like the Gothic tale they employed natural terrors such as mouldering castles and subterranean vaults, they differed from the tales in that they typically began *in medias res*, revelled in the use of the supernatural and the unexplained, and broke off at a crucial moment.[7] Tales and fragments in these formats appeared continually in magazines such as the *Lady's*, the *General*, the *Monthly Mirror*, and a host of others, while magazines such as the *Marvellous* were devoted exclusively to this kind of fiction. But, as Mayo notes, as early as 1791 both the Gothic tale and fragment 'were well on the way to being stereotypes . . . and during the succeeding decades imitators in the magazines were to ring endless changes on the old forms and motifs'.[8] Not until about 1820 did sensation fiction begin to shed the trappings of the Radcliffean school of the Gothic, as some of the most popular and influential authors of the day were drawn to the magazine tale of terror, and began to transform its range and potential.

The leading exponent of the newer kinds of terror fiction was *Blackwood's Magazine*, which turned away from the Gothic tradition and offered in its stead a fresh realism and concentration of sensational effect in its best tales. In such stories as John Galt's 'The Buried Alive' (1821), William Maginn's 'The Man in the Bell' (1821), and Henry Thomson's 'Le Revenant' (1827), a powerful new formula emerged for the modern tale of terror, in which the protagonist—usually the first-person narrator of the story—would record the extreme psychological effects of being trapped, incarcerated, or even entombed in unbearable conditions of confinement and panic. These fictional possibilities of claustrophobia were exploited to the full in William Mudford's *Blackwood's* tale 'The Iron Shroud' (1830), in which a prisoner discovers that his metallic cell is gradually shrinking and will thus certainly crush him to death. It was upon the basis of these works that Edgar Allan Poe soon developed the hysterical intensity

[7] Robert Mayo, 'Gothic Romance in the Magazines' in *PMLA*, 65 (Sept. 1950), 776–8.
[8] Ibid. 778–9.

of his most memorable stories, notably 'The Pit and the Pendulum' (1843), which is indebted directly to Mudford's tale. However, despite the influential prominence of these claustrophobic narratives, the terror fiction of *Blackwood's* transcended any predictable formulae, and included a range of material, from traditional Scottish ghost stories to narratives of murder, famine, and shipwreck. A second distinctive feature of its fictional fare was the exploitation of public curiosity about the grisly secrets of the medical profession: *Blackwood's* highly successful series of *Passages from the Diary of a Late Physician* (1830–7), written by the former Edinburgh medical student Samuel Warren, provided numerous lurid deathbed scenes along with startling pictures of lunacy, catalepsy, *delirium tremens*, amputation, and similar horrors, all presented in the form of 'inside' knowledge. In a similar vein, other *Blackwood's* tales would recount, from the privileged point of view of a clergyman, the final confessions and ravings of madmen and murderers. In one way or another, the most powerful and characteristic effects of the *Blackwood's* tale of terror derived from the impression of being 'inside'— either an alarmingly enclosed space, or a secret realm of suffering. Neither the *New Monthly* nor its various competitors in London and Dublin ever evolved a distinctive formula for the tale of terror in the way that *Blackwood's* had done, to the extent of attracting imitation and parody, in its early years; but they renewed and extended the possibilities of such fiction, most obviously in inaugurating the modern tradition of vampire stories, but also in adapting real-life incidents of terror to fictional forms, and in refreshing—as *Blackwood's* had neglected to do—the mainstream of Gothic fiction itself. In general, although with some scope for exceptions, it may be said that where the hallmark of *Blackwood's* terror fiction was a shrill intensity, the equivalent work of the London and Dublin monthlies was more composed, in both the psychological and the artistic senses of the word.

In the frantically competitive world of the magazines in the 1820s and 1830s, imitation was not just the sincerest form of flattery but the surest route to commercial survival. It should not, then, surprise us to find some echoes of the successful

Blackwood's tradition in the productions of its monthly rivals. For instance, two of the tales selected here could be mistaken easily enough for *Blackwood's* material: 'My Hobby,—Rather', by the American author N. P. Willis, which describes the gruesome desecration of a corpse, is a short and violent excursion beyond the bounds of good taste, while Charles Lever's 'Post-Mortem Recollections of a Medical Lecturer' uses the familiar device of the cataleptic trance which threatens the narrator with the fate of live burial. Each employs the convention of first-person testimony to suddenly overwhelming fright. On the other hand, many magazinists in Dublin and London diverged clearly from the school of Blackwood by developing more old-fashioned Gothic materials, either in the archaic mode of 'Sir Guy Eveling's Dream' by Horace Smith, or in Letitia Landon's elegant tale 'The Bride of Lindorf'. The final story in this collection, Sheridan Le Fanu's 'Passage in the Secret History of an Irish Countess', derives its plot from those founding texts of Gothic fiction, Walpole's *The Castle of Otranto* and Ann Radcliffe's *The Mysteries of Udolpho* (1794), while looking ahead to the high Victorian Gothic of Le Fanu's own novel *Uncle Silas* (1864), which is in fact an expanded version of the same tale.

A more general and substantial feature which several of the tales collected here share with a good number of their counterparts in *Blackwood's*, and indeed with fiction and theatrical melodrama outside the magazines, is their moral impetus, directed chiefly at the thoughtlessness of the fashionable and dissolute young rake or libertine. As Samuel Warren and several other *Blackwood's* contributors presented their tales of terror either straightforwardly or disingenuously as 'moral tales' serving the function of *memento mori* to the idle young man-about-town, so the authors of macabre fiction in the rival magazines adopted the conventional figure of the rake, devising various means of warning readers against his example and his fate. In some versions, as in Smith's 'Sir Guy Eveling's Dream' and Allan Cunningham's 'The Master of Logan', the young firebrand utters a rash oath that conjures up demonic terrors to punish his sexual licence; in others, such as the anonymous 'Life in Death', a more calculating and

jaded kind of debauchee attempts to recapture the sinful energies of his youth by unhallowed means. In this last-mentioned
tale, the youthful protagonist lapses, while watching over his
father's corpse and looking forward to squandering his inher-
ited wealth, into an odd kind of reverie: 'Strange images of
death and pleasures mingled together; now it was a glorious
banquet, now the gloomy silence of a church-yard; now bright
and beautiful faces seemed to fill the air, then by a sudden
transition they became the cadaverous relics of the charnel-
house.' A clue is given here to the admonitory ambitions and
to the imaginative instabilities of the 'moral' tale of terror,
which typically brings into harsh juxtaposition the dimly
evoked realm of Vice (a world of brandy, actresses, and card-
tables, always safely offstage) and the more starkly drawn
images of mortality. Le Fanu's 'Passage in the Secret History
of an Irish Countess' illustrates a further variation upon the
stock figure of modern dissipation, in the character of Sir
Arthur, a supposedly 'reformed rake' with his card-playing
days behind him.

The recurrence of this *topos* in so many tales may serve to
illuminate an often overlooked dimension of the lead story in
this collection, Polidori's *The Vampyre*. For obvious reasons,
it has been the connections of this work with previous vampiric lore and with subsequent literary and cinematic adapta-
tions that have occupied most discussion of the tale. Yet the
significance of Polidori's momentous transformation of the
figure of the vampire from bestial ghoul to glamorous aris-
tocrat cannot be grasped fully without recognizing that his
Lord Ruthven is really the conventional rakehell or libertine
with a few vampiric attributes grafted onto him. For Ruthven,
at least, vampirism is merely a continuation of rakery by other
means; and for Polidori, the 'vampire story' is conceived as
a variant upon the moral tale, a tale designed principally as a
warning—here, against the fascinating power of the libertin-
ism represented by his employer Byron. The significance of
this monitory motive, incidentally, can be felt in the tale's
strongest tension, which is between the hero's urgent need
to warn his sister and others against Ruthven, and the even
stronger force which prevents him from giving that warning

utterance. The story is notably—and for some modern readers disappointingly—deficient in vampire-lore and its now customary paraphernalia, but this is because the figure of the vampire here has a restricted function, serving principally as a vivid metaphor for that kind of womanizer who may be said to 'prey upon' his victims, or to be, in a phrase that had recently come into use in Polidori's day, a 'lady-killer'. Polidori has received fairly earned credit for ennobling and glamorizing the vampire; but to look at the same transformation from this other side is to see that he just as certainly revamped (more precisely, vamped for the first time) the stock figure of the upper-class rake, which is perhaps the more significant mythic feat.

In the context of the broad range of macabre fiction, the vampire is merely one special version of the *revenant* or returner from the dead, who has numerous other guises. It is a noteworthy feature of the short fiction in the London magazines that it so frequently resorts to such figures, while the most characteristic *Blackwood's* tales usually avoided them. There are weaker and stronger variations upon this theme: at one end of the spectrum, a skeleton hand will resurface sixty years later in a scrap-metal shop, or a woman believed to have died years ago turns out to be alive in the deserted wing of a Gothic castle, or a man about to be buried will awaken from his coma and spring upright in his coffin; at the other end, full-blown supernaturalism asserts itself as the truly dead are summoned from their graves as ghosts or worse. In one of Hogg's 'Terrible Letters from Scotland', the narrator, after escaping premature burial, complains that his neighbours 'called me the man that was dead and risen again, and shunned me as a being scarcely of this earth'. To present his predicament in just those terms is, of course, to draw attention to the way in which the grim 'resurrections' of macabre fiction darkly travesty the central myth of Christian theology itself, inverting its heavenly promises into hellish curses. A pervasive theological gloom hangs over many of these stories, especially those of Scottish authors—Hogg, Cunningham, and (we must suppose) the anonymous author of 'The Curse'—whose historical memory is still overshadowed by the religious wars and persecutions of the seventeenth century. Darker still is the vision of the Irish writer William Carleton, who presents the murderous conspiracy in his 'Confessions of a Reformed Ribbonman' as a satanic mass.

Carleton's tale exemplifies most powerfully an important tendency, almost inherent in the miscellaneous and sensation-hungry nature of these magazines, to incorporate elements of the recent 'true crime' material into the tale of terror, eroding the boundaries between fact and fiction. His 'Confessions' revisit an actual massacre in County Louth that had taken place fourteen years before their publication. Similarly, Catherine Gore's 'The Red Man' starts with an account of an execution that had indeed taken place in Paris less than two years before she published the story. The anonymous tale 'The Victim' again draws upon readers' recent recollections of Edinburgh's most notorious murder case, the Burke and Hare trial of 1829, in which it emerged that a shortage of suitable corpses for anatomical dissection in the medical schools had been made good by the random abduction and suffocation of living victims. The extreme case of such ghoulish opportunism is reached in Hogg's 'Terrible Letters', which exploit the widespread anxieties about the spread of cholera, initially from Sunderland and Newcastle to Edinburgh and Glasgow in the winter of 1831/2. Placing these morbid little tales in the London *Metropolitan* was a particularly cruel stunt at a time—April 1832—when the English capital was daily expecting its own death toll (currently only six hundred) to escalate to unknown heights, and when the *Metropolitan* itself was providing monthly updates on the ravages of the epidemic in England, and deliberating on the vulnerability of the East End to a repetition of the Scottish disaster. In another way, the opportunistic exploitation of recent true-life marvels was also a feature of Colburn's use of Polidori's *The Vampyre*, which traded on the notoriety of Lord Byron.

These features of magazine fiction may appear scurrilous and reprehensibly commercial, remote from the higher possibilities of literary art. And yet it was upon the basis of such unwholesome traffic that the modern short story emerged as an internationally significant form in these decades—in the productions of Hoffman, Pushkin, Mérimée, Balzac, Hawthorne, and Poe. That the British and Irish writers from Polidori to Le Fanu could contribute to this process their own satisfyingly crafted works, the macabre tales that follow should demonstrate for themselves.

NOTE ON THE TEXT

THE fourteen tales reprinted in the main section of this volume were first published in a British or Irish magazine between 1819 and 1838, and in each instance the magazine text is the copy text. Details of dates and the magazine of publication appear in the explanatory notes, as does information regarding the various reprintings of specific tales. In the case of Polidori's *The Vampyre*, no manuscript has been discovered, and though the tale appeared in book form shortly after it was published in the *New Monthly Magazine*, both the magazine and the book text were almost certainly printed without Polidori's knowledge. In the text of *The Vampyre*, two obvious errors in tense have been corrected, and the punctuation has been altered in a small number of cases in order to improve the sense; this usually involves a comma being changed to either a semicolon or a full stop. In all other instances, the *New Monthly* text has been followed. For a full discussion of the textual history of *The Vampyre*, see Henry R. Viets, 'The London Editions of Polidori's *The Vampyre*' in *Papers of the Bibliographical Society of America*, 63 (1969), 83–103, and *The Vampyre and Ernestus Berchtold*, eds. D. L. Macdonald and Kathleen Scherf (Toronto, 1994), 21–6.

The text of all fourteen tales has been modernized in a number of ways: double quotation marks have been changed to single, a standard format has been adopted for the headings, and, where necessary, square brackets have been changed to round. In James Hogg's 'Some Terrible Letters from Scotland' the brief editorial introductions to the second and third letters have been taken out of square brackets and put into italics, and in the anonymous tale 'The Curse' rows of asterisks used as ellipses and to subdivide the text have been eliminated. In several of the tales obvious errors in spelling and punctuation have been silently corrected. Prefatory letters or statements have been omitted from the front of some of the tales and signatures have been removed from the end of the tales. Details of the signatures appear in the explanatory notes.

The copy text for the material reprinted in the three appendices to this volume is the first published version. The 'Preliminaries' for *The Vampyre* were first printed in the *New Monthly Magazine* immediately preceding the text of *The Vampyre*. The 'Note on *The Vampyre*' was first published as part of the Introduction to Polidori's only full-length novel, *Ernestus Berchtold* (1819); for details of the novel's publication, see Macdonald and Scherf, *The Vampyre and Ernestus Berchtold* (Toronto, 1994), 26–9. Byron's 'Augustus Darvell' originally appeared, without his permission, at the end of his poem *Mazeppa* (1819); for details of the tale's textual history, see *Lord Byron: The Complete Miscellaneous Prose*, ed. Andrew Nicholson (Oxford, 1991), 329–34.

Like the texts of the fourteen tales, the texts of the appendices have been modernized in several ways: in particular, double quotation marks have been changed to single, asterisks have been eliminated, and a standard format has been adopted for the headings.

SELECT BIBLIOGRAPHY

FOR critical discussions of John Polidori's *The Vampyre*, see Richard Sharp Astle, 'Ontological Ambiguity and Historical Pessimism in Polidori's *The Vampyre*' in *Sphinx*, 2 (1977), 8–16; Judith Barbour, 'Dr John William Polidori, Author of *The Vampyre*' in *Imagining Romanticism: Essays on English and Australian Romanticism*, eds. Deidre Coleman and Peter Otto (West Cornwall, Conn., 1992), 85–110; James Rieger, 'Dr Polidori and the Genesis of *Frankenstein*' in *Studies in English Literature*, 3 (1963), 461–72; Roxana Stuart, 'Ruthven' in *Stage Blood: Vampires of the 19th-Century Stage* (Bowling Green, Ohio, 1994), 11–175; Richard Switzer, 'Lord Ruthven and the Vampires' in *The French Review*, 29 (1955), 107–12; Henry R. Viets, 'The London Editions of Polidori's *The Vampyre*' in *Papers of the Bibliographical Society of America*, 63 (1969), 83–103.

The best general studies of the vampire include: Nina Auerbach, *Our Vampires, Ourselves* (Chicago, 1995); Margaret Carter, *The Vampire in Literature: A Critical Bibliography* (Ann Arbor, Mich., 1989); Christopher Frayling, 'Introduction' in *Vampyres: Lord Byron to Count Dracula*, ed. Christopher Frayling (London, 1991), 3–84; Brian J. Frost, *The Monster with a Thousand Faces: Guises of the Vampire in Myth and Literature* (Bowling Green, Ohio, 1989); Ken Gelder, *Reading the Vampire* (London, 1994); Peter D. Grudin, *The Demon Lover* (New York, 1987); Carol Senf, *The Vampire in Nineteenth-Century English Literature* (Bowling Green, Ohio, 1988); James Twitchell, *The Living Dead: A Study of the Vampire in Romantic Literature* (Durham, NC, 1981).

There has been no detailed study of the nineteenth-century magazine tale of terror. For background discussion, see Edith Birkhead, *The Tale of Terror* (London, 1921); Noël Carroll, *The Philosophy of Horror or Paradoxes of the Heart* (London, 1990); William Patrick Day, *In the Circles of Fear and Desire* (Chicago, 1985); Benjamin Franklin Fisher IV, *The Gothic's Gothic* (New York, 1988); Terry Heller, *The Delights of Terror* (Urbana, Ill., 1987); David Punter, *The Literature of Terror* (London, 1980); and Donald Ringe, *American Gothic* (Lexington, Ky., 1982).

For discussions of the development and significance of magazine fiction in the late Romantic and early Victorian periods, see Michael Allen, *Poe and the British Magazine Tradition* (New York, 1969); Elliott Engell and Margaret King, *The Victorian Novel Before Victoria:*

1830–1837 (New York, 1984); Lee Erickson, *The Economy of Literary Form* (Baltimore, 1996); Benjamin Lease, *Anglo-American Encounters: England and the Rise of American Literature* (Cambridge, 1981); Harold Orel, *The Victorian Short Story: Development and Triumph of a Literary Genre* (Cambridge, 1986); Carol Polsgrove, 'They Made it Pay: British Short-Fiction Writers, 1820–1840' in *Studies in Short Fiction*, 11 (1974), 417–21; Lance Schachterle, '*Oliver Twist* and its Serial Predecessors' in *Dickens Studies Annual*, 3 (1974), 1–13.

For individual magazines, see Linda B. Jones, 'The *New Monthly Magazine*, 1821–1830', unpublished thesis (Colorado University, 1970); William Kilbourne, 'The Role of Fiction in *Blackwood's Magazine* from 1817 to 1845', unpublished thesis (Northwestern University, 1966); Michael Sadleir, *Dublin University Magazine: Its History, Contents and Bibliography* (Dublin, 1938); Austin Seckersen, 'The Dublin Literary Gazette' in *British Literary Magazines: The Romantic Age*, ed. Alvin Sullivan (London, 1983), 112–14; Lance Schachterle, 'The Metropolitan Magazine' in *British Literary Magazines: The Romantic Age*, 304–8; M. M. H. Thrall, *Rebellious Fraser's* (New York, 1934).

For individual authors, see Bonnie Anderson, 'The Writings of Catherine Gore' in *Journal of Popular Culture*, 10 (1976), 404–23; Courtland P. Auser, *Nathaniel Parker Willis* (New York, 1969); Arthur H. Beavan, *James and Horace Smith* (London, 1899); James Campbell, *Edward Bulwer-Lytton* (Boston, 1986); Eileen A. Sullivan, *William Carleton* (Boston, 1983); Barbara Hayley, *Carleton's Traits and Stories and the 19th Century Anglo-Irish Tradition* (Gerrards Cross, Bucks., 1983); David Hogg, *The Life of Allan Cunningham, With Selections from His Works and Correspondence* (London, 1875); D. L. Macdonald, *Poor Polidori: A Critical Biography of the Author of The Vampyre* (Toronto, 1991); W. J. McCormack, *Sheridan Le Fanu and Victorian Ireland* (Oxford, 1980); Lewis Simpson, *James Hogg: A Critical Study* (Edinburgh, 1962); Glennis Stephenson, *Letitia Landon: The Woman behind L. E. L.* (Manchester, 1995); Lionel Stevenson, *Doctor Quicksilver: The Life of Charles Lever* (London, 1939).

CHRONOLOGY OF THE MAGAZINES

1796 Feb. *Monthly Magazine* established, edited by John Aikin.

1814 Feb. *New Monthly Magazine* established, edited by John Watkins.

1817 Oct. *Blackwood's Edinburgh Magazine* established, edited by William Blackwood.

1819 Apr. John William Polidori's *The Vampyre* in the *New Monthly*; James Hogg's *The Shepherd's Calendar* in *Blackwood's* (thirteen instalments ending in Apr. 1828).

1820 Jan. *London Magazine* established, edited by John Scott.

June. William Hazlitt's *Table Talk* in the *London* (thirteen instalments ending in Dec. 1821); John Galt's *The Ayrshire Legatees* in *Blackwood's* (eight instalments ending in Feb. 1821).

Aug. Charles Lamb's *Essays of Elia* in the *London* (twenty-eight instalments ending in Nov. 1822).

1821 Jan. Thomas Campbell becomes editor of the *New Monthly*.

Feb. John Scott of the *London* is killed in a duel after weeks of feuding between *Blackwood's* and the *London*.

Sept. Thomas De Quincey's *Confessions of an English Opium-Eater* in the *London* (second instalment Oct. 1821).

1822 Mar. J. G. Lockhart's *Noctes Ambrosianae* in *Blackwood's* (seventy-one instalments ending in Feb. 1835; most written by John Wilson, with help from several others).

1824 Jan. Hazlitt's 'The Spirits of the Age' in the *New Monthly* (five instalments ending in June 1824).

1826 Jan. Stendhal's *Sketches of Parisian Society, Politics and Literature* in the *New Monthly* (twenty-nine instalments ending in July 1829).

1829 June. *London Magazine* ceases publication.

Sept. Michael Scott's *Tom Cringle's Log* in *Blackwood's* (twenty-three instalments ending in Aug. 1833).

1830 Jan. William Carleton's 'Confessions of a Reformed Ribbonman' in the *Dublin Literary Gazette*.

1830 Feb. *Fraser's Magazine* established, edited by William Maginn.

Aug. Samuel Warren's *Passages from the Diary of a Late Physician* in *Blackwood's* (eighteen instalments ending in Aug. 1837).

1831 May. *Metropolitan Magazine* established, edited by Thomas Campbell.

Nov. Edward Bulwer becomes editor of the *New Monthly*.

1832 Feb. William Godwin the Younger's 'The Executioner' in *Blackwood's* (second instalment Mar. 1832).

Apr. *Tait's Edinburgh Magazine* established, edited by William Tait.

1833 Jan. *Dublin University Magazine* established, edited by Charles Stanford.

Nov. Carlyle's *Sartor Resartus* in *Fraser's* (eight instalments ending in Aug. 1834).

1834 July. Benjamin Disraeli's *The Infernal Marriage* in the *New Monthly* (four instalments ending in Oct. 1834).

1835 June. Catherine Gore's 'The Red Man' in the *New Monthly*.

1836 Aug. Letitia Landon's 'The Bride of Lindorf' in the *New Monthly*.

1837 Jan. *Bentley's Miscellany* established, edited by Charles Dickens; Theodore Hook becomes editor of the *New Monthly*, which is renamed the *New Monthly Magazine and Humorist*.

Feb. Dickens's *Oliver Twist* in *Bentley's* (twenty-four instalments ending in Apr. 1839).

Mar. Marryat's *The Phantom Ship* in the *New Monthly* (seventeen instalments ending in Aug. 1839).

Nov. William Thackeray's *The Yellowplush Correspondence* in *Fraser's* (nine instalments ending in Aug. 1838).

1838 Nov. Joseph Sheridan Le Fanu's 'Passage in the Secret History of an Irish Countess' in the *Dublin University Magazine*.

1839 Mar. W. H. Ainsworth becomes editor of *Bentley's*.

May. Thackeray's *Catherine* in *Fraser's* (seven instalments ending in Feb. 1840).

THE VAMPYRE
AND OTHER TALES OF
THE MACABRE

THE VAMPYRE

John Polidori

IT HAPPENED that in the midst of the dissipations attendant upon a London winter, there appeared at the various parties of the leaders of the *ton** a nobleman, more remarkable
for his singularities, than his rank. He gazed upon the mirth
around him, as if he could not participate therein. Apparently,
the light laughter of the fair only attracted his attention, that
he might by a look quell it, and throw fear into those breasts
where thoughtlessness reigned. Those who felt this sensation
of awe, could not explain whence it arose: some attributed it
to the dead grey eye, which, fixing upon the object's face, did
not seem to penetrate, and at one glance to pierce through to
the inward workings of the heart; but fell upon the cheek
with a leaden ray that weighed upon the skin it could not
pass. His peculiarities caused him to be invited to every house;
all wished to see him, and those who had been accustomed
to violent excitement, and now felt the weight of *ennui*, were
pleased at having something in their presence capable of en-
gaging their attention. In spite of the deadly hue of his face,
which never gained a warmer tint, either from the blush of
modesty, or from the strong emotion of passion, though its
form and outline were beautiful, many of the female hunters
after notoriety attempted to win his attentions, and gain, at
least, some marks of what they might term affection; Lady
Mercer, who had been the mockery of every monster shewn
in drawing rooms since her marriage, threw herself in his way,
and did all but put on the dress of a mountebank, to attract
his notice;—though in vain:—when she stood before him,
though his eyes were apparently fixed upon her's, still it
seemed as if they were unperceived—even her unappalled
impudence was baffled, and she left the field.* But though
the common adultress could not influence even the guidance
of his eyes, it was not that the female sex was indifferent to
him: yet such was the apparent caution with which he spoke

to the virtuous wife and innocent daughter, that few knew he ever addressed himself to females. He had, however, the reputation of a winning tongue; and whether it was that it even overcame the dread of his singular character, or that they were moved by his apparent hatred of vice, he was as often among those females who form the boast of their sex from their domestic virtues, as among those who sully it by their vices.

About the same time, there came to London a young gentleman of the name of Aubrey: he was an orphan left with an only sister in the possession of great wealth, by parents who died while he was yet in childhood. Left also to himself by guardians, who thought it their duty merely to take care of his fortune, while they relinquished the more important charge of his mind to the care of mercenary subalterns, he cultivated more his imagination than his judgment. He had, hence, that high romantic feeling of honour and candour, which daily ruins so many milliners' apprentices. He believed all to sympathise with virtue, and thought that vice was thrown in by Providence merely for the picturesque effect of the scene, as we see in romances; he thought that the misery of a cottage merely consisted in the vesting of clothes, which were as warm, but which were better adapted to the painter's eye by their irregular folds and various coloured patches. He thought, in fine, that the dreams of poets were the realities of life. He was handsome, frank, and rich: for these reasons, upon his entering into the gay circles, many mothers surrounded him, striving which should describe with least truth their languishing or romping favourites: the daughters at the same time, by their brightening countenances when he approached, and by their sparkling eyes, when he opened his lips, soon led him into false notions of his talents and his merit. Attached as he was to the romance of his solitary hours, he was startled at finding that except in the tallow and wax candles, that flickered not from the presence of a ghost, but from want of snuffing, there was no foundation in real life for any of that congeries of pleasing pictures and descriptions contained in those volumes, from which he had formed his study. Finding, however, some compensation in his gratified vanity, he was about to relinquish his dreams, when the extraordinary being we have above described, crossed him in his career.

He watched him; and the very impossibility of forming an idea of the character of a man entirely absorbed in himself, who gave few other signs of his observation of external objects, than the tacit assent to their existence, implied by the avoidance of their contact: allowing his imagination to picture every thing that flattered its propensity to extravagant ideas, he soon formed this object into the hero of a romance, and determined to observe the offspring of his fancy, rather than the person before him. He became acquainted with him, paid him attentions, and had so far advanced upon his notice, that his presence was always recognized. He gradually learnt that Lord Ruthven's affairs were embarrassed, and soon found, from the notes of preparation in —— Street, that he was about to travel.* Desirous of gaining some information respecting this singular character, who, till now, had only whetted his curiosity, he hinted to his guardians, that it was time for him to perform the tour, which for many generations has been thought necessary to enable the young to take some rapid steps in the career of vice, towards putting themselves upon an equality with the aged, and not allowing them to appear as if fallen from the skies, whenever scandalous intrigues are mentioned as the subjects of pleasantry or of praise, according to the degree of skill shewn in carrying them on. They consented: and Aubrey immediately mentioning his intentions to Lord Ruthven, was surprised to receive from him a proposal to join him. Flattered, by such a mark of esteem from him, who, apparently, had nothing in common with other men, he gladly accepted it, and in a few days they had passed the circling waters.

Hitherto, Aubrey had had no opportunity of studying Lord Ruthven's character, and now he found, that, though many more of his actions were exposed to his view, the results offered different conclusions from the apparent motives to his conduct. His companion was profuse in his liberality;—the idle, the vagabond, and the beggar, received from his hand more than enough to relieve their immediate wants. But Aubrey could not avoid remarking, that it was not upon the virtuous, reduced to indigence by the misfortunes attendant even

upon virtue, that he bestowed him alms;—these were sent from
the door with hardly suppressed sneers; but when the profligate came to ask something, not to relieve his wants, but
to allow him to wallow in his lust, or to sink him still deeper
in his iniquity, he was sent away with rich charity. This was,
however, attributed by him to the greater importunity of the
vicious, which generally prevails over the retiring bashfulness
of the virtuous indigent. There was one circumstance about
the charity of his Lordship, which was still more impressed
upon his mind: all those upon whom it was bestowed, inevit-
ably found that there was a curse upon it, for they all were
either led to the scaffold, or sunk to the lowest and the most
abject misery. At Brussels and other towns through which
they passed, Aubrey was surprized at the apparent eagerness
with which his companion sought for the centres of all fashionable vice; there he entered into all the spirit of the faro
table:* he betted, and always gambled with success, except
where the known sharper was his antagonist, and then he lost
even more than he gained; but it was always with the same
unchanging face, with which he generally watched the society around: it was not, however, so when he encountered the
rash youthful novice, or the luckless father of a numerous
family; then his very wish seemed fortune's law—this apparent abstractedness of mind was laid aside, and his eyes sparkled
with more fire than that of the cat whilst dallying with the
half dead mouse. In every town, he left the formerly affluent
youth, torn from the circle he adorned, cursing, in the solitude of a dungeon, the fate that had drawn him within the
reach of this fiend; whilst many a father sat frantic, amidst the
speaking looks of mute hungry children, without a single farth-
ing of his late immense wealth, wherewith to buy even sufficient to satisfy their present craving. Yet he took no money
from the gambling table; but immediately lost, to the ruiner
of many, the last gilder he had just snatched from the convulsive grasp of the innocent: this might but be the result of
a certain degree of knowledge, which was not, however, capable of combating the cunning of the more experienced. Aubrey
often wished to represent this to his friend, and beg him to
resign that charity and pleasure which proved the ruin of all,

and did not tend to his own profit;—but he delayed it—for each day he hoped his friend would give him some opportunity of speaking frankly and openly to him; however, this never occurred. Lord Ruthven in his carriage, and amidst the various wild and rich scenes of nature, was always the same: his eye spoke less than his lip; and though Aubrey was near the object of his curiosity, he obtained no greater gratification from it than the constant excitement of vainly wishing to break that mystery, which to his exalted imagination began to assume the appearance of something supernatural.

They soon arrived at Rome, and Aubrey for a time lost sight of his companion; he left him in daily attendance upon the morning circle of an Italian countess, whilst he went in search of the memorials of another almost deserted city. Whilst he was thus engaged, letters arrived from England, which he opened with eager impatience; the first was from his sister, breathing nothing but affection; the others were from his guardians, the latter astonished him; if it had before entered into his imagination that there was an evil power resident in his companion, these seemed to give him almost sufficient reason for the belief. His guardians insisted upon his immediately leaving his friend, and urged, that his character was dreadfully vicious, for that the possession of irresistible powers of seduction, rendered his licentious habits more dangerous to society. It had been discovered, that his contempt for the adultress had not originated in hatred of her character; but that he had required, to enhance his gratification, that his victim, the partner of his guilt, should be hurled from the pinnacle of unsullied virtue, down to the lowest abyss of infamy and degradation: in fine, that all those females whom he had sought, apparently on account of their virtue, had, since his departure, thrown even the mask aside, and had not scrupled to expose the whole deformity of their vices to the public gaze.

Aubrey determined upon leaving one, whose character had not yet shown a single bright point on which to rest the eye. He resolved to invent some plausible pretext for abandoning him altogether, purposing, in the mean while, to watch him more closely, and to let no slight circumstance pass by unnoticed. He entered into the same circle, and soon perceived, that his Lordship was endeavouring to work upon the inexperience of the daughter of the lady at whose house he chiefly frequented. In Italy, it is seldom that an unmarried female is met with in society; he was therefore obliged to carry on his plans in secret; but Aubrey's eye followed him in all his windings, and soon discovered that an assignation had been appointed, which would most likely end in the ruin of an innocent, though thoughtless girl. Losing no time, he entered the apartment of Lord Ruthven, and abruptly asked him his intentions with respect to the lady, informing him at the same time that he was aware of his being about to meet her that very night. Lord Ruthven answered, that his intentions were such as he supposed all would have upon such an occasion; and upon being pressed whether he intended to marry her, merely laughed. Aubrey retired; and, immediately writing a note, to say, that from that moment he must decline accompanying his Lordship in the remainder of their proposed tour, he ordered his servant to seek other apartments, and calling upon the mother of the lady, informed her of all he knew, not only with regard to her daughter, but also concerning the character of his Lordship. The assignation was prevented. Lord Ruthven next day merely sent his servant to notify his complete assent to a separation; but did not hint any suspicion of his plans having been foiled by Aubrey's interposition.

Having left Rome, Aubrey directed his steps towards Greece, and, crossing the Peninsula, soon found himself at Athens. He then fixed his residence in the house of a Greek; and soon occupied himself in tracing the faded records of ancient glory upon monuments that apparently, ashamed of chronicling the deeds of freemen only before slaves, had hidden themselves beneath the sheltering soil or many coloured lichen. Under the same roof as himself, existed a being, so beautiful and delicate, that she might have formed the model for a painter wishing to pourtray on canvass the promised hope of the faithful in Mahomet's paradise, save that her eyes spoke too much mind for any one to think she could belong to those who had no souls.* As she danced upon the plain, or tripped along the mountain's side, one would have thought the gazelle a poor type of her beauties, for who would have exchanged her eye, apparently the eye of animated nature, for that sleepy luxurious look of the animal suited but to the taste of an epicure. The light step of Ianthe often accompanied Aubrey in his search after antiquities, and often would the unconscious girl, engaged in the pursuit of a Kashmere butterfly, show the whole beauty of her form, floating as it were upon the wind, to the eager gaze of him, who forgot the letters he had just decyphered upon an almost effaced tablet, in the contemplation of her sylph-like figure. Often would her tresses falling, as she flitted around, show in the sun's ray such delicately brilliant and swiftly fading hues, as might well excuse the forgetfulness of the antiquary, who let escape from his mind the very object he had before thought of vital importance to the proper interpretation of a passage in Pausanias.* But why attempt to describe charms which all feel, but none can appreciate?—It was innocence, youth, and beauty, unaffected by crowded drawing rooms, and stifling balls. Whilst he drew those remains of which he wished to preserve a memorial for his future hours, she would stand by, and watch the magic effects of his pencil, in tracing the scenes of her native place; she would then describe to him the circling dance upon the open plain, would paint to him in all the glowing colours of youthful memory, the marriage pomp she remembered viewing in her infancy; and then, turning to subjects that had evidently made a greater impression upon her mind, would tell him all the supernatural tales of her nurse. Her earnestness and apparent belief of what she narrated, excited the interest even of Aubrey; and often, as she told him the tale of the living vampyre, who had passed years amidst his friends, and dearest ties, forced every year, by feeding upon the life of a lovely female to prolong his existence for the ensuing months, his blood would run cold, whilst he attempted to laugh her out of such idle and horrible fantasies; but Ianthe cited to him the names of old men, who had at last detected one living among themselves, after several of their near relatives and children had been found marked with the stamp of the fiend's appetite; and when she found him so incredulous, she begged of him to believe her, for it had been remarked, that those who had dared to question their existence, always had some proof given, which obliged them, with grief and heartbreaking, to confess it was true. She detailed to him the traditional appearance of these monsters, and his horror was increased, by hearing a pretty accurate description of Lord Ruthven; he, however, still persisted in persuading her, that there could be no truth in her fears, though at the same time he wondered at the many coincidences which had all tended to excite a belief in the supernatural power of Lord Ruthven.

Aubrey began to attach himself more and more to Ianthe; her innocence, so contrasted with all the affected virtues of the women among whom he had sought for his vision of romance, won his heart; and while he ridiculed the idea of a young man of English habits, marrying an uneducated Greek girl, still he found himself more and more attached to the almost fairy form before him. He would tear himself at times from her, and, forming a plan for some antiquarian research, he would depart, determined not to return until his object was attained; but he always found it impossible to fix his attention upon the ruins around him, whilst in his mind he retained an image that seemed alone the rightful possessor of his thoughts. Ianthe was unconscious of his love, and was ever the same frank infantile being he had first known. She always seemed to part from him with reluctance; but it was because she had no longer any one with whom she could visit her favourite haunts, whilst her guardian was occupied in sketching or uncovering some fragment which had yet escaped the destructive hand of time. She had appealed to her parents on the subject of Vampyres, and they both, with several present, affirmed their existence, pale with horror at the very name. Soon after, Aubrey determined to proceed upon one of his excursions, which was to detain him for a few hours; when they heard the name of the place, they all at once begged of him not to return at night, as he must necessarily pass through a wood, where no Greek would ever remain after the day had closed, upon any consideration. They described it as the resort of the vampyres in their nocturnal orgies, and denounced the most heavy evils as impending upon him who dared to cross their path. Aubrey made light of their representations, and tried to laugh them out of the idea; but when he saw them shudder at his daring thus to mock a superior, infernal power, the very name of which apparently made their blood freeze, he was silent.

Next morning Aubrey set off upon his excursion unattended; he was surprised to observe the melancholy face of his host, and was concerned to find that his words, mocking the belief of those horrible fiends, had inspired them with such terror.—When he was about to depart, Ianthe came to the side of his horse and earnestly begged of him to return, ere night allowed the power of these beings to be put in action —he promised. He was, however, so occupied in his research that he did not perceive that day-light would soon end, and that in the horizon there was one of those specks which in the warmer climates so rapidly gather into a tremenduous mass and pour all their rage upon the devoted country.—He at last, however, mounted his horse, determined to make up by speed for his delay: but it was too late. Twilight in these southern climates is almost unknown; immediately the sun sets, night begins; and ere he had advanced far, the power of the storm was above—its echoing thunders had scarcely an interval of rest—its thick heavy rain forced its way through the canopying foliage, whilst the blue forked lightning seemed to fall and radiate at his very feet. Suddenly his horse took fright, and he was carried with dreadful rapidity through the entangled forest. The animal at last, through fatigue, stopped, and he found, by the glare of lightening, that he was in the neighbourhood of a hovel that hardly lifted itself up from the masses of dead leaves and brushwood which surrounded it. Dismounting, he approached, hoping to find some one to guide him to the town, or at least trusting to obtain shelter from the pelting of the storm. As he approached, the thunders, for a moment silent, allowed him to hear the dreadful shrieks of a woman mingling with the stifled exultant mockery of a laugh, continued in one almost unbroken sound; he was startled: but, roused by the thunder which again rolled over his head, he with a sudden effort forced open the door of the hut. He found himself in utter darkness; the sound, however, guided him. He was apparently unperceived; for though he called, still the sounds continued, and no notice was taken of him.

He found himself in contact with some one, whom he immediately seized, when a voice cried 'again baffled,' to which a
loud laugh succeeded, and he felt himself grappled by one
whose strength seemed superhuman: determined to sell his
life as dearly as he could, he struggled: but it was in vain: he
was lifted from his feet and hurled with enormous force against
the ground:—his enemy threw himself upon him, and kneeling upon his breast, had placed his hands upon his throat,
when the glare of many torches penetrating through the hole
that gave light in the day, disturbed him—he instantly rose and,
leaving his prey, rushed through the door, and in a moment
the crashing of the branches, as he broke through the wood,
was no longer heard.—The storm was now still; and Aubrey,
incapable of moving, was soon heard by those without.—
They entered; the light of their torches fell upon the mud walls,
and the thatch loaded on every individual straw with heavy
flakes of soot. At the desire of Aubrey they searched for her
who had attracted him by her cries; he was again left in darkness; but what was his horror, when the light of the torches
once more burst upon him, to perceive the airy form of his
fair conductress brought in a lifeless corse. He shut his eyes,
hoping that it was but a vision arising from his disturbed
imagination; but he again saw the same form, when he unclosed
them, stretched by his side. There was no colour upon her
cheek, not even upon her lip; yet there was a stillness about
her face that seemed almost as attaching as the life that once
dwelt there:—upon her neck and breast was blood, and upon
her throat were the marks of teeth having opened the vein:—
to this the men pointed, crying, simultaneously struck with
horror, 'a Vampyre, a Vampyre!' A litter was quickly formed,
and Aubrey was laid by the side of her who had lately been
to him the object of so many bright and fairy visions, now
fallen with the flower of life that had died within her. He
knew not what his thoughts were—his mind was benumbed
and seemed to shun reflection and take refuge in vacancy—
he held almost unconsciously in his hand a naked dagger of
a particular construction, which had been found in the hut.—
They were soon met by different parties who had been engaged
in the search of her whom a mother had soon missed.—Their

lamentable cries, as they approached the city, forewarned the parents of some dreadful catastrophe.—To describe their grief would be impossible; but when they ascertained the cause of their child's death they looked at Aubrey and pointed to the corpse.—They were inconsolable; both died broken-hearted.

Aubrey being put to bed was seized with a most violent fever, and was often delirious; in these intervals he would call upon Lord Ruthven and upon Ianthe—by some unaccountable combination he seemed to beg of his former companion to spare the being he loved.—At other times he would imprecate maledictions upon his head, and curse him as her destroyer. Lord Ruthven chanced at this time to arrive at Athens, and, from whatever motive, upon hearing of the state of Aubrey, immediately placed himself in the same house and became his constant attendant. When the latter recovered from his delirium he was horrified and startled at the sight of him whose image he had now combined with that of a Vampyre; but Lord Ruthven by his kind words, implying almost repentance for the fault that had caused their separation, and still more by the attention, anxiety, and care which he showed, soon reconciled him to his presence. His Lordship seemed quite changed; he no longer appeared that apathetic being who had so astonished Aubrey; but as soon as his convalescence began to be rapid, he again gradually retired into the same state of mind, and Aubrey perceived no difference from the former man, except, that at times he was surprised to meet his gaze fixed intently upon him with a smile of malicious exultation playing upon his lips; he knew not why, but this smile haunted him. During the last stage of the invalid's recovery, Lord Ruthven was apparently engaged in watching the tideless waves raised by the cooling breeze, or in marking the progress of those orbs, circling, like our world, the moveless sun;—indeed he appeared to wish to avoid the eyes of all.

Aubrey's mind, by this shock, was much weakened, and that elasticity of spirit which had once so distinguished him now seemed to have fled for ever.—He was now as much a lover of solitude and silence as Lord Ruthven; but much as he wished for solitude, his mind could not find it in the neighbourhood of Athens; if he sought it amidst the ruins he had formerly frequented, Ianthe's form stood by his side—if he sought it in the woods, her light step would appear wandering amidst the underwood, in quest of the modest violet; then suddenly turning round would show, to his wild imagination, her pale face and wounded throat with a meek smile upon her lips. He determined to fly scenes, every feature of which created such bitter associations in his mind. He proposed to Lord Ruthven, to whom he held himself bound by the tender care he had taken of him during his illness, that they should visit those parts of Greece neither had yet seen. They travelled in every direction, and sought every spot to which a recollection could be attached; but though they thus hastened from place to place yet they seemed not to heed what they gazed upon.—They heard much of robbers, but they gradually began to slight these reports, which they imagined were only the invention of individuals, whose interest it was to excite the generosity of those whom they defended from pretended dangers. In consequence of thus neglecting the advice of the inhabitants, on one occasion they travelled with only a few guards, more to serve as guides than as a defence.—Upon entering, however, a narrow defile, at the bottom of which was the bed of a torrent, with large masses of rock brought down from the neighbouring precipices, they had reason to repent their negligence—for, scarcely were the whole of the party engaged in the narrow pass, when they were startled by the whistling of bullets close to their heads, and by the echoed report of several guns. In an instant their guards had left them, and placing themselves behind rocks had begun to fire in the direction whence the report came. Lord Ruthven and Aubrey, imitating their example, retired for a moment behind a sheltering turn of the defile; but ashamed of being thus detained by a foe, who with insulting shouts bade them advance, and being exposed to unresisting slaughter, if any of the robbers should climb above and take them in the rear, they determined at once to rush forward in search of the enemy.—Hardly had they lost the shelter of the rock, when Lord Ruthven received a shot in the shoulder that brought him to the ground. —Aubrey hastened to his assistance, and no longer heeding the contest or his own peril, was soon surprised by seeing the robbers' faces around him; his guards having, upon Lord Ruthven's being wounded, immediately thrown up their arms and surrendered.

By promises of great reward, Aubrey soon induced them to convey his wounded friend to a neighbouring cabin, and having agreed upon a ransom he was no more disturbed by their presence, they being content to merely guard the entrance till their comrade should return with the promised sum for which he had an order.—Lord Ruthven's strength rapidly decreased; in two days mortification ensued, and death seemed advancing with hasty steps.—His conduct and appearance had not changed; he seemed as unconscious of pain as he had been of the objects about him; but towards the close of the last evening his mind became apparently uneasy, and his eye often fixed upon Aubrey, who was induced to offer his assistance with more than usual earnestness—'Assist me! you may save me—you may do more than that—I mean not my life, I heed the death of my existence as little as that of the passing day; but you may save my honour, your friend's honour.'—'How, tell me how; I would do any thing,' replied Aubrey. 'I need but little—my life ebbs apace—I cannot explain the whole— but if you would conceal all you know of me, my honour were free from stain in the world's mouth—and if my death were unknown for some time in England—I—I—but life.'— 'It shall not be known.'—'Swear!' cried the dying man, raising himself with exultant violence, 'Swear by all your soul reveres, by all your nature fears, swear that for a year and a day you will not impart your knowledge of my crimes or death to any living being in any way, whatever may happen, or whatever you may see.'—His eyes seemed bursting from their sockets: 'I swear!' said Aubrey; he sunk laughing upon his pillow and breathed no more.

Aubrey retired to rest, but did not sleep; the many circumstances attending his acquaintance with this man rose upon his mind, and he knew not why; when he remembered his oath a cold shivering came over him, as if from the presentiment of something horrible awaiting him. Rising early in the morning he was about to enter the hovel in which he had left the corpse, when a robber met him, and informed him that it was no longer there, having been conveyed by himself and comrades, upon his retiring, to the pinnacle of a neighbouring mount, according to a promise they had given his lordship, that it should be exposed to the first cold ray of the moon that rose after his death. Aubrey was astonished, and taking several of the men, determined to go and bury it upon the spot where it lay. But, when he had mounted to the summit he found no trace of either the corpse or the clothes, though the robbers swore they pointed out the identical rock on which they had laid the body. For a time his mind was bewildered in conjectures, but he at last returned, convinced that they had buried the corpse for the sake of the clothes.

Weary of a country in which he had met with such terrible misfortunes, and in which all apparently conspired to heighten that superstitious melancholy that had seized upon his mind, he resolved to leave it, and soon arrived at Smyrna.* While waiting for a vessel to convey him to Otranto, or to Naples, he occupied himself in arranging those effects he had with him belonging to Lord Ruthven. Amongst other things there was a case containing several weapons of offence, more or less adapted to ensure the death of the victim. There were several daggers and ataghans.* Whilst turning them over, and examining their curious forms, what was his surprise at finding a sheath apparently ornamented in the same style as the dagger discovered in the fatal hut; he shuddered; hastening to gain further proof, he found the weapon, and his horror may be imagined when he discovered that it fitted, though peculiarly shaped, the sheath he held in his hand. His eyes seemed to need no further certainty—they seemed gazing to be bound to the dagger; yet still he wished to disbelieve; but the particular form, the same varying tints upon the haft and sheath were alike in splendour on both, and left no room for doubt; there were also drops of blood on each.

He left Smyrna, and on his way home, at Rome, his first inquiries were concerning the lady he had attempted to snatch from Lord Ruthven's seductive arts. Her parents were in distress, their fortune ruined, and she had not been heard of since the departure of his lordship. Aubrey's mind became almost broken under so many repeated horrors; he was afraid that this lady had fallen a victim to the destroyer of Ianthe. He became morose and silent, and his only occupation consisted in urging the speed of the postilions, as if he were going to save the life of some one he held dear. He arrived at Calais; a breeze, which seemed obedient to his will, soon wafted him to the English shores; and he hastened to the mansion of his fathers, and there, for a moment, appeared to lose, in the embraces and caresses of his sister, all memory of the past. If she before, by her infantine caresses, had gained his affection, now that the woman began to appear, she was still more attaching as a companion.

Miss Aubrey had not that winning grace which gains the gaze and applause of the drawing-room assemblies. There was none of that light brilliancy which only exists in the heated atmosphere of a crowded apartment. Her blue eye was never lit up by the levity of the mind beneath. There was a melancholy charm about it which did not seem to arise from misfortune, but from some feeling within, that appeared to indicate a soul conscious of a brighter realm. Her step was not that light footing, which strays where'er a butterfly or a colour may attract—it was sedate and pensive. When alone, her face was never brightened by the smile of joy; but when her brother breathed to her his affection, and would in her presence forget those griefs she knew destroyed his rest, who would have exchanged her smile for that of the voluptuary? It seemed as if those eyes,—that face were then playing in the light of their own native sphere. She was yet only eighteen, and had not been presented to the world; it having been thought by her guardians more fit that her presentation should be delayed until her brother's return from the continent, when he might be her protector. It was now, therefore, resolved that the next drawing room,* which was fast approaching, should be the epoch of her entry into the 'busy scene'.* Aubrey would rather have remained in the mansion of his fathers, and fed upon the melancholy which overpowered him. He could not feel interest about the frivolities of fashionable strangers, when his mind had been so torn by the events he had witnessed; but he determined to sacrifice his own comfort to the protection of his sister. They soon arrived in town, and prepared for the next day, which had been announced as a drawing room.

The crowd was excessive—a drawing room had not been held for a long time, and all who were anxious to bask in the smile of royalty, hastened thither. Aubrey was there with his sister. While he was standing in a corner by himself, heedless of all around him, engaged in the remembrance that the first time he had seen Lord Ruthven was in that very place—he felt himself suddenly seized by the arm, and a voice he recognized too well, sounded in his ear—'Remember your oath.' He had hardly courage to turn, fearful of seeing a spectre that would blast him, when he perceived, at a little distance, the same figure which had attracted his notice on this spot upon his first entry into society. He gazed till his limbs almost refusing to bear their weight, he was obliged to take the arm of a friend, and forcing a passage through the crowd, he threw himself into his carriage, and was driven home. He paced the room with hurried steps, and fixed his hands upon his head, as if he were afraid his thoughts were bursting from his brain. Lord Ruthven again before him—circumstances started up in dreadful array—the dagger—his oath.—He roused himself, he could not believe it possible—the dead rise again!—He thought his imagination had conjured up the image his mind was resting upon. It was impossible that it could be real—he determined, therefore, to go again into society; for though he attempted to ask concerning Lord Ruthven, the name hung upon his lips, and he could not succeed in gaining information. He went a few nights after with his sister to the assembly of a near relation. Leaving her under the protection of a matron, he retired into a recess, and there gave himself up to his own devouring thoughts. Perceiving, at last, that many were leaving, he roused himself, and entering another room, found his sister surrounded by several, apparently in earnest conversation; he attempted to pass and get near her, when one, whom he requested to move, turned round, and revealed to him those features he most abhorred. He sprung forward, seized his sister's arm, and, with hurried step, forced her towards the street: at the door he found himself impeded by the crowds of servants who were waiting for their lords; and

while he was engaged in passing them, he again heard that
voice whisper close to him—'Remember your oath!'—He did
not dare to turn, but, hurrying his sister, soon reached home.

Aubrey became almost distracted. If before his mind had
been absorbed by one subject, how much more completely
was it engrossed, now that the certainty of the monster's living again pressed upon his thoughts. His sister's attentions
were now unheeded, and it was in vain that she intreated him
to explain to her what had caused his abrupt conduct. He only
uttered a few words, and those terrified her. The more he
thought, the more he was bewildered. His oath startled him;
—was he then to allow this monster to roam, bearing ruin
upon his breath, amidst all he held dear, and not avert its progress? His very sister might have been touched by him. But
even if he were to break his oath, and disclose his suspicions,
who would believe him? He thought of employing his own
hand to free the world from such a wretch; but death, he
remembered, had been already mocked. For days he remained
in this state; shut up in his room, he saw no one, and eat only
when his sister came, who, with eyes streaming with tears,
besought him, for her sake, to support nature. At last, no
longer capable of bearing stillness and solitude, he left his
house, roamed from street to street, anxious to fly that image
which haunted him. His dress became neglected, and he wandered, as often exposed to the noon-day sun as to the midnight damps. He was no longer to be recognized; at first he
returned with the evening to the house; but at last he laid him
down to rest wherever fatigue overtook him. His sister, anxious for his safety, employed people to follow him; but they
were soon distanced by him who fled from a pursuer swifter
than any—from thought. His conduct, however, suddenly
changed. Struck with the idea that he left by his absence the
whole of his friends, with a fiend amongst them, of whose
presence they were unconscious, he determined to enter again
into society, and watch him closely, anxious to forewarn, in
spite of his oath, all whom Lord Ruthven approached with
intimacy. But when he entered into a room, his haggard and
suspicious looks were so striking, his inward shudderings so
visible, that his sister was at last obliged to beg of him to

abstain from seeking, for her sake, a society which affected him so strongly. When, however, remonstrance proved unavailing, the guardians thought proper to interpose, and, fearing that his mind was becoming alienated, they thought it high time to resume again that trust which had been before imposed upon them by Aubrey's parents.

Desirous of saving him from the injuries and sufferings he had daily encountered in his wanderings, and of preventing him from exposing to the general eye those marks of what they considered folly, they engaged a physician to reside in the house, and take constant care of him. He hardly appeared to notice it, so completely was his mind absorbed by one terrible subject. His incoherence became at last so great, that he was confined to his chamber. There he would often lie for days, incapable of being roused. He had become emaciated, his eyes had attained a glassy lustre;—the only sign of affection and recollection remaining displayed itself upon the entry of his sister: then he would sometimes start, and, seizing her hands, with looks that severely afflicted her, he would desire her not to touch him. 'Oh, do not touch him—if your love for me is aught, do not go near him!' When, however, she inquired to whom he referred, his only answer was—'True! true!' and again he sank into a state, whence not even she could rouse him. This lasted many months: gradually, however, as the year was passing, his incoherences became less frequent, and his mind threw off a portion of its gloom, whilst his guardians observed, that several times in the day he would count upon his fingers a definite number, and then smile.

The time had nearly elapsed, when, upon the last day of the year, one of his guardians entering his room, began to converse with his physician upon the melancholy circumstance of Aubrey's being in so awful a situation when his sister was going next day to be married. Instantly Aubrey's attention was attracted; he asked anxiously to whom. Glad of this mark of returning intellect, of which they feared he had been deprived, they mentioned the name of the Earl of Marsden. Thinking this was a young earl whom he had met with in society, Aubrey seemed pleased, and astonished them still more by his expressing his intention to be present at the nuptials, and desiring to see his sister. They answered not, but in a few minutes his sister was with him. He was apparently again capable of being affected by the influence of her lovely smile; for he pressed her to his breast, and kissed her cheek, wet with tears, flowing at the thought of her brother's being once more alive to the feelings of affection. He began to speak with all his wonted warmth, and to congratulate her upon her marriage with a person so distinguished for rank and every accomplishment; when he suddenly perceived a locket upon her breast; opening it, what was his surprise at beholding the features of the monster who had so long influenced his life. He seized the portrait in a paroxysm of rage, and trampled it under foot. Upon her asking him why he thus destroyed the resemblance of her future husband, he looked as if he did not understand her—then seizing her hands, and gazing on her with a frantic expression of countenance, he bade her swear that she would never wed this monster, for he——But he could not advance—it seemed as if that voice again bade him remember his oath—he turned suddenly round, thinking Lord Ruthven was near him, but saw no one. In the meantime the guardians and physician, who had heard the whole, and thought this was but a return of his disorder, entered, and forcing him from Miss Aubrey, desired her to leave him. He fell upon his knees to them, he implored, he begged of them to delay but for one day. They, attributing this to the insanity they imagined had taken possession of his mind, endeavoured to pacify him, and retired.

Lord Ruthven had called the morning after the drawing room, and had been refused with every one else. When he heard of Aubrey's ill health, he readily understood himself to be the cause of it: but when he learned that he was deemed insane, his exultation and pleasure could hardly be concealed from those among whom he had gained this information. He hastened to the house of his former companion, and, by constant attendance, and the pretence of great affection for the brother and interest in his fate, he gradually won the ear of Miss Aubrey. Who could resist his power? His tongue had dangers and toils to recount—could speak of himself as of an individual having no sympathy with any being on the crowded earth, save with her to whom he addressed himself; —could tell how, since he knew her, his existence had begun to seem worthy of preservation, if it were merely that he might listen to her soothing accents;—in fine, he knew so well how to use the serpent's art, or such was the will of fate, that he gained her affections. The title of the elder branch falling at length to him, he obtained an important embassy, which served as an excuse for hastening the marriage, (in spite of her brother's deranged state,) which was to take place the very day before his departure for the continent.

Aubrey, when he was left by the physician and his guardian, attempted to bribe the servants, but in vain. He asked for pen and paper; it was given him; he wrote a letter to his sister, conjuring her, as she valued her own happiness, her own honour, and the honour of those now in the grave, who once held her in their arms as their hope and the hope of their house, to delay but for a few hours, that marriage, on which he denounced the most heavy curses. The servants promised they would deliver it; but giving it to the physician, he thought it better not to harass any more the mind of Miss Aubrey by, what he considered, the ravings of a maniac. Night passed on without rest to the busy inmates of the house; and Aubrey heard, with a horror that may more easily be conceived than described, the notes of busy preparation. Morning came, and the sound of carriages broke upon his ear. Aubrey grew almost frantic. The curiosity of the servants at last overcame their vigilance, they gradually stole away, leaving him in the custody of an helpless old woman. He seized the opportunity, with one bound was out of the room, and in a moment found himself in the apartment where all were nearly assembled. Lord Ruthven was the first to perceive him: he immediately approached, and, taking his arm by force, hurried him from the room, speechless with rage. When on the staircase, Lord Ruthven whispered in his ear—'Remember your oath, and know, if not my bride to day, your sister is dishonoured. Women are frail!' So saying, he pushed him towards his attendants, who, roused by the old woman, had come in search of him. Aubrey could no longer support himself; his rage, not finding vent, had broken a blood-vessel, and he was conveyed to bed. This was not mentioned to his sister, who was not present when he entered, as the physician was afraid of agitating her. The marriage was solemnized, and the bride and bridegroom left London.

Aubrey's weakness increased; the effusion of blood produced symptoms of the near approach of death. He desired his sister's guardians might be called, and when the midnight hour had struck, he related composedly what the reader has perused—he died immediately after.

The guardians hastened to protect Miss Aubrey; but when they arrived, it was too late. Lord Ruthven had disappeared, and Aubrey's sister had glutted the thirst of a VAMPYRE!

SIR GUY EVELING'S DREAM

Horace Smith

'Now that we be upon this subject of dreams and apparitions, I may nohow forbear to mention that full strange and terrible one of Sir Guy Eveling, and the consequences tragical issuing therefrom, which do I the more willingly pen, forasmuch as the dismal tale was hushed and smothered up at the time by the great families with whom he was consanguined, people of worshipful regard and jeopardous power, whereby folks only whispered of the story in corners, and peradventure bruited* about many things which were but fond imaginings. How I learned the real sooth and verity of that awesome event, and came to be consulted thereupon, ye shall presently see, when I unfold to you that the Lady Rivers, the favourite sister of Sir Guy, then dwelt in the close of Westminster Abbey, in the next house to mine own, which abutteth upon the great cloisters; who first being only a near neighbour, became at last a fast friend, and claimed my advisement in all that touched herself and that most unhappy gentleman her brother. Albeit my lips were vowed to a locked secrecy while she lived, yet can they now divulge what they have so long concealed; for that right worthy lady (whom God absolve!) having withdrawn to the Rookery, by Fountains Abbey* in Yorkshire, did there erewhile give up the ghost in all godliness of faith and abundancy of hope.

'Now wot ye well that Sir Guy had received a good and clerkly schooling at Oxenforde, and was well learned in all that doth beseem a gentleman, yet, maugre this his knowledge, he was of a haute and orgulous stomach that would not agnize* the wisdom of beadsmen, nor even brook the tender counsellings of friends and kinsmen, whereby he waxed wild, and readily fell to mischief and riot, giving up his mornings to dicers, racqueters, and scatterlings, and casting away the night with ribalds, wasselers, and swinge-bucklers, when he was not worse bestowed (though better to his liking) with giglots* and gold-wasting wantons, upon whom he lavished his substance, and then betook himself to the dice to repair his fortune—for ever one wickedness begetteth another. In this evil wise did he live, reckless of reproof and deaf to fond entreatment, to the sore discomfort and aggrieving of all his honourable house: howbeit that few now took busy concernment about him except the Lady Rivers, who did often, with all the compassment of wit and loving-kindness of heart, beseech him to abandon the crafty mermaids and chamberers with whom he consorted, and choose some chaste and discreet mate, so to establish himself in such a goodly household as became his ancestry. Verily, Alice, (would he say) if ye any thing earthly regard, I do entreat ye forbear this manner of speech, which nought availeth thee to utter and irketh me to hear, for I will not quit my ronyons and bonarobas* till it pleaseth me of my own free will; and for a wife, never have I yet seen the eyes that could bribe me to put the neck of my liberty into the collar of a wedding ring. And therewithal he again plunged into his riotous and deboshed courses.

'It chanced once, that returning home from a wild revel as the sun was dawning and the apprentices afoot, he betook himself to his lodging at the Flower-de-luce, next to the French Embassador's, on the outside of Temple Bar, where, being heavy with his carouse, he cast himself upon his bed, in his cassock as he was, and forthwith fell asleep, as it is surmised, and had a troublous and astounding dream; though he himself ever stoutly did maintain that being right well awake, and having just then heard the Temple clock strike eight of the morning, he looked to his bed-foot, and lo! there stood before him a strange lady of stately presence and surpassingly beauteous. More especially was he astonied at her large, round, glistering dark eyes, with two goodly arcs of black thereover spreading, the which seemed to him a more noble and majestical vision withal than he had ever encountered upon earth. Her cheer was not the less fraught with dignity than comeliness, albeit that her visage was passing wan, and of somewhat melancholic and tristful ostent;* and so she gazed earnestly upon him, who in like wise did glue his looks upon her, much marvelling what this might mean. But incontinent* after, sith

she neither moved nor spake, he being ever of a right courage-
ous heart, and deeming moreover that it might be some prank
of his irregulous and profane companions, did raise himself
up on the bed, and drawing nigh unto the figure, so to convince himself by touch of hand whether it might be real flesh
and blood, in this wise said unto it:—"Most sweetly fair and
wondrously delectable lady! whom I more admire and love
than may my tongue upon so short a summons worthily confess; suffer that I doff from thy throat that ungainly ruff
wherein thy beauty is muffled, sith it is an unseemly fashion
that I did ever marvellously mislike."—Whom when she saw
approaching as if to untie the ruff, a sudden great terror and
change of countenance fell upon her, so that she clasped both
her hands round her throat as if to hold it fast, and, uttering
a piteous soul-piercing shriek, the spectre or apparition, for
such in good sooth might it seem, straight vanished away!

'Now Sir Guy was of that stubborn and misbelieving spirit
that holdeth not faith in ghostly things, so he arose and cautelously* searched throughout the chamber and in the cup-
boards thereof; but nothing might he discover, the windows
being double-latched, and the door locked even as he had left
it. So anon he heard a knocking thereat, and opening he found
his servant, who came in fear that some mishap might have
befallen, sith he had also heard the shrieking of the vision,
whereby his master was right well assured that it was not a
dream. Nathless he was in no wise amort* or forlorn in mind,
but entertaining the misadventure with a merry and regardless mockery, as was in all things his wont, he betook himself to the Lady Rivers, whom he thus greeted in laughing
guise—"Ods Pitikins! sister mine, happy man be my dole,*
for I have seen the eyes that shall bribe me to thy wishes, and
thou shalt presently dance at my spousal, if thou wilt find me
the queen of the bright crystals that did draw my curtains
this morn, but would not tarry my embracing." Whereupon
he recounteth what he had seen, concluding with a Styx-sworn
oath, that none other would he marry but she whom once seeing he would never forget nor forbear to love. "Now God and
good provision forbid!" quoth his sister; "for yet ye wot not
what manner of vision this may be, nor whether, if a mortal

woman, she be not a harlot and a Jesabel."—"Of that I reck not," said Sir Guy; "be she of chaste and holy approof, be she besmirched with sin, I tell thee in all sooth none other will I wed"; and to this his unmastered resolve did he conjure himself by many irreverent and profane protests which it were not seemly that I should repeat.

'On the evening of the day next following, as he went homeward, he was overtaken of a sudden by a perilous and rageful storm, wherein the whole welkin did seem to vomit forth fire and water, while men did stop up their ears because of the splitting roar of the thunder. This was that self tempest which there be many now living may remember, sith it followed hard upon the Proclamation of our late King Edward,* and even then was the tower of St Mary Woolnoth Church* split by the lightning, as to this day it remaineth. Sir Guy, I say, running with much speed to evitate this hurricane, passed so fleetly into the porch of his dwelling, that he might hardly be aware of a female standing thereon, having her head sheathed in a wimple; but as she drew somewhat on one side so to let him pass, he glimpsed beneath her hood, and lo! there were the twain large black eyes, above all measure lustrous, and that visage of fair sorrow, more beautiful than beauty, which had stood before him in his chamber. Judge you if he were not fixed like a statue, while she with a modest courtesy besought him that she might there abide the return of her servant, whom, being surprised by the foul weather, she had sent within the Bar* for a carriage, nothing mistrusting that he would speedily appear therewith. There was no lack of earnest and passionate entreatment from Sir Guy that she would take shelter in his parlour upstairs; but it booted not, for ever with sweet but grave denial she thanked him for his proffer, still resolving there to tarry till her laggard servant should come back. Howbeit, while they were discoursing, the storm blowing into the passage where they stood, wrested open the door at the other end, where was a small garden, in such wise that the wind rushed in from the street side, and much rain therewith; whereupon the lady, already somewhat bemoiled, consented to withdraw upstairs from that rude blustering of the weather. Whom, when she was seated, Sir Guy

did courteously invite to doff her wimple, which done he
might mark the self ruff that misliked him in his dream, and
again making show to remove it, her visage waxed wroth and
fearful, she clasped her throat with her hands, and Sir Guy
might hear a faint shriek, as at a distance, which he bethought
on such a noisome night might peradventure be of some pas-
senger in the streets smitten by the then thickly falling tiles.
Nathless he mused much why she should thus cautelously
enwrap her throat.

'So fell they forthwith into pleasant discourse, and if he
admired much her facete entertainment and argute compassment* of wit, much more was he astonied at her honey-sweet
voice, which to his enchanted ears did seem more tuneably
melodious than ever was the dulcimer of Miriam* or Orpheus
his lute. With every look from those majestical eyes, and every
sound from her music-breathing mouth, love gained a greater
empery over his soul; and forasmuch as he well wist that
opportunity and likelihood of sphere* were not to be lost, he
straightway confessed his passion, and did woo her with many
oaths and much amorous entreatment. Whereat, by blushing,
she confessed at once her shamefacedness and somewhat angry
surprise, rebuking him gravely, but sweetly withal; alway pro-
testing she was of discreet virtuous bearing and goodly parent-
age, which warranted not any light or immodest encountering.
Whereat he forbore furthermore to press her: whereas her servant came not, neither the carriage, he dispread before her a
small supper of picked pullets, applejohns, marchpane, com-
fits and other dainty cates, and therewith a beaker of charneco
wine, and a sherris sack-posset,* whereof she frugally did
partake.

'"Sith my varlet, who, in sooth, is but a dullard," quoth
the lady, "cometh not, and the storm seemeth to be in good
measure abated, and beside it waxeth late, I will bid you good
night, and seek my dwelling a-foot, much thanking you for
your hospitable bearing." But Sir Guy, nowise willing so to
part, led her to the window, inviting her to mark the pitchy
darkness of the welkin: incontinent whereupon the black
caverns of the sky opened, and the live lightning leaped forth
like a flaming sword, by whose flash they saw through the

Temple-bar up into Fleet-street, which was like a river of
raging water clinquant with light; and, anon, all was again
shrouded in inky blackness, and the deafening thunder bel-
lowed as if it would fain burst asunder the solid earth. So,
seeing there was no safe mean of then seeking her abode, and
Sir Guy tendering to her use a small bed-room above his own,
with pledge of safe and worthy dealing, she, much lamenting the chance of so forced intrusion upon a stranger, albeit
thankful of his right courteous bearing, did there consent to
pass the night. Straight whereupon Sir Guy, with unwilling
steps, yet not without hope of more prosperous stead thereafter, ushered her to her chamber, and with a lover's beni-
son, committing her to the sleepful god, did sorrowing take
his leave.

'In his own room scarce had he tarried five minutes, much
pondering upon this occurrent and the so strange mystery
of the ruff, when he bethought him that he had left with his
fair guest no lamp, whereof in a house unknown, and a night
so fitful, she might well have special need. Wherewith he took
one from the mantel, and ascending the stairs went into the
lady's room, whom he found already in part unapparelled;
her muffler and tirevolant* being laid aside from her head,
which as she moved, the black locks did bridle up and down
upon her white shoulders, like a company of ravens newly
alighted upon the snow. But, above all, what did rivet his eyes
was to see that her ruff was doffed, and about her throat was
there a full broad roundure of black velvet, thickly broidered
with pearls and jacinths, close clasped to the skin, which
(being moved thereunto by a not-to-be-subdued curiosity) he
did again approach with offer to unlock, whereat her visage
was again overshadowed with affrightment, she upraised her
hands to her neck, and a distant shriek sounded through the
air as aforetime. Nathless, so passing beauteous and bewitching sweet did she appear in that disordered gear, which seemed
to celestify her charms, that Sir Guy, more than ever overcome with love, fell upon his knee, and with divers oaths and
protestations, not sparing tears withal, did call all the saints
to witness that he gave himself up to her with plight of hand,
and took her for his betrothed wife, movingly beseeching her

to compassionate his case. Nor did the lady, intenerated* by
his tears and piteous looks, and having moreover taken his
plighted troth, which verily is a real spousal, any longer with
cold denial repudiate his suit.

'Awaking full early next day, and finding the lady still asleep,
Sir Guy bethought him of an appointment on that self morning to receive a sum of gold, which he had won on the yester
from one of the diceing cavaleros, and kenning him to be a
Bezonian and a lozel,* he feared he might blench from his
engagement did he not meet him; which he the less willed,
forasmuch as having latterly been free of dispense, his purse
was somewhat more than usual disfurnished. So, slipping
deftly from the bed, he donned his gear in silence, and hied
with all speed to the White Rose, beside the Duke's-garden,
at the Cross of Charing, where he received the purse of
gold; wherewith as he hurried homeward, he conned over in
thought what brooches, gimmal rings, carkanets, and jewelled
gawds and braveries* he should buy, to prank out her whom
he termed his alder-liefest love. Whom not to awaken, he did
full gently ope the door, and by the glooming light through
the shutters oozing, saw her fair round arm, which Venus
might envy, distended upon the counterpoint of the bed. So,
taking it hushingly up with fond intent to kiss it—lo! it was
key-cold!—he felt the pulse, and it did not beat;—he let go
the arm, and it lumped deadly down! Amort with fearful misgivings, he threw back the shutters, when the new-risen sun
shone bright upon the bed, and drawing aside the curtains—
O, God of mercy! he beheld a soul-sickening corpse!—Those
late glorious eyes were now bloodshot and well nigh brast
from their sockets, and albeit that the sun glared full upon
them, they were stony and unlustrous; clenched were the teeth,
wherefrom the bloodless lips started back; the visage was
ghastly wan; the hair wildly spread about the pillow; and all
bore semblance of one who with a violent and sudden death
had painfully struggled!

'Rushing, with a loud cry, from that chamber of death, he
encountered his host, who, much astonied at his agony, and
yet more when he kenned the cause thereof, betook him with
right good speed to the Temple, searching a chirurgeon and

the officers of justice, who coming with their posse to the house, made prisoner of Sir Guy, and with him straightway entered into the fatal room. But no sooner did they set eye upon the body, than backward, shuddering with much horror and consternation, while they crossed their foreheads, and called upon God and the saints to shield them, several voices did at once cry out—"That is the Italian lady which was hanged on Thursday last!"—(Seemeth it that this misfortuned woman was the leman of the Italian ambassador, whom having in a passion of jealousy stabbed, she was judged therefore, and suffered the death at Tybourn). So unbuckling the broad velvet necklace, behold! her livid throat was all over sore, discoloured, and bruised, and writhled,* and deep cut into by the cruel and despiteous rope.

'Sir Guy, who had awhiles stood aghast in a voiceless dismay, now heaved forth a deep and dread groan,—for well might he remember, when his sister would fain dissuade him from wedding any semblance of the vision, that he profanely did say:—"Soothly, Alice, were a she devil to tempt me in such winning wise, I would certes wed her"; and he sorely trembled to think that some demon, peradventure Sathan himself, had incorporated himself in that now loathed form, to receive his plight and so delude and win his sinful soul. Thenceforward his gaysome heart and right merry cheer did altogether fail him; he 'gan to wail and dump, shunning converse of man, and in lonesome corners would paddle his neck with his hand, saying he could lay his finger in the wound, as if himself had been hanged; and in this wise gat worse and worse, until at the last he went stark distraught and was mewed up in the Spittal for the crazed,* where, some three or four weeks thereafter, he gave up the ghost in great wildness and agony of soul.'

CONFESSIONS OF A REFORMED RIBBONMAN

William Carleton

I HAD read the anonymous summons, but from its general import, I believed it to be one of those special meetings convened for some purpose affecting the general objects and proceedings of the body. At least the terms in which it was conveyed to me, had nothing extraordinary or mysterious in them, beyond the simple fact that it was not to be a general, but a select meeting; this mark of confidence flattered me, and I determined to attend punctually. I was, it is true, desired to keep the circumstance entirely to myself, but there was nothing startling in this, for I had often received summonses of a similar import. I therefore resolved to attend, according to the letter of my instructions, 'on the next night, at the solemn hour of midnight, to deliberate and act upon such matters as should, then and there, be submitted to my consideration.' The morning after I received this message, I arose and resumed my usual occupations; but from whatever cause it may have proceeded, I felt a sense of approaching evil hang heavily upon me; the beats of my pulse were languid, and an undefinable feeling of anxiety pervaded my whole spirit; even my face was pale, and my eye so heavy, that my father and brothers concluded me to be ill; an opinion which I thought at the time to be correct; for I felt exactly that kind of depression which precedes a severe fever. I could not understand what I experienced, nor can I yet, except by supposing that there is in human nature some mysterious faculty, by which, in coming calamities, the approach throws forward the shadow of some fearful evil, and that it is possible to catch a dark anticipation of the sensations which they subsequently produce. For my part I can neither analyze nor define it; but on that day I knew it by painful experience, and so have a thousand others in similar circumstances.

It was about the middle of winter. The day was gloomy and tempestuous almost beyond any other I remember; dark clouds rolled over the hills about me, and a close sleet-like rain fell in slanting drifts that chased each other rapidly to the earth on the course of the blast. The out-lying cattle sought the closest and calmest corners of the fields for shelter; the trees and young groves were tossed about, for the wind was so unusually high that it swept its hollow gusts through them, with that hoarse murmur which deepens so powerfully on the mind the sense of dreariness and desolation.

As the shades of night fell, the storm if possible increased. The moon was half gone, and only a few stars were visible by glimpses, as a rush of wind left a temporary opening in the sky. I had determined, if the storm should not abate, to incur any penalty rather than attend the meeting; but the appointed hour was distant, and I resolved to be decided by the future state of the night.

Ten o'Clock came, but still there was no change; eleven passed, and on opening the door to observe if there were any likelihood of it clearing up, a blast of wind mingled with rain, nearly blew me off my feet; at length it was approaching to the hour of midnight, and on examining a third time, I found it had calmed a little, and no longer rained.

I instantly got my oak stick, muffled myself in my great coat, strapped my hat about my ears, and as the place of meeting was only a quarter of a mile distant, I presently set out.

The appearance of the heavens was louring and angry, particularly in that point where the light of the moon fell against the clouds from a seeming chasm in them, through which alone she was visible. The edges of this were faintly bronzed, but the dense body of the masses that hung piled on each side of her, was black and impenetrable to sight. In no other point of the heavens was there any part of the sky visible; for a deep veil of clouds overhung the horizon, yet was the light sufficient to give occasional glimpses of the rapid shifting which took place in this dark canopy, and of the tempestuous agitation with which the midnight storm swept to and fro beneath.

At length I arrived at a long slated house, situated in a solitary part of the neighbourhood; a little below it ran a small stream, which was now swollen above its banks, and rushing with mimic roar over the flat meadows beside it. The appearance of the bare slated building in such a night was particularly sombre, and to those like me who knew the purpose to which it was then usually devoted, it was, or ought to have been, peculiarly so. There it stood, silent and gloomy, without any appearance of human life or enjoyment about, or within it: as I approached, the moon once more had broken out of the clouds, and shone dimly upon the glittering of the wet slates and window, with a death-like lustre, that gradually faded away as I left the point of observation, and entered the folding door. It was the parish chapel.

The scene which presented itself here, was in keeping not only with the external appearance of the house, but with the darkness, the storm, and the hour,—which was now a little after midnight. About eighty persons were sitting in dead silence upon the circular steps of the altar; they did not seem to move, and as I entered and advanced, the echo of my footsteps rang through the building with a lonely distinctness, which added to the solemnity and mystery of the circumstances about me. The windows were secured with shutters on the inside, and on the altar a candle was lighting, which burned dimly amid the surrounding darkness, and lengthened the shadow of the altar itself, and of six or seven persons who stood on its upper steps, until they mingled in the obscurity which shrouded the lower end of the chapel. The faces of those who sat on the altar steps were not distinctly visible, yet the prominent and more characteristic features were in sufficient relief, and I observed, that some of the most malignant and reckless spirits in the parish, were assembled. In the eyes of those who stood at the altar, and whom I knew to be invested with authority over the others, I could perceive gleams of some latent and ferocious purpose, kindled, as I soon observed, into a fiercer expression of vengeance, by the additional excitement of ardent spirits, with which they had stimulated themselves to a point of determination that mocked at the apprehension of all future responsibility, either in this world or the next.

The welcome which I received on joining them, was far different from the boisterous good humour which used to mark our greetings on other occasions; just a nod of the head from this or that person, on the part of those *who sat*, with a *ghud dhemur tha thu*,* in a suppressed voice, even below a common whisper; but, from the standing group, who were evidently the projectors of the enterprise, I received a convulsive grasp of the hand, accompanied by a fierce and desperate look, that seemed to search my eye and countenance, to try if I was a person not likely to shrink from whatever they had resolved to execute. It is surprising to think of the powerful expression which a moment of intense interest or great danger is capable of giving to the eye, the features, and slightest actions, especially in those whose station in society does not require them to constrain nature, by the force of social courtesies, into habits of concealment of their natural emotions. None of the standing group spoke, but as each of them wrung my hand in silence, his eye was fixed on mine, with an expression of drunken confidence and secrecy, and an insolent determination not to be gainsayed without peril. If looks could be translated with certainty, they seemed to say, 'we are bound upon a project of vengeance, and if you do not join us, remember that we *can* revenge.' Along with this grasp, they did not forget to remind me of the common bond by which we were united, for each man gave me the secret grip of Ribbonism in a manner that made the joints of my fingers ache for some minutes after.

There was one present, however—the highest in authority —whose actions and demeanour were calm and unexcited; he seemed to labour under no unusual influence whatever, but evinced a serenity so placid and philosophical, that I attributed the silence of the sitting group, and the restraint which curbed in the out-breaking passions of those who *stood*, entirely to his presence. He was a school-master, who taught his daily school in that chapel, and acted also, on Sunday, in the capacity of clerk to the priest—an excellent and amiable old man, who knew little of his illegal connection, and atrocious conduct.

When the ceremonies of brotherly recognition and friendship were past, the Captain, by which title I will designate the last-mentioned person, stooped, and raising a jar of whiskey on the corner of the altar, held a wine glass to its neck, which he filled, and with a calm nod handed it to me to drink. I shrunk back, with an instinctive horror, at the profaneness of such an act, in the house, and on the altar of God, and peremptorily refused to taste the proffered draught. He smiled, mildly, at what he considered my superstition, and added quietly, and in a low voice, 'You'll be wantin' it, I'm thinkin', afther the wettin' you got.'—'Wet or dry,' said I—'Stop, man' he replied in the same tone—'spake lower; but why would'nt you take the whiskey? Sure there's as holy people to the fore as you—did'nt they all take it?—an' I wish we may never do worse than dhrink a harmless glass of whiskey, to keep the could out, any way.' 'Well,' said I, 'I'll just trust to God, and the consequinces, for the could, Paddy, ma bouchal; but a blessed dhrop ov it wo'nt be crossin' my lips, avick; so no more gosther* about it—dhrink it yerself, if you like; maybe you want it as much as I do—wherein I've the patthern of a good big-coat upon me, so thick, yer sowl, that if it was rainin' bullocks, a dhrop would'nt get undher the nap ov it.' He gave me a calm, but keen glance, as I spoke. 'Well, Jim,' said he, 'it's a good comrâde you've got for the weather that's in it—but in the mane time, to set you a dacent patthern, I'll just take this myself,'—saying which, with the jar still upon its side, and the fore-finger of his left hand in its neck, he swallowed the spirits. 'It's the first I dhrank to-night,' he added, 'nor would I dhrink it now, only to shew you that I've heart and sperrit to do a thing that we're all bound and sworn to, when the proper time comes'—saying which, he laid down the glass, and turned up the jar, with much coolness, upon the altar.

During this conversation, those who had been summoned to this mysterious meeting were pouring in fast; and as each person approached the altar, he received from one to two or three large glasses of whiskey, according as he chose to limit himself—and, to do them justice, there were not a few of those present, who, in despite of their own desire, and the Captain's express invitation, refused to taste it in the house of God's worship. Such, however, as were scrupulous, he afterwards recommended to take it on the outside of the chapel door, which they did—as by that means, the sacrilege of the act was supposed to be evaded.

About one o'clock they were all assembled except six—at least so the Captain, on looking at a written paper, asserted. 'Now, boys,' said he, in the same low voice, 'we are all present except the thraitors whose names I am goin' to read to you; not that we are to count thim as thraitors, till we know whether or not it was in their power to come; any how, the night is terrible—but, boys, you're to know, that neither fire nor wather is to privint yees, when duly summonsed to attind a meeting—particularly whin the summons is widout a name, as you have been tould that there is always something of consequence to be done *thin*.' He then read out the names of those who were absent, in order that the real cause of their absence might be ascertained—declaring, that they would be dealt with accordingly. After this he went, and with his usual caution shut and bolted the door, and having put the key in his pocket, he ascended the steps of the altar, and for some time traversed the little platform from which the priest usually addresses the congregation.

Until this night I never contemplated the man's countenance with any particular interest, but as he walked the platform, I had an opportunity of observing him more closely. He was a little man, apparently not thirty; and on a first view seemed to have nothing remarkable either in his dress or features. I, however, was not the only person whose eye was rivetted upon him at that moment; in fact every one present observed him with equal interest, for hitherto he had kept the object of the meeting perfectly secret, and of course we all felt anxious to know it. It was while he traversed this platform that I scrutinized his features with a hope, if possible, to glean from them some indication of what was passing within; I could, however, mark but little, and that little was at first rather from the intelligence which seemed to subsist between him and those whom I have already mentioned as *standing* against the altar, than from any indications of his own; their gleaming eyes were fixed upon him with an intensity of savage and demon-like hope, which blazed out in flashes of malignant triumph, as upon turning, he threw a cool but rapid glance at them, to intimate the progress he was making in the subject to which he devoted the undivided energies of his mind. But in the course of this meditation, I could observe on one or two occasions a dark shade come over his countenance that contracted his brow into a deep furrow, and it was then, for the first time, that I saw the satanic expression of which his face, by a very slight motion of its muscles, was capable; his hands, during this silence, closed and opened convulsively; his eyes shot out two or three baleful glances, first to his confederates, and afterwards vacantly into the deep gloom of the lower part of the chapel; his teeth ground against each other, like those of a man whose revenge burns to reach a distant enemy, and finally, after having wound himself up to a certain determination, his features relaxed into their original calm and undisturbed expression.

At this moment a loud laugh, having something supernatural in it, rang out wildly from the darkness of the chapel; he stopped, and putting his open hand over his brows, peered down into the gloom, and said calmly in Irish, *bee dhu hust ne wulh anam inh*—'hold your tongue, it is not yet the time.' —Every eye was now directed to the same spot, but, in consequence of its distance from the dim light on the altar, none could perceive the object from which the laugh proceeded. It was by this time, near two o'clock in the morning.

He now stood for a few moments on the platform, and his chest heaved with a depth of anxiety equal to the difficulty of the design he wished to accomplish; 'brothers,' said he, 'for we are all brothers—sworn upon all that's sacred an' holy, to obey whatever them that's over us, maning among ourselves, wishes us to do—are you now ready, in the name of God, upon whose althar I stand, to fulfil yer oath?'

The words were scarcely uttered, when those who had *stood* beside the altar during the night, sprung from their places, and descending its steps rapidly, turned round, and raising their arms exclaimed, 'By all that's sacred an' holy we're willin'.'

In the mean time, those who *sat* upon the steps of the altar, instantly rose, and following the example of those who had just spoken, exclaimed after them, 'to be sure—by all that's sacred an' holy we're willin'.'

'Now boys,' said the Captain, 'ar'nt yees big fools for your pains? an' *one* of yee's does'nt know what I mane.'

'You're our Captain,' said one of those who had stood at the altar—'an' has yer ordhers from higher quarthers, of coorse whatever ye command upon us we're bound to obey you in.'

'Well,' said he, smiling, 'I only wanted to thry yees an' by the oath yees tuck, there's not a Captain in the county has as good a right to be proud of his min as I have—well yees won't rue it, may be when the right time comes; and for that same rason every one of yees must have a glass from the jar; thim that won't dhrink it *in* the chapel can dhrink it *widout*; an' here goes to open the door for them'—he then distributed another large glass to every man who would accept it, and brought the jar afterwards to the chapel door, to satisfy the scruples of those who would not drink within. When this was performed, and all duly excited, he proceeded:

'Now, brothers, you are solemnly sworn to obey me, an' I'm sure there's no thraithur here that 'id parjure himself for a trifle, any how, but *I'm* sworn to obey them that's above me—manin' still among ourselves—an' to shew you that I don't scruple to do it, here goes'—he then turned round, and taking the Missal between his hands, placed it upon the holy altar. Hitherto, every word was uttered in a low precautionary tone; but on grasping the book, he again turned round, and looking upon his confederates with the same satanic expression which marked his countenance before, exclaimed in a voice of deep determination;——

'By this sacred an' holy book of God, I will perform the action which we have met this night to accomplish, be that what it may—an' this I swear upon God's book, an' God's altar!' At this moment the candle which burned before him went suddenly out, and the chapel was wrapped in pitchy darkness; the sound as if of rushing wings fell upon our ears, and fifty voices dwelt upon the last words of his oath, with wild and supernatural tones that seemed to echo and to mock what he had sworn. There was a pause, and an exclamation of horror from all present, but the Captain was too cool and steady to be disconcerted; he immediately groped about until he got the candle, and proceeding calmly to a remote corner of the chapel, took up a half-burned turf which lay there, and after some trouble, succeeded in lighting it again. He then explained what had taken place; which indeed was easily done, as the candle happened to be extinguished by a pigeon which sat exactly above it. The chapel, I should have observed, was at this time, like many country chapels, unfinished inside, and the pigeons of a neighbouring dove-cote, had built nests among the rafters of the unceiled roof, which circumstance also explained the rushing of the wings, for the birds had been affrighted by the sudden loudness of the noise. The mocking voices were nothing but the echoes, rendered naturally more awful by the scene, the mysterious object of the meeting, and the solemn hour of the night.

When the candle was again lighted, and these startling circumstances accounted for, the persons whose vengeance had been deepening more and more during the night, rushed to the altar in a body, where each in a voice trembling with passionate eagerness, repeated the oath, and as every word was pronounced, the same echoes heightened the wildness of the horrible ceremony, by their long and unearthly tones. The countenances of these human tigers were livid with suppressed rage—their knit brows, compressed lips, and kindled eyes, fell under the dim light of the taper, with an expression calculated to sicken any heart not absolutely diabolical.

As soon as this dreadful rite was completed, we were again startled by several loud bursts of laughter, which proceeded from the lower darkness of the chapel, and the captain on hearing them, turned to the place, and reflecting for a moment, said in Irish, *gutsho nish, avoh elhee*—'come hither now, boys'. A rush immediately took place from the corner in which they had secreted themselves all the night—and seven men appeared, whom we instantly recognized as brothers and cousins of certain persons who had been convicted some time before, for breaking into the house of an honest poor man in the neighbourhood, from whom, after having treated him with barbarous violence, they took away such fire arms as he kept for his own protection.

It was evidently not the captain's intention to have produced these persons until the oath should have been generally taken, but the exulting mirth with which they enjoyed the success of his scheme betrayed them, and put him to the necessity of bringing them forward somewhat before the concerted moment.

The scene which now took place was beyond all power of description; peals of wild fiend-like yells rang through the chapel, as the party which *stood* on the altar, and that which had crouched in the darkness met; wringing of hands, leaping in triumph, striking of sticks and fire arms against the ground and the altar itself, dancing and cracking of fingers, marked the triumph of some hellish propensity. Even the captain for a time was unable to restrain their fury; but at length he mounted the platform before the altar once more, and with a stamp of his foot, recalled their attention to himself and the matter in hand.

'Boys,' said he, 'enough of this, and too much; an' well for us it is that the chapel is in a lonely place, or our foolish noise might do us no good—let thim that swore so manfully jist now, stand a one side, till the rest kiss the book one by one.'

The proceedings, however, had by this time taken too alarming a shape, for even the captain to compel them to a blindfold oath; the first man he called flatly refused to swear, until he should first hear the nature of the service that was required. This was echoed by the remainder, who taking courage from the firmness of this person, declared generally, that until they first knew the business they were to execute, none of them should take the oath. The captain's lip quivered slightly, and his brow once more knit with the same hellish expression, which I have remarked gave him so much the appearance of an embodied fiend; but this speedily passed away, and was succeeded by a malignant sneer, in which lurked, if there ever did in a sneer, 'a laughing devil,' calmly, determinedly, atrocious.

'It was'nt worth yer whiles to refuse the oath,' said he, mildly, 'for the thruth is, I had next to nothing for ye's to do—not a hand, maybe, would have to *rise*, only jist to look on, an', if any resistance would be made, to shew yerselves; yer numbers would soon make them see that resistance would be no use whatever in the present case. At all evints the oath of *secrecy must* be taken, or woe be to him that will refuse *that*, he wont know the day, the hour, nor the minute, when he'll be made a spatch-cock ov.' He then turned round, and placing his right hand on the Missal, swore 'in the presence of God, and before his holy altar, that whatever might take place that night he would keep secret, from man or mortal, except it was the holy priest on his dying day, and that neither bribery, nor imprisonment, nor death, would wring it from his heart'; having done this, he struck the book violently, as if to confirm the energy with which he swore, and then calmly descending the steps, stood with a serene countenance, like a man conscious of having performed a good action. As this oath did not pledge those who refused to take the other to the perpetration of any specific crime, it was readily taken by all present; preparations were then made to execute what was intended; the half burned turf was placed in a little pot—another glass of whiskey was distributed, and the door being locked by the captain, who kept the key as parish master and clerk, the crowd departed silently from the chapel.

The moment that those who lay in the darkness during the night, made their appearance at the altar, we knew at once the persons we were to visit; for, as I said before, these were related to the miscreants whom one of these persons had convicted, in consequence of their midnight attack upon himself and his family. The Captain's object in keeping them unseen was, that those present, not being aware of the duty about to be imposed on them, might have less hesitation against swearing to its fulfilment. Our conjectures were correct, for on leaving the chapel we directed our steps to the house in which this man (the only Protestant in the parish) resided.

The night was still stormy, but without rain; it was rather dark too, though not so as to prevent us from seeing the clouds careering swiftly through the air. The dense curtain which had overhung and obscured the horizon, was now broken, and large sections of the sky were clear, and thinly studded with stars that looked dim and watery, as did indeed the whole firmament, for in some places large clouds were still visible threatening a continuance of severe tempestuous weather. The road appeared washed and gravelly, every dike was full of yellow water, and each little rivulet and larger stream dashed its hoarse music in our ears; the blast, too, was cold, fierce, and wintry, sometimes driving us back to a stand still, and again, when a turn in the road would bring it in our backs, whirling us along for a few steps, with involuntary rapidity. At length the fated dwelling became visible, and a short consultation was held in a sheltered place, between the Captain and the two parties who seemed so eager for its destruction. Their fire arms were now charged, and their bayonets and short pikes, the latter shod and pointed with iron, were also got ready: the live coal which was brought in the small pot, had become extinguished, but to remedy this, two or three persons from the remote parts of the parish, entered a cabin on the wayside, and under pretence of lighting their own and their comrade's pipes, procured a coal of fire, for so they called a lighted turf. From the time we left the chapel until this moment, a most profound silence had been maintained, a circumstance, which, when I considered the number of persons present, and the mysterious and dreaded object of their journey, had a most appalling effect upon my spirits.

At length we arrived within fifty perches of the house, walking in a compact body, and with as little noise as possible; but it seemed as if the very elements had conspired to frustrate our design, for on advancing within the shade of the farm-hedge, two or three persons found themselves up to the middle in water, and on stooping to ascertain more accurately the state of the place, we could see nothing but one immense sheet of it spread like a lake over the meadows which surrounded the spot we wished to reach.

Fatal night! the very recollection of it, when associated with the fearful tempest of the elements, grows, if that were possible, yet more wild and revolting. Had we been engaged in any innocent or benevolent enterprize, there was something in our situation, just now, that had a touch of interest in it to a mind imbued with a relish for the savage beauties of nature. There we stood, about a hundred and thirty in number, our dark forms bent forwards peering into the dusky expanse of water, with its dim gleams of reflected light, broken by the weltering of the mimic waves into ten thousand fragments, whilst the few stars that overhung it in the firmament, appeared to shoot through it in broken lines, and to be multiplied fifty-fold in the many-faced mirror on which we gazed.

Over this was a stormy sky, and around us a darkness through which we could only distinguish, in outline, the nearest objects, whilst the wild wind swept strongly and dismally upon us. When it was discovered that the common pathway to the house was inundated, we were about to abandon our object, and return home; the Captain, however, stooped down low for a moment, and almost closing his eyes, looked along the surface of the waters, and then raising himself very calmly, said, in his usual quiet tone, 'yees need'nt go back, boys, Iv'e found a path, jist follow me.' He immediately took a more circuitous direction, by which we reached a causeway that had been raised for the purpose of giving a free passage to and from the house, during such inundations as the present. Along this we had advanced more than half way, when we discovered a break in it, which, as afterwards appeared, had that night been made by the strength of the flood. This, by means of our sticks and pikes, we found to be about three feet deep, and eight yards broad. Again we were at a loss how to proceed, when the fertile brain of the Captain devised a method of crossing it: 'boys,' said he, 'of course you've all played at leap-frog— very well, strip and go in a dozen of you,—lean one upon the shoulders of another from this to the opposite bank, where one must stand facing the outside man, both their shoulders agin one another, that the outside man may be supported— then *we* can creep over you, an' a decent bridge you'll be, any way.' This was the work of only a few minutes, and in less than ten we were all safely over.

Merciful heaven! how I sicken at the recollection of what is to follow—on reaching the dry bank, we proceeded instantly, and in profound silence, to the house; the Captain divided us into companies, and then assigned to each division its proper station. The two parties who had been so vindictive all the night, he kept about himself, for of those who were present they only were in his confidence, and knew his nefarious purpose; their number was about fifteen. Having made these dispositions, he, at the head of about five of them, approached the house on the windy side, for the fiend possessed a coolness which enabled him to seize upon every possible advantage; that he had combustibles about him was evident, for in less than fifteen minutes nearly one half of the house was enveloped in flames. On seeing this, the others rushed over to the spot where he and his gang were standing, and remonstrated earnestly, but in vain; the flames now burst forth with renewed violence, and as they flung their strong light upon the faces of the foremost group, I do think hell itself could hardly present any thing more satanic than their countenances, now worked up into a paroxysm of infernal triumph, at their own revenge. The Captain's look had lost all its calmness, every feature started out into distinct malignity, the curve in his brow was deep, and ran up to the root of the hair, dividing his face into two sections, that did not seem to have been designed for each other. His lips were half open, and the corners of his mouth a little brought back on each side, like those of a man expressing intense hatred and triumph over an enemy, who is in the death-struggle under his grasp. His eyes blazed from beneath his knit eye-brows, with a fire that seemed to have been lighted up in the infernal pit itself. It is unnecessary and only painful to describe the rest of his gang; demons might have been proud of such horrible visages as they exhibited; for they worked under all the power of hatred, revenge, and joy; and these passions blended into one terrific scowl, enough almost to blast any human eye that would venture to look upon it.

When the others attempted to intercede for the lives of the inmates, there were at least fifteen loaded guns and pistols levelled at them; 'another word,' said the Captain, 'an' you're a corpse where you stand, or the first man who will dare to speak for them: no, no, it was'nt to spare them we came here—"No Mercy" is the pass word for the night, an' by the sacred oath I swore beyant in the chapel, any one among yees that will attimpt to shew it, will find none at my hand. Surround the house boys, I tell ye, I hear them stirring—*No Mercy*—no quarther—is the ordher of the night.'

Such was his command over these misguided creatures, that in an instant there was a ring round the house to prevent the escape of the unhappy inmates, should the raging element give them time to attempt it; for none present dare withdraw themselves from the scene, not only from an apprehension of the Captain's present vengeance, or that of his gang, but because they knew that even had they then escaped, an early and certain death awaited them from a quarter against which they had no means of defence. The hour now was about half past two o'clock. Scarcely had the last words escaped from the Captain's lips, when one of the windows of the house was broken, and a human head having the hair in a blaze, was descried, apparently a woman's, if one might judge by the profusion of burning tresses, and the softness of the tones, notwithstanding that it called, or rather shrieked aloud, for help and mercy. The only reply to this was the whoop from the Captain and his gang of no mercy—'No mercy,' and that instant the former, and one of the latter rushed to the spot, and ere the action could be perceived, the head was transfixed with a bayonet and a pike, both having entered it together. The word mercy was divided in her mouth; a short silence ensued, the head hung down on the window, but was instantly tossed back into the flames.

This action occasioned a cry of horror from all present, except the *gang* and their leader, which startled and enraged the latter so much, that he ran towards one of them, and had his bayonet, now reeking with the blood of its innocent victim, raised to plunge it in his body, when dropping the point, he said in a piercing whisper that hissed in the ears of all: 'Its no use *now*, you know, if one's to hang, all will hang; so our safest way, you persave, is to lave none of them to tell the story: ye *may* go now if you wish; but it wont save a hair of your heads. You cowardly set! I knew if I had tould yees the sport, that none of ye except my *own* boys would come, so I jist played a thrick upon you; but remember what you are sworn to, and stand to the oath ye tuck.'

Unhappily, notwithstanding the wetness of the preceding weather, the materials of the house were extremely combustible; the whole dwelling was now one body of glowing flame, yet the shouts and shrieks within, rose awfully above its crackling and the voice of the storm, for the wind once more blew in gusts, and with great violence. The doors and windows were all torn open, and such of those within, as had escaped the flames rushed towards them, for the purpose of further escape, and of claiming mercy at the hands of their destroyers—but whenever they appeared, the unearthly cry of no mercy rung upon their ears for a moment, and for a moment only, for they were flung back at the points of the weapons which the demons had brought with them to make the work of vengeance more certain.

As yet there were many persons in the house, whose cry for life was strong as despair, and who clung to it with all the awakened powers of reason and instinct; the ear of man could hear nothing so strongly calculated to stifle the demon of cruelty and revenge within him, as the long and wailing shrieks which rose beyond the element, in tones that were carried off rapidly upon the blast, until they died away in the darkness that lay behind the surrounding hills. Had not the house been in a solitary situation, and the hour the dead of night, any persons sleeping within a moderate distance must have heard them, for such a cry of sorrow deepening into a yell of despair, was almost sufficient to have awakened the dead. It was lost however upon the hearts and ears that heard it: to them, though in justice be it said, to only comparatively a few of them, it was as delightful as the tones of soft and entrancing music.

The claims of the poor sufferers were now modified; they supplicated merely to suffer death *at the hands of their enemies*; they were willing to bear that, provided they should be allowed to escape from the flames; but no, the horrors of the conflagration were calmly and malignantly gloried in by their merciless assassins, who deliberately flung them back into all their tortures. In the course of a few minutes a man appeared upon the side-wall of the house, nearly naked; his figure, as he stood against the sky in horrible relief, was so finished a picture of woe-begone agony and supplication, that it is yet as distinct in my memory as if I were again present at the scene. Every muscle, now in motion by the powerful agitation of

his sufferings, stood out upon his limbs and neck, giving him
an appearance of desperate strength, to which by this time he
must have been wrought; the perspiration poured from his
frame, and the veins and arteries of his neck were inflated to
a surprising thickness. Every moment he looked down into
the thick flames which were rising to where he stood; and
as he looked, the indescribable horror which flitted over his
features might have worked upon the devil himself to relent.
His words were few; 'my child,' said he, 'is still safe, she is
an infant, a young creature that never harmed you nor any
one—she is still safe. Your mothers, your wives have young
innocent children like it—Oh, spare her, think for a moment
that its one of your own, spare it, as you hope to meet a just
God, or if you dont, in mercy shoot me first, put an end to
me, before I see her burned.'

The Captain approached him coolly and deliberately. 'You
will prosecute no one now, you bloody informer,' said he;
'you will convict no more boys for taking an ould rusty gun
an' pistol from you, or for givin' you a neighbourly knock
or two into the bargain.' Just then from a window opposite
him, proceeded the shrieks of a woman who appeared at it
with the infant in her arms. She herself was almost scorched
to death; but with the presence of mind and humanity of her
sex, she was about to thrust the little babe out of the window.
The Captain noticed this, and with characteristic atrocity,
thrust, with a sharp bayonet, the little innocent, along with
the person who endeavoured to rescue it, into the red flames,
where they both perished. This was the work of an instant.
Again he approached the man; 'your child is a coal now,' said
he, with deliberate mockery, 'I pitched it in myself on the
point of this,' showing the weapon, 'and now is your turn,'
saying which he clambered up by the assistance of his gang,
who stood with a front of pikes and bayonets bristling to receive the wretched man, should he attempt in his despair to
throw himself from the wall. The Captain got up, and placing
the point of his bayonet against his shoulder, flung him into
the fiery element that raged behind him. He uttered one wild
and piercing cry, as he fell back, and no more; after this nothing was heard but the crackling of the fire, and the rushing

of the blast; all that had possessed life within were consumed, amounting either to eleven or fifteen persons.

When this was accomplished, those who took an active part in the murder, stood for some time about the conflagration, and as it threw its red light upon their fierce faces and rough persons, soiled as they now were with smoke and black streaks of ashes, the scene seemed to be changed to hell, and the murderers to spirits of the damned, rejoicing over the arrival and the torture of a guilty soul. The faces of those who kept aloof from the slaughter, were blanched to the whiteness of death; some of them fainted—and others were in such agitation that they were compelled to leave their comrades. They became actually stiff and powerless with horror; yet to such a scene were they brought by the pernicious influence of Ribbonism.

It was only when the last victim went down, that the conflagration shot up into the air with most unbounded fury. The house was large, deeply thatched, and well furnished; and the broad red pyramid rose up with fearful magnificence towards the sky. Abstractedly it had sublimity, but now it was associated with nothing in my mind but blood and terror. It was not, however, without a purpose that the Captain and his guard stood to contemplate its effect. 'Boys,' said he, 'we had better be sartin' that all's safe; who knows but there might be some of the sarpents crouchin' under a hape of rubbish, to come out and gibbet us to-morrow or next day; we had better wait a while, any how, if it was only to see the blaze.'

Just then the flames rose majestically to a surprising height; our eyes followed their direction, and we perceived for the first time, that the dark clouds above, together with the intermediate air, appeared to reflect back, or rather to have caught the red hue of the fire; the hills and country about us appeared with an alarming distinctness; but the most picturesque part of it, was the effect or reflection of the blaze on the floods that spread over the surrounding plains. These, in fact, appeared to be one broad mass of liquid copper, for the motion of the breaking waters, caught from the blaze of the high waving column, as reflected in them, a glaring light, which eddied and rose, and fluctuated, as if the flood itself had been a lake of molten fire.

Fire, however, destroys rapidly; in a short time the flames sank—became weak and flickering—by and bye, they only shot out in fits—the crackling of the timbers died away—the surrounding darkness deepened; and ere long, the faint light was overpowered by the thick volumes of smoke, that rose from the ruins of the house, and its murdered inhabitants.

'Now, boys,' said the Captain, 'all is safe, we may go. Remember, every man of you, what you've sworn this night on the book and altar of God—not on a heretic Bible. If you perjure yourselves, you may hang us; but let me tell you for your comfort, that if you do, there is them livin' that will take care the lase of your own lives will be but short.' After this we dispersed, every man to his own home.

Reader, not many months elapsed ere I saw the bodies of this Captain, whose name was Paddy Devan, and all those who were actively concerned in the perpetration of this deed of horror, withering in the wind, where they hung gibbetted, near the scene of their nefarious villainy; and while I inwardly thanked heaven for my own narrow and almost undeserved escape, I thought in my heart how seldom, even in this world, justice fails to overtake the murderer, and to enforce the righteous judgment of God, 'that whoso sheddeth man's blood, by man shall his blood be shed'.

MONOS AND DAIMONOS

Edward Bulwer

I AM English by birth, and my early years were passed in
—— I had neither brothers nor sisters; my mother died when
I was in the cradle; and I found my sole companion, tutor,
and playmate in my father. He was a younger brother of a
noble and ancient house: what induced him to forsake his
country and his friends, to abjure all society, and to live in a
rock, is a story in itself, which has nothing to do with mine.

As the Lord liveth, I believe the tale that I shall tell you
will have sufficient claim on your attention, without calling
in the history of another to preface its most exquisite details,
or to give interest to its most amusing events. I said my father
lived on a rock—the whole country round seemed nothing
but rock!—wastes, bleak, blank, dreary; trees stunted, herbage
blasted; caverns, through which some black and wild stream
(that never knew star or sunlight, but through rare and hideous chasms of the huge stones above it) went dashing and
howling on its *blessed* course; vast cliffs, covered with eternal
snows, where the birds of prey lived, and sent, in screams and
discordance, a grateful and meet music to the heavens, which
seemed too cold and barren to wear even clouds upon their
wan, grey, comfortless expanse: these made the characters of
that country where the spring of my life sickened itself away.
The climate which, in the milder parts of —— relieves the nine
months of winter with three months of an abrupt and autumn-
less summer, never seemed to vary in the gentle and sweet
region in which *my* home was placed. Perhaps, for a brief interval, the snow in the valleys melted, and the streams swelled,
and a blue, ghastly, unnatural kind of vegetation, seemed here
and there to mix with the rude lichen, or scatter a grim smile
over minute particles of the universal rock; but to these
witnesses of the changing season were the summers of my
boyhood confined. My father was addicted to the sciences—
the physical sciences—and possessed but a moderate share of

learning in any thing else; he taught me all he knew; and the rest of my education, Nature, in a savage and stern guise, instilled in my heart by silent but deep lessons. She taught my feet to bound, and my arm to smite; she breathed life into my passions, and shed darkness over my temper; she taught me to cling to her, even in her most rugged and unalluring form, and to shrink from all else—from the companionship of man, and the soft smiles of woman, and the shrill voice of childhood; and the ties, and hopes, and socialities, and objects of human existence, as from a torture and a curse. Even in that sullen rock, and beneath that ungenial sky, I had luxuries unknown to the palled tastes of cities, or to those who woo delight in an air of odours and in a land of roses! What were those luxuries? They had a myriad varieties and shades of enjoyment—they had but a common name. What were those luxuries? *Solitude!*

My father died when I was eighteen; I was transferred to my uncle's protection, and I repaired to London. I arrived there, gaunt and stern, a giant in limbs and strength, and to the tastes of those about me, a savage in bearing and in mood. They would have laughed, but I awed them; they would have altered *me*, but I changed *them*; I threw a damp over their enjoyment and a cloud over their meetings. Though I said little, though I sat with them, estranged and silent, and passive, they seemed to wither beneath my presence. Nobody could live with me and be happy, or at ease! I felt it, and I hated them that they could love not me. Three years passed —I was of age—I demanded my fortune—and scorning social life, and pining once more for loneliness, I resolved to journey into those unpeopled and far lands, which if any have pierced, none have returned to describe. So I took my leave of them all, cousin and aunt—and when I came to my old uncle, who had liked me less than any, I grasped his hand with so friendly a gripe, that, well I ween, the dainty and nice member was but little inclined to its ordinary functions in future.

I commenced my pilgrimage—I pierced the burning sands —I traversed the vast deserts—I came into the enormous woods of Africa, where human step never trod, nor human voice ever started the thrilling and intense solemnity that broods over the great solitudes, as it brooded over chaos before the world was! There the primeval nature springs and perishes; undisturbed and unvaried by the convulsions of the surrounding world; the leaf becomes the tree, lives through its uncounted ages, falls and moulders, and rots and vanishes, unwitnessed in its mighty and mute changes, save by the wandering lion, or the wild ostrich, or that huge serpent—a hundred times more vast than the puny boa that the cold limners of Europe have painted, and whose bones the vain student has preserved, as a miracle and marvel. There, too, as beneath the heavy and dense shade I couched in the scorching noon, I heard the trampling as of an army, and the crush and fall of the strong trees, and beheld through the matted boughs the behemoth pass on its terrible way, with its eyes burning as a sun, and its white teeth arched and glistening in the rabid jaw, as pillars of spar glitter in a cavern; the monster, to whom only those wastes are a home, and who never, since the waters rolled from the Dædal* earth, has been given to human gaze and wonder but my own! Seasons glided on, but I counted them not; they were not doled to me by the tokens of man, nor made sick to me by the changes of his base life, and the evidence of his sordid labour. Seasons glided on, and my youth ripened into manhood, and manhood grew grey with the first frost of age; and then a vague and restless spirit fell upon me, and I said in my foolish heart, 'I will look upon the countenances of my race once more!' I retraced my steps—I recrossed the wastes—I re-entered the cities—I took again the garb of man; for I had been hitherto naked in the wilderness, and hair had grown over me as a garment. I repaired to a sea-port, and took ship for England.

In the vessel there was one man, and only one, who neither avoided my companionship nor recoiled at my frown. He was an idle and curious being, full of the frivolities, and egotisms, and importance of them to whom towns are homes, and talk has become a mental aliment. He was one pervading, irritating, offensive tissue of little and low thoughts. The only meanness he had not was fear. It was impossible to awe, to silence, or to shun him. He sought me for ever; he was as a blister to me, which no force could tear away; my soul grew faint when my eyes met him. He was to my sight as those creatures which from their very loathsomeness are fearful as well as despicable to us. I longed and yearned to strangle him when he addressed me! Often I would have laid my hand on him, and hurled him into the sea to the sharks, which, lynx-eyed and eager-jawed, swam night and day around our ship; but the gaze of many was on us, and I curbed myself, and turned away, and shut my eyes in very sickness; and when I opened them again, lo! he was by my side, and his sharp quick voice grated, in its prying, and asking, and torturing accents, on my loathing and repugnant ear! One night I was roused from my sleep by the screams and oaths of men, and I hastened on deck: we had struck upon a rock. It was a ghastly, but, oh Christ! how glorious a sight! Moonlight still and calm —the sea sleeping in sapphires; and in the midst of the silent and soft repose of all things, three hundred and fifty souls were to perish from the world! I sat apart, and looked on, and aided not. A voice crept like an adder's hiss upon my ear; I turned, and saw my tormentor; the moonlight fell on his face, and it grinned with the maudlin grin of intoxication, and his pale blue eye glistened, and he said, 'We will not part even here!' My blood ran coldly through my veins, and I would have thrown him into the sea, which now came fast and fast upon us; *but the moonlight was on him, and I did not dare to kill him*. But I would not stay to perish with the herd, and I threw myself alone from the vessel and swam towards a rock. I saw a shark dart after me, but I shunned him, and the moment after he had plenty to sate his maw. I heard a crash, and a mingled and wild burst of anguish, the anguish of three hundred and fifty hearts that a minute afterwards were stilled, and I said in my *own* heart, with a deep joy, '*His* voice is with the rest, and we *have* parted!' I gained the shore, and lay down to sleep.

The next morning my eyes opened upon a land more beautiful than a Grecian's dreams. The sun had just risen, and laughed over streams of silver, and trees bending with golden and purple fruits, and the diamond dew sparkled from a sod covered with flowers, whose faintest breath was a delight. Ten thousand birds, with all the hues of a northern rainbow blended in their glorious and glowing wings, rose from turf and tree, and loaded the air with melody and gladness; the sea, without a vestige of the past destruction upon its glassy brow, murmured at my feet; the heavens without a cloud, and bathed in a liquid and radiant light, sent their breezes as a blessing to my cheek. I rose with a refreshed and light heart; I traversed the new home I had found; I climbed upon a high mountain, and saw that I was in a small island—it had no trace of man—and my heart swelled as I gazed around and cried aloud in my exultation, 'I shall be alone again!' I descended the hill: I had not yet reached its foot, when I saw the figure of a man approaching towards me. I looked at him, and my heart misgave me. He drew nearer, and I saw that my despicable persecutor had escaped the waters, and now stood before me. He came up with his hideous grin, and his twinkling eye; and he flung his arms round me,—I would sooner have felt the slimy folds of the serpent—and said, with his grating and harsh voice, 'Ha! ha! my friend, we shall be together still!' I looked at him with a grim brow, but I said not a word. There was a great cave by the shore, and I walked down and entered it, and the man followed me. 'We shall live so happily here,' said he; 'we will never separate!' And my lip trembled, and my hand clenched of its own accord. It was now noon, and hunger came upon me; I went forth and killed a deer, and I brought it home and broiled part of it on a fire of fragrant wood; and the man eat, and crunched, and laughed, and I wished that the bones had choked him; and he said, when we had done, 'We shall have rare cheer here!' But I still held my peace. At last he stretched himself in a corner of the cave and slept. I looked at him, and saw that the slumber was heavy, and I went out and rolled a huge stone to the mouth of the cavern, and took my way to the opposite part of the island; it was my turn to laugh then! I found out another cavern; and I made a bed of moss and of leaves, and I wrought a table of wood, and I looked out from the mouth of the cavern and saw the wide seas before me, and I said, 'Now I shall be alone!'

When the next day came, I again went out and caught a kid, and brought it in, and prepared it as before, but I was not hungered, and I could not eat, so I roamed forth and wandered over the island: the sun had nearly set when I returned. I entered the cavern, and sitting on my bed and by my table was that man whom I thought I had left buried alive in the other cave. He laughed when he saw me, and laid down the bone he was gnawing.

'Ha, ha!' said he, 'you would have served me a rare trick, but there was a hole in the cave which you did not see, and I got out to seek you. It was not a difficult matter, for the island is so small; and now we *have* met, and we will part no more!'

I said to the man, 'Rise, and follow me!' So he rose, and I saw that of all my food he had left only the bones. 'Shall this thing reap and I sow?' thought I, and my heart felt to me like iron.

I ascended a tall cliff: 'Look round,' said I; 'you see that stream which divides the island; you shall dwell on one side, and I on the other; but the same spot shall not hold us, nor the same feast supply!'

'That may never be!' quoth the man; 'for I cannot catch the deer, not spring upon the mountain kid; and if you feed me not, I shall starve!'

'Are there not fruits,' said I, 'and birds that you may snare, and fishes which the sea throws up?'

'But I like them not,' quoth the man, and laughed, 'so well as the flesh of kids and deer!'

'Look, then,' said I, 'look: by that grey stone, upon the opposite side of the stream, I will lay a deer or a kid daily, so that you may have the food you covet; but if ever you cross the stream and come into my kingdom, so sure as the sea murmurs, and the bird flies, I will kill you!'

I descended the cliff, and led the man to the side of the stream. 'I cannot swim,' said he; so I took him on my shoulders and crossed the brook, and I found him out a cave, and I made him a bed and a table like my own, and left him. When I was on my own side of the stream again, I bounded with joy, and lifted up my voice; 'I shall be alone *now!*' said I.

So two days passed, and I *was* alone. On the third I went after my prey; the noon was hot, and I was wearied when I returned. I entered my cavern, and behold the man lay stretched upon my bed. 'Ha, ha!' said he, 'here I am; I was so lonely at home that I have come to live with you again!'

I frowned on the man with a dark brow, and I said, 'So sure as the sea murmurs, and the bird flies, I will kill you!' I seized him in my arms; I plucked him from my bed; I took him out into the open air, and we stood together on the smooth sand, and by the great sea. A fear came suddenly upon me; I was struck with the awe of the still Spirit which reigns over solitude. Had a thousand been round us, I would have slain him before them all. I feared now because we were alone in the desert, with silence and GOD! I relaxed my hold. 'Swear,' I said, 'never to molest me again: swear to preserve unpassed the boundary of our several homes, and I will *not* kill you!' 'I cannot swear,' answered the man; 'I would sooner die than forswear the blessed human face—even though that face be my enemy's!'

At these words my rage returned; I dashed the man to the ground, and I put my foot upon his breast, and my hand upon his neck, and he struggled for a moment—and was dead! I was startled; and as I looked upon his face I thought it seemed to revive; I thought the cold blue eye fixed upon me, and the vile grin returned to the livid mouth, and the hands which in the death-pang had grasped the sand, stretched themselves out to me. So I stamped on the breast again, and I dug a hole in the shore, and I buried the body. 'And now,' said I, 'I am alone at last!' And then *the sense of loneliness*, the vague, vast, comfortless, objectless sense of desolation passed into me. And I shook—shook in every limb of my giant frame, as if I had been a child that trembles in the dark; and my hair rose, and my blood crept, and I would not have stayed in that spot a moment more if I had been made young again for it. I turned away and fled—fled round the whole island; and gnashed my teeth when I came to the sea, and longed to be cast into some illimitable desert, that I might flee on for ever. At sunset I returned to my cave—I sat myself down on one corner of the bed, and covered my face with my hands—I thought I heard a noise; I raised my eyes, and, as I live, I saw on the other end of the bed the man whom I had slain and buried. There he sat, six feet from me, and nodded to me, and looked at me with his wan eyes, and laughed. I rushed from the cave—I entered a wood—I threw myself down—there opposite to me, six feet from my face, was the face of that man again! And my courage rose, and I spoke, but he answered not. I attempted to seize him, he glided from my grasp, and was still opposite, six feet from me as before. I flung myself on the ground, and pressed my face to the sod, and would not look up till the night came on and darkness was over the earth. I then rose and returned to the cave; I laid down on my bed, and the man lay down by me; and I frowned and tried to seize him as before, but I could not, and I closed my eyes, *and the man lay by me.* Day passed on day and it was the same. At board, at bed, at home and abroad, in my uprising and my down-sitting, by day and at night, there, by my bed-side, six feet from me, and no more, was that ghastly and dead thing. And I said, as I looked upon the beautiful land and the still heavens, and then turned to that fearful comrade, 'I shall never be alone again!' And the man laughed.

At last a ship came, and I hailed it—it took me up, and I thought, as I put my foot on the deck, 'I shall escape from my tormentor!' As I thought so, I saw him climb the deck too, and I strove to push him down into the sea, but in vain; he was by my side, *and he fed and slept with me as before!* I came home to my native land! I forced myself into crowds— I went to the feast, and I heard music—and I made thirty men sit with me, and watch by day and by night. So I had thirty-*one* companions, and one was more social than all the rest.

At last I said to myself, 'This is a delusion, and a cheat of the external senses, and the thing is *not*, save in my mind. I will consult those skilled in such disorders, and I will be— *alone again!*'

I summoned one celebrated in purging from the mind's eye its films and deceits—I bound him by an oath to secrecy— and I told him my tale. He was a bold man and a learned, and he promised me relief and release.

'Where is the figure now?' said he, smiling; 'I see it not.'

And I answered, 'It is six feet from us!'

'I see it not,' said he again; 'and if it were real, my senses would not receive the image less palpably than yours.' And he spoke to me as schoolmen speak. I did not argue nor reply, but I ordered the servants to prepare a room, and to cover the floor with a thick layer of sand. When it was done, I bad the Leech follow me into the room, and I barred the door. 'Where is the figure now?' repeated he; and I said, 'Six feet from us as before!' And the Leech smiled. 'Look on the floor,' said I, and I pointed to the spot; 'what see you?' And the Leech shuddered, and clung to me that he might not fall. 'The sand,' said he, 'was smooth when we entered, and now I see on that spot the print of human feet!'

And I laughed, and dragged my *living* companion on; 'See,' said I, 'where we move what follows us!'

The Leech gasped for breath; 'The print,' said he, 'of those human feet!'

'Can you not minister to me then?' cried I, in a sudden and fierce agony, 'and must I *never* be alone again?'

And I saw the feet of the dead thing trace one word upon the sand; and the word was—NEVER.

THE MASTER OF LOGAN

Allan Cunningham

Even in our ashes live our wonted fires.—GRAY*

ONE summer's eve, as I passed through a burial-ground on
the banks of the Nith,* I saw an old man resting on a broad
flat stone which covered a grave. The church itself was gone
and but a matter of memory: yet the church-yard was still
reverentially preserved, and several families of name and standing continued to inter in the same place with their fathers.
Some one had that day been buried, and less care than is usual
had been taken in closing up the grave, for, as I went forward, my foot struck the fragment of a bone. I lifted it hastily, and was about to throw it away, when the old man said,
'Stay, thoughtless boy, that which you touch so carelessly was
once part of a living creature, born in pain and nursed tenderly, was beloved, and had a body to rot in the grave, and
a soul to ascend into heaven—touch not, therefore, the dust
of thy brother rudely.' So he took the bone, and, lifting a
portion of the green sod, which covered the grave, replaced
it in the earth. I was very young, and maybe thoughtless, but
I was touched with the patriarchal look of the man, and also
by his scriptural mode of expressing himself. I remained by
him, and was in no haste to be gone.

'My child,' he said, 'I have a melancholy kind of pleasure
in wandering about this old burial-place. In my youth I have
sat with hundreds of the old and young in the church to
which this ground belonged—they are all lying here save one
whom the sea drowned and two who perished in a foreign
battle, and I am the last of the congregation who lives to say
it. I am grown sapless, and I am become leafless. There is not
one hair on a head ninety years old and odd—look, my child,
it was once covered with locks as dark as the back of yon
hooded-crow.' He removed his hat as he spoke, and his bald

head shone, in the light of the sun, like that of an apostle in a religious painting. 'I love to converse,' he said, 'with children such as yourself. The young men of this generation mock the words of age; it would be well if they mocked nothing else; but what can we expect of those who doubt all and believe nothing? If you will sit down on this grave-stone and listen patiently, I shall relate a tradition, pertaining to this burial-ground, which has the merit of a beneficial moral:—A tale which you will remember at eighty, as well as I do now, and which will show what befalls those who meddle, unwisely, with the dust of poor mute human nature.' I sat down as he desired, and he told me the following story.

'In the summer of the last year of the reign of James Stuart,* it happened that John Telfer was making a grave in this burial-ground. The church was standing then, and there were grave-stones in rank succeeding rank—for this is a place of old repute, and Douglases and Maxwells and Morrisons and Logans lie round ye thick and threefold. John, as I said, was digging a grave, and as he shovelled out the black mould, mixed with bones, he muttered, "Ay! Ay! It was a sad and an eerie day when the earth was laid over the fair but sinful body which I put here last. The clouds lowered, the thunder-plump* fell, and the fire flew, and heaven and earth seemed ready to come together. It's no' for nought that Nature expresses her wrath—the very gaping ground shuddered as if unwilling to take such sinful dust into its bosom." I remember the day well, though an old story now. He was a douce* man, John Telfer, and had fought in the great battles which the people waged with the nobles, in the days of Montrose and David Lesley.* He continued to dig till a skull appeared; he looked at it and said, "Thou empty tabernacle, sore art thou changed since I saw thee amongst the splendid Madams of thy day! Where are thy bright eyes, thy long tresses, which even monarchs loved, and the lips which spoke so witchingly and sang so sweet? Thou art become hideous to behold!— How art thou fallen since the days of thy youth, and how ghastly thou art in the sunny air, amid the church-yard grass!" And he threw it with his shovel among the grass and daisies growing thick around.

'Now there came to the kirk-yard a young man of an ancient kindred, who had blood in his veins of those who had wrought good deeds of old for Scotland. But he was a wild and a dissolute youth, who loved gay dresses and drunken companions: his blood was hot, his hand often on the sword-hilt, and his chief delight was in chambering* and in visits at midnight to the ladies' bower. Your father and your mother have warned you to beware of the folly of the Master of Logan—his name hath become a proverb and a warning in the land. It is of him I speak.

'And he came, as I said, into the kirk-yard, and as he came he whistled. He touched the fleshless skull with the toe of his Turkey shoe* till the earth fell out of the eye-holes, and he said, "John, whose skull is this?"—"A woman's Sir," said John, and wrought away with his shovel; for he was a good man, and disliked to be questioned by one whom he hated. "A woman's!" said the Master of Logan, "some presser of curd and creamer of milk! yet a dainty one in her day, I'll warrant."—"Deed, Sir," answered John, "the woman was well to look at, and a dainty one was she. I have seen gowd and jewels aboon that brow, and such a pair of een beneath, as would have wiled the bird from the brier or the lark from the sky."—"O, I can guess the rest," said the Master of Logan —"an alluring damsel, with sinful black eyes—who excelled in the dance—could sing a merry ballad—had made no captious vow against the company of men—was sometimes visited by the minister, and came to the kirk when the Sessions sat. Am I right?"

'John looked at him for half-a-minute's space, and then answered, "Ay! right—wool sellers, ken wool buyers—wha would have thought, now, that the living could look on a sample of gross dust and claim relationship in spirit? It's e'en a true tale, Master of Logan—so go home and repent. Dust is what ye maun come to; some unhallowed foot will yet kick your skull, and cry, 'Here was a man who had wit in his day, but what is he now?' "—"Why, John, ye can preach nearly as well as the parson"—"Preach!" said John; "I have preached, Sir, in my day—it was during the times of the Godly Covenant, and I behoved to speak; for one of Cromwell's troopers pulled that hen-hearted body, Bryce Bornagain, out of the pulpit, and set up his southern crest.* I trow I sobered him— I trow I sobered him—what I couldna do with the word I accomplished with anither weapon," and John threw the earth into the air, out of the bottom of a ten-foot deep grave, with an energy which those days of double controversy recalled.— "Ye would like to have those days back again, I think, John?" inquired the other. "Back again! na troth, no," said he, "I would have nought back again that's anes awa—the days of Cromwell are weel away, if they bide—and so is Phemie Morison there, whase skull ye're handling—she's well awa, too, if she bide."—"Bonnie Phemie Morison!" replied the Master of Logan, "and is this her!—she seems fairly enough away. What should bring her back again?"—"Oh just love of evil," said the conqueror of Cromwell's preaching dragoon,— "to visit the haunts of early joys, maybe—or of unrepented sins. It's said her spirit finds a pleasure of its own in coming back to the good green earth. We're no dead when we are dust, Master of Logan." And he laid his hand on the brink of the lowly dwelling he had prepared, and leaped out with an avidity which seemed to arise from an apprehension that the dust on which he trode was ready to be re-animated.

'The Master of Logan placed the skull on the tomb-stone of one of his ancestors, and said, "Now, John, between you and me, do you really think that our fair friend, here, takes a walk in the spirit occasionally—saunters, as she did of old, in the cool of the summer twilight—stalks round the grave of some unhappy youth, whom her charms consigned to early rest, and enjoys again, in idea, the love which she inspired?" —"Ha' done," said John, "ha' done, Master of Logan, now but ye talk fearfully. Look an' yere wild words be not inspiring that crumbling bone as if with life. I could maist take my oath that it looked at me." John's brow grew moist, and he said, "I wish the corpse would come, for this is an unsonsie* place."—"Particularly," said the other, "when Phemie Morison, here, walks about and pays visits."—"O heart-hardened creature!" cried John, "yere folly will get a sobering.—I have kenned as bold lads as your honour made humble enough in spirit about the middle watches of the night. There was Frank

Wamfray, a soldier, who neither feared God nor man. A spirit, in likeness of a woman, came to him in the dead hour of the night, and caroused with him out of his canteen, at the gates of Proud Preston*—I could go blindfold to the spot—and what came of him? He lived and died demented—he was a humbling spectacle." Loud laughed the Master of Logan, and cried "Here's fair Phemie Morison. I wish she would come and sup with me to-night!" He was observed to change colour, he turned to walk away, and the old man exclaimed, "See! there is an unearthly light in the sockets. Sir, repent and pray, else ye will sup with an evil spirit."

'The Master went away, and as he spurred his horse he could not prevent his thoughts from returning to the scene which he had just witnessed. He imagined that he saw the old man, the open grave, and the mouldering skull placed on the tombstone. He slackened the rein of his horse, and after a fit of unusual moodiness, muttered, "I am as mad as Cromwell's old adversary, John the Bedrell, himself—there can be no life in a rotten bone, nor light in the eyes of an empty skull"—he galloped away, and his mind was soon occupied with gayer subjects, and looks of another kind than those of death and the grave.

'He had a cup of wine to drink with a companion, a fair dame to visit, and when he reached the gate of his own tower the clock was striking ten. He threw his rein to his servant and entered—rang his bell violently, as was his wont when angry, and said, "Lockerbie, how is this?—here is a table covered and dishes set for two—fool! I sup alone—how comes this?"—"Even so as was ordered," replied Lockerbie; "between light and dark, a messenger rode to the gate, rang the porch bell, and said, 'A lady sups with the Master to-night, so let a table be spread for two.' This, as your honour knows, is a message neither sae startling nor uncommon, sae I gied orders, and moreover I said, ladies love music, nor do they hate wine, let both be had, and"—"Lockerbie," said his young master, "what manner of person was this messenger?"—"Oh, a pleasant man, with a red face," replied the servant, "but he merely delivered the message, and rode. I wish he had stopped, had it only been to eschew the thunder-plump which fell when the loud clap was. And that's weel minded—there's Dick Sorbie swears through the castle wa', and yere honour kens it's twelve feet thick, that the messenger was a braw bouncing lass, with a scarlet cloak on and een like elf candles—but I say a man, a pleasant man, with a ruddy countenance."

'The Master, when he heard this, wore a serious brow—he paced up and down the room—looked at the covered table— gazed out into the night—the moon was there with all her stars; the stream was running its course—the owl was hooting on the castle wall, and the relics of the thundercloud were melting slowly away on the hills of Tinwold. "A wild delusion!" he muttered to himself—"my ear was poisoned by weak old Martha who nursed me. See! nature continues her course—the moon shines—the stars are all abroad—the stream runs—and how can I imagine that a wild word, said in jest, should change the common course of nature. I cannot, shall not believe it!"

'He threw himself on a settee of carved oak, and looked on the walls and on the ceiling of the apartment. On the former hung the arms and the portraits of his ancestors—and grim and stately they looked. On the latter was painted a rude representation of the Day of Judgment—from which this room had, in early days, acquired the name of the Judgment-hall. Graves were opening and giving up their dead, and some were ascending to a sad and some to a saving sentence. He had never looked seriously on this composition before—nor did he desire to peruse it now; but he could not keep his eyes off it. From one of the graves which opened on the left-hand of the Great Judge, he saw a skull ascend—and he thought there was a wild light in its eyeless sockets, resembling what he had seen that afternoon in the burial-ground.

'The Master of Logan went to a cabinet of ebony and took out a Bible with clasps of gold—he touched it now for the second time, and opened it for the first—it had belonged to his mother—but of his mother he seldom thought, and if he remembered his fathers, it was but to recall their deeds in battle and dwell on those actions which had more affinity to violence than to virtue. He opened the Bible, but he did not read:—the sight of his mother's writing, and the entry of his own birth and baptism, in her small and elegant hand, made his eyes moist, though no tears fell:—as he sat with it open on his knee, he thought there was more light in the chamber than the candles shed, and lifting his head, he imagined that a female form, shadowy and pure, dissolved away into air as he looked. "That was, at least, a real phantom of the imagination," he said mentally—"the remembrance of my mother created her shape—and it is thus that our affections fool us." He closed and clasped the Bible, and lifting a small silver bell from the table rang it twice. A venerable and gray-headed man came tottering in, saying, "What is your will?"

'"I rang for you, Rodan, to ask your advice," said he,—"sit down and listen."—"Alas! Sir, it's lang lang now since ony body asked it," said the other, with a shake of his silvery hairs, "though I have given advice, as your good and gallant father, rest his soul, experienced, both in the house and on the edge of battle."—"But this," said the Master, "is neither matters of worldly wisdom, nor pertaining to battle." —"Then," said the old man, rising, "it's no' for me, it's no' for me. If it's a question of folly, ask yere sworn companion, young Darisdeer—if it be a matter of salvation, whilk I rather hope than expect, ask the minister, godly Gabriel Burgess—he'll make darkness clear t' ye, he'll rid up the mystery of death and the grave, and for laying spirits!—but we're no fashed* with spirits, I trow, and am no' sure that I ever saw ane, unless I might call the corpse light of old Nanse Kennedy a spirit. I would rather trust my cause with Gabriel Burgess than with ony dozen divines of these dancing and fiddling days."—"Bid Sorbie saddle a horse, a quiet one and quick-footed," said the Master, "and lead it over the hill, to Kirk-Logan, and bring the minister to me. He will show this Bible, and say the owner desires to see him as fast as speed can bring him." The old man bowed, and retired.

'"I have often ridden on an errand to a lady," said Sorbie, "and it seems natural that an errand to the parson should follow—though what my master can want with him is beyond my knowledge—he's nane of the praying sort—as little is he of the marrying sort—and, I think he wadna send for a good divine, to make fun of him over the bottle with his wild comrades. He mauna try to crack his fun on godly Gabriel Burgess. I wad rather face the Master of Logan himself, when kindled with drink and inflamed with contradiction. The minister's the man for handling a refractory sinner. I think I see him fit to spring out of the pulpit, like a fiery dragon—his hands held out, his eyes shining, his grey hair rising up like eagles' wings, and his voice coming down among sinners like a thunder-clap. And then there is a power given him of combating the spirits of darkness—an open Bible, a drawn sword, a circle of chalk and some wise words—so Gabriel prevails. I wonder what puts spirits in my head in this lonesome place." He spurred his horse, and looking right and left, before and behind, like one keeping watch in suspicious places, entered a wild ravine, partly occupied by a brook, and wound his way along the banks chanting the Gallant Graemes,* with all the courage he could muster; he pitched the tune low, for he desired to have the entire use of ear and eye in his ride down the Deadman's Gill, for so the glen was called.

'His horse snorted and snuffed, and Sorbie saw, to his infinite delight, that a lady riding on a little palfrey, and attended by a single servant, had entered the gorge of the glen, and was coming towards him. "Now, in the name of fun, what soft customer can this be?" said he to himself: "she's mantled and veiled as if afraid of the night air. But what the fiend is the matter with the beasts?—softly, softly, Galloway Tam, else ye'll tumble me and coup* the lady—damn the horses, that I should say sae, and me in a eerie place and in the way to the minister too—softly, softly." The road luckily widened at the place where he met this wandering dame, else, such was the irritable temper of the horses which he rode and led, that he would have certainly lost his seat. He bowed as she came up, and said, "Good even, fair Mistress, ye ride late."—"And good even to thee, good fellow," said the lady, in a voice of great natural sweetness, "it is late, but I have not far to go, if the Master of Logan be at home?"—"He's at home, and alone," answered Dick, with a low bow, "and expecting some one, for I saw a table spread for two: I know not who is the invited guest." The lady laughed, and lifting her veil, showed a youthful and lovely face, with bright eyes and flaxen ringlets

—then dropped the veil, and continued her journey. "It's a face I have never seen before," said Sorbie to himself, "but such a face as that will aye be welcome to the Master of Logan. I maun spur on for the minister, since such a sweet dame as yon is on a visit. My master will scarcely wait for his coming to say grace afore meat—she's a shiner." And away rode the messenger at a round pace.

'Just as he emerged from the glen, he saw a dark figure riding slowly towards him; and it seemed to his sight that horse and rider were one, for both were dark. "Now," muttered he, "the auld saying's come to pass,—'Meet wi' a woman at night and then ye're fit to meet with the Deil'—for here He comes —riding, I dare be sworn, on Andrew Johnston of Elfsfield." The rider approached, and said, "Turn—turn—I am on my way to thy master." "Be merciful, but this is wondrous!" exclaimed the other, in ecstasy. "Is this you, Minister? O, but ye are welcome!" and he took off his hat and shook back his hair, more to cool his burning brow, on which drops of terror had gathered, than out of respect to the clergyman. "Come, turn thy bridle back, Richard Sorbie," said Gabriel, —"Thou hast seen something, such as human sight cannot behold without fear, which hath moved thee thus."

'Sorbie had, however, recovered all his ordinary audacity, and answered very gaily, "Indeed, Minister, to tell ye the truth, ye were the object of terror yourself; for seeing ye coming, riding along in this haunted place, all dark, horse and man, I e'en set ye down for the Enemy instead of the friend o' mankind, and I'm free to own that I did na like to face ye. Faith, but my horses, poor things, were wiser than me; they took it calmly enough, and ye ken yourself a horse is no' willing to ride up to an emissary of the other world, or emissaries of this world either, Minister, else Galloway Tam wouldna have made sic a work. He nearly laid me on the gowans,* when I met a wandering Queen of Sheba,* in the Deadman's Gill, some ten minutes since." "A wandering lady, at this hour, in this wild glen!" said Gabriel: "and what manner of woman was she?"—"Oh a lass wi' manners enough, Minister," said Sorbie; "and veiled, as ye may guess, with an armful of lint-white locks about her bonnie blue een. But ye'll see her,

Minister, ye'll see her; she's awa to sup with the Master of Logan, and if ye makena the mair speed, he'll hae commenced the meat. I was sent off with such speed, to bring ye, as I never was sent afore—mair by token, there's a memorial that the Master's in earnest." And he put the little clasped Bible into his hands. "Let us ride faster," said the Minister, "I may be too late"; and they rode onward.

'"It was here," said Sorbie, pointing to a wider part of the way, "that I met the lady with the lint-white locks—and this too is the place, they say, Minister, where the Lords of Logan had a summer-bower of old, and where one of them had for his companion, one of the wanton lasses of Ae, a frail twig o' the auld tree of the Morisons." "Hush!" said Gabriel— "give not the thought utterance—such scenes should not be recalled. Bid what is good live again—let the memory of what is evil perish."—"Aweel," said Sorbie, "e'en let it be sae— but such things canna aye be accomplished—an' yonder's the lights of Logan tower, a glad sight in such a lonesome place as this: but will ye tell me, Minister, how ye came to ken that the Master wanted ye?—I was sent to bring ye—and I'm sure the tower sent out no other messenger."—"A blessed creature warned me," said Gabriel—"yea, a blessed creature." And he looked at the Bible as he spoke. "I would have gone to the uttermost ends of the earth to do her bidding, while she lived, and now shall I refuse her when she is a ministering spirit?"—"He's got into one of his fits of communings with the invisible world," thought Sorbie, "and it's wisdom to let him alone, lest he should cause me to see something whilk I have no wish to see. Yet I marvel who this blessed creature could be who told him—he's owre deep for me to deal with, this Minister of ours."

'While they were on their way down the Deadman's Gill, the Master of Logan heard the neighing of a palfrey at his tower gate, and a bustle amongst his servants. He presently heard the sound of a woman's voice—very low, very soft, and as liquid as music, giving some directions to the attendants; and soon a light foot, accompanied by the rustling of silks, approached his apartment. The door opened, and a young Lady, richly dressed and of great beauty, was ushered in—she lifted her veil from her person, threw it backwards over her shoulders, carrying with it a whole stream of ringlets, and occupying the settee of oak, to which she was conducted, said, "Master of Logan, I must be your guest for an hour. You have your table ready furnished—your silver censers burning, and the wine ready. Ah, Sir, was this feast spread for a lady?" And she gave her head, with its innumerable curls, a pleasant toss, and threw a comic archness into the glance of her eye, and waited for an answer. "Truly, Lady Anne," said he, "I must not say that it was spread for you, since I did not expect this honour, but it could not be spread for any one more lovely or more welcome."—"Master," answered the young lady, with some dignity, "I am not now as I have been —I am now mistress of my own actions, with no guardian to control me. I go where I wish, and journey as I will—but I am not here altogether of my own choice—for, look out on the night—yon huge black cloud cannot choose but rain by pailfuls, and I would rather throw myself on your hospitality than trust the treacherous storm. It would have no mercy upon our female falderols and our round tires* like the moon."

'"Dear Lady Anne," replied the Master of Logan, "whatever be the cause of your coming, your presence here is most welcome—not the less so since the elements constrained a little that dear quick-silvering disposition of thine—which, now I think on't, used to wrong me with suspicions and attack me with sarcasms. But all that only renders the present visit more welcome. Lay your veil aside, and allow those fair prisoners, those luxuriant tresses, a little liberty—the cloud, which you dreaded, grows darker and darker; and you may be thankful if you are released till midnight." She unveiled, and removed a broad fillet which enclosed her tresses, allowing them to descend in abundance on her shoulders—then, raising her white arms, caught them up ringlet after ringlet, and confined them around her brows and beneath the fillet, only allowing a tress or two to scatter negligently down her long white neck. He knew enough of human nature to know that all this apparent care was but a stratagem to show her charms to advantage, and he looked at her with much earnestness and an encreasing regard, which he did not desire to conceal.

It is true that once or twice he said, mentally, "What but admiration of me would have possessed this young and modest lady—she who always repelled, with cold tranquillity, the compliments and attentions I paid her,—what has happened to induce her to overstep the limits of maidenly discretion? But nature's nature, and I have often seen the will that was restrained by parents set itself free with a vengeance, and make ample amends for early constraint. I must comfort her as well as I can; I wish I had not sent for that severe divine— this will furnish a text for another lecture—he will make me the common speech of the pulpit—and, what is worse, this young lady too will be a sufferer." The Master seemed to have dismissed from his mind all the fears which lately distressed him; the intoxication of woman's beauty o'ermastered all other emotions.

'The domestics of the Tower meanwhile indulged in abundance of wild speculations. "I marvel what will happen next?" said the first servant. "Our master has sent for a divine; and young Lady Anne Dalzel has come wandering hither under the cloud o'night, like an errant damsel in the auld ballads— it canna be for good that he's grown godly and she's grown daft."—"I wonder what puts it into your head," said the second servant, "that this young tramping lass, with the lint-white hair and licentious een, is Lady Anne Dalzel? Do you think that her douce mother's ae daughter would sae far forget rank and virtue, and e'en prudence, as to come cantering awa here in the dark hour o' the night? Na, na! the dove will never flee into the nest of the gore-falcon."—"Ye say true," said a third menial; "this quean, whoe'er she may be—and for looks, she might be an earl's daughter—savours nothing of the auld house of Dalzel. Why, man, there's a saucy sort of grace—a kind of John-come-woo-me-now kind of look about her, which never belonged to the name."—"And who, then, can she be?" inquired a dozen of domestics, gathering round the other speakers in a circle.

'"I ken what I ken," said an old woman, who had charge of the poultry; "and I know what I know! Ay! ay! they're well guided whom God guides; and yet all that we see is not of his making. Ah, sirs, there's mony a queer thing permitted in the earth! and this cummer, for all so young and so rosie as she looks, has nae touch of natural flesh and blood. Wha has nae heard of fair May Morison, who erred wie one o'the auld Lords of Logan, and was a dweller in the summer bower down in the Deadman's Gill? I mind her weel when I was a gilpin* of a lassie, in the year saxteen hundred and fifty and sax—and wha was then like Madam? But she erred sair, and sank far, and died when she was in her prime, in unrepented sin, they say, for it's certain she came back and haunted the Deadman's Gill—and who would come back if they could bide away!"—"Hoot! hoot! Dame Clocken," said several tongues at once; "this is all wynted* milk, woman; ye set your imagination wi' rotten eggs, and canna bring out a wholesome brood."—"Troth, and it would have been well for me," said the old woman, "had the whole been a matter of fancy; but I saw her spirit, ye unbelievers—a sight I thought I sould never hae coost the cauld of.* It was eleven at night—the place, the auld Bower—and I was on a tryste with Willie Gowdie of Gulliehill. Awa' I went, light o' heart and quick o' foot, and when I came to the appointed place, wha saw I but cummer! There she sat, wi' her lang links of flaxen hair flowing oure her shoulders like a deluge. I thought it was one of Willie's pranks, and up I went, but through God's strength refrained frae speaking. O, sirs, she looked up!—Its head was a skull, and the lights o' perdition in its eyne-holes! I shrieked, and dropped down; and when I came to myself, I thought there was some ane giving me queer grips. I looked and it was Willie Gowdie." To this interminable stream of wild story, the clatter of horses' hoofs first in the avenue, and then at the gate, brought a termination. Some hurried out with lights, and presently returned, showing in Gabriel Burgess, with more than a common proportion of solemnity on his brow.

'Old Rodan showed the preacher the way to the Chamber of Judgment; and as he stopped to set his hose and neckcloth in order at one of the mirrors, he heard a soft, mild voice say, "You are witty and you are pleasant, Master, and, like some of your ancestors, have little mercy on woman. So this is your kirk-yard legend; it explains why your looks are hollow and your manners austere—how unlike the gayest dancer at the assembly and the rashest rider in the chase. But why should such shallow imaginings disturb a mind so strong as your's?— Can the wisest or the wildest human word raise the dead— clothe their bones with beauty—fill their hollow eyes with the light of heaven, and put the breath o' God between their lips—give them a taste for table dainties, and a turn for conversation?" He held the wine-glass in his hand, when the steps of the preacher were heard in the passage and the door began to open. "Appear, in likeness of a priest!" exclaimed the young lady, laughing; and Gabriel Burgess entered, and took a seat between her and the Master of Logan.

' "I am glad to see you, Reverend Sir," said the Master. "I have sent for you on a matter which moved me much; but I am easier now."—"Indeed, my young friend," said the divine, "no wonder that you wished for me; such a companion suggests thoughts of the altar, doubtless. And is this young lady to get command over the Tower? What fair name will she lose for the sake of the house of Logan?"—"A name of old repute," said the Master, "even Anne Dalzel."—"Ah! young lady," said the Preacher, "I reverence thee for thy mother's sake. But thou art of another Church, and I have not seen thee some years. Dalzel, a bold name and an old name; but I'm the man who changes the fair names of ladies—I hope I shall be permitted to find thee another name before we part?" The young lady looked down, the Master looked at the lady, and the Preacher at both, and then said, "More of this presently; but I hope Lady Anne will forgive me for appearing before her in these homely garments, unlike the splendid dresses of her favourite Church."* And he sedulously smoothed up his hose, and seemed anxious to appear acceptable in the sight of a fastidious lady.

' "Truly, Parson," said the lady, laughing, "I am afraid you will think me vain and frivolous; these curled locks and jewelled clothes are not according to the precepts of your Church. Will you not hesitate to bind the foolish daughter of a laxer Church to one of the chosen of your own?"—"Ah! Madam," answered the Preacher, smiling, "your jewelled robes and curled locks become you; and I might as well quarrel with a rose because it blooms bonnie, or with a lily because it smells sweet, as with woman because of her loveliness. And as for marriage, some thirty score and three have I wedded in my day, and may do the good office to many yet."—"A laborious divine," said the young lady, "and I dare say one who makes durable work. This Scotland of ours is, indeed, a pleasant land for matrimonial inclinations. The Kirk, with reverence be it said, is at the head of the bridal establishment; but if the parson weds his thousands, the magistrate marries his tens of thousands; and those who are too bashful to reveal their loves to the whole congregation, or too poor to pay the fees of the Justice—why, they make an exchange of matrimonial missives and set up their household. We have no such indulgence in our Episcopal Church."

' "Lady," replied the Preacher, "ye have laid your delicate hand on one of the sore-places of our Zion. The carnal power of the State measures its strength too much with the spiritual power of the Church; and when we war with those self-seeking people, we are accused of desiring to engross the entire disposal of man's body here and of his soul hereafter. Our Church is poor and humble; the lowliest roof in the land is that which covers the house of God, and the commonest vestments in Scotland are those which cover her clergy. Concerning this, I repine not; for there are powers which even our poverty and humility give us, which exalt and strengthen us. How could I war with the effeminacy of embroidered garments, and the monstrous lavishness of our nobles and our gentry, were I to be rolled up to the controversy in a cushioned coach, attended by footmen in laced jackets?"

' "That is so well and so wisely said," answered the young lady, "that I could wish the etiquette of the table admitted of our tasting of wine together before the bell rings for supper; but the Master is become abstemious of late, he passes the cup, and shuns pleasant converse."—"Perchance he hath something on his mind, which weighs heavily," replied the Preacher; "and wine to the sick of heart is an addition of heaviness. Is there aught in which the wisdom of the devout, or the kindness of the beautiful, can be of advantage unto thee? Here we are both," he said, smiling,—"what hurteth my son? says the Church of Scotland; and what vexeth my brother? saith this fair vassal of a laxer kirk."—"I say," answered the lady, "that we are two oracles, infallible in our way, and that our son and brother cannot open his heart, or reveal his sorrows, to two more wise and sagacious people. In truth, in some sort, he was about the unburthening of his heart when he heard your footsteps, but he wisely reserved the marrow of his misery for one more ancient in knowledge, and more confirmed in understanding. Something hath happened in the burial-ground of Logan kirk to disquiet his mind."—"Speak, my son," said the Preacher; "there is healing for all sorrows, whether of mind or of body." The Master of Logan, in a tone sometimes affectedly pleasant, related what had passed, and spake lightly of the gay invitation given to the dust of Phemie Morison.

'The Preacher listened attentively, but like one who had heard the tale before. "My son," said he, "the evils which beset thee arise from the living, and not from the dead, and you are more in jeopardy from one ripe and rosy madam in warm flesh and blood, than from all the bones of all the dames that ever graced the courts of the Stuarts. The words which you uttered were indeed unguarded, and must be repented of; but they were uttered in a dull ear—death and the grave listen to no voice, save that of the archangel. No, no, my son, imagine not that rash words can call dust into life; can summon the spirit from the realms of bliss or of woe, or that thou art so supremely blessed, or so splendidly wicked, as to have spirits of good, or of evil, for thy boon companions. In the blinded and melancholy days of Popery, when men made their own gods, then evil spirits were rife in the land; but since the pure light of Presbyterianism arose, they have been chased into their native darkness.* Even I, weak and imperfect as I am, and unworthy of being named with some of the chosen sons of the sanctuary, have driven the children of perdition before me. So, my son, clear thy brow, say thy prayers, seek thy pillow, and thy rest shall be sound—I have said it."

'"Holy man," said the young lady, "how fortunate was I in coming into this tower to-night; how much shall I profit by thy discourse! Ah, the professors of my Church are full fed, and of a slothful nature, and are not rigid in their visitations nor frequent in their admonitions. You have driven, you say, the children of darkness before you—excuse the forwardness of ignorance—may a daughter of a less gifted Church inquire how this miraculous undertaking was accomplished?" —"Oh, most willingly, Madam," answered the Preacher— "there was no magic in it, all was plain, and easily understood; but here comes supper, sending up a savour such as would waken hunger in an anchorite. I hope, Master, that you have not tempted me with superstitious meats or drinks—with pudding stuffed with blood, for that is unclean, or porridge made with plums, for that is Episcopalian."

'The dishes were arranged on the table while the Preacher was still speaking; he stretched his hands over them, and over the wine, which was sparkling in silver flagons, and said, "God be present at this table to-night, and bless the meat and bless the drink, and let every mouthful of the one, and every drop of the other, be to thy glory alone.—Now, my fair foe," said the Clergyman, "to what shall I help thee? A wing of this fowl, or a slice of this salmon?"—"Most reverend and learned Sir," said she, with a smile, "I consider supper to be an undue indulgence, which inflames the blood, and makes the complexion coarse. As I desire to be loved, I avoid the vulgar practice, and am surprised to see it countenanced by a stickler for all manner of simple and plain things."—"Madam," replied the Preacher, "corrupt and craving nature must be relieved; to fast entirely is Popish, to have a meal of particular and stated dishes is Prelatical, but to take what comes is a trusting in Providence, and is Presbyterian. This wild-fowl, now," he said, smiling, "has fattened itself on the heather top, and might supper a prophet; and this sauce is fit for the General Assembly,* and ought to be restricted to divines." He ate away with an excellent appetite, neither looking to the right nor to the left, till he had rendered the bones worthy of admission to a museum of anatomy.

' "Most holy Preacher," said the lady, "there is a fair fish before you and a flagon of wine; as they are both permitted by your Church, they will, no doubt, be agreeable to your stomach. While you are occupied silently and laboriously upon them, allow me, a daughter of self-denial, to touch this little musical instrument, and chaunt you a song; and as I make it while I sing it, it shall be measured by your meal." The Preacher had helped himself to a weighty slice of salmon; had deluged it in sauce; had filled up his glass to the brim in a challenge from his entertainer—and giving an approving nod, fell anxiously on, lest the poetic resources of the lady should fail early. Thus permitted, she lifted a cittern,* touched it with exquisite skill, and began to sing the following ballad, in a voice which could only be matched by the united notes of the blackbird and the thrush.

SANDY HARG

The night-star shines clearly,
　　The tide's in the bay,
My boat, like the sea-mew,
　　Takes wing and away.
Though the pellock* rolls free
　　Through the moon-lighted brine,
The silver-finn'd salmon
　　And herling are mine—
My fair one shall taste them,
　　May Morley of Larg,
I've said and I've sworn it,
　　Quoth young Sandy Harg.

He spread his broad net
　　Where, 'tis said, in the brine
The mermaidens sport
　　Mid the merry moonshine:
He drew it and laugh'd,
　　For he found 'mongst the meshes
A fish and a maiden
　　With silken eyelashes—
And she sang with a voice,
　　Like May Morley's of Larg,
"A maid and a salmon
　　For young Sandy Harg!"

Oh white were her arms,
　　And far whiter her neck—
Her long locks in armfuls
　　Overflow'd all the deck:

One hand on the rudder
　She pleasantly laid,
Another on Sandy,
　And merrily said—
"Thy halve-net has wrought thee
　A gallant day's darg*—
Thou'rt monarch of Solway,
　My young Sandy Harg."

Oh loud laugh'd young Sandy,
　And swore by the mass,
"I'll never reign king,
　But mid gowans and grass."
Oh loud laugh'd young Sandy,
　And swore, "By thy hand,
My May Morley, I'm thine,
　Both by water and land;
'Twere marvel if mer-woman,
　Slimy and slarg,*
Could rival the true love
　Of young Sandy Harg."

She knotted one ringlet,
　Syne knotted she twain,
And sang—lo! thick darkness
　Dropp'd down on the main—
She knotted three ringlets,
　Syne knotted she nine,
A tempest stoop'd sudden
　And sharp on the brine,
And away flew the boat—
　There's a damsel in Larg
Will wonder what's come of thee,
　Young Sandy Harg.

"The sky's spitting fire,"
　Cried Sandy—"and see
Green Criffel* reels round
　And will choke up the sea;
From their bottles of tempest
　The fiends draw the corks,
Wide Solway is barmy,
　Like ale when it works;

There sits Satan's daughter,
  Who works this dread darg,
To mar my blythe bridal,"
  Quoth young Sandy Harg.

From his bosom a spell
  To work wonders he took,
Thrice kiss'd it, and smiled,
  Then triumphantly shook
The boat by the rudder,
  The maid by the hair,
With wailings and shrieks
  She bewilder'd the air;
He flung her far seaward—
  Then sailed off to Larg
There was mirth at the bridal
  Of young Sandy Harg!

'The Master of Logan was unable to resist the influence of this wild ballad, and the sweet and bewitching voice which embodied it. The supper table, the wines and fine dishes, were unregarded things: his hands, as the infection stole through him, kept temperate time, and his right foot beat, but not audibly, an accompaniment to the melody. Nor did the lady seem at all unconscious of her delicate witchery; she gradually silenced the cittern as the song proceeded, and before it ended, her voice, and her voice alone, was heard; and filled the chamber, and penetrated to the remotest rooms and galleries. The servants hung listening in a crowd over each other's shoulders at the door of the room. The Preacher alone seemed untouched by the song and the voice; his hand and mouth kept accurate time; with a knowing eye and a careful hand did he minister to his own necessities, giving no other indication of his sense of the accompaniment than an acquiescent nod, as much as to say, "Good, good!" At length he desisted; leaned back on the chair, and reposed, thankful and appeased. The Master wondered to see a man, accounted austere and abstemious, yield so pleasantly to the temptations of carnal comforts; and the domestic who attended—a faithful follower of the Kirk—shook his head amongst his companions, and said, "There's an awful meaning in the Minister's way of eating this blessed night." The young lady seemed to take much pleasure in what she called drawing the black snail out of its shell. No sooner had she finished her song—which concluded with the supper—than she took her seat at the table, and the conversation was resumed.

'It was now nigh twelve o'clock; the night, which had hitherto been wild and gusty, refused to submit to the rule of morning without strife: the wind grew louder; the rain fell faster; the thunder of the augmenting streams increased; and now and then a flash of lightning rushed from a cloud in the east to one in the west, showing, by a momentary flame, the rustling agitation of the pines, and the foaming plunges which the mountain streams made from precipice to precipice. "The prince and power of the air is at work to-night," said old Rodan, "and there will be sad news from the sea."— "From the sea, said ye?" replied a matron, who presided over the duties of the dairy; "him whom ye speak of, and I mauna name, is none sae far off as the sea. I wouldna gang down the Deadman's Gill this blessed night for the worth of Scotland's crown."—"Whisht, for God's sake! whisht," said the dame who ruled amongst the poultry; "the fiend has long lugs,* and is a sad listener; but, cummers, there's something about to come to pass in this tower to-night, that will be tauld in tale and ballad when the youngest of us is stiff and streeket.* But we're safe—the buckler of the Gospel is extended before us, and the thick tempest will fall from us, like rain from a wild swan's wings. Lord send that the auld Tower may haud aboon our heads!"

'Never, from the time the Tower was founded, did it contain a more joyous party: the Master had drowned the memory of his fears in song and wine; the Preacher had, apparently, sweetened down the severity of his manners by converse with the young lady and by the social cup; and the lady herself gave a loose to her mirth and her eyes, and was willing to imagine that she had laid upon both the necks of her companions the pleasing yoke of her bondage. "Minister," said she, "I have long mistaken your character. I thought you a melancholy, morose man, given to long preachments and much abstinence, and one who thought that a gladsome heart was an offence worthy of punishment hereafter. Come, now, let me ask you a question or two in your own vocation. What manner of woman was the Witch of Endor?"* There was a sparkling humour in the lady's eye when she asked this—there was a still slyer humour in the Preacher's when he answered it: "On her personal looks, scripture is silent; but I conceive her to have been a lovely young widow with a glorious jointure."—"Well, now, Parson," she said, "I like you for this; we must be better acquainted; you must come and visit me; I have heard that you are famous for discomfiting evil spirits, and for warring hand to hand with aërial enemies."—"Ay, truly, young lady," answered the Preacher; "but that was when this land was in the bonds of iniquity: with our Kirk establishment, a new dispensation hath come upon the land.* Master, the wine tarries with you."

' "Well, now," said the young lady, "there's our friend of the Tower here—he imagined to-night that something evil would break right through all your new dispensations: he expected a visit from the grave—a social dame, in her winding-sheet, was invited to supper. Parson, are you man enough for her, should she come bounce in upon us? I am alarmed at the very image I have drawn."—"And let her come," said the Preacher, pouring out a brimming cup of wine—"e'en, young lady, let her come—I trow I should soon sort her—this wine is exquisite now, and must be as old as the accession of the Stuarts*—I trow I should sort her—I know the way, lady, how to send refractory spirits a-trooping—I have learned the art frae a sure hand. It would do your heart good, were a spirit to appear, to see how neatly I would go to work. Ah! the precious art will perish for want of subjects—witchcraft will die a natural death for lack of witches, and my art will perish from the same cause. I hope the art of making wine will be long remembered—for this is worthy of Calvin."*

' "Minister," said the young lady, looking slyly while she spoke at the Master, "let not such gifts perish. Suppose this chair, with the saint carved on the back, to be a spirit, and show us how you would deal with it."—"Ye are a cunning dame," said the Preacher; "d'ye think that I can make a timber utensil dissolve and depart like a spirit? Awa with your episcopal wit—and if you will grow daft, drink wine." He took another sip.—"Thou art a most original parson," said the young lady, laughing; "but I am desirous of becoming a disciple. Come! this chair is a spirit—take to your tools."— "Weel, weel, lady," said the Preacher, impatiently, "I shall e'en waste so much precious time for your amusement. But ye must not grow feared as I grow bold and serious."—"Are you sure that you will not be afraid yourself?—such things have happened," said the young lady. He only answered, "Verily, I have heard so," and then began.

'He took a sword from the wall, and described a circle, in the centre of which he stood himself. "Over a line drawn with an instrument on which the name of God is written, nought unholy can pass. Master, stand beside me, and bear ye the sword." He next filled a cup with water, and said, "Emblem of purity, and resembling God, for he is pure, as nought unholy can pass over thee whilst thou runnest in thy native fountain, neither shall aught unholy abide thy touch, thus consecrated—as thou art the emblem of God, go and do his good work—Amen." So saying, he turned suddenly round and dashed the cupful of water in the face and bosom of the young lady—fell on his knees, and bowed his head in prayer. She uttered scream upon scream; her complexion changed; her long locks twined and writhed like serpents; the flesh seemed to shrivel on her body; and a light shone in her eyes which the Master trembled to look upon. She tried to pass the circle towards him, but could not; a burning flame seemed to encompass and consume her; and as she dissolved away, he heard a voice saying, "But for that subtle priest, thou hadst supped with me in hell!"

'"Young man," said the Preacher, rising from his knees, "give praise to God, and not to me—we have vanquished, through him, one of the strongest and most subtle of Satan's emissaries. Thy good angel, thy blessed mother, sent me to thee in thy need, and it behoved me to deal warily with the artificer of falsehood. Aid me in prayer, I beseech thee, for forgiveness for putting on the sinful man to-night—for swilling of wine and wallowing in creature-comforts, and for uttering profane speeches. Ah! the evil one thought he had put on a disguise through which even penetration could not penetrate; but I discerned him from the first, and could scarce forbear assailing him at once, so full was I of loathing. He was witty to his own confusion." The Master knelt, and prayed loud and fervently; the domestics were called in, and the worship of God was, from that night, established in his household.

'Look on me, my child,' said the old man, when he had concluded his wild story; 'I could have told this tale in a soberer fashion—yea, I could even have told it to thee in a merrier shape—nathless the end and upshot would have been the same. I tell it to thee now, lest its memory should perish on the earth and its moral warning cease. Tell it to thy children, and to thy children's children, as I have told it, and do not lend an ear to the glozing* versions which the witty and profane relate. Hearken to them, and you will believe that this fair and evil spirit was a piece of lascivious flesh and blood, and that the power which the Preacher and the Master of Logan laboured to subdue was a batch of old wine, which proved the conqueror, and laid them in joy side by side, while the head domestic, a clever and a sagacious man, invented this wondrous tale to cover their infirmities. Nay, an thou smilest, even relate it as thou wilt. Laughter is happiness, and sorrow is admonition—and why should not a story have its merry side and its sad, as well as human life? Farewell, my son— when thou tellest this story, say it was related to thee by an old man with a grey head, whose left foot was in the grave and the right one breaking the brink—the last of the house of Logan.'

THE VICTIM

Anonymous

SOME years ago, myself and a fellow-student went to Daw-lish* for the summer months. An accident, which I need not narrate, and which was followed by a severe attack of pleur-isy, chained me a prisoner to my room for several weeks. My companion, whose name was St Clare, was a young man of high spirits and lively temper; and though naturally kind and affectionate, escaped, as often as he could, from the restraint of a sick room. In one of his walks, he chanced to encounter a young lady, whom he fell in love with, as the phrase is, at first sight, and whose beauty he dwelt upon with a warmth of enthusiasm not a little tantalizing to one, like myself, who could not even behold it. The lady, however, quitted Dawlish very suddenly, and left my friend in ignorance of every other particular concerning her than that her name was Smith, and her residence in London. So vague a direction he, however, resolved to follow up. We returned to town sooner than we otherwise should have done, in order that the lover might commence his inquiries. My friend was worthy of the roman-tic name that he bore, Melville St Clare—a name that was the delight of all his boarding-school cousins, and the jest of all his acquaintance in the schools.

He was the sole son of Thomas St Clare, of Clare Hall, in the county of ——, No. ——, in Hanover-square, and Banker, No. ——, Lombard-street. An eccentric man did the world account him. 'Very odd,' remarked the heads of houses for wholesale brides, 'that the old man should insist upon his son studying medicine and surgery, when every one knows he will inherit at least ten thousand a-year.'—'Nothing to do with it,' was the argument of the father; 'who can tell what is to happen to funded, or even landed property, in England? The empire of disease takes in the world; and in all its quar-ters, medical knowledge may be made the key to competency and wealth.'

While quietly discussing in my own mind the various relative merits between two modes of operation for poplitical aneurism, at my lodgings in town, some three weeks after our return from the country of hills and rain, (some ungallantly add, of thick ancles also,) my studies were broken in upon by a messenger, who demanded my immediate compliance with the terms of a note he held in his hand. It ran thus:—

'Let me pray you to set off instantly with the bearer in my carriage to your distressed friend—

'M. St Clare.'

On reaching the house, the blinds were down and the shutters closed; while the knocker muffled, bespoke a note of ominous preparation. 'How are you?' I inquired, somewhat relieved by seeing my friend up; and though looking wan, bearing no marks of severe illness. 'I hope nothing has happened?'

'Yes, the deadliest arrow in Fortune's quiver has been shot —and found its mark. At three, this morning, my father's valet called me up, to say his master was in convulsions. Suspecting it to be a return of apoplexy, I despatched him off for Abercrombie,[†] and on reaching his room, I found my fears verified. Abercrombie arrived; he opened the temporal artery, and sense returned, when my unfortunate parent insisted on informing me what arrangements he had made in my favour respecting the property; and on my suggesting that his books might previously require to be looked over, he interrupted me by saying it was useless. "You are the son of a ruined man." I started. "Yes, such have I been for the last twenty years! I have secured to you a *thousand pounds*, to finish your education—and that is all that calamity has left it in my power to bestow." For some moments I was led to doubt his sanity.

'"What, then, can be contained within those two massive chests, so carefully secured?"—"Old parchment copies of my mortgages. Your fortune has only changed in aspect; before you were in existence, the author of your being was a *beggar*! My credit alone has supported me. I have with difficulty

---

[†] Abercrombie is the chief surgical writer on diseases of the brain.*

been able to invest in the funds for your wants the paltry
sum I mentioned. May you prosper better than your father,
and the brightness of your day make up for the darkness of
his closing scene. God's blessing ——" His head sank on the
pillow, and falling into a comatose state he slept for four or
five hours, when his transition from time to eternity was as
gentle as it was unnoticed.

'For my part, I merely remain here till the last offices are
performed. All his affairs will be committed to his solicitors,
when the fortune and residence which I looked forward to
enjoying as my own must be left to others.'

'Courage, my dear fellow,' said I, 'there is no space too
great to allow of the sun's rays enlivening it—neither is that
heart in existence which hope may not inhabit.'

The funeral was over, the mansions of his father relinquished, and St Clare himself duly forgotten by his *friends*.
The profession, which he before looked on as optional in its
pursuit, was now to become his means of existence; and in
order to pursue it with greater comfort to ourselves, we took
spacious rooms, which enabled us to live together, in ——
street, Borough, in the neighbourhood of our hospital. One
morning, it so happened that I had something to detain me
at home, and St Clare proceeded by himself to his studies.
From the brilliant complexion and handsome countenance of
a former day, his appearance had degenerated into the pale
and consumptive look of one about to follow the friend for
whom his 'sable livery of woe was worn'.

'Give me joy, Dudley! Joy, I say, for life is bright once
more!' exclaimed St Clare, returning late in the evening, while
his face was beaming with gladness.

'I rejoice to hear it,' said I. 'What has happened?' I inquired.

St Clare explained. He had met his unforgotten mistress of
Dawlish; she had introduced him to her father, with whom
she was walking, and whom he recognized as a Mr Smith, an
eccentric and wealthy acquaintance of his deceased parents.
Mr Smith invited him to dinner the next day. To cut short my
story, St Clare soon received permission to pay his addresses
to the lady he had so long secretly loved; and Mr Smith,
who had originally been in trade, and was at once saving and

generous, promised 16,000*l.* to the young couple, on the condition that St Clare should follow up his profession. The marriage was to be concluded immediately after St Clare had passed the College of Surgeons, which he expected to do in six months.

'Dudley, I have an engagement to-day, and shall not be at home till the evening,' said St Clare, returning from the Hospital one morning; 'but as we must dissect the arteries of the neck somewhat more minutely before we go up for examination, I wish you would get a subject. I am told you can have one within two days, by applying to this man,' giving me the card of an exhumator in the Borough.

'Very well,' I returned, setting off.

'Which will you have, Sir?' asked the trafficker in human clay, whose lineaments bespoke the total absence of every human feeling from his heart:—'a lady or a jemman?'

'Whichever you can procure with least trouble,' I replied. 'When can you bring it to my lodgings?'

'The day after to-morrow, Sir.'

'Good! What is your price?'

'Why, Sir, the market's very high just now, as there's a terrible rout about those things; so I must have twelve guineas.'

'Well, then, at eleven, the evening after to-morrow, I shall expect you.'

The night passed, no St Clare appeared;—the next, still he came not—and eleven on the following evening found him yet absent. Surrounded with books, bones, skulls, and other requisites for surgical study, midnight surprised me, when a gentle tap at the door put my reveries to flight.

'Two men in the street, Sir, wish to see you there.'

'Very well,' said I; and recollecting the appointment, I descended, and found the exhumator and another.

'We called you down, Sir, to get the woman out of the way; because, you know, these things don't do to gossip about. Shall we take it up-stairs?'

'Yes, and I will follow behind. Make as little noise as possible.'

'No, no, Sir, trust us for that—we're pretty well used to this sort of work. Jem, give the signal': when the party addressed, stepping into the street, gave a low whistle on his fingers, and something advanced with a dull, rustling noise, which proved to be a wheelbarrow containing a sack. They had filled the gutter with straw, and over this driven the barrow. In an instant two of them seized the sack, and without making any more disturbance than if they had been simply walking up-stairs, they carried it into my apartment, and the vehicle it was brought in was rapidly wheeled off.

It is usual for students to carry on their dissections solely in the theatre to which they belong, but as there are many annoyances from the low and coarse set too often mixed up in these places, St Clare and myself had determined to choose a lodging where we could pursue this necessary, but revolting, part of the profession in private. Within my bedroom was a dressing-closet, which, as it was well lighted, we devoted to this purpose. Having carried in their burden and laid it down, they returned to the sitting-room, through which was the only communication with the other.

'Couldn't get ye a jemman, Sir; so we brought ye a lady this time,' said the man.

'Very well. I hope the subject is a recent one, because I may not be able to make use of the body for a day or two.'

'As to the time she has been buried, Sir, that's *none* to speak of'; while a grin of dark expression gathered round his mouth; and though ignorant of its meaning it made me recoil, from the air of additional horror it flung over features already so revolting in expression. I went into the closet to take a glance at the subject, fearing they might attempt to deceive me. They had lain it on the table, and a linen cloth swathed round was the only covering. I drew aside the corner which concealed the face, and started, for never till that instant had I seen aught that came so near to my most ideal picture of female loveliness; even though the last touches had been painted by the hand of Death. As the light of the candle fell on the shrouded figure before me, it composed the very scene that Rembrandt would have loved to paint,* and you, my reader, to have looked on. Her hair was loose and motionless, while its whole length, which had strayed over her neck and shoulders, nestled in a bosom white as snow, whose pure, warm tides were now at rest for ever! One thing struck me as singular—her rich, dark tresses still held within them a thin, slight comb. An oath of impatience from the men I had left in the next room drew me from my survey.

'Where did you get the subject, my men?' I inquired, as I put the money into the man's hand.

'Oh, we hadn't it from a town churchyard, Sir. It came up from the country, didn't it, Jem?'

'Yes,' replied the man addressed, and both moved quickly to depart; while I returned to gaze on the beauteous object I had left, and which afforded me a pleasure, so mixed up with all that was horrid, that I sincerely hope it will never fall to my lot to have a second experience of the same feeling.

To me she was as nothing, less than nothing; and though, from long habit, I had almost brought myself to meet with indifference the objects which are found on the dissecting-table, I could not gaze on one so young, so very fair, without feeling the springs of pity dissolve within me; and tears, fast and many, fell on those lips; I refrained not from kissing, notwithstanding Mortality had set its seal upon them; as yet—

'Before Decay's effacing fingers
Had swept the lines where beauty lingers.'

Her eyes were closed beneath the long lashes. I lifted one lid; the orb beneath was large and blue—but 'soul was wanting there.'* So great was the impression her beauty made upon me, that, stepping into the next room, I took my materials, and made a drawing of the placid and unconscious form so hushed and still. I look upon it at this moment, and fancy recalls the deep and unaccountable emotions that shook me as I made it. It must have been an instinctive——But, to proceed, I saw but one figure in my sleep—the lovely, but unburied dead. I awoke—what could it be that felt so moist and cold against my face?—where was I?—what light was glimmering through the windows?—it was the break of day. Worn with fatigue, I had fallen asleep over my drawing, while the candle had burnt out in the socket, and my head was resting on the inanimate breast, which had been deprived too soon of existence to know the pure joy of pillowing a fellow-heart it loved. I arose, and retired to a sleepless couch. In the evening, while over my modicum of coffee, in came St Clare. He appeared haggard and wild, whilst every now and then his eye would gaze on vacancy, and closing, seem to shut out some unpleasant thought, that haunted him in ideal reality.

'Well, St Clare, what has detained you?'

'Death!' said he, solemnly. 'The sole remaining relative to whom Nature has given any claim on my affections, is no more. A sudden despatch called me down to soothe the expiring hours of my mother's sister, and not a soul is left me now on earth to love, save Emily and my friend. I feel most unaccountably oppressed—a dread sense of ill pervades me; but let me hope that ill is past.'

'Well, think of it no more,' I replied, and changed the conversation. 'I have procured a subject—female, beautiful and young; but I feel more inclined to let it rest and rot amidst its fellow-clods of clay, than bare so fair a bosom to the knife. It is well that the living hold a pre-occupancy of my heart, or such a beauteous form of death ——'

'This note has just been left for you, Sir, from Mr Smith, who requests an immediate answer,' said my servant, entering. I read aloud its contents:—

'Though unknown to you, save by name and the mention of another, I call upon you, as the friend of one who was my friend, to assist me in unravelling this horrid mystery. On Tuesday, at two, my dearest Emily went out, with the intention of returning at four. Since that hour, I have been unable to obtain the slightest information respecting her. I have called in your absence for St Clare twice; he was unexpectedly out. Surely I have not mistaken *him! He* cannot have filled up the measure of mankind's deceit, and abused the trust reposed in him! Let me pray you, for the love of Heaven! to give me the least clue you are possessed of that may lead to her discovery.

'I know not what I have written, but you can understand its meaning.

'Your's, &c.
'JOHN SMITH.'

Starting from his seat with an air of a maniac, St Clare abstractedly gazed on empty air, as if to wait conviction. Too soon it came, and seizing a light, he dashed towards the closet where he knew the body was to be. For the first time a dark suspicion flashed upon me, and taking the other candle I followed. The face had been again covered, and St Clare, setting the light upon the table, stood transfixed,—just as we feel the pressure of some night-mare-dream,—without the power of drawing his eyes away, or by dashing aside the veil, to end this suspense of agony, in the certainty of despair.

Every muscle of his body shook, while his pale lips could only mutter—'It must be so! it must be so!' and his finger pointing to the shrouded corpse, silently bade me to disclose the truth: mute, motionless horror pervaded me throughout; when, springing from his trance, he tore away the linen from the features it concealed. One glance sufficed;—true, the last twenty-four hours had robbed them of much that was lovely, but they were cast in a mould of such sweet expression that *once seen*, was to be *remembered for ever*.

With indescribable wildness he flung himself upon the body, and embracing the pallid clay, seemed vainly trying to kiss it back to life. I watched his countenance till it became so pale, there was only one shade of difference between the two. In an instant, from the strained glare of his fixed glance, his eyes relaxed, and a lifeless, inanimate expression of nonentity succeeded their former tension, while with his hand still retaining the hair of the deceased in his grasp, he sunk upon the ground.

Assistance was called, and from a state of insensibility he passed into one of depression.

All our efforts to disentangle the locks he had so warmly loved from his fingers were in vain; the locks were, therefore, cut off from the head. Through all the anguish of his soul he never spoke; the last words to which his lips gave utterance, were these—'It must be so, it must be so.' For hours he would stare at one object, and his look was to me so full of horror and reproach, I could not meet it. Suddenly he would turn to the hair, and fastening his lips upon it, murmur some inarticulate sounds, and weep with all the bitterness of infantine sorrow.

The reader will remember it so chanced, that I never was introduced to the heroine of my tale; but all doubt was now removed as to the identity of the subject for dissection with the unfortunate Emily Smith. How she came by her death was a mystery that nothing seemed likely to unravel.

Not the slightest marks of violence could be found about her person; the arms were certainly in an unnatural position, being bent with the palms upward, as if to support a weight; and seemed to have been somewhat pressed, but this might be accounted for by the packing of the body. All beside wore the appearance of quiescent death.

She was opened, and not the slightest trace of poison presented itself. Immediate search had been made for the men; they had absconded, and all apparent means of inquiry seemed hushed with the victim of science in its grave.

Some years passed—St Clare was dead—the father of the unfortunate Emily was no more. Fortune had thriven with me, and being independent of practice, I had settled in the West-end of London, and married the object of my choice. I was soon occupied with the employments of my profession, and amongst the rest, that of surgeon to the —— dispensary.

Seven years after my first commencement, I had to attend a poor man who was attacked with inflammation of the brain. The violence of the disease had been subdued, but some strange wanderings of delirium still haunted him. In a paroxysm of this sort he one day exclaimed to me, as I was feeling his pulse, 'Cut it off! Cut it off! it says so: off with it!' Paying no attention to this, I replaced his arm within the coverlid, but dashing it out, he seized mine and demanded, 'does it not say if thy right hand offend thee, cut it off?'* 'Yes, my man, but yours is a useful member; take my advice and keep it on.'

'I will not; it has offended me, ay, damned me to eternity. It is a murderous right hand!' But I will not drag the reader through the incoherent ravings of guilty delirium; it suffices to say, that after some considerable pains I elicited the following story from him.

'It's just ten years to-morrow (that's Tuesday) since I was discharged from four months imprisonment in the House of

Correction. I was then just twenty. In the same place I met a gang of resurrection men, and they said what a jolly life they led, plenty of money, and all that, when one of 'em told the rest he knew a better way to get the rhino* quickly than what they did, and if so be as they wouldn't split, he'd tell 'em. Well, after making me take an oath (I trembles now to think of it) that I wouldn't tell, they let me into it. This was to kidnap all the greenhorns, that didn't know their way about town, and carry them to a house the gang had in —— alley, near Blackfriars, where they were to be suffocated, and sold to you doctors for cutting up.* Well, it took a long time to bring my mind to such a thing, but they persuaded me we were *all destined to go to heaven or hell*, before we were born, and that *our actions had nothing to do with it*. So I agreed, when the time came round, to enter the gang.

'On the day we were *let loose*, there were four of us loitering near the coach stand in —— street. A gentleman was walking up and down before an inn, looking at his watch every now and then, and casting his eyes round to see if a coach was coming which he seemed to expect. Presently he met some one who knowed 'un, and I saw him take a letter and read it, and then say to the other "I can't come this instant, because I expect a friend in half an hour, and must wait for her; but stay, I can write a note, and put her off," when he stepped inside the inn, and came out in ten minutes, with a note in his hand. One of us had been servant in a cutting-up house in the Borough, and knowed him afore: stepping up, he asked if he could carry the note for him? The other was in a hurry, and said "yes," giving him half-a-crown to take it into the Borough, then got into the coach and drove off. Instead of going with it, he had larnt to read, and breaking the note open, found some lady was coming to meet the gentleman by half-past two. "I tell ye what, my boys," says he, "here's a fish come to our net without looking for it, so we'll have her first." Shortly after, up comes the coach with a lady in it; meanwhile one of our gang had got another coach belonging to us *for the purpose*, which was in waiting; so the villain tells her that the gentleman had been obliged to go somewhere else, but he was an old servant, and if she would get into his coach, he would drive her to the house where the gemman was waiting to receive her. She, never suspecting, got in, and was driven off to the *slaughter house*, as we called it. She entered by a back yard, and frightened by the dark, dirty way, and lonely-looking rooms, and not seeing him she expected, she attempted to run off, but that was of no use, and taking her to a room for the purpose, in the middle of the house, where no one could hear her screaming, she was locked up for the night. Well, I was uncommon struck with her beautiful looks, and begged very hard to let her go: they said it would not do, because as how they would all be found out. *So die she must, the next order they had for a corpse.* That very night came an order, and they swore I should have the killing of her, for being spooney enough to beg her life. I swore I would not do it; but they said if I didn't they would send me instead, and, frightened at their threats, I agreed.

'In the room where she slept was a bed, with a sliding top to let down and smother the person who was lying beneath, while the chain which let it down was fastened in the room above. They had given her a small lamp in order to look at her through a hole, that they might see what she was about. After locking the door inside, (for they left the key there to keep 'em *easy*, while it was bolted on the out,) and looking to see there was no one in the room, nor any other door, she knelt by the bed-side, said her prayers, and then laid down in her clothes. This was at ten—they watched her till twelve; she was sleeping soundly, but crying too, they said, when they took me up into the room above, and with a drawn knife at my throat, insisted on my letting go the chain which was to smother her beneath—I did it! Oh, I did it!—hark!' starting up, 'don't you hear that rustling of the clothes? a stifled cry? no, all is quiet! She is done for—take her and sell her!' and from that he fell into his old raving manner once more.

The next day he was again lucid, and pulling from his bosom an old purse, he said, 'I managed to get these things without their knowledge.' It contained a ring with a locket engraven 'E. S.' and the silver plate of a dog's collar with the name of 'Emily' on it; 'that,' he remarked, 'came from a little spaniel which we sold.'

I made a finished miniature from the rough drawing taken on the first evening of my seeing Emily Smith. This had been set in the lid of a snuff-box, and anxious to see if he would recognise it, I brought it in my pocket. After looking an instant at the contents of the purse, I silently placed the snuff-box in his hand. His mind but barely took time to comprehend and know the face, when flinging it from him with a loud cry, his spirit took its flight to final judgment—and I vowed from that day a renunciation of the scalpel for ever.

SOME TERRIBLE LETTERS FROM
SCOTLAND

James Hogg

DEAR SIR,—As I knew you once, and think you will remember me,—I having wrought on your farm for some months with William Colins that summer that Burke was hanged,*— I am going to write you on a great and trying misfortune that has befallen to myself, and hope you will publish it, before you leave London, for the benefit of all those concerned.

You must know that I have served the last three years with Mr Kemp, miller, of Troughlin;* and my post was to drive two carts, sometimes with corn to Dalkeith market, and sometimes with flour-meal to all the bakers in Musselburgh and the towns round about. I did not like this very well; for I often thought to myself, if I should take that terrible Cholera Morbus, what was to become of me, as I had no home to go to, and nobody would let me within their door. This constant fright did me ill, for it gave my constitution a shake: and I noticed, whenever I looked in my little shaving-glass, that my face was grown shilpit* and white, and blue about the mouth; and I grew more frightened than ever.

Well, there was one day that I was at Musselburgh with flour; and when I was there the burials were going by me as thick as droves of Highland cattle; and I thought I sometimes felt a saur* as if the air had thickened around my face. It is all over with me now, thought I, for I have breathed the Cholera! But when I told this to Davison, the baker's man, he only laughed at me, which was very ungracious and cruel in him; for before I got home I felt myself manifestly affected, and knew not what to do.

When I came into the kitchen, there was none in it but Mary Douglas: she was my sweetheart like, and we had settled to be married. 'Mary, I am not well at all to-night,' said I, 'and I am afraid I am taking that deadly Cholera Morbus.'

'I hope in God that is not the case!' said Mary, letting the tongs fall out of her hand; 'but we are all in the Almighty's hands, and he may do with us as seemeth good in his sight.'

She had not well repeated this sweet, pious submission, before I fell a-retching most terribly, and the pains within were much the same as if you had thrust seven or eight red-hot pokers through my stomach. 'Mary, I am very ill,' said I, 'and I well know Mr Kemp will not let me abide here.'

'Nay, that he will not,' said she; 'for he has not dared to come in contact with you for weeks past: but, rather than you should be hurried off to an hospital, if you think you could walk to my mother's, I will go with you, and assist you.'

'Alas! I cannot walk a step at present,' said I; 'but the horses are both standing yoked in the carts at the stable-door, as I was unable to loose them.' In a few minutes she had me in a cart, and drove me to her mother's cot, where I was put to bed, and continued very ill. There was never any trouble in this world like it: to be roasted in a fire, or chipped all to pieces with a butcher's knife, is nothing to it. Mary soon had a doctor at me, who bled me terribly, as if I had been a bullock, and gave me great doses of something, which I suppose was laudanum; but neither of them did me any good: I grew worse and worse, and wished heartily that I were dead.

But now the rest of the adjoining cotters rose in a body, and insisted on turning me out. Is it not strange, Sir, that this most horrible of all pestilences should deprive others, not only of natural feeling, but of reason? I could make no resistance although they had flung me over the dunghill, as they threatened to do; but the two women acted with great decision, and dared them to touch me or any one in their house. They needed not have been so frightened; for no one durst have touched me more than if I had been an adder or a snake. Mary, and her mother, old Margaret, did all that they could for me: they bathed the pit of my stomach with warm camomile, and rubbed my limbs and hands with hard cloths, shedding many tears over me; but the chillness of death had settled on my limbs and arms, and all the blood in my body had retreated to its conquered citadel; and a little before daylight I died.

For fear of burying me alive, and for fear of any violence being done to my body by the affrighted neighbours, the two women concealed my death; but poor Mary took the sheets, which had been bought for her bridal bed, and made them into dead-clothes for me; and in the afternoon the doctor arrived, and gave charges that I should be coffined and buried without loss of time. At this order Mary wept abundantly, but there was no alternative; for the doctor ordered a coffin to be made with all expedition at the wright's, as he went by, and carried the news through the parish, that poor Andrew, the miller's man, had died of a most malignant Cholera.

The next morning very early, Johnie, the elder, came up with the coffin, his nose plugged with tobacco, and his mouth having a strong smell of whisky; and, in spite of all Mary's entreaties, nailed me in the coffin. Now, Sir, this was quite terrible; for all the while I had a sort of half-consciousness of what was going on, yet had not power to move a muscle of my whole frame. I was certain that my soul had not departed quite away, although my body was seized with this sudden torpor, and refused to act. It was a sort of dream, out of which I was struggling to awake, but could not; and I felt as if a fall on the floor, or a sudden jerk of any kind, would once more set my blood a-flowing, and restore animation. I heard my beloved Mary Douglas weeping and lamenting over me, and expressing a wish that, if it were not for the dreadfulness of the distemper, that she had shared my fate. I felt her putting the robes of death on me, and tying the napkin round my face; and, O, how my spirit longed to embrace and comfort her! I had great hopes that the joiner's hammer would awake me; but he only used it very slightly, and wrought with an inefficient screw-driver: yet I have an impression that if any human eye had then seen me, I should have been shivering; for the dread of being buried alive, and struggling to death in a deep grave below the mould, was awful in the extreme!

The wright was no sooner fairly gone, than Mary unscrewed the lid, and took it half off, letting it lie along the coffin on one side. O, how I wished that she would tumble me out on the floor, or dash a pail of water on me! but she did neither, and there I lay, still a sensitive corpse. I determined, however, to make one desperate effort, before they got me laid into the grave.

But between those who are bound together by the sacred ties of love, there is, I believe, a sort of electrical sympathy, even in a state of insensibility. At the still hour of midnight, as Mary and her mother were sitting reading a chapter of the New Testament, my beloved all at once uttered a piercing shriek,—her mother having fallen down motionless, and apparently lifeless. That heart-rending shriek awakened me from the sleep of death!—I sat up in the coffin, and the lid rattled on the floor. Was there ever such a scene in a cottage at midnight? I think never in this island. Mary shrieked again, and fainted, falling down motionless across her mother's feet. These shrieks, which were hardly earthly, brought in John Brunton and John Sword, who came rushing forward towards the women, to render them some assistance; but when they looked towards the bed, and saw me sitting in my winding-sheet, struggling in the coffin, they simultaneously uttered a howl of distraction and betook them to their heels. Brunton fainted, and fell over the threshold, where he lay groaning till trailed away by his neighbour.

My ancles and knees being tied together with tapes, and my wrists bound to my sides, which you know is the custom here, I could not for a while get them extricated, to remove the napkin from my face, and must have presented a very awful appearance to the two men. Debilitated as I was, I struggled on, and in my efforts overturned the coffin, and, falling down upon the floor, my face struck against the flags, which stunned me, and my nose gushed out blood abundantly. I was still utterly helpless; and when the two women began to recover, there was I lying wallowing and struggling in my bloody sheet. I wonder that my poor Mary did not lose her reason that night; and I am sure she would, had she not received supernatural strength of mind from Heaven. On recovering from her swoon, she ran out, and called at every door and window in the hamlet; but not one would enter the cottage of the plague. Before she got me divested of my stained grave-clothes and put to bed, her mother was writhing in the Cholera, her mild countenance changed into the appearance of withered clay, and her hands and feet as if they had been boiled. It is amazing that the people of London should mock at the fears of their brethren for this terrible and anomalous plague; for though it begins with the hues and horrors of death, it is far more frightful than death itself; and it is impossible for any family or community to be too much on their guard against its baleful influence. Old Margaret died at nine next morning; and what could I think but that I had been her murderer, having brought infection to her homely and healthy dwelling? and the calamity will hang as a weight on my heart for ever. She was put into my coffin, and hurried away to interment; and I had no doubt that she would come alive again below the earth;—but the supposition is too horrible to cherish!

For my part, as far as I can remember, I did not suffer any more pain, but then I felt as if I had been pounded in a mill,—powerless, selfish, and insensible. I could not have remembered aught of the funeral, had it not been that my Mary wept incessantly, and begged of the people that they would suffer the body of her parent to remain in the house for one night; but they would not listen to her, saying that they dared not disobey the general order, and even for her own sake it was necessary the body should be removed.

Our cottage stood in the middle of a long row of labourers' houses, all of the same description; and the day after the funeral of old Margaret, there were three people in the cottage next to ours seized with the distemper, and one of them died. It went through every one of the cottages in that direction, but all those in the other end of the row escaped. On the Monday of the following week my poor Mary fell down in it, having, like myself and her mother, been seized with it in its worst form; and in a little time her visage and proportions were so completely changed, that I could not believe they were those of my beloved. I for a long time foolishly imagined that she was removed from me, and a demon had taken her place; but reason at length resumed her sway and convinced me of my error. There was no one to wait on or assist Mary but me, and I was so feeble I could not do her justice: I did all that I was able, however; and the doctor gave me hopes that she would recover. She soon grew so ill, and her pangs, writhings, and contortions, became so terrible, that I wished her dead:—yes, I prayed that death would come and release her! but it was from a conviction that she would revive again, and that I should be able to wake her from the sleep of death. I did not conceive my own revival as any thing supernatural, but that which might occur to every one who was suddenly cut off by the plague of Cholera; and I prayed that my dear woman would die. She remained quite sensible; and, taking my hand, she squeezed it and said, 'Do you really wish me dead, Andrew?' I could make no reply; but she continued to hold my hand, and added, 'Then you will not need to wish for it long. O Lord, thy will be done in earth as it is in heaven!'

She repeated this last sentence in a whisper, and spoke no more, for the icy chillness had by this time reached the region of the heart; and she expired as in a drowsy slumber. Having no doubts of her revival I did not give the alarm of her death, but continued my exertions to restore animation. When the doctor arrived he was wroth with me, and laughed me to scorn, ordering the body to be directly laid out by matrons, preparatory for the funeral; and that night he sent two hired nurses for the purpose. They performed their task; but I would in no wise suffer the body to be coffined after what had happened to myself, until I saw the farthest. I watched her night and day, continuing my efforts to the annoyance of my neighbours until the third day, and then they would allow it no longer; but, despite all my entreaties, they took my beloved from me, nailed her in the coffin, and buried her; and now I am deprived of all I loved and valued in this world, and my existence is a burden I cannot bear, as I must always consider myself accessary to the deaths of those two valuable women.

The worst thing of all to suffer is the dreadful apprehension that they would come alive again below the earth, which I cannot get quit of; and though I tried to watch Mary's grave, I was so feeble and far-spent, that I could not but always fall asleep on it. There being funerals coming every day, when the people saw me lying on the grave with my spade beside me, they thought I had gone quite deranged, and, pitying me, they, half by force, took me away; but no one offered me an asylum in his house, for they called me the man that was dead and risen again, and shunned me as a being scarcely of this earth.

Still the thought that Mary would come alive haunts me,— a terror which has probably been engendered within me by the circumstances attending my own singular resuscitation. And even so late as the second night after her decease, as I was watching over her with prayers and tears, I heard a slight gurgling in her throat, as if she had been going to speak: there was also, I thought, a movement about the breast, and one of the veins of the neck started three or four times. How my heart leaped for joy as I breathed my warm breath into her cold lips! but movement there was no more. And now, Sir, if you publish this letter, let it be with an admonition for people to be on their guard when their friends are suddenly cut off by this most frightful of all diseases, for it is no joke to be buried alive.

I have likewise heard it stated, that one boy fell a-kicking the coffin on his way to the grave, who is still living and life-like, and that a girl, as the doctors were cutting her up, threw herself off the table. I cannot vouch for the truth of these singular and cruel incidents, although I heard them related as facts; but with regard to my own case there can be no dispute.

It does a great deal of ill to the constitution to be too frightened for this scourge of God; but temerity is madness, and caution prudence: for this may be depended on, that it is as infectious as fire. But then, when fire is set to the mountain, it is only such parts of its surface as are covered with decayed garbage that is combustible, while over the green and healthy parts of the mountain the flame has no power; and any other reasoning than this is worse than insanity.

For my part, I have been very hardly used, there having been few harder cases than my own. In Lothian every one shunned me; and the constables stopped me on the road, and would not even suffer me to leave the county,—the terror of infection is so great. So dreadful are the impressions of fear on some minds, that it has caused a number of people both in Scotland and England to hang themselves, or otherwise deprive themselves of life, as the only sure way of escaping its agonies.

Finding myself without a home and without employment, I made my escape over the tops of the Lammermuirs,* keeping out of sight of any public road, and by that means escaped into Teviotdale,* where I changed my name to Ker, and am now working at day-labour in the town of Roxburgh, and on the farms around; and though my name was Clapperton when I wrought with you, I must now sign myself your humble servant,

ANDREW KER.

The next is in some degree different, though likewise narrating very grievous circumstances. It is written by the mate of The Jane Hamilton of Port Glasgow.

SIR,—I now sit down to give you the dismal account of the arrival of the Cholera in the west of Scotland. I sent it a month ago to a friend in London, to put into the newspapers, but it never appeared; so if you think it worth while, you may publish it. But if there be any paper or periodical that Campbell or Galt* is connected with, I would rather it were sent to one of them, as they are both acquaintances and old schoolfellows, and will remember me very well.

Well then, Sir, you must know that in our passage from Riga to Liverpool, in January, we were attacked by very squally weather off the western coast of Scotland, and were obliged to put into one of those interminable narrow bays denominated lochs, in Argyleshire, where we cast anchor on very bad ground.

I cannot aver that our ship was perfectly clean, for we lost one fine old fellow by the way, and several others were very bad; so I was sent off to a mining or fishing village, to procure some medicine and fresh meat. Our captain had an immensely large black Newfoundland dog, whose name was Oakum, and who always attached himself to me, and followed me; but that day he chanced not to go ashore with me. Some time afterwards, some of the sailors going on shore to play themselves, Oakum went with them, and coming on the scent of my track he followed it. Now the natives had some way heard that the Cholera was come with the ship; but so little did they conceive what it was, that they were nothing afraid of coming in contact with me.

The village grocer, draper, hatter, and apothecary, had no medicines on hand, save Glauber's salts,* and of these he had two corn-sacks full. I bought some; and while I was standing and bargaining about the price of a pig, I beheld a terrible commotion in the village: the men were stripped, and running as for a race; and the women were screaming and running after them, some of them having a child on their backs, and one below each arm, while the Gaelic was poured and shouted from every tongue. 'What is it? What in the world is it?' said I to the merchant, who had a little broken English. 'Oh, she pe tat tam bhaist te Collara Mòr,'* said he; and away he ran with the rest.

It so happened that one Donald M'Coll was going down the coast on some errand, and meeting with Oakum with his broad gilded collar about his neck, he instantly knew who he was; and, alarmed beyond expression, he took to his heels, threw off his coat and bonnet and ran, giving the alarm all the way as he went; and men, women, and children, betook them to flight into the recesses of the mountains, where they lay peeping over the rocks and the heath, watching the progress of this destroying angel.

Honest Oakum was all the while chopping out of one cottage into another, enjoying the scraps exceedingly, which the people had left behind them in their haste. Yea, so well satisfied was he with his adventure, that he did not return until after dark, so that the Highlanders did not know he had returned at all. The people had not returned to their houses when we came away.

But the most singular circumstance is yet to relate. On our return to the Clyde from Liverpool, where we rode quarantine, we learnt that the Cholera Morbus had actually broken out in that village,—at least a most inveterate diarrhoea, accompanied with excessive pains and vomiting, which carried off a number of the inhabitants; but, the glen being greatly overstocked, they were not much missed. Such a thing as

Cholera Morbus or sending for a doctor never entered their heads, but a terrible consumption of the merchant's Glauber's salts ensued; and when no more could be done for their friends, they buried them, and then there was no more about it. Whether the disease was communicated to them by the dog, by myself, by the fright, or the heat they got in running, I cannot determine; but it is certain the place suffered severely. They themselves alleged as the cause, their having 'peen raiter, and te raiter too heafy on te herring and pot-hato.'* It was from thence that the disease was communicated to Kirkintilloch by a single individual. Oakum continues in perfect health; but was obliged to undergo fumigation and a bath, by way of quarantine, which he took highly amiss.

I am, Sir, your obedient servant,

ALEXANDER M'ALISTER.

The next is the most hideous letter of all. We wish the writer may be quite in his right mind. But save in a little improvement in the orthography and grammar, we shall give it in his own words.

SIR,—Although I sent the following narrative to an Edinburgh newspaper, with the editor of which I was well acquainted; yet he refused to give it publicity, on the ground that it was only a dream of the imagination: but if a man cannot be believed in what he hears and sees, what is he to be believed in? Therefore, as I am told that you have great influence with the printers in London, I will thank you to get this printed; and if you can get me a trifle for it, so much the better.

I am a poor journeyman tradesman in the town of Fisherrow,* and I always boarded with my mother and two sisters, who were all in the trade;† but my mother was rather fond of gossiping and visiting, and liked to get a dram now and then. So when that awful plague of Cholera came on us for the punishment of our sins, my mother would be running to every one that was affected; and people were very glad of her assistance, and would be giving her drams and little presents;

† Probably the fish trade.

and for all that my sisters and I could say to her, she would not be hindered.

'Mother,' said I to her, one night, 'gin ye winna leave aff rinning to infectit houses this gate, I'll be obliged to gang away an' leave ye an' shift for mysel' some gate else; an' my sisters shall gang away an' leave ye too. Do ye no consider, that ye are exposing the whole o' your family to the most terrible of deaths; an' if ye should bring infection among us, an' lose us a', how will ye answer to God for it?'

'Hout, Jamie, my man, ye make aye sic a wark about naething!' quoth she; 'I am sure ye ken an' believe that we are a' in our Maker's hand, and that he can defend us frae destruction that walketh at noonday, and from the pestilence that stealeth in by night?'

'I allow that, mother,' quoth I; 'I dinna misbelieve in an overruling Providence. But in the present instance, you are taking up an adder, and trusting in Providence that the serpent winna sting you and yours to death.'

'Tush! Away wi' your grand similitudes, Jamie,' said she; 'ye were aye ower-learned for me. I'll tell ye what I believe. It is, that if we be to take the disease an' dee in it, we'll take the disease an' dee in it; and if it is otherwise ordained, we'll neither take it nor dee in it: for my part, I ken fu' weel that I'll no be smittit, for the wee drap drink, whilk ye ken I always take in great moderation, will keep me frae taking the infection; an' if ye keep yoursels a' tight an' clean, as ye hae done, the angel o' Egypt will still pass by your door an' hurt you not.'

'I wot weel,' said my sister Jane, 'I expect every day to be my last, for my mither will take nae body's advice but her ain. An' weel do I ken that if I take it I'll dee in it. I hae the awfu'est dreams about it! I dreamed the last night that I dee'd o' the plague, an' I thought I set my head out o' the cauld grave at midnight, an' saw the ghosts of a' the Cholera fok gaun trailing about the kirk-yard wi' their white withered faces an' their glazed een; an' I thought I crap* out o' my grave an' took away my mother and brother to see them, an' I had some kind o' impression that I left Annie there behind me.'

'O! for mercy's sake, haud your tongue, lassie,' cried Annie; 'I declare ye gar a' my flesh creep to hear you. It is nae that I'm ony feard for death in ony other way but that. But the fearsome an' loathsome sufferings, an' the fearsome looks gars a' ane's heart grue* to think o'. An' yet our mither rins the hale day frae ane to anither, and seems to take a pleasure in witnessing their cries, their writhings, and contortions. I wonder what kind o' heart she has, but it fears me it canna be a right ane.'

My poor dear sister Annie! she fell down in the Cholera the next day, and was a corpse before midnight; and, three days after, her sister followed her to the kirk-yard, where their new graves rise side by side thegither among many more. To describe their sufferings is out of my power, for the thoughts of them turns me giddy, so that I lose the power of measuring time, sometimes feeling as if I had lost my sisters only as it were yesterday, and sometimes an age ago. From the moment that Annie was seized, my state of mind has been deplorable; I expected every hour to fall a victim to it myself: but as for my mother, she bustled about as if it had been some great event in which it behoved her to make an imposing figure. She scolded the surgeon, the officers of the Board of Health, and even the poor dying girls, for their unearthly looks and cries. 'Ye hae muckle to cry for,' cried she; 'afore ye come through what I hae done in life, ye'll hae mair to cry for nor a bit cramp i' the stomach.'

When they both died she was rather taken short, and expressed herself as if she weened that she had not been fairly dealt with by Providence, considering how much she had done for others; but she had that sort of nature in her that nothing could daunt or dismay, and continued her course— running to visit every Cholera patient within her reach, and going out and coming in at all times of the night.

After nine or ten days, there was one Sabbath night that I was awoke by voices which I thought I knew; and on looking over the bed, I saw my two sisters sitting one on each side of my mother, conversing with her, while she was looking fearfully first to the one and then to the other; but I did not understand their language, for they seemed to be talking keenly of a dance.

My sisters having both been buried in their Sunday clothes, and the rest burnt, the only impression I had was, that they had actually come alive and risen from the grave; and if I had not been naked at the time I would have flown to embrace them, for there were reports of that kind going. But when I began to speak, Jane held up her hand and shook her head at me; and I held my peace, for there was a chilness and terror came over me; yet it was not for my sisters, for they had no appearance of being ghosts: on the contrary, I thought I never saw them look so beautiful. They continued talking of their dance with apparent fervour; and I heard one of them saying, it was a dance of death, and held in the churchyard. And as the plague of Cholera was a breath of hell, they who died of it got no rest in their graves, so that it behoved all, but parents in particular, to keep out of its influences till the vapour of death passed over.

'But now, dear mother, you must go with us and see,' said Annie.

'Oh, by all means!' said Jane, 'since you have introduced us into such splendid company, you must go with us, and see how we act our parts.' 'Come along, come along,' cried both of them at the same time; and they led my mother off between them: she never spoke, but continued to fix the most hideous looks first on the one and then on the other. She was apparently under the power of some supernatural influence, for she manifested no power of resistance, but walked peaceably away between them. I cried with a tremulous voice, 'Dear, dear sisters, will you not take me with you too?' But Annie, who was next me, said, 'No, dearest brother, lie still and sleep till your Redeemer wakes you—We will come for you again.'

I then felt the house fall a-wheeling round with me, swifter than a mill-wheel, the bed sank, and I fell I knew not whither. The truth is, that I had fainted, for I remember no more until next day. As I did not go to work at my usual time, my master had sent his 'prentice-boy to inquire about me, thinking I had been attacked by Cholera. He found me insensible, lying bathed in cold sweat, and sent some of the official people to me, who soon brought me to myself. I said nothing of what I had seen; but went straight to the churchyard, persuaded that I would find my sisters' graves open, and they out of them; but, behold! they were the same as I left them, and I have never seen mother or sisters more. I could almost have persuaded myself that I had been in a dream, had it not been for the loss of my mother; but as she has not been seen or heard of since that night, I must believe all that I saw to have been real. I know it is suspected both here and in Edinburgh, that she has been burked,* as she was always running about by night; but I know what I saw, and must believe in it though I cannot comprehend it.

Yours most humbly,
JAMES M'L——.

THE CURSE

Anonymous

——'The deed was foul,
But grievously the forfeit has been paid.'
ASTOLPHO

I AM again free—free, save from the torture of my own thoughts, which, like the furies of old, are ever present to lash me. I am once more in the deserted home of my fathers—I am no longer a fettered maniac, crouching spaniel-like before the glare of my savage keeper. There is no one to whom I dare open my mind. It may be a childish morbid feeling, but still I dare not, cannot do it. The presence of man is hateful to me—all seem to look on me with loathing and hatred. I must unload my breast—I must give some vent to the fire which burns within me, and record my tale of desolation; any thing is preferable to unbroken silence; and it is matter of consolation that when I am gone, some perchance may pity me, when they peruse the strange record of my blasted fate.

The second son of a family more distinguished for unblemished antiquity than possessions or wealth, I was early thrown, in a great measure, on my own resources, and sought in foreign climes that fortune which there was no chance of finding at home. I was successful beyond hope or expectation; and, ere my health had been lost and strength wasted by the withering influence of a tropical clime, I was on my way homeward, rich almost beyond my wildest desires.

'Now am I indeed happy,' I exclaimed as the palm-clad hills of Bombay faded from my sight—'now am I happy indeed.' For home, with all its ecstatic associations, rushed full and strong on my mind; I had a father whom I revered—a brother whom I loved as brother never was loved before; I was going to see them, to live with them, never more to part. But there was one in whom was concentrated the love of father and of

brother, and more than both—one who for years, ay 'even
from my boyish days,'* had ever formed a part of my mus-
ings by day, my dreams by night; the thoughts of whose love
and constancy had been my guiding polar star in all difficult-
ies, the zest of my prosperity, the solace of my darker hours;—
deprived of whom life seemed but a 'salt-sown desert,' though
invested with all that was glorious or great, and with whom
a crust of brown bread and a squalid hovel seemed richer than
the banquet of a Roman emperor, or the palace of an eastern
magician whose slaves were mighty genii, and to whom the
elements themselves were ministering spirits.

Helen Vere—my hand shakes like palsied age as I trace
her name—Helen Vere was my first, my only love; I loved
her before I knew what the passion was, and it grew with my
years, and strengthened with my strength. I see her at this
moment before me, plain and distinct, as if she 'were still in
the flesh.'* Her slender, exquisitely formed person; her glorious bust, faultlessly white as uncontaminated snow, delicately intersected with veins vying with the dreamy azure of an
Italian sky; her large dark swimming eyes, where passionate
love and maiden bashfulness dwelt, twin sisters; her hand—
her—but I injure by this attempt at description—her peerless
beauty might be dreamt of, but never, never could be painted by poet or limner.

We were young when we parted—she was but a girl, and
I but few steps beyond boyhood—and we loved almost as
children love, without a dream of change or alteration. We
pledged no vows, made no sworn promises;

> 'For never having dream'd of falsehood, we
> Had not one word to say of constancy.'*

I never dreamt of change; I would as soon have thought that
the sun could cease to shine, or the planets keep their nightly
watch among the countless armies of heaven.

I had not heard from her for some time; the communication with the East, especially with that quarter where I was
situated, was irregular and uncertain, and many months had
passed since I had heard from home. I learned afterwards that

a letter had come a day after I sailed—would to God I had received it!—but I must not anticipate.

My passage home was long and tedious, but at last the welcome cry from the mast-head was heard, and in a few hours my foot pressed the sacred soil of Britain: I felt as if inspired by a new existence; the air seemed richer and more balmy than the aromatic gales of Ceylon, for Helen Vere breathed it. That delicious moment richly repaid me for years of toil and privation and grief—I was *happy*: how strange the word seems *now!*

I lost not a moment, but pressed homeward; and soon the proud, free, cloud-mantled mountains of my native Scotland rose before me. The sight brought back my home associations with redoubled force and vividness; and then, for the first time, the thought struck me, what if Helen be sick—be dead? I never dreamt of picturing her as changed—my heart swelled almost to bursting—I trembled like a man at whose strength a raging fever has scoffed—a cold clammy perspiration burst from every pore, and though but twelve miles from home, I felt as if I could as easily have travelled a million—I could not go on, were death itself the penalty of my delay.

I turned off the road and entered a little country churchyard. It had long been deserted, the village to which it had been attached having long since gone to decay; a few grey, moss-covered stones alone remained to chronicle where the house of God had been; but the hand of time had spared the dwellings of mouldering mortality, and the damp, rude headstones still remained, to tell that the dust and 'dry bones'* which they covered had once been living and breathing man. Our hereditary family tomb was here; a strange, old, gloomily fantastic pile, largely furnished, by some rural sculptor, with angels and cross bones and armorial bearings. It was the last place I had visited when I left home; and I sat down on one of the projecting angles, and mused on the chances which had befallen me since then. A sabbath-like calm pervaded the scene; nothing was heard save the slight breeze rustling the clumps of withered hemlock, or, at intervals, the sweet wild murmur of the humble-bee, gathering its treasure from the buttercups and blue-bells. No one can resist the sympathies of nature altogether, and my mind soon grew calm and tranquil as the scene around me.

While I thus sat in my musing mood, I heard some one behind me repeat those noble words of inspiration, 'Blessed are the dead who die in the Lord';* and, on turning round, I beheld an old man, a peasant as his dress betokened, leaning on his staff and gazing on a little grave almost concealed by the charnel herbage which encircled it on every side. 'Ay,' he continued, as if unaware of my presence, 'blessed indeed are they who die in the Lord; but the wicked man and the persecutor has no bonds in his death; he may flourish for a season as a green bay-tree; he may enlarge his bounds, and cast forth his arms in his pride; but the time shall come when they will seek him, but shall not find him, and the place which knew him once shall know him no more for ever:*

> "For why? the way of godly men
>   Unto the Lord is known;
> Whereas the way of wicked men
>   Shall quite be overthrown." '*

So saying, he began to clear away the grass and weeds from the little stone; and having done so, he sat down, as if musing on those who slept below.

Absorbed as I was with my own thoughts, my curiosity at last prevailed, and I said to him, 'Good morrow, old man; I see you are, like myself, a visitor of the dead: may I ask whose resting-place you contemplate with such an interest?'

He now for the first time seemed aware of my presence, and, looking up and touching his broad blue bonnet, he replied: 'They who sleep here, sir, were those of whom the world was not worthy—the true salt of the earth, even they who wandered about on the earth desolate, afflicted, tormented; and having come out of great tribulation, and washed their robes white in the blood of the Lamb, are now set down at the right hand of God.'* Here he took off his cap, and looked for a moment or two up to the bright blue heavens, as if he beheld the glorious situation he described. 'In a word,' he continued, 'they who sleep here are two martyrs, who wrote their testimony against the defections of the land and the breaking of the covenant, even in the precious letters of their blameless blood. They fell unknown, unlamented, and unrevenged, by a world lying in sin; but there is One above before whom even a sparrow cannot fall to the ground unmarked; and *He* will avenge the innocent blood even in *His* own good time; for the blood of his saints is precious in his eyes.'

My curiosity being excited by this exordium, I requested him to tell me the story to which he referred. 'It's a simple tale,' he said, 'and little different from hundreds of other passages which our land had the misfortune to see when the bloody giant of prelacy triumphed in his pride and cruelty; but ye are a young man, and who knows but God in providence may yet call you to act in defence of his laws and his prerogative, even as they did? Surely all these things were given as an ensample to us, to act as they did, if ever the stern necessity of the times demand; which may a gracious God in his providence forfend!'

THE STORY OF JOHN CRAIG AND ISOBEL ROSS

It was in those days when the bloody persecutor of God's saints, Charles the Second, was striving to root out all religion from our land, and when the booted and spurred apostles of prelacy went about like roaring lions seeking whom they might devour,* that John Craig, a singular godly youth, did take to wife Isobel Ross, a maiden fair as to worldly externals, but, what was far better, of an enlightened and sober piety, not in any way tainted with the defections or errors which then so rifely prevailed. They loved and were beloved more than usually falls to the lot of us poor shreds; and, not without reason, they promised themselves many, many days of happiness and joy. But a continuance of prosperity is not to be looked for in this vale of sorrow and tears; every month the persecution grew more and more bitter, and honest men durst no more worship God after the manner of their fathers, but were compelled to pray among glens and the rocks and caves of the earth, as if they were evil-doers, breaking and setting at nought the laws of the land.

Ye see that tomb there—it is the burial-place of the Erskines of Rath—(here I started—it was the tomb of my fathers the old man pointed to, but I said nothing). Sir John Erskine, who sleeps there, grandfather to the present laird, was one of the most violent persecutors in this part of the country. The folk said he had a looking to some post under the king, which made him the more active in hunting out the rebels, as they were called; and he exceeded even the rude hirelings of soldiers themselves in his oppressions and violences; some of them indeed clean shrunk from participating in many of his deeds, which however was milk and honey to that bloodthirsty apostate James Sharp,* whose appetite for carnage nothing could quench or slacken.

Well, sir, to keep to our tale: word was brought him early one morning that there was a conventicle, or field-preaching, in a glen up among the hills: see yonder it is, where a clump of black fir-trees are growing. This was an opportunity of serving the king not to be lost; so he got his servants to arm, called out the military who were quartered in the village, and set out at full speed to the place. But God had other things in reserve for those at that meeting; for, getting timely notice from a herd-boy who had seen the host advancing, they all escaped save and excepting John Craig, who fell suddenly, before he was aware, into the hands of the persecutors.

Being but a young man, and never before convicted of correspondence with the hill-folks, many thought that he would get free, or a short imprisonment, or small fine; but Sir John was enraged at the ill success of his expedition, and determined to wreak his vengeance on the poor lad, as a fearful example to the rest of the country. So he commanded him to be tied on a trooper's horse, and led him down the hill till they came to his own little cottage, where his wife Isobel was waiting his arrival to breakfast.

It was a fine, calm, clear, winter morning, the ground was covered with snow hardened by a keen frost, and the sun shone brightly and cheerily, as if on a scene of joy and festivity. His wife hearing the noise ran out to welcome her John, and beheld him a fettered prisoner, and in the hands of those whose tender mercies she well knew were horrid cruelties!

But the God whom she served did not forsake her in this her moment of bitterness and despair; she felt nerved with a strength which no human power could ever invest her with; and she went up to her husband firmly and tearlessly, as if she knew not that he was soon to be a bleeding corse, and she a friendless, houseless widow. She whispered a word of courage and consolation in his ear, she chafed his stiff, half-frozen hands, she parted his long brown hair over his brow—for his arms were tied—and with the corner of her apron she wiped the sweat from his cheek, and the foam of pain and agony from those lips from which she had often drained deep draughts of love and delight.

The murderous ruffian now tendered the test, as the only means of escape from death—instant death; and what a test! a compromise of conscience, a trampling on the tenderest feelings of devotion and principle. The agonized husband cast an eye of bitter meaning on his wife, and she at once understood the appeal, and nobly she answered it. 'John Craig,' she said, with a voice slightly broken, for the woman and the wife were holding a fearful strife in her breast,—'John Craig, care not for me; I am friendless, I am poor, I have none on earth to care for me but you, but God will care for me, John; He is the father of the fatherless, and the husband of the widow; *He* who has cared for me up till this time will give me strength to witness this last trial—to drain to the dregs this cup of unmixed bitterness and grief. We have often prayed together, dear John, when we were safe in our own sweet cottage, when we feared no danger and suffered no evil; and shall we not pray now when the shades of death compass us around, and hem us in on every side? come, John, let us pray to *Him* who is the hearer of prayer, and who hath not told any of the seed of Jacob to seek *His* face in vain.' And he looked on her and was comforted, and shook away the first and only tear he had shed; and there they knelt on the frozen ground, the husband and the wife, and prayed a prayer which made even the rude and thoughtless troopers turn aside and weep.

But Sir John's heart was hardened; he rudely broke in on their devotions, cursed their canting whine, and commanded the helpless and manacled man to kneel down on a little stone, and the troopers to prepare their carbines. He obeyed without a murmur; but when he rose to take his place as commanded, all men wondered at the change which that short season of prayer had wrought on his countenance. His eye was no longer clouded and downcast, but gleamed with an exultation and light which seemed to reflect something beyond the grave—brighter and more glorious than the sun in his unclouded pride; he kissed the pale and bloodless cheek of his Isobel, and walked with a stately and unflinching step to the appointed place; but, before he kneeled down, he looked steadily at Erskine castle, the windows of which were glittering in the morning sun, and many thought that a shade of sorrow passed over his manly brow. He stood as if entranced for a moment or two, and then spake in tones more sorrowful than angry. 'We are commanded to pray for our enemies, and from my soul I beseech that my blood may not be laid to the charge of this man, but I may not conceal what God commands me to speak: I shall indeed fall by your hands, but I will not fall unavenged; you will not see it—none here present will see it—but as surely as I speak, it will come to pass. Yet three generations, and the proud house of Rath will cease to be, and fearful will the curse fall: would I could avert it! but God has decreed it, and what mortal shall stay *His* hand, or say unto *Him*, What doest thou? Farewell, time—farewell, all created comforts; welcome, eternity—welcome, heaven—welcome, eternal life. Father, into thy hands I commend my spirit. Amen! and amen!'[†]

Here he bent his head and ceased to speak. The troopers unslung their muskets and took aim, and the miserable wife kneeled down also, covering her eyes firmly with both hands. She saw nothing—she heard nothing; and when she came to her recollection, the band had retired, and her young goodman was lying at her feet, with his brains sprinkled over his fair and manly face. She stretched the body out on the snow, for she had now no home—the wretches had burned the cottage to the ground—and after closing those eyes which had

---

[†] These concluding exclamations are almost verbatim from the *Scots Worthies*.*

never spoken to her but in the language of peace and love and joy, she prayed to their common God, and found comfort such as the world can neither give nor take away.

The rest of the tale is short, and will not tire out your patience. The murdering crew spent the whole of that day in the village, and none dared to visit the widowed mourner, lest they should be suspected of treasonable communing; such was the nature of these fearful times. That night a storm raged, such as no one remembered ever having witnessed. The wind howled, and swept over the hills and down the glens, as if the prince of darkness had been riding in triumph at the good services rendered him by his liege vassals. The snow fell fast and thick, and the mountain burns foamed and boiled, and roared like mighty rivers diverted from their proper channels. The next morning some pitying neighbours sought the lone cottage on the hill; but what a scene presented itself! There lay the martyr, calm as when he first entered into his rest, half shrouded in the drifted snow, and by his side his young widowed wife, cold and stiff and dead, the big tear-drops frozen on her wan cheek. But they had been tears of holy rapture and joy; she had found comfort in death, for a calm smile still seemed to linger about her mouth, and, like the holy Stephen, those who stood around 'saw *her* face as it had been the face of an angel.'*

They both lie here, doubtless in hope of a glorious and blessed resurrection, and in that tomb sleeps their murderer, till the thunder of the last dread trumpet call the oppressor and the oppressed before His throne, who will judge all men according to the deeds done in the flesh, whether they be good or whether they be evil. God alone knows his fate; but, sir, not for all the wealth of the Indies ten times told, would I change that little neglected hillock of earth for yonder proud sculptured tomb. The curse has not yet fallen on the house of the spoiler; but as sure as that noontide sun is shining over our heads, it will come, and that quickly. The blood of Abel cried not in vain from the earth, neither will that of John Craig and Isobel Ross; for precious in God's sight is the blood of his saints.

It was long after the old man had ceased to speak, that I looked up, and when I did so he was gone. I was sitting alone, between the patrician tomb and the humble earthen mound, through the long rank grass of which the piping wind whistled in wild fitful gusts, as if the inhabitants of the tombs were lamenting their destinies and woes.

When at last I rose, I felt as if I were recovering from some strange sickness or troubled dream. '*The third generation*,' I continued repeating, over and over to myself,—'the third generation. 'Tis indeed come. What if the strange legend of that old dotard should be true? But no! 'tis but an idle tale—the invention of credulous superstition—an old wife's fable, to frighten children withal. May the curse light on the inventor of such an improbable farrago!' But for all this, I felt a kind of nameless awe and apprehension hang over me, and I half wished that I had never seen the peasant, and never heard his tale.

When going out of the enclosure, I saw some farmers ride past in the direction of my father's house, with favours in their hats, as if for a bridal; and between intervals of joyous shouts of laughter, I heard mention made of Rath house, as the scene of some such festivity. I could not prevail on myself to question the many groups as to particulars, but rode on, congratulating myself on my good fortune in reaching home on such an occasion, when all would be mirth, and happiness, and festivity.

Rath house, the seat of my fathers, stands at the extremity of a steep perpendicular line or curtain of rock, which, without break or stay, goes sheer down full twenty fathoms, till it ends in a deep and rapid stream, rushing through a narrow gorge, and scantily studded with a sort of dwarfish stunted brushwood, through which the boiling and bubbling of the water is seen at broken intervals.

Along the ridge of this steep it was the custom, when any marriage occurred in the family, for the bridal procession to ride to church, which stood in a glen about half a mile distant; and on such an occasion the bride and bridegroom rode double, that is, on one horse, the lady sitting behind, on an ancient pad used only for that purpose. 'Twas one of those old antiquated observances which almost every family of any standing has, and which is kept up merely because practised by former generations; and as the ceremony generally took place a little after mid-day, so I fully calculated on meeting the joyous throng midway at least. 'It will be my brother's bridal,' said I, 'and my father will be there—and my old uncle, Heaven bless him! will be there—and Helen Vere, perchance, will be there as bridemaid. Little does she dream how soon she may ride the principal feature in a similar solemnity.' The thought of Helen inspired me with new vigour; the legend of the churchyard was all forgotten. I spurred up my horse, and ere long the gray towers and turrets of my fathers rose before me, gloriously sprinkled by the fervid beams of an unclouded July sun. I recognised a friend in every stone, an old acquaintance in every tree. I even thought I knew the crows'-nests which I had so often despoiled; and I could swear to the initials of my name, which, with Helen's assistance, I had feloniously carved out of the smooth bark of a huge chestnut-tree.

But other thoughts now occupied my mind, for I heard the joyous shouts of many a light-hearted boy and maiden; and presently, turning a corner of the way, I saw indeed a bridal procession, advancing in all its glittering circumstance and panoply. My heart beat high. 'I will meet them on foot,' I said, 'as an unknown individual, and their joy and surprise will be the greater.' So I turned my horse in to an adjoining field, and, mantling my face in my capacious cloak, I pursued my way, filled with a variety of contending feelings, which I can neither analyse nor describe.

On came the procession. My father (according to usage) rode first, on an ancient steed, which had faithfully served him for more than twenty years. The old man was feeble, and more bent than when I parted with him; yet still I was rejoiced to see that time had laid his hand but gently on his honoured head. His eye had waxed dim, however, and he rode past me without stop or recognition. Then came my relations,— distant connexions, whom I had never seen, or, having seen them merely as children, did not know. The ignorance was mutual. I was merely regarded as a spectator of the solemnity of the day. At last the bridegroom appeared, on a gallant piebald steed, which proudly pranced beneath his joyful burden, as if he gloried in the weight. I could not be mistaken;

it was indeed my brother, my only darling brother, who, from a laughing lad, had grown up into a noble man,—a man whom in a crowded street you would turn back and gaze upon, as a perfect model of his race. Grace and power were in every motion and look; the light ease of the Apollo was admirably blended with the nerve and muscle of the Hercules.

He rode up, and, as usual, the bride sat behind him, tall, slender, and nobly fashioned, and bashfully retiring as the graceful gazelle. I was about to speak, when a passing gust of wind blew aside her veil, and there I beheld Helen! ay, Helen Vere, my first, my only love, and my all but pledged bride. What misery, and despair, and rage, were concentrated in that little moment! All my hopes, all the wanderings, and toils, and privations, became but as empty wind by that look. I seemed in a moment to live over fifteen long years of my life. My first feelings of love—my parting kiss—my dreams of her when far away, danced wildly in my brain. She was another's bride! The sudden shock was too much for feeble frail reason to sustain. I forgot where I was—what I was doing. I rushed forward; I threw out my arms, like one battling with some tempest-vexed sea. I screamed, I laughed, I shouted ha, ha, ha! till the rocks echoed as with the howling of a thousand wolves. My blood felt like liquid fire; my eyes seemed starting from their burning sockets; my veins were swollen to agony, and my heart seemed glowing and crackling, as if the infernal fire of a whole eternity were concentrated in its narrow limits. 'Welcome, my love! welcome, my lady bride!' I shouted, 'you have kept your troth bravely—we shall have a merry bridal —ha, ha, ha,! But who laughs?' I exclaimed, startled at the hideous sound of my own maniac voice—'who dares laugh at us—ha! she rides with a demon—'tis death, death himself —see you not the fleshless limbs through the bravery of his crimson robes—down, down fiend!—down, in God's name or the devil's, to your native hell!' And, possessed with the wild fantasy which my whirling brain had conjured up, I rushed at my brother to pull him from his seat. I had the nerve of a giant—I was blind with the fury of raging madness: the horse with its riders were near the edge of the rock —I sprung forward at the imaginary enemy, and oh, horror!

horror! horror! over they went, horse and riders, over the naked craggy precipice. All I have described passed in a moment of time—the pair, thank God! never, on this earth at least, knew their murderer.

The moment they fell, my reason returned like a flash of light—I was fascinated, rooted to the spot, gazing into the abyss of death and horror. I saw, I marked every thing; I saw the steed with its burden dash from point to point; I even noted the sparks which the hoofs of the agonised brute struck from the flinty side of the ravine, and I distinctly heard a low but terribly clear shriek of mortal agony mingling with the sullen crash which told they had reached their grave at the bottom.

The frenzy again came upon me; I lost all thought, all fear: regardless of the tremendous height, I swung myself down by bush and stone, getting footing and holding which in no other circumstances I could have found or availed myself of. I heard a confused murmur of voices above me, the gradual diminishment of which was the only index to my progress; and at length, bruised and breathless, but strong with fever and madness, I reached the bottom.

At first I could discern nothing; my eye was bloodshot and dim—I was dizzy too, and sick and faint; for the first excitation had begun to wear away. At last I saw something dark mingled with white; it grew plainer and plainer, like the phantasmagorical scene of a magic lantern; my sight gradually regained its wonted power—my reason and consciousness returned, and I saw what will haunt me till the spirit hath parted with the flesh—even longer, it may be.

It was very terrible to be sitting there in that wild fastness beside the dead, who but minutes—moments ay, had been rioting in life, and health, and joy—and I had caused the change; but for me, they still had been tenants of this glad and sunny earth, had still felt the blessed freshness of the western breeze which now whirled the withered oak leaves around their unconscious forms. The solitude was awful. I have been in the wild battle, where death held his bloodiest carnival,—I have been at sea when the masts were sprung, and the breakers a-head were already baptising the bows of the devoted ship,—and I have been in a city whose walls were crumbling, and whose palaces were sinking under the tornado and earthquake;—at that moment I would have rushed into the whole of these united, if that could be, as a blessed refuge from the calm, still quiet of death and desolation which that lonely gulf now presented.

Helen's face, by some chance, was untouched; unmutilated; her head resting on the side of the horse, she seemed as if peacefully gazing at me, as she was wont in bygone years, when reposing with me on the sunny side of some green *gowan*-decked hill. I could not believe that what had happened was real—I spoke to her—I grasped her hand yet warm with recent life—I laughed, I upbraided her for her cold apathy and neglect. 'What! not one word, Helen, after our long absence? Is this kind? 'Tis but to try, my love—speak, Helen, speak but one word to say that you are still my own little black-haired laughing Helen.' My eye glanced on the fearfully mutilated form of my brother—the damning reality at once pressed upon my brain—for an instant I felt torments to which the severest bodily agony would be pleasure and ease—but madness, blessed madness, came to my relief; and I awoke, as after a long and troubled sleep, in the very room where I had slept when a child.

A strange fancy struck me: I thought for a moment that I was still a boy, that my residence in India, the fearful crag, and the lapse of fifteen long years, were but the visionary creations of the erratic dream of a single night; and I almost expected to hear the laughing voice of Helen Vere outside my chamber-door, chiding me for lying so long a-bed, when the sun had risen two hours before, and the tame stock-doves would be wearying for their accustomed food.

Two old withered hags, sick-nurses I presume, sat on each side of my couch in earnest converse, and I gently raised myself on my elbow to listen. 'In truth,' said one, ''tis an awful story; 'tis lucky the old man died before he knew it was his son.' 'What strange fancies he had, to be sure,' quoth the other; 'because the bride was timersome, and did not like riding a-horseback, he must needs have the bridemaid to take her place: well, well, old folks will have their fancies; the laird was ever particular in keeping up the freaks of the family.' I could hear no more—'She *was* true then!' I yelled, and sunk back stunned and senseless, like one stricken by a million thunderbolts.

I found myself naked and chained in a dungeon of a madhouse; it was cold, piercing cold; the night was wild and stormy, a high hoarse-voiced wind shook the dark tall trees which grew around the window, and their shadows, reflected by the bright moonlight, danced and flickered on the roof and walls of my cell like demons laughing at me, and mocking my distress; a great moping screech-owl was perched outside the gratings of the window; and as the neighbouring church-clock chimed the hour of one, it slowly and sluggishly raised its head for a moment, opened its heavy dull eye, and then slumbered as before: the clanking of chains was sullenly heard at intervals; and above, and below, and from every side, came fearful demoniac-like gusts of screaming and laughter, and shrieks of insensate agony, and wild dark blasphemies and execrations.

Thanks be to God, I am again in my sound mind—the fierce remembrance of the above fearful passages has softened down into a settled permanent melancholy. I cannot bear society—I see no one but the old clergyman of the village, whose pious communings have tended in no small degree to make me bear my lot with patience. But when I look at the desolation which pervades my paternal mansion and lawns, when I look at my worn-out frame, and my hair prematurely gray with sorrow and watching, and think that with me one of the oldest families in the land will cease to exist, a feeling of unspeakable loneliness will ever and anon steal upon me; and I think with chastened wonder upon the ways of that God which are past finding out, and which baffle and put to fault the wisest imaginings of our poor, erring, short-sighted race.

LIFE IN DEATH

Anonymous

'Who shall deny the mighty secrets hid
In Time and Nature?'

'But can you not learn where he sups?' asked the dying man,
for at least the twentieth time; while the servants again repeated the same monotonous answer—'Lord, sir, we never
know where our young master goes.'

'Place a time-piece by the bed-side, and leave me.'

None was at hand; when one of the assembled group
exclaimed—'Fetch that in Mr Francis's room.'

It was a small French clock, of exquisite workmanship, and
a golden Cupid swung to and fro,—fitting emblem for the
light and vain hours of its youthful proprietor, but a strange
mockery beside a death-bed! Yet the patient watched it with
a strange expression of satisfaction, mingled, too, with anxiety, as the glittering hands pursued their appointed round. As
the minutes passed on, an ejaculation of dismay burst from
Mr Saville's lips: he strove to raise his left hand with a ges-
ture of impatience; he found it powerless too; the palsy, which
had smitten his right side, had now attacked the left. 'A thousand curses upon my evil destiny—I am lost!'

At this moment the time-piece struck four, and began to
play one of the popular airs of that day; while the cord on
which the Cupid was balanced moved, modulated by the fairy-
like music. 'He comes!' almost shrieked the palsied wretch,
making a vain effort to rise on his pillow. As if the loss of
every other sense had quickened that of hearing seven-fold,
he heard the distant tramp of horses, and the ring of wheels,
on the hard and frosty road. The carriage stopped; a young
man, wrapped in furs, sprang out, opened the door with his
own key, and ran up the stairs, gaily singing,

'They may rail at this earth: from the hour I began it,
  I have found it a world full of sunshine and bliss;
And till I can find out some happier planet,
  More social and bright, I'll content me with this.'*

'Good God, sir, don't sing—your father's dying!' exclaimed the servant who ran to meet him. The youth was silenced in a moment; and, pale and breathless, sprang towards the chamber. The dying man had no longer power to move a limb: the hand which his son took was useless as that of the new-born infant; yet all the anxiety and eagerness of life was in his features.

'I have much to say, Francis; see that we are alone.'

'I hope my master does not call this dying like a Christian,' muttered the housekeeper as she withdrew. 'I hope Mr Francis will make him send for a priest, or at least a doctor. People have no right to go out of the world in any such heathen manner.'

The door slammed heavily, and father and son were left alone.

'Reach me that casket,' said Mr Saville, pointing to a curiously carved Indian box of ebony. Francis obeyed the command, and resumed his kneeling position by the bed.

'By the third hand of that many-armed image of Vishnu is a spring, press it forcibly.'

The youth obeyed and the lid flew up, within was a very small glass phial containing a liquid of delicate rose colour. The white and distorted countenance of the sufferer lighted up with a wild unnatural joy.

'Oh youth, glad beautiful youth, art thou mine again, shall I once more rejoice in the smile of woman, in the light of the red wine cup, shall I delight in the dance, and in the sound of music?'

'For heaven's sake compose yourself,' said his son, who thought that his parent was seized with sudden insanity. 'In truth I am mad to waste breath so precious!—Listen to me, boy! A whole existence is contained in that little bottle; from my earliest youth I have ever felt a nameless horror of death, death yet more loathsome than terrible: you have seen me engrossed by lonely and mysterious studies, you knew not that they were devoted to perpetual struggle with the mighty conqueror—and I have succeeded. That phial contains a liquid which rubbed over my body, when the breath has left it seemingly for ever, will stop the progress of corruption, and restore all its pristine bloom and energy. Yes, Francis, I shall rise up before you like your brother. My glorious secret! how could I ever deem life wasted in the search? Sometimes when I have heard the distant chimes tell the hour of midnight, the hour of others' revelry or rest, I have asked, is not the present too mighty a sacrifice to the future; had I not better enjoy the pleasures within my grasp? but one engrossing hope led me on; it is now fulfilled. I return to this world with the knowledge of experience, and the freshness of youth; I will not again give myself up to feverish studies and eternal experiments. I have wealth unbounded, we will spend it together, earth holds no luxury which it shall deny us.'

The dying man paused, for he observed that his son was not attending to his words, but stared as if his gaze was spellbound by the phial which he held.

'Francis,' gasped his father.

'There is very little,' muttered the son, still eying the crimson fluid.

The dews rose in large cold drops on Saville's forehead—with a last effort he raised his head, and looked into the face of his child—there was no hope there; cold, fixed, and cruel, the gentleness of youth seemed suddenly to have passed away, and left the stern features rigid as stone; his words died gurgling in the throat, his head sank back on the pillow, in the last agony of disappointment, despair, and death. A wild howl filled the chamber, and Francis started in terror from his knee; it was only the little black terrier which had been his father's favourite. Hastily he concealed the casket, for he heard the hurrying steps of the domestics, and rushing past them, sought his own room, and locked the door. All were struck by his altered and ghastly looks.

'Poor child,' said the housekeeper, 'I do not wonder he takes his father's death so to heart, for the old man doated on the very ground he trod upon. Now the holy saints have mercy upon us,' exclaimed she, making the sign of the cross, as she caught sight of the horrible and distorted face of the deceased.

Francis passed the three following days in the alternate stupor and excitement of one to whom crime is new, and who is nevertheless resolved on its commission. On the evening of the fourth he heard a noise in the room where the corpse lay, and again the dog began his loud and doleful howl. He entered the apartment, and the two first men he saw were strangers, dressed in black with faces of set solemnity; they were the undertakers, while a third in a canvass apron, and square paper cap, was beginning to screw down the coffin, and while so doing was carelessly telling them how a grocer's shop, his next-door neighbour's, had been entered during the night, and the till robbed.

'You will leave the coffin unscrewed till to-morrow,' said the heir. The man bowed, asked the usual English question which suits all occasions, of 'Something to drink, sir?' and then left young Saville to his meditations. Strange images of death and pleasures mingled together; now it was a glorious banquet, now the gloomy silence of a church-yard; now bright and beautiful faces seemed to fill the air, then by a sudden transition they became the cadaverous relics of the charnel-house. Some clock in the neighbourhood struck the hour, it was too faint for Francis to hear it distinctly, but it roused him; he turned towards the little time-piece, there the golden cupid sat motionless, the hands stood still, it had not been wound up; the deep silence around told how late it was; the fire was burning dead, the candles were dark with their large unsnuffed wicks, and strange shadows, gigantic in their proportions, flitted round the room.

'Fool that I am to be thus haunted by a vain phantasy. My father studied overmuch; his last words might be but the insane ravings of a mind overwrought. I will know the truth.'

Again his youthful features hardened into the gladiatorial expression of one grown old in crime and cruelty. Forth he went and returned with the Indian casket; he drew a table towards the coffin, placed two candles upon it, and raised the lid: he started, some one touched him; it was only the little black terrier licking his hand, and gazing up in his face with a look almost human in its affectionate earnestness. Francis put back the shroud, and then turned hastily away, sick and faint at the ghastly sight. The work of corruption had begun, and the yellow and livid streaks awoke even more disgust than horror. But an evil purpose is ever strong; he carefully opened the phial, and with a steady hand, let one drop fall on the eye of the corpse. He closed the bottle, replaced it in the casket, and then, but not till then, looked for its effect. The eye, large, melancholy, and of that deep violet blue, which only belongs to early childhood, as if it were too pure and too heavenly for duration on earth, had opened, and full of life and beauty was gazing tenderly upon him. A delicious perfume filled the air; ah, the old man was right! Others had sought the secret of life in the grave, and the charnel-house; he had sought it amid the warm and genial influences of nature; he had watched the invigorating sap bringing back freshness to the forest tree; he had marked the subtile spring wakening the dead root and flower into bloom—the essence of a thousand existences was in that fragile crystal. The eye now turned anxiously towards the casket, then with a mute eloquence towards the son; it gazed upon him so piteously, he saw himself mirrored in the large clear pupil; it seemed to implore, to persuade, and at last, the long soft lash glistened, and tears, warm bright tears, rolled down the livid cheek. Francis sat and watched with a cruel satisfaction; a terrible expression of rage kindled the eye like fire, then it dilated with horror, and then glared terribly with despair. Francis shrank from the fixed and stony gaze. But his very terror was selfish.

'It must not witness against me,' rushed into his mind. He seized a fold of the grave clothes, crushed the eye in the socket, and closed the lid of the coffin. A yell of agony rose upon the silent night. Francis was about to smite the howling dog, when he saw that it lay dead at his feet. He hurried with his precious casket from the chamber, which he never entered again.——Years have passed away, and the once gay and handsome Francis Saville is a grey and decrepit man, bowed by premature old age, and with a constitution broken by excess. But the shrewd man has been careful in his calculations; he knew how selfish early indulgence and worldly knowledge had made himself, and he had resolved that so his children should not be corrupted: he had two, a boy and a girl, who had been brought up in the strictest ignorance and seclusion, and in the severest practices of the Catholic faith. He well knew that fear is a stronger bond than love, and his children trembled in the presence of the father, whom their mother's latest words had yet enjoined them to cherish. Still the feeling of dutiful affection is strong in the youthful heart, though Mr Saville resolved not to tempt it, by one hint of his precious secret.

'I cannot bear to look in the glass,' exclaimed Mr Saville, as he turned away from his own image in a large mirror opposite; 'why should I bear about this weight of years and deformity? My plan is all matured, and never will its execution be certain as now. Walter must soon lose his present insecure and devout simplicity, and on them only can I rely. Yes, this very night will I fling off the slough of years, and awake to youth, warm, glad, and buoyant youth.'

Mr Saville now rang the bell for his attendants to assist him to bed.

When comfortably settled, his children came as usual to wish him good night, and kneel for his blessing; he received them with the most touching tenderness. 'I feel,' said he, 'unusually ill to-night. I would fain, Edith, speak with your brother alone.'

Edith kissed her father's hand, and withdrew.

'You were at confession to-day when I sent for you,' continued the invalid, addressing the youth, who leant anxiously by his pillow. 'Ah, my beloved child, what a blessed thing it is to be early trained to the paths of salvation. Alas! at your age I was neglected and ignorant; but for that, many things which now press heavily on my conscience had, I trust, never been. It was not till after my marriage with that blessed saint your mother that my conscience was awakened. I made a pilgrimage to Rome, and received from the hands of our holy Father the Pope, a precious oil, distilled from the wood of the true cross, which, rubbed over my body as soon as the breath of life be departed, will purify my mortal remains from

sin, and the faith in which I die will save my soul from pur-
gatory. May I rely upon the dutiful obedience of my child to
the last wishes of his parent?'

'Oh, my father!' sobbed the youth.

'Extinguish the lights, for it is not fitting that humanity
should watch the mysteries of faith; and, by your own hope
of salvation, anoint the body the moment life is fled. It is
contained in this casket,' pointing to the little ebony box; 'and
thus you undo the spring. Leave me now, my child. I have
need of rest and meditation.'

The youth obeyed; when, as he was about to close the door,
he heard the voice of Mr Saville, 'Remember, Walter; my blessing or my curse will follow you through life, according as
you obey my last words. My blessing or my curse!'

The moment he left the room Mr Saville unfastened the
casket, and from another drawer took a bottle of laudanum:
he poured its contents into the negus on his table, and drank
the draught!—The midnight was scarce passed when the nurse,
surprised at the unwonted quiet of her usually querulous and
impetuous patient, approached and undrew the curtain: her
master was dead! The house was immediately alarmed. Walter
and his sister were still sitting up in the small oratory which
had been their mother's, and both hastened to the chamber
of death. Ignorance has its blessing; what a world of corruption and distrust would have entered those youthful hearts,
could they have known the worthlessness of the parent they
mourned with such innocent and endearing sorrow.

Walter was the first to check his tears. 'I have, as you know,
Edith, a sacred duty to perform; leave me for awhile alone,
and we will afterwards spend the night in prayer for our
father's soul.'

The girl left the room, and her brother proceeded with
his task. He opened the casket and took out the phial; the
candles were then extinguished, and, first telling the beads of
his rosary, he approached the bed. The night was dark, and the
shrill wind moaned like a human being in some great agony,
but the pious son felt no horror as he raised the body in his
arms to perform his holy office. An exquisite odour exhaled
from the oil, which he began to rub lightly and carefully over

the head. Suddenly he started, the phial fell from his hand and was dashed to atoms on the floor.

'His face is warm—I feel his breath! Edith, dear Edith! come here. The nurse was wrong: my father lives!'

His sister ran from the adjacent room, where she had been kneeling before an image of the Madonna in earnest supplication, with a small taper in her hand: both stood motionless from terror as the light fell on the corpse. There were the contracted and emaciated hands laid still and rigid on the counterpane; the throat, stretched and bare, was meagre and withered; but the head was that of a handsome youth, full of freshness and life. The rich chestnut curls hung in golden waves on the white forehead, a bright colour was on the cheek, and the fresh, red lips were like those of a child; the large hazel eyes were open, and looked from one to the other, but the expression was that of a fiend,—rage, hate, and despair mingling together, like the horrible beauty given to the head of Medusa. The children fled from the room, only, however, to return with the priest, who deemed that sudden sorrow had unsettled their reason. His own eyes convinced him of the truth: there was the living head on the dead body!

The beautiful face became convulsed with passion, froth stood upon the lips, and the small white teeth were gnashed in impotent rage.

'This is, surely, some evil spirit,' and the trembling priest proceeded with the form of exorcism, but in vain.

Walter then, with a faltering voice, narrated his last interview with his father.

'The sinner,' said the old chaplain, 'is taken in his own snare. This is assuredly the judgment of God.'

All night did the three pray beside that fearful bed: at length the morning light of a glad day in June fell on the head. It now looked pale and exhausted, and the lips were wan. Ever and anon, it was distorted by sudden spasms,—youth and health were maintaining a terrible struggle with hunger and pain. The weather was sultry, and the body showed livid spots of decomposition; the beautiful head was still alive, but the damps stood on the forehead, and the cheeks were sunken. Three days and three nights did that brother and sister maintain their ghastly watch. The head was evidently dying. Twice the eyes opened with a wild and strong glare; the third time they closed for ever. Pale, beautiful, but convulsed, the youthful head and the aged body,—the one but just cold, the other far gone in corruption,—were laid in the coffin together!

MY HOBBY,—RATHER

N. P. Willis

'*Antonio.* Get me a conjuror, I say! Inquire me out a
man that lets out devils!'

*Old Play**

SUCH a night! It was like a festival of Dian,*—a burst of a
summer shower at sunset, with a clap or two of thunder, had
purified the air to an intoxicating rareness, and the free breathing of the flowers, and the delicious perfume from the earth
and grass, and the fresh foliage of the new spring, showed
the delight and sympathy of inanimate Nature in the night's
beauty. There was no atmosphere—nothing between the eye
and the pearly moon,—and she rode through the heavens
without a veil, like a queen as she is, giving a glimpse of her
nearer beauty for a festal favour to the worshipping stars.

I was a student at the famed university of Connecticut,*
and the bewilderments of philosophy and poetry were strong
upon me, in a place where exquisite natural beauty, and the
absence of all other temptation, secure to the classic neophite
an almost supernatural wakefulness of fancy. I contracted a
taste for the horrible in those days, which still clings to me.
I have travelled the world over, with no object but general
observation, and have dwindled my hour at courts and operas
with little interest, while the sacking and drowning of a
woman in the Bosphorus, the impalement of a robber on the
Nile, and the insane hospitals from Liverpool to Cathay, are
described in my capricious journal with the vividness of the
most stirring adventure.

There is a kind of *crystallization* in the circumstances of
one's life. A peculiar turn of mind draws to itself events fitted
to its particular nucleus, and it is frequently a subject of wonder why one man meets with more remarkable things than
another, when it is owing merely to a difference of natural

character. I have been thus a singular adventurer in the strange and unnatural. As I intend making my observations in this way the subjects of several papers, I will introduce them at present with my slighter beginnings.

It was, as I was saying, a night of wonderful beauty. I was watching a corpse. In that part of the United States the dead are never left alone till the earth is thrown upon them, and, as a friend of the family, I had been called upon for this melancholy service on the night preceding the interment. It was a death which had left a family of broken hearts; for, beneath the sheet which sank so appallingly to the outline of a human form, lay a wreck of beauty and sweetness whose loss seemed to the survivors to have darkened the face of the earth. The ethereal and touching loveliness of that dying girl, whom I had known only a hopeless victim of consumption, springs up in my memory even yet, and mingles with every conception of female beauty.

Two ladies, friends of the deceased, were to share my vigils. I knew them but slightly, and, having read them to sleep an hour after midnight, I performed my half-hourly duty of entering the room where the corpse lay, to look after the lights, and then strolled into the garden to enjoy the quiet of the summer night. The flowers were glittering in their pearl-drops, and the air was breathless.

The sight of the long, sheeted corpse, the sudden flare of lights as the long snuffs were removed from the candles, the stillness of the close-shuttered room, and my own predisposition to invest death with a supernatural interest, had raised my heart to my throat. I walked backwards and forwards in the garden-path, and the black shadows beneath the lilacs, and even the glittering of the glow-worms within them, seemed weird and fearful.

The clock struck, and I re-entered. My companions still slept, and I passed on to the inner chamber. I trimmed the lights, and stood and looked at the white heap lying so fearfully still within the shadow of the curtains; and my blood seemed to freeze. At the moment when I was turning away with a strong effort at a more composed feeling, a noise like a flutter of wings, followed by a rush and a sudden silence, struck on my startled ear. The street was as quiet as death, and the noise, which was far too audible to be a deception of the fancy, had come from the side toward an uninhabited wing of the house. My heart stood still. Another instant, and the fire-screen was dashed down, and a *white cat* rushed past me, and with the speed of light sprang like a hyena upon the corpse. The flight of a vampyre into the chamber would not have more curdled my veins. A convulsive shudder ran cold over me, but, recovering my self-command, I rushed to the animal (of whose horrible appetite for the flesh of the dead I had read incredulously*), and attempted to tear her from the body. With her claws fixed in the breast, and a *yowl* like the wail of an infernal spirit, she crouched fearlessly upon it, and the stains already upon the sheet convinced me that it would be impossible to remove her without shockingly disfiguring the corpse. I seized her by the throat, in the hope of choking her, but, with the first pressure of my fingers, she flew into my face, and the infuriated animal seemed persuaded that it was a contest for life. Half-blinded by the fury of her attack, I loosed her for a moment, and she immediately leaped again upon the corpse, and had covered her feet and face with blood before I could recover my hold upon her. The body was no longer in a situation to be spared, and I seized her with a desperate grasp to draw her off; but to my horror, the half-covered and bloody corpse rose upright in her fangs, and, while I paused in fear, sat with drooping arms, and head fallen with ghastly helplessness over the shoulder. Years have not removed that fearful spectacle from my eyes!

The corpse sank back, and I succeeded in throttling the insane monster, and threw her at last lifeless from the window. I then composed the disturbed limbs, laid the hair away once more smoothly on the forehead, and, crossing the hands over the bosom, covered the violated remains, and left them again to their repose. My companions, strangely enough, slept on, and I paced the garden-walk alone, till the day, to my inexpressible relief, dawned over the mountains.

THE RED MAN

Catherine Gore

A CERTAIN popular French tradition would lead us to believe that the palace of the Tuileries has been for centuries past the resort of a demon, familiarly known by the name of '*L'Homme Rouge*,' or the Red Man; who is seen wandering in all parts of the Château whenever some great misfortune menaces its regal inhabitants; but who retreats at other periods to a small niche in the *Tour de l'Horloge*, the central tower built by Catherine de Medicis, and especially devoted to the use of her royal astrologers.

Béranger* has described the royal Red Man as

> 'Un diable habillé d'écarlate,
>   Bossu, louche, et roux,
> Un serpent lui sert de cravate;
>   Il a le nez crochu,—
>   Il a le pied fourchu.'—

But, as it happens, other red men are to be met with in Paris besides the celebrated scarlet devil of the Tuileries; who, after all, is but a sort of metropolitan Zamiel, and little better than the *Feuergeist** of a high Dutch melodrama. Whoever, for instance, has chanced to visit the Quai Desaix with the intention of finding the *Marché aux Fleurs*, or Flower-Market, on any other day than the official Wednesdays and Saturdays when it presents so charming an aspect, may have been startled by the sight of half a hundred reddish men and women, the old iron-vendors who on ordinary occasions ply their unattractive trade beneath the dwarf acacia-trees of La Vallée. Even these, however, are the mere half-castes of the calling; but should some courteous reader be smitten, like ourselves, with a taste for the by-ways rather than the highways of a great city, let him dive into one of those tortuous, fetid, narrow, ten-storied streets of the ancient cité of Paris, where Nôtre Dame uplifts its Gothic towers, and the hospital of the

Hôtel Dieu bathes its leprous feet in the polluted waters of the Seine, which ought to have been devoted to the exclusive purpose of dispensing salubrity and purification to the capital,—there, either in the Rue de la Boucherie or Rue de la Huchette,—it matters not to give the exact locality,—he will discover a retreat, something between the modern shop and ancient *échoppe*, the front open to the narrow street in order to display to view its rust-bitten contents,—viz., heaps, bunches, and trays full of old iron, of every form and mould,—old locks, old keys, old implements and instruments of every trade and calling,—exhibited to the admiration of the public with as dainty a spirit of arrangement as in the curiosity and *virtù* shops of the Quai Voltaire, and presided in proper person by the proprietor,—the identical and especial RED MAN.

Fifty years has Balthazar followed the business. Fifty years have done their work in imparting to his face that copper-coloured complexion,—to his hair, beard, whiskers, habiliments, even down to his leathern apron, a hue of dingy red, which now appears to be engrained into his very nature. The walls, the floors, the ceiling of his dusky habitation, are red; nay, the very atmosphere he breathes is impregnated and coloured by the particles of rust thrown off from the ever-shifting materials of his trade. Between his buyings and sellings, the timeworn rods and bars, hooks and nails, blades and staples, are in perpetual motion. He has always some worn-out pot or cauldron to examine,—some lock, or hinge, or bolt, or bar, to dislocate; some jack-chain or fetter to unrivet,—some trap or springe to pull to pieces. For Balthazar is an amateur, as well as a man of business. Custom has rendered his rusty occupation second nature to him. He can breathe no other than the ferruginated atmosphere of his shop; and the lilacs of the Bois de Romainville, or the thorns of the Près St Gervais, stink, by comparison, in his nostrils. He would rather behold some piece of complicated machinery, oxided here and there into the rusty hue, marking it out as likely to become his property, than cast his eyes on all the Raphaels of the Louvre,—all the Rubenses of the Luxembourg. He has not yet travelled northward from his shop so far as to view that chef-d'œuvre of modern architecture, the *Bourse*; nor westward, to behold the Corinthian portico of the Madelaine with its matchless frieze. Of the Arc de l'Etoile he has heard rumours, and the Suspension Bridge has been duly reported to him. But till their iron stanchions become rusty, they will acquire no interest in the sight of Balthazar; whose cares and enjoyments are alike bounded within the narrow sphere compassed between his den behind the Hôtel Dieu, and his sleeping room in the most ancient house of the most ancient Rue St Jacques, where stand the Sorbonne, the Val de Grace, with other and numberless monuments of the olden time. He is unluckily too much a man of business, and finding his pleasure therein, to be much of a gossip; nevertheless, take the old man at the right moment, when he has achieved a lucky bargain, and is making the stifling red particles fly around him in clouds, while handling some worn-out piece of machinery before consigning it to his treasury, or appending it to a stall-hook of the *échoppe*, and you may cajole a world of information out of the RED MAN.

It was at some such auspicious conjunction of the planets, that it was in the first instance our fortune to accost him. We were returning with sickened soul and bewildered eyes, from the Barrière St Jacques—a spot appointed (since the Place de la Grève underwent consecration by a libation of the blood of heroes*) as the place of public execution; and whither, enclosed in a machine resembling a colossal baker's basket, condemned criminals are now trundled from the Conciergerie through the frequented streets of the Pays Latin, that the guillotine may do its hasty work under the awful auspices of 'Monsieur de Paris,' the celebrated Samson of the bloody hand.*

The grand spectacle of the heavy day in question was the judicial assassination of the supposed murderer of Madame Dupuytren's cook, of whose innocence sufficient evidence has since been adduced.* But innocent or guilty, we had seen blood—human blood—poured forth like water,—had looked upon the horror-struck aspect of a man before whom death stood face to face arrayed,—had witnessed the cunning artifices of the priest of a new sect,* who sought to render the martyrdom of the victim an evidence of the sanctity of his own charlatanic professions. All this we had seen: the shuddering

of the crowd; the deadly swoon of the inquisitive female whose
spirit was intrepid, but whose flesh was weak; and the almost
instantaneous relaxation of that intense feeling of excitement
which, until the great moment, had suspended the very breath
of the populace, as by a spell irresistible. For the throng was
already dispersed from the spot; the executioner and his two
assistants, protected in their loathsome operations by a few
municipal guards, had withdrawn the bolts and screws from
the murderous framework; the headless trunk and gasping
head were on their way to the dissecting room; and the blood-
gorged spectators, consisting chiefly of artizans out of work,
'ambitious students,' and the lowest *gamins* of Paris, were off
in various directions in search of breakfast; some wrangling,
some singing, some preaching, some yawning; some declaring
that the supposed assassin had died like a heathen,—others
that he had died like a hero.

For ourselves, who had been witnessing for the first time
the operation of the knife, we must plead guilty to a certain
perturbation of the senses leaving every sensation indistinct;
a whizzing in the ears,—a mistiness of vision,—a parchedness
of tongue,—a throbbing of heart, rendering the very way
before us hard to follow. We had a mind to visit Nôtre Dame
for early mass. Our spirit hungered after the pealing of the
organ and the music of those pure young voices which speak
the promises of peace in heavenliest diapason. We had been
present at the passing of a human soul, (guilty or guiltless,
God alone could determine,) from time to eternity. We longed
for the murmurs of a requiem; the tranquillity of a holy place;
for the security of the sanctuary; for the groined roof, the
echoing aisle, the word of God, the promises of salvation. In
such a mood of mind, it was our destiny to stumble into the
stall of the RED MAN!

For a moment, indeed, we fancied that our eyes deceived
us; that the hue of the blood we had seen spilled had attached
itself to the whole external creation. And probably the horror
of the impression depicted itself in our countenance; for the
old man, having gazed for a moment in silence, laid down the
rusty chain he was shaking into form, and having humanely
demanded if we were not indisposed, tendered the Evangelic

offering of a glass of water; which was gratefully accepted and swallowed, before we became accurately cognizant of our whereabout. Under all the circumstances, Balthazar's wooden chair seemed a luxurious refuge. We were glad to sit there, and pour into sympathizing ears the confession of our blood-hatred. The old man happened to have religious scruples of his own anent prison discipline and the penitentiary system; *he* too was an eschewer of the punishment of death; and as an inhabitant for sixty years of the Quartier St Jacques, resented with much bitterness the indignity inflicted upon his parish by the transposition of the guillotine.

Our minds were mutually attuned for horrors; we could talk of nothing but killing,—nothing but death. Balthazar had witnessed the execution of the monomaniac Papavoine;* and we, after tossing off another glass of *eau filtre*, had our own anecdotes to relate of Tyburn, of Newgate, of Jack Ketch, of the condemning cap of the judge, the condemned sermon of the felon, the cart, the toll of the bell, the ordinary, the sheriff, the coffin,—even unto the seething of the strangled corse, and the admonitory glass-case in Surgeons'-hall!*

Balthazar was perhaps jealous of our adeptitude in these tales of terror; for, at the close of our narrative of the fearful tragedy of Gill's Hill and fate of Thurtell,* he suddenly disappeared towards the back of his *échoppe*, and having penetrated into one of the subterranean recesses containing the choicer specimens of his trade, hobbled back to place in our hands a rusty complication of iron machinery, one portion of which seemed to be formed of pieces of bone or ivory. After turning it over and over without much enlightenment of our ignorance as to its nature and destination, we ventured to cast an upward glance of inquiry towards the old iron-dealer's face.

What a study for Rembrandt! The otter-skin cap of Balthazar, foxy as his own iron-dyed hair and whiskers, was pulled close upon one eye, while the other peered out, bleared and fiery from the excitement of its habitual atmosphere, with the leathern cheek around puckered into a peculiar expression of cunning and exultation. His thin lips were compressed, as if waiting the irrepressible interrogations of our curiosity; and while he stood leaning against a fascis* of jarring rods, he rolled unconsciously within his red hands a corner of his rusty leathern apron, from which the ferruginous particles flew off in volleys.

'Well, Sir?' said he, at last, tired of our perversity of silence: and—

'Well, my good friend?' was all the question we chose to vouchsafe in reply.

'Why, what I have to say,' was his somewhat more explicit rejoinder, 'is, that the Armada-armoury of the Tower of London which you have been describing, contains no choicer instrument of torture than the one you regard so carelessly.'

'Instrument of torture! Is this piece of rusty iron, then, a relique of the Inquisition?' was our involuntary exclamation.

'Not exactly. But you have not examined it. You have not observed the artist-like manner in which the springs close upon the bones—You do not perceive that it is one of the cleverest gins ever formed by the cunning of man—Try to extricate the skeleton hand! Try!'

'The skeleton hand?—the *bones?*'

'Ay! attempt to liberate them from the trap!'

And the effort, when made, was, as he had announced, unaccomplishable.

'But do you really mean,' was our next inquiry, 'that these pieces of bleached bone are, in truth, a portion of some human skeleton?'

'What else?' cried the old man, chuckling. 'It needs no Cuvier* to decide the point. Any student of anatomy between this and the Jardin des Plantes shall teach you as much.'

The skeleton of a human hand, and inclosed in an intricate fetterlock of rusty iron!

'The bones are diminutive; the hand must surely have been that of a female?' was the fruit of our cogitations upon this ugly instrument of barbarity;—'of a female,—probably young, —perhaps beautiful;—one who must have lived, or rather died, a captive. But where? Not, surely, in France;—not in gallant, refined, chivalrous Paris? This curious specimen may have been imported from the East,—from Tunis, or Tripoli, or Fez?'

'No such thing!' interrupted Balthazar. 'The ironwork does honour to a trusty workman, who must have served his time to a master-mechanic of the *cité*; the hand is that of a woman French-born,—Parisian-bred. The victim was, in short, one who lived and died almost within sight and sound of the very spot where we are standing.'

'Centuries ago, of course. The times of the Frédégondes and Brunéhauts* have probably legends of domestic horror to match with the crimes of their historical archives.'

'Bah, bah!' cried the old man petulantly. 'Human nature is the same in all ages and countries. Every day—every city— produces some monstrous wickedness, secret or discovered, arising from the triumphs of ungoverned passion;—from hatred,—lust,—revenge,—or mere blood-thirstiness. The crime in which this piece of ruthless machinery had its rise, was done in my own lifetime, in a place which I weekly and calmly traverse. The perpetrator went down to the grave, I will not say unpunished, but undiscovered. No one pitied the victim,—no one cursed the assassin. The whole story is, and is better, buried in oblivion.'

'Impossible, impossible!' we exclaimed, again carefully examining the whitened bones and their fiendish inclosure. 'Since you profess yourself acquainted with the origin and destination of this mysterious instrument, you must not tantalize our curiosity.'

'What avails it to rake up memoirs of the frailties of our fellow-creatures?' said the Red Man, dropping the corner of his leathern apron, replacing his cap horizontally over his brows, and turning towards a tray of screws and hinges, as if provokingly bent on devoting his attention to indifferent objects. 'Let the dead bury their dead! To-morrow it were cruelty to speak of the last throes of the unhappy wretch whom this morning you saw precipitated into eternity. Yet his life was given for a life, according to the decree of the Almighty, according to the laws of the land.'

'Nevertheless, the lesson to be imparted by such examples were lost,' we remonstrated, 'were the deed hidden behind a curtain. It is for the good of mankind, not to gratify an individual craving for retribution, that the penalty is paid. No man has a right to connive in the concealment of crime.'

'Unless when, as in the present instance, Time, the universal avenger, has swallowed up the offender and the offence,' rejoined Balthazar. 'All that could be done now in atonement were to curse with bell and book the place where the crime was perpetrated. And to what avail? You would affix an eternal stigma upon a spot of earth, the work of the Almighty's hands, fast by his holy house, and sanctified by the daily echoes of his holy word.'

'The *Parvis de Nôtre Dame!*'* we exclaimed, certain of having now attained the heart of the matter.

'The *Parvis de Nôtre Dame!*' reiterated the Red Man, in an affirmative tone. 'And since you appear so obstinately interested in the subject, it may save my time and your own to enter at once into explanation. Know, then, that this relique came not into my hands in the way of traffic. At the epoch of the first revolution,* when the very name of priest had become abomination in the ears of the people, and so many venerable servants of the church were arrested and sacrificed in every part of the kingdom, the greater number of the canons of Nôtre Dame were wise enough to seek safety in flight or in concealment. One, however, there was—an aged man, familiarly and favourably known to the poor of the island by the name of Père Anselme, who disdained to follow the example of the fashionable abbés or beneficed nobles; and attached beyond all power of separation to the old towers and aisles of the cathedral, or, as some thought, to the little, gloomy, official habitation wherein, for thirty years, he had abided, refused to stir,—surrendered himself, as it were, to his destinies,—and was eventually numbered among the victims of the massacre at the prison of L'Abbaye.* It was on the evening following his arrest that a decrepit mulatto serving-man, attired in shabby mourning, entered my *échoppe*, entreating my assistance in opening the springs of the fetterlock in question, one end of which was still attached to a chain and staple, which had evidently been wrenched by force from a stone wall. Vain, however, were the utmost endeavours of my skill; the cunning of the springs effectually defied my artificership; and having rendered it back to the old man to be re-enveloped in the cloth in which he had transported it to my dwelling, I could not forbear an inquisitive remark or two concerning the mysterious task he had sought to impose upon me, and the inexplicable nature of the instrument.

'He shook his head mournfully in reply; but at length admitted that the trap was connected with certain family secrets, which he was desirous of screening from the scrutiny of the National officers in a house to which, that morning, the seals of office had been affixed.

' "It required some exertion of strength, as you may perceive," said the poor old mulatto, opening his shrivelled hands and displaying the mangled palms, "to wrench the staple from the wall. Thank Heaven, however, I succeeded: and all that now remains for me to accomplish is to unclose the springs, —consign these wretched bones to consecrated earth, and this wicked instrument to the furnace;—that so may finish all memory of one of the cruellest deeds darkening the history of human kind."

'Smitten with an interest in the business, almost equal to that you now evince, I instantly proffered a renewal of my efforts in so pious a cause; and promised, if the lock could be left in my possession, to apply the whole of my leisure to the task. Christophe's first impulse was a decided negative to this proposal; but, on consideration, he admitted that the trap would be safer from observation in my hands than in his own, and having extorted from me a promise of secrecy, he departed with the intention of returning in the course of a week. Many weeks elapsed, however, before I saw the mulatto again; and when he once more entered the shop, I could scarcely bring to remembrance my former visiter. He was so worn, so wasted, so tremulous, so fearful, that I had scarcely courage to refer to the painful secret by which we had been originally brought into collision. But Christophe was the first to recur to the fetter-lock; and after a vehement burst of almost childish tears, admitted that the great motive for secrecy was now at an end. "God has avenged all—God, in his own good time, has poured down retribution!" was his reiterated exclamation. "My poor old master was butchered in the massacre of the 2nd of September. All is over!—I have nothing now to care for!—let those come and see who list! My own days are numbered:—to others lie the accomplishment of my tasks—to you, Sir, if it be the will of Heaven, the expiatory deed of opening this fatal springe, and consigning the bones of Lucile to hallowed ground!"

'Touched by the helplessness of his grief, no less than by the fidelity of his attachment, I undertook to fulfil, as far as my powers might avail, the task proposed; and in the process of another week's acquaintance with old Christophe (the last week of his mortal existence), derived from his lips the particulars of a family history of unequalled interest and horror connected with the lock. You seem at leisure to listen;—hear, and moralize upon the tale.

'Anselme Lanoue, Sir, was the only son of respectable parents, occupying a small property in the neighbourhood of St Etienne; destined from his infancy to follow in their footsteps as the unaspiring cultivator of his paternal estate. Having, however, at a very early age, distinguished himself among his fellow-students at the Lycée of St Etienne by a remarkable proficiency in mathematics, and, at his leisure hours, by a singular tendency to mechanical pursuits, the proprietor of one of the chief engine-foundries in the country, a distant kinsman of Madame Lanoue, persuaded his father and mother to bind the boy in apprenticeship to a calling for which he evinced so marked a vocation, and which afforded such auspicious prospects of future fortune. Anselme accordingly became an engineer, and soon confirmed the prognostications of his new master by striking out various improvements and inventions of high account. At three and twenty he had achieved the post of chief engineer in the establishment, and at eight and twenty was not only a partner but the affianced husband of his master's daughter. His parents did not survive to witness the consummation of his prosperity—both were already in the grave, and Anselme's patrimony disposed of to augment the capital of his thriving trade.

'Nothing now remained for him to desire. Lucile Moronval was a lovely girl of eighteen, whom he had fondly watched from childhood, with a gradually increasing hope of being enabled, at some future time, to aspire to her hand; and although it was whispered among the commercial coteries, that she had for some time testified considerable repugnance to the marriage arranged for her by her parents, on the grounds that Anselme, in spite of his enlightenment and high moral principles, was of a silent, stern, jealous, and even at times morose disposition, mistrustful in his temper and sullen in his deportment,—all was finally reconciled; and ere the bride had attained her nineteenth year, they were settled as man and wife in a pleasant house in the suburbs of St Etienne, the dwelling attached to the foundry being supposed disadvantageously situated for the health of the young matron. Lanoue seemed indeed to derive double happiness when established in his cheerful home at the close of his labours of the day, from the circumstance of their temporary separation. Lucile had household cares to occupy her time during the interim, and at the close of the first year of their marriage, had a pretty little Lucile of her own to display to her husband and father on their return from the foundry.

'Still it was remarked by the same prying gossips who had been the first to notice her disinclination to become the wife of Anselme, that after the first few months of her motherly triumph, Madame Lanoue appeared to take little pleasure in her child. She grew dispirited, indifferent, negligent in her person and household; and the more her husband evinced his discontent at these changes in her deportment, the more her spirits were depressed. Some of her neighbours were prompt to attribute the mischief to the arrival of a young cousin, a certain Clement Manoury, who had been the companion of Lucile's early years, and for some time past detained by the arrangement of his family affairs in the island of Martinique. It was even said that her kinsman had returned with the intention of claiming her hand; and that Lanoue, on discovering his abortive pretensions, had forbidden Clement the house, insisting on an absolute rupture of the family connexion.

'Certain it was that the door of Anselme was closed upon his supposed rival; and certain also it was said to be, that Lanoue, who had hitherto contented himself with returning home at the close of his day's labours to his evening meal, was now frequently seen traversing the town, from his foundry at the river-side to his cheerful habitation in the suburbs, with hurried step and gloomy countenance, at various unaccustomed periods of the day. Those who were busiest on the watch managed to ascertain that he had, at different times, broken in suddenly on the solitude of Lucile—but, happily, only to find it solitude. Nothing transpired to justify his suspicions, but nothing seemed to pacify the disturbance of his mind.

'For often does a husband or a wife possess confirmation strong of fickleness or infidelity, which less interested persons account as nothing—symptoms of coldness, of estrangement, of loathing in moments once devoted to endearment —tears where smiles should be, or smiles of scorn instead of the playful self-abandonment sanctioned by reciprocal tenderness. And Anselme had good reason to see that he was no longer beloved. Had he not, therefore, reason to suspect that another had already superseded him in the affections of his wife?

'He *did* at least suspect it, and the suspicion maddened him. He read it in the averted eye, the quivering lip, the hand withdrawn from his own; and when at length he gathered from his wife that he was about again to become a father, the admission, instead of filling his heart with the rapture which had preceded the birth of little Lucile, struck him with disgust. Perplexed in the extreme by the agonizing misgivings which had taken possession of his mind, he soon became brutal, wild, ungovernable in his exasperations against his unhappy victim. Yet strange enough it was that Lucile never resented his violence—never appealed to her neighbours' compassion or her father's protection. She suffered all in silence—too mild to murmur, too gentle to resist. It was even hinted that harsh words had been followed by hard blows; yet still the humbled creature uttered not a syllable of complaint!

'At length the time was accomplished, and Madame Lanoue brought forth a son. Her father eagerly desired that it might be named "Anselme," after her husband, and Lanoue stood eagerly waiting in the hope that Lucile would second the request. But amid all her exhaustion and debility, the young mother found strength to implore that her father, who was to be its Christian sponsor, would bestow his own name on the infant; and that name happened, unluckily, to be no other than "Clement!" From that moment it was a fearful sight to watch the glances cast by Lanoue upon his unwelcome offspring.

'Not long, however, did Lucile find courage to encounter the concentrated wrath of the now desperate man; and exactly five weeks after her confinement, she disappeared from St Etienne. One evening, on returning from the foundry, Anselme found his little home abandoned—the cradle empty—the nurse dismissed—while a few lines, in the hand-writing of Lucile, acquainted him that he would see her face no more, and that his little daughter was deposited with her former nurse, at a village two leagues distance from Lyons;—for *that* child, at least, was his own.

'By this fatal announcement the miserable truth became manifest to all the world. Anselme was pardoned his former mistrust, his previous jealousy, when it was seen that Madame Lanoue had eloped with the object of her early attachment, and embarked for Martinique—that her father's name and her husband's roof were dishonoured—that Lucile was an adultress!

'Poor old Moronval!—he had not long to support his load of obloquy, or the consciousness that his daughter's former declarations of attachment to another ought to have prevented him from interposing his parental authority to complete her union with Anselme Lanoue. He died repentant and self-accusing, driven to despair by the accusations of his indignant son-in-law. And thus, freed from all engagements, and bereft of almost every tie to life, Anselme grew weary of his former haunts, his former avocations, and resolved at once to dispose of the foundry, and seek happiness in some province where his name and misfortunes did not serve to point him out to public notice. It was expected that his child would bear him company, but having visited the little girl shortly after the disappearance of his wife, the unhappy man discerned or fancied he discerned some resemblance to her kinsman Manoury in the countenance of the infant Lucile, and thenceforward resolved to exclude it from his home. A liberal annuity was accordingly settled upon the nurse;—it was arranged

that Lucile should be reared as her own; and Lanoue became
a Cain and a wanderer!

'From that period all trace of the once thriving engineer
was lost at St Etienne. Rumours prevailed that he had entered
into the ecclesiastical state, that he was even a member of the
confraternity of La Trappe; and one fellow-townsman, who
happened to have business in the West Indies, protested that
he had seen Anselme Lanoue fulfilling the duties of a mission-
ary in the island of Martinique. The lapse of a dozen years, however, tended to obliterate all curiosity respecting him or his
movements—his very name came to be forgotten at St Etienne;
and little Lucile, reared in all the simplicity of a Lyonnese
farmer's daughter began to think of her unknown father as
numbered with the dead.

'Scarcely, however, had she attained her fifteenth year, when
there arrived at the village a priest of severe but venerable
aspect, who proceeded to exhibit to Nanette and her husband
the necessary proofs empowering him to claim the guardianship
of Lucile Lanoue. For many hours was the stranger closetted
with the afflicted couple; who, at the close of the conference,
announced him to their charge as her uncle and future protector. Lucile, who had been hitherto taught to consider her
father an only son, and her mother an only daughter, could
by no means reconcile herself to this unlooked-for tie of con-
sanguinity. But Nanette soon satisfied her beloved nurseling
that so it was and was to be;—that her only chance of happiness lay in unlimited submission to the will of her new
uncle, with whom she was to reside in Paris, where he enjoyed
a small benefice under the metropolitan see; and who, although
a stern man and reserved, regarded her with the tenderest
affection. Nothing remained but to submit; and Lucile, still
bewildered by the sudden transition in her destinies, bade
adieu to her native province, and accompanied her uncle to
his gloomy abode in the *Parvis Nôtre Dame*.

'For many months the gay-hearted and bright-eyed girl
found little in her new home to replace the simple occupations and affectionate tending of her childhood. Waited upon
by a decrepit mulatto servant, who seemed to regard her as
an intruder, immured from the sunshine and the free range

of nature, she became weary of life, even unto the utmost heart-sickness of weariness. But in course of time, the studies to which her uncle began to claim her attention acquired interest in her eyes; she was taught new languages,—sciences hitherto undreamed of;—the page of history unrolled its wonders to her eyes,—the mysteries of nature unfolded their miracles to her comprehension. The gentle mind of Lucile became fascinated by her uncle's lessons of wisdom; she had long listened with reverence to his exhortations from the pulpit; she now began to admit the extent of his attractions as a companion, the value of his regard as a friend and monitor.

'There was but one point on which his lessons were distasteful. It struck her that the stern ascetic insisted too often and too strongly on the virtue of chastity, and the pure mind of Lucile revolted from the frequency of a charge she deemed superfluous. Père Anselme persisted in warning her against unclean thoughts, when her soul was spotless as that of a nun; and inveighed against the attraction of temptations, which to *her* were foul and offensive. He seemed, in fact, to invest the whole force of female excellence in a virtue which to Lucile appeared a necessary and spontaneous obligation; for the white rose in its first expansion of purity, was not more spotless than Lucile Lanoue!

'At length she revolted against these iterations of his daily sermon.—"You talk to me, dear uncle," said she, "of crimes that enter not into my apprehension. What pleasure can you suppose me to find in seeking after books, images, ideas, expressions of an immodest nature? What sense of enjoyment can possibly attach itself to things which bring a blush to the cheek, and confusion to the heart?"

' "Nevertheless, beware!" rejoined the stern pastor; "circumstances may arise to invest with unknown charms these very accessories of evil. And remember, Lucile,—remember, my niece,—remember, my beloved child, that sooner than see thee yield to the backslidings by which so many of thy sex sink into the gulf of perdition, I would tear thee limb from limb,—behold thee perish inch by inch, and minute by minute. The soul of woman is the brightest emanation of the eternal fountain of light and life; but the smallest blemish upon its spotlessness, and corruption and utter darkness ensue. Either thou must be as the angels of Heaven, secure from the influence of every grosser passion, or fall under the domination of the worst, and become a thing for men to trample on and fiends to scoff at. Half the mischiefs, half the crimes of this world of woe, are produced by the levity of woman. And though I love thee, Lucile,—love thee with a yearning spirit of tenderness, greater than can be dreamed of by the imagining of thy young experience,—know, that should a day of contamination come, thou must look to find in me a ruthless judge,—a stone-hearted executioner. There would be no mercy in my soul for an offence of thine."

'Harsh as were these denunciations, they sounded more like the ravings of fanaticism, than the remonstrances of a spiritual teacher, in the ears of Lucile. She had no power to attach them to a foregone conclusion, or to the shadowing forth of ideal evil. Even when, about a year after the first outpouring of the strenuous exhortations of Père Anselme, she became acquainted with the brilliant aide-de-camp of the King of France, who was charged to command a solemn service of Te Deum at the metropolitan cathedral, on occasion of the birth of a Dauphin, and the young and handsome Count de Valençay contrived shortly afterwards to entangle her in a secret correspondence and clandestine meetings, Lucile saw no occasion to connect the honourable expressions of attachment of her impassioned admirer with the prohibitions of her uncle! Valençay beheld in the bright cynosure of the Parvis Nôtre Dame the nominal niece of a hypocritical abbé, and far too fair a creature to be consigned to so ignoble and degrading a destiny; while Lucile beheld in Valençay her future husband, and the noblest and most captivating of mankind. They stood relatively in a false position. Mademoiselle Lanoue was too much afraid of the harsh interpretation of her uncle to infringe her lover's injunctions by acquainting the old man with the secret of their engagement. She dared not even involve in her confidence the old mulatto servant, Christophe, lest at any time he might be induced to betray them to the animadversions of Père Anselme.

'Time passed. It is needless, and would be painful to relate how often, during her uncle's discharge of his official duties, Lucile managed to escape from her gloomy home, and accompany her noble admirer on expeditions to the heights of Romainville, or the unfrequented banks of the Marne; to evening promenades in the Royal Gardens, to obscure spots and secret resorts, even *she* scarcely knew where. It was in vain she implored Valençay's permission to acquaint her legal guardian with their engagements, and at length with the union they had secretly contracted. The Count pleaded the opposition of his family—the resentment of the King;—and Lucile felt too happy in the homage, the tender affection of the man she deemed her husband, to examine with caution into his arguments, or investigate the motives of his evasions.

'It chanced that, while these mysteries were proceeding unsuspected in the quiet household of the canon of Nôtre Dame, Père Anselme was requested by one of the ministrants of the church of St Sulpice to undertake for a few days the clerical charge for which he was incapacitated by sudden and severe indisposition. The active priest, rejoicing in an opportunity of augmenting the sum of those duties which he had adopted as a sort of expiation—a species of mysterious atonement—readily complied: and thus, for several days, Lucile was left more than ever at liberty to pursue her favourite avocations, and cement her rash connections, little apprehending the consequences of her uncle's ex-official occupation. Nay, little indeed did Père Anselme himself anticipate, when he entered the confessional of his unaccustomed church, to how painful an exercise of his priestly functions he was about to be submitted.

'For behold! there came to his judgment seat a young noble of the court of the Trianon, the associate of the Lauzuns and Polignacs,* who, engaged in a duel of deadly provocation, had chosen to address himself to a strange confessor for a remission of his mortal sins. Count Valençay admitted himself to be every way an offender;—intemperate, debauched, a gambler, a seducer of innocence; and among other crimes which he charged against himself, was a pretended marriage with a pretended niece of a canon of Nôtre Dame; for whom he admitted the

utmost violence of a criminal attachment.—"Lucile is about
to become a mother," said he, in the unreservedness of confession; "and her child will become fatherless, and herself a
castaway, should I fall to-morrow. *Am* I to be forgiven?"

'Père Anselme wrung his hands and sobbed aloud at this
declaration; while Valençay, attributing the good man's despair
to the unction of his zeal, implored his intercessions with
Heaven for the more than widow who was about to be left
to the evil-dealing of a cruel world. He demanded also abso-
lution, and Père Anselme trembled while he pronounced the
words of grace; he had not, indeed, *so* trembled since the day
when he first learned the elopement of his wife with Clement
Manoury, of Martinique!

'That night, on his return home, Christophe the mulatto
received orders from his master to light the fire of a small
furnace erected at one end of the little garden attached to the
Canon's house, where, during the winter days, he was wont
to amuse himself by the exercise of his skill in smithery, such
as the manufacture of curious locks and safety-bolts, which
he often caused to be sold for the benefit of the poor. During
the summer, he usually devoted his leisure to other pursuits;
and what might be the cause of his selecting a fine midsum-
mer night for the renewal of his occupation no one could guess.
Till morning, however, the bellows of the forge were heard
in operation, and then, instead of retiring to rest after his unaccountable exertions, Père Anselme went forth to his daily
duties, having charged his servants with certain household services to be performed during his absence, and taken with him
the key of the house-door, in order to enforce the commands
he had already issued, that none should pass the threshold
during his absence. He desired also that the morning and evening meal of Lucile might be served to her as usual; nor did
he return at night till his daughter had retired to rest. But
there was nothing in all this to occasion surprise to Lucile; her
thoughts indeed were otherwise engrossed, and had they been
free for cogitation, she knew that the time of the Canon was
just then doubly engaged with the duties of his brother Curé.

'She was wrapt in sleep when, at midnight, he re-entered
the house, and a sleep so heavy, that she observed not an

unusual sound in an uninhabited chamber on the opposite side
of the corridor from her own, the walls of which abutted
against those of a public hospital. Heavy, ay, heavy indeed
must those slumbers have been, that heard not stones displaced and replaced—the blows of the heavy mallet—the smart
strokes of the sledge hammer, which so strangely disturbed
the rest of the old mulatto.

'On the morrow, at an early hour, a hired *berline** stood
at the Canon's door; and when the lovely but pale and wan
Lucile made her appearance at the breakfast-table, the Canon
bid her with a grim smile prepare for a holiday. Together they
ascended the carriage, but her eager inquiries could obtain no
clue to their destination. "Be satisfied," replied Anselme in a
hoarse voice; "you will discover anon. I have secured to you
a day of pleasure."

'At length she perceived that they had passed the barriers
of the city, and were ascending the heights of Charonne. In
another minute's space they were following a splendid funeral
procession, that took its way towards the cemetery of Mont
Louis. The hearse was covered with gorgeous escutcheons
—the noblest armorial bearings of ancient France graced the
long train of carriages following the dead—and as the cortège
stopped at the gates of the cemetery, Lucile perceived that a
sword and belt, a coronet and cushion, were placed upon the
coffin.

'Involuntarily she gave vent to expressions of interest, as
with a pale face she gazed upon the solemn scene—involuntarily evinced her curiosity as to the name of the hero about
to be consigned to the dust. She addressed herself to her
"uncle," but Père Anselme was reciting aloud his prayers for
the dead, whom the priests, with their crosses and banners,
had come forth to welcome to the grave. Their driver now prepared to let down the steps, having received previous orders
from the canon.

'"Whose obsequies are these?" inquired Lucile with faltering accents, as she prepared to place her foot on the step.

'"'Tis the burial of the young Count Valençay, Aide-
de-Camp to his Majesty, who fell yesterday in a duel at
Montrouge," replied the man in a careless tone; "he was the

only son of his mother, and she was a widow; yet 'tis said that he hazarded his life in a drunken quarrel, for a worthless actress."

'But he spoke to unheedful ears; Lucile lay senseless at the bottom of the carriage, and when the miserable girl recovered her powers of recollection, she found herself in a strange room, chained by her right hand to a bare wall, a loaf of bread, a vessel of water, and a missal, lying by her side. Even then, she neither heard, nor saw, nor felt distinctly; strange words sounded in her ears—a figure which she deemed to be that of her uncle stalked before her, proclaiming himself her father, and addressing her in opprobrious terms and with fearful denunciations that fell meaningless upon her heart. Yet the accusations were full, *too* full of truth; and the invectives with which he accosted the dying girl were such as defile the ears of the lowest of her fallen sex.

' "True child of an abandoned mother," cried he—"of a mother who deserted thy cradle for the arms of a paramour—of a mother whom I abandoned all ties of nature and country to punish as she deserved—thy doom is decreed! I forewarned *her*, yet she fell! I told her that so surely as she dared to outrage her vows of matron chastity, the hand of my vengeance should be heavy on her—that her blood should flow drop by drop in atonement for her sin; and so it did, and I beheld it, and was content. Then returned I to Europe, in the hope that the sorrows of my youth might be compensated by a tranquil old age, passed in the bosom of my child. And thou, too, Lucile, did I forewarn! I ventured not to assume over thee a father's authority, lest peradventure the babbling of those who surrounded thy childhood should have described him to thee as harsh and intemperate; but as a near kinsman—as a spiritual teacher—my voice was loud in thine ears, with exhortations against the evil promptings of the salt blood of thy mother flowing in thy veins; yet thou hast fallen, and the ruin of my house is accomplished—my last hope withered—my last joy defiled! Out on thee, castaway, out on thee! For thee, even for thee, shall there be no mercy—no ear of pity for thy bewailing—no heart of flesh for thine anguish. My own hand, a father's hand, forged the snares that hold thee fast; and now will I feast mine eyes on the sufferings of thy penance. *Despair and die!*"

'To all these outrages Lucile had no other reply than the name of him whom she believed to have been her husband. To die was all indeed that she desired; but despair she could not, for she trusted that death would reunite her to the object of her soul's affections. Her mind was at times perturbed, at times lucid; but of her peculiar jeopardy she knew and could comprehend nothing. It was all a miserable confusion of suffering—of terror—of darkness—of desperation!

'At length came the appointed hour—the hour of a mother's agony; and all night the lonely creature writhed and struggled with her pain, her miserable right hand still fettered within the master-bolt; but towards morning her moans grew fainter, and the feeble wail of a new-born child was added to the sound. Lucile was still alive when her father entered the room, and her dying eyes re-opened in fearful dilation only to witness the paroxysm of disgust with which he crushed into nothingness the tender frame of that offspring of shame. It was well perhaps the miserable babe should die, for already it was an orphan.

'That night, Anselme Lanoue watched beside the dead— the young mother with her little infant laid upon her arm, and a bloody cloth enveloping the right hand of the corpse! When placed in her coffin, and the bier brought forth from that hateful chamber, the Canon of Nôtre Dame closed its door for ever, that no one might look upon the mangled hand still fixed within the manacle left hanging to the wall; and it was Christophe the mulatto who, on the apprehension of the old priest, nearly twenty years after the fatal catastrophe, bethought him of the mysteries to be revealed in that deserted room, and found strength to wrench the staple from the stones.

'Look upon it again,' said Balthazar, replacing the terrible relique in my hand at the close of his narrative, 'and tell me, Sir, whether your country contains a more fearful testimonial of the ascendancy of ungovernable passion?'

The gathering tears in our eyes prevented our discerning so clearly as we could wish the delicacy of those blanched and fragile bones; but it was clear that the hand had been divided above the wrist by some sharp instrument; it was clear that two fingers had been previously broken in a desperate struggle for self-extrication. That hand which the hand of love alone had pressed—which had been from infancy uplifted to Heaven in the fervent supplications of innocence—had been crushed and tortured by the vengeance of a father!

Our hearts revolted against the spectacle; and right glad were we to behold the instrument of torture finally consigned to the dark and rusty treasury of—THE RED MAN.

POST-MORTEM RECOLLECTIONS OF
A MEDICAL LECTURER

Charles Lever

'To die—to sleep—perchance to dream:—
Ay; there's the rub.'

*Hamlet**

IT WAS already near four o'clock ere I bethought me of
making any preparation for my lecture. The day had been,
throughout, one of those heavy and sultry ones autumn so
often brings in our climate, and I felt from this cause much
oppressed and disinclined to exertion; independently of the
fact, that I had been greatly over-fatigued during the preceding week,—some cases of a most trying and arduous nature
having fallen to my lot—one of which, from the importance
of the life to a young and dependent family, had engrossed
much of my attention, and aroused in me the warmest anxiety for success. In this frame of mind I was entering my carriage, to proceed to the lecture-room, when an unsealed note
was put into my hands: I opened it hastily, and read that poor
H——, for whom I was so deeply interested, had just expired.
I was greatly shocked. It was scarcely an hour since I had seen
him, and from the apparent improvement since my former
visit, had ventured to speak most encouragingly; and had even
made some jesting allusion to the speedy prospect of his once
more resuming his place at 'hearth and board.' Alas! how
short-lived were my hopes destined to be! how awfully was
my prophecy to be contradicted!

No one but he who has himself experienced it, knows anything of the deep and heartfelt interest a medical man takes
in many of the cases which professionally come before him; I
speak here of an interest perfectly apart from all personal regard
for the patient or his friends. Indeed, the feeling I allude to, has
nothing in common with this, and will often be experienced

as thoroughly for a perfect stranger as for one known and respected for years.

To the extreme of this feeling I was ever a victim. The heavy responsibility, often suddenly and unexpectedly imposed—the struggle for success, when success was all but hopeless—the intense anxiety for the arrival of those critical periods which change the character of a malady, and divest it of some of its dangers, or invest it with new ones—the despondence when that period has come only to confirm all the worst symptoms, and shut out every prospect of recovery—and, last of all, that most trying, of all the trying duties of my profession, the breaking to the perhaps unconscious relatives, that my art had failed, my resources were exhausted, in a word, that there was no longer a hope.

These things have preyed on me for weeks, for months long, and many an effort have I made in secret to combat this feeling, but without the least success, till at last I absolutely dreaded the very thought of being sent for, to a dangerous and critical illness. It may then be believed how very heavily the news I had just received came upon me: the blow, too, was not even lessened by the poor consolation of my having anticipated the result, and broken the shock to the family.

I was still standing with the half-opened note in my hands, when I was aroused by the coachman asking, I believe for the third time, whither he should drive to?—I bethought me for an instant, and said, 'To the lecture-room.'

When in health, lecturing had ever been to me more of an amusement than a labour; and often, in the busy hours of professional visiting, have I longed for the time when I should come before my class, and divesting my mind of all individual details, launch forth into the more abstract and speculative doctrines of my art. It so chanced, too, that the late hour at which I lectured, as well as the subjects I adopted, usually drew to my class many of the advanced members of the profession, who made this a lounge after the fatigues of the morning.

Now, however, I approached this duty with fear and trembling: the events of the morning had depressed my mind greatly, and I longed for rest and retirement. The passing glance I threw at the lecture-room, through the half-opened door, showed it to be crowded to the very roof; and as I walked along the corridor, I heard the name of some foreign physician of eminence, who was among my auditory. I cannot describe the agitation of mind I felt at this moment. My confusion, too, became greater as I remembered that the few notes I had drawn up, were left in the pocket of the carriage, which I had just dismissed, intending to return on foot. It was already considerably past the usual hour, and I was utterly unable to decide how to proceed. I hastily drew out a portfolio that contained many scattered notes, and hints for lectures, and hurriedly throwing my eye across them, discovered some singular memoranda on the subject of insanity. On these I resolved at once to dilate a little, and if possible eke out the materials for a lecture.

The events of the remainder of that day are wrapt in much obscurity to my mind, yet I well remember the loud thunders of applause which greeted me on entering the lecture-room, and how, as for some moments I appeared to hesitate, they were renewed again and again, till, at last summoning resolution, I collected myself sufficiently to open my discourse. I well remember, too, the difficulty the first few sentences cost me,—the doubts, the fears, the pauses, which beset me at every step, as I went on. My anxiety to be clear and accurate in conveying my meaning, making me recapitulate and repeat, till I felt myself, as it were, working in a circle. By degrees, however, I grew warmed as I proceeded, and the evident signs of attention my auditory exhibited, gave me renewed courage, while they impressed me with the necessity to make a more than common exertion. By degrees, too, I felt the mist clearing from my brain, and that even without effort, my ideas came faster, and my words fell from me with ease and rapidity. Simile and illustration came in abundance; and distinctions, which had hitherto struck me as the most subtle and difficult of description, I now drew with readiness and accuracy. Points of an abstruse and recondite nature, which, under other circumstances, I should not have wished to touch upon, I now approached fearlessly and boldly, and felt that in the very moment of speaking, they became clearer and clearer to myself. Theories and hypotheses, which were of old, and acknowledged acceptance, I glanced hurriedly at as I went on, and with a perspicuity and clearness I never before felt exposed their fallacies, and unmasked their errors. I thought I was rather describing events, and things passing actually before my eyes at the instant, than relating the results of a life's experience and reflection. My memory, usually a defective one, now carried me back to the days of my early childhood; and the whole passages of a life long, lay displayed before me like a picture. If I quoted, the very words of the author rushed to my mind as palpably, as though the page lay open before me. I have still some vague recollection of an endeavour I made to trace the character of the insanity in every case to some early trait of the individual in childhood, when overcome by passion or overbalanced by excitement, the faculties run wild into all those excesses, which, in after years, develope eccentricities of character, and in some weaker temperaments, aberrations of intellect. Anecdotes illustrating this novel position came thronging to my mind; and events in the early years of some who subsequently died insane, and seemed to support my theory, came rushing to my memory. As I proceeded, I became gradually more and more excited—the very ease and rapidity with which my ideas suggested themselves, increased the fervour of my imaginings—till at last, I felt my words came without effort, and spontaneously, while there seemed a co-mingling of my thoughts, which left me unable to trace connexion between them, while I continued to speak as fluently as before. I felt at this instant a species of indistinct terror of some unknown danger which impended me, yet which was impossible for me to avert or avoid. I was like one who, borne on the rapid current of a fast flowing river, sees the foam of a cataract before him, yet waits passively for the moment of his destruction, without an effort to save. The power which maintained my mind in its balance had gradually forsaken me, and shapes and fantasies of every odd and fantastic character flitted around and about me. The ideas and descriptions my mind had conjured up, assumed a living, breathing vitality—and I felt like a necromancer waving his wand over the living and the dead. I paused—there was a dead silence in the lecture room—a thought rushed like a meteor flash across my brain, and, bursting forth into a loud laugh of hysteric passion, I cried—and I, and I—too, am a maniac. My class rose like one man—a cry of horror burst through the room. I know no more.

I was ill, very ill, and in bed. I looked around me—every object was familiar to me. Through the half closed window curtain there streamed one long line of red sunlight—I felt it was evening. There was no one in the room, and, as I endeavoured to recall my scattered thoughts sufficiently to find out why I was thus, there came an oppressive weakness over me —I closed my eyes, and tried to sleep. I was roused by some one entering the room—it was my friend Dr G——; he walked stealthily towards my bed, and looked at me fixedly for several minutes. I watched him closely, and saw that his countenance changed as he looked on me; I felt his hand tremble slightly as he placed it on my wrist, and heard him mutter to himself, in a low tone, My God! how altered! I heard now a voice at the door, saying in a soft whisper—may I come in. The doctor made no reply, and my wife glided gently into the apartment. She looked deathly pale, and appeared to have been weeping. She leaned over me, and I felt the warm tears fall one by one upon my forehead. She took my hand within both of her's, and putting her lips to my ear, said, 'Do you know *me*, William?' There was a long pause. I tried to speak; but I could not—I endeavoured to make some sign of recognition, and stared her fully in the face; but I heard her say in a broken voice, 'he does not know *me* now'; and then I felt it was in vain. The doctor came over, and, taking my wife's hand, endeavoured to lead her from the room. I heard her say, 'not now, not now'; and I sank back into a heavy unconsciousness.

I awoke from what appeared to have been a long and deep sleep. I was, however, unrefreshed and unrested. My eyes were dimmed and clouded—and I in vain tried to ascertain if there was any one in the room with me. The acute sensation of fever had subsided, and left behind the most lowering and depressing debility. As by degrees I came to myself, I found that the doctor was sitting beside my bed—he bent over me and said—'Are you better, William?' Never till now, had my inability to reply given me any pain or uneasiness—now, however, the abortive struggle to speak was torture. I thought and felt that my senses were gradually yielding beneath me, and a cold shuddering at my heart told me that the hand of death was upon me. The exertion now made to repel the fatal lethargy, must have been great—for a cold, clammy perspiration broke profusely over my body, a rushing sound, as if water filled my ears—a succession of short convulsive spasms, as if given by an electric machine, shook my limbs. I grasped the doctor's hand firmly in mine, and starting to the sitting posture, I looked wildly about me. My breathing became shorter and shorter: my grasp relaxed: my eyes swam: and I fell back heavily in the bed: the last recollection of that moment was the muttered expression of my poor friend G——, saying—'It is over at last.'

Many hours must have elapsed ere I returned to any consciousness. My first sensation was feeling the cold wind across my face, which seemed to come from an open window. My eyes were closed, and my lids felt as if pressed down by a weight. My arms lay along my side, and though the position in which I lay was constrained and unpleasant, I could make no effort to alter it—I tried to speak, but could not.

As I lay thus, the footsteps of many persons traversing the apartment, broke upon my ear, followed by a heavy dull sound, as if some weighty body had been laid upon the floor—a harsh voice of one near me now said, as if reading, 'William H——, aged 38 years—I thought him much more.' The words rushed through my brain, and with the rapidity of a lightning flash, every circumstance of my illness came before me, and I now knew that I had died, and for my interment were intended the awful preparations about me. Was this then death? Could it be, that though coldness wrapt the suffering clay, passion and sense should still survive—and that while every external trace of life had fled, consciousness should still cling to the cold corpse destined for the earth. Oh! how horrible, how more than horrible! the terror of that thought. Then I thought it might be what is termed a trance, but that poor hope deserted me, as I brought to mind the words of the doctor, who knew too well all the unerring signs of death to be deceived by its counterfeit, and my heart sank as they lifted me into the coffin, and I felt that my limbs had stiffened, and I knew this never took place in a trance. How shall I tell the heart-cutting anguish of that moment, as my mind looked forward to a futurity too dreadful to think upon; when memory should call up many a sunny hour of existence, the loss of friends, the triumph of exertion, and then fall back upon the dread consciousness of the ever busied life the grave closed over—and then I thought that perhaps sense but lingered round the lifeless clay, as the spirits of the dead are said to hover around the places and homes they had loved in life, ere they leave them for ever—and that soon the lamp should expire upon the shrine, when the temple that sheltered it lay mouldering and in ruins.—Alas! how fearful to dream of even the happiness of the past, in that cold grave where the worm only is a reveller—to think that though—

> Friends, brothers, and sisters, are laid side by side,
> Yet none have e'er questioned, nor none have replied.

Yet that all felt in their cold and mouldering hearts the loves and the affections of life, budding and blossoming as though the stem was not rotting to corruption that bore them. I brought to mind the awful punishment of the despot, who chained the living to the dead man, and thought it mercy when compared to this.*

How long I lay thus I know not, but the dreary silence of the chamber was again broken, and I found that some of my dearest friends were come to take a farewell look of me, ere the coffin was closed on me for ever. Again the horror of my state struck me with all its forcible reality; and like a meteor there shot through my heart, the bitterness of years of misery, condensed into the space of a minute. And then I remembered how gradual is death, and how by degrees it creeps over every portion of the frame—like the track of the destroyer, blighting as it goes—and said to my heart, all may yet be still within me, and the mind as lifeless as the body it dwelt in; and yet these feelings partook of life in all their strength and vigour. There, was the *will* to move, to speak, to see, to live —and yet all was torpid and inactive, as though it had never lived. Was it that the nerves, from some depressing cause, had ceased to transmit the influence of the brain? had these winged messengers of the mind refused their office?—and then I called to mind the almost miraculous efficacy of the will, exerted under circumstances of great exigency, and with a concentration of power, that some men are only capable of. I had heard of the Indian father who suckled his child at his own bosom,* when he had laid its mother in the grave; yet was it not the will had wrought this miracle? I myself had seen the paralytic limb awake to life and motion, by the powerful application of the mind stimulating the nervous channels of communication, and awakening the dormant powers of vitality to their exercise. I knew of one whose heart beat fast or slow as he did will it. Yes! thought I, in a transport, the will to live, is the power to live; and only when this faculty has yielded with bodily strength, need death be the conqueror over us. The thought of reanimation was extatic;—but I dare not dwell upon it—the moments passed rapidly on, and even now the last preparations were about to be made, ere they committed my body to the grave. And how was the effort to be made? If the will did indeed possess the power trusted in, how was it to be applied? I had often wished to speak or move during my illness, yet was unable to do either. I then remembered that in those cases where the will had worked its wonders, the powers of the mind had entirely centered themselves in the one heart-filling desire to accomplish a certain object—as the athlete in the games strains every muscle to lift some ponderous weight. And thus, I knew, that if the heart could be so subjected to the principle of volition, as that, yielding to its impulse, it would again transmit the blood along its accustomed channels, and that then the lungs should be brought to act upon the blood, by the same agency, the other functions of the body would more readily be restored, by the sympathy with these great ones. Besides, I trusted, that so long as the powers of the mind existed in the vigour I felt them in, that much of what might be called, latent vitality, existed in the body;—then I set myself to think upon those nerves which preside over the action of the heart

—their origin, their course, their distribution, their relation, their sympathies. I traced them as they arose in the brain, and tracked them till they were lost in millions of tender threads upon the muscle of the heart. I thought, too, upon the lungs as they lay flaccid and collapsed within my chest—the life blood stagnant in their vessels, and tried to possess my mind with the relation of these two parts, to the utter exclusion of every other. I endeavoured then to transmit along the nerves, the impulse of that faculty my whole hope rested on; alas, it was in vain—I tried to heave my chest and breathe, but could not—my heart sank within me—and all my former terrors came thickening around me, more dreadful by far, as the stir and bustle in the room indicated, they were about to close the coffin. At this moment, my dear friend B—— entered the room—he had come many miles to see me once more, and they made way for him to approach me as I lay. He placed his warm hand upon my breast, and, oh! the throb it sent through my heart. Again, but almost unconsciously to myself, the impulse rushed along my nerves—a bursting sensation seized my chest—a tingling ran through my frame—a crashing, jarring sensation, as if the tense nervous cords were vibrating to some sudden and severe shock, took hold on me; and then after one violent convulsive throe, which brought the blood from my mouth and eyes, my heart swelled at first slowly, then faster; and the valves reverberated, clank!—clank!—responsive to the stroke, at the same time the chest expanded, the muscles strained like the cordage of a ship in a heavy sea, and I breathed once more. While thus the faint impulse to returning life was given, the dread thought flashed on me that it might not be real, and that to my own imagination alone, were referable, the phenomena I experienced. At the very instant the gloomy doubt crossed my mind, it was dispelled, for I heard a cry of horror through the room, and the words—He is alive—he still lives—from a number of voices around me. The noise and confusion increased: I heard them say, carry out B—— before he sees him again—he has fainted! Directions, and exclamations of wonder, and dread followed one upon another, and I can but call to mind the lifting me from the coffin, and the feeling of returning warmth I experienced, as I was placed before a fire, and supported by the arms of my friends.

I will only add, that after some weeks of painful debility, I was again restored to health—having tasted the full bitterness of death.

THE BRIDE OF LINDORF

Letitia E. Landon

MIDNIGHT is a wonderful thing in a vast city—and midnight was upon Vienna. The shops were closed, the windows darkened, and the streets deserted—strange that where so much of life was gathered together there could be such deep repose; yet nothing equals the stillness of a great town at night. Perhaps it is the contrast afforded by memory that makes this appear yet more profound. In the lone valley, and in the green forest, there is quiet even at noon—quiet, at least, broken by sounds belonging alike to day and night. The singing of the bee and the bird, or the voice of the herdsman carolling some old song of the hills—these may be hushed; but there is still the rustle of the leaves, the wind murmuring in the long grass, and the low perpetual whisper of the pine. But in the town —the brick and mortar have no voices of their own. Nature is silent—her soft, sweet harmonies are hushed in the great human tumult—man, and man only, is heard. Through many hours of the twenty-four, the ocean of existence rolls on with a sound like thunder—a thousand voices speak at once. The wheels pass and re-pass over the stones—music, laughter, anger, the words of courtesy and of business, mingle together —the history of a day is the history of all time. The annals of life but repeat themselves. Vain hopes, vainer fears, feverish pleasure, passionate sorrow, crime, despair, and death— these make up the eternal records of Time's dark chronicle. But this hurried life has its pauses—once in the twenty-four come a few hours of rest and silence.

Vienna was now still as the grave, whose darkness hung over a few lamps swung dimly to and fro, and a few dark shadows—which the crimes of men make needful. The weary watchers of the night paced with slow and noiseless steps the gloomy streets. God knows that many of those hushed and darkened houses might have many a scene of waking care within—many a pillow might be but a place of unrest for the aching head—still the outward seeming of all was repose.

One house, and one only, obeyed not the general law. It was a magnificent hotel in the largest square, and was obviously the scene of a splendid fête. Light and music streamed from the windows, the courtyard was filled with equipages, and a noisy crowd—part servants, part spectators—thronged the gates. Within, all was pomp and gaiety. The Countess von Hermanstadt was unrivalled in her fêtes. She knew how to give them—a knowledge very few possess. The generality labour under the delusion, that when they have lighted and filled their rooms, they have done their all. They never were more in error. Lighting is much—crowding is much also—but there lacks 'something more exquisite still.'* This something the countess possessed in its perfection. Any can assemble a crowd, but few can make it mingle. But Madame von Hermanstadt had a skill which a diplomatist might have studied. She saw—she heard everything; she knew who would and who would not understand each other; she caught at a glance the best position for one lady's velvets, and for the diamonds of another; she never interrupted those who were engaged—she never neglected those who were not; she took care that great people should be amused, and little people astonished. Moreover, she had an object in whatever she did—hence the incentive of interest was added to the pride of art.

The ball of to-night was given in honour of Pauline von Lindorf, her niece, who had just left the convent of St Therese; —her education, as it is called, completed—that education which is but begun. How many cares—how much sorrow will it take to give the stern and bitter education of actual life! Pauline had just finished a waltz, having pleaded fatigue sooner than might have been expected from a foot so light—a form so fairy-like. She wore a robe of white satin, trimmed with swansdown; large pearls looped back the folds, and a band of diamonds scarcely restrained the bright hair that fell over her neck and shoulders in a thousand natural ringlets. It was of that rare rich golden so seldom seen—almost transparent, like rain with the sunbeams shining through it. At the first glance, that slight and graceful girl—with the rose on her cheek a little flushed by exercise, her glittering curls falling round her, golden as those of Hope—might have seemed the very ideal of youth and pleasure;—so much for the first glance, and how few go beyond! But whoso had looked closer would have seen that the soft red on the cheek was feverish; and there was that tremulous motion of the lip which bespeaks a heart ill at ease. At first she was looking down, and the long shadow of the curled eyelash rested on the rounded cheek; but there was something in the expression of the eyes, when raised, that caught even the most careless passer-by. They were large—unusually large—and of that violet blue which so rarely out-lasts the age of childhood, while they wore that wild and melancholy look whose shadows have a character of fate;—they are omens of the heart.

It was growing late, and a furtive gaze of the young bar-oness wandered more and more frequent round the rooms, and each time sought the ground with a deeper shade of dis-appointment. The Countess von Hermanstadt observed the look, and her own haughty brow curved with a scarcely per-ceptible frown. It was smoothed away instantly; and passing with a bland smile through the assembled groups, she left the ball-room.

The upper part of the magnificent house was in darkness, but in one window burned a still and lonely lamp. It lighted a small chamber sufficiently removed from the scene of the festival to be quite undisturbed by its tumult, though a dis-tant sound of music floated in, ever and anon, at the open window. The chamber was panelled with old carved oak, and the arches thus formed were filled with books. Books, too, of all sizes, were piled on the ground, and papers and writ-ing materials covered a table in the middle. There were also some pictures: a sombre landscape of Salvator Rosa*—just a desolate rock, grey and barren, standing out amid old dark trees, where many a branch was bare with the lightning's fiery visitings. Beneath them stood a single figure—pale, bare-headed, with long black hair that had not yet lost the motion of the wind. He looked what he was—an outlaw; the blood which he had shed, yet warm upon his hand, and his foot yet quivering with its flight for life or death. Near this was a dark,

grave portrait by Velasquez: one of those faces whereon time
has written the lesson of the prophet king—'All is vanity and
vexation of spirit.'* Others were scattered round, but all more
or less of a sombre character, and marking the taste of their
possessor. He was a young man of some twenty-two years
of age. The richness of part of his costume ill suited the apparently studious recluse; but the task of dressing had been hastily suspended. He had flung a loose robe of sables around
him, and leaned back in a large arm-chair, thinking of anything but the festival for which he had begun to prepare. His
eye sometimes dwelt on an old history of chivalry, whose silver clasps lay open before him—sometimes on the last sparks
of the fire that was dying away on the hearth, but oftener on
a copy of a well known Italian picture, the portrait of Beatrice
Cenci.*

'Yes,' said he, half aloud, 'a few links bring all life before
us: here is adventure—excitement—the toil and the triumph
of the body. I wish I had been born in those stirring times—
life spent half on horseback, half at the banquet board—when
you had but to look round the tournament, fix on the brightest smile, and then win your lady with your sword. Action—
action in the sunshine—passion—but little feeling, and less
thought: such was meant to be our existence. But we refine—
we sadden and we subdue—we call up the hidden and evil
spirits of the inner world—we wake from their dark repose
those who will madden us. The heart is like the wood on
yonder flickering hearth: green and fresh, haunted by a thousand sweet odours, bathed in the warm air, and gladdened by
the summer sunshine—so grew it at first upon its native soil.
But nature submitteth to art, and man has appointed for it
another destiny; it is gathered, and cast into the fire. It seems,
then, as if its life had but just begun. A new spirit has crept
into the kindled veins—a brilliant light dances around it—it
is bright—it is beautiful—and it is consumed! What remains?
—A warmth on the atmosphere soon passing away, and a
heap of blackened ashes! What more will remain of the heart?'

At this moment a burst of sudden flame sprung up from
the mouldering embers, and fell with singular effect on the wan
and lovely likeness of Beatrice Cenci. 'Why does that face

haunt me?' exclaimed the youth. 'Why, when others younger and brighter are near, does it glide between them and me like a shadow? I remember finding it as a child in the old deserted gallery. I loved it then, I know not why—save that it brought to my memory a face I fancy watched my sleep when I was a little child. I recollect a large, dark room—a bed whose gloomy curtains were drawn aside—and some one bent over me and kissed me. I put my arms around her neck, and went to sleep, for I had been afraid. She came every night then; but my memory is faint and confused—I can recall nothing more. How beautiful is that picture, with its clear, colourless cheek—with the imperial brow, and the large black eyes filled with melancholy tenderness! Holy Madonna, what a destiny was hers! —A childhood whose sweetest affections were crushed! I can fancy the little pale trembler crouching beneath her angry father's fierce eyes; and at last, as if those soft eyes grew desperate gazing on their slain, who shall say what madness of despair led to the fearful crime—avenging one yet more fearful? Why do I keep it here? It makes me sad—too sad!' And he turned aside, and leant his head upon his hand.

Ernest, for such was the young student's name, was singularly handsome; but it was the heart and the mind that gave their own nameless charm. The heart sent the flushed crimson to the cheek—the mind lighted up the clear white forehead, around which darkened the blackest hair: that deep black hair whose comparisons are all so gloomy, the poet likens it to midnight—to the shadow of the grave—to the tempest— to the raven's wing. Brought from the south, our cold climes just serve to dash the passionate temperament which it indicates with the despondency and the reverie of our sad and misty skies. All women would have called him interesting— the woman who loved him would have called him beautiful. Had the word fascinating never been used before, it would have been invented for him. Like all of his susceptible organization, Ernest was very variable: sometimes the life of society, with every second word an epigram; at others, grave and absorbed—no stimulus, no flattery, could rouse him to animation. His intimate, his very few intimate friends, said that nothing could exceed his eloquence in graver converse: carried away by his feelings, how could he help being eloquent? He was made of all nature's most dangerous ingredients: he thought deeply—he felt acutely; and for such this world has neither resting-place nor contentment.

The door of Ernest's chamber suddenly opened, and its threshold was crossed by a step that certainly had never crossed it before. Stately and slow, as usual, the Countess von Hermanstadt just raised her robe with an air of utter disdain, as she swept by the heavy folios that lay scattered on the ground.

'What! not dressed yet, Ernest?—Certainly the Count von Hermanstadt is well employed, sitting there like a moonstruck dreamer. Pray, am I to have the distinguished honour of a poet or a painter, or,'—added she, pointing sneeringly to a volume of planetary signs that lay open at her feet—'or even an astrologer, as my son?'

Ernest coloured, and rose hastily from his seat. 'I do so hate,' said he, 'those crowds where no one cares for the other; where'—

'No one,' interrupted the Countess, 'can be so great a simpleton as yourself. Who, in a crowd or elsewhere, will care about one whom they never see? What friends will you ever make in this little, miserable room? The Archduke Charles has twice inquired after you. I managed as well as I could; but I really have something else to do to-night than just to make excuses for you.'

'Ah! my mother, you cannot think how unfitted I am for the mock gaiety of to-night. Let me stay where I am.'

'Nonsense!—Why, there has been your pretty cousin waiting, till I forbade it, to dance with you. I left her waltzing with Prince Louis.'

'The less need of me.'

'Nay, my dear child!' said his mother, in those caressing tones she well knew how to assume, 'think what a slight it will be to our guests if you do not appear; and so many old friends of our house among them. I want assistance. Come, Ernest, would you be the only son in Vienna who would refuse his mother the slight favour of appearing at a ball which is given to introduce him to old friends, whom she at least loves and values?'

Ernest rose hastily and silently from his seat. 'I will be there almost as soon as yourself,' exclaimed he; and indeed the Countess had scarcely resumed her place at the upper end of the room, before she saw her son enter, and noted with delight, hidden under an air of proud humility, his graceful and high-born bearing. 'He is odd, reserved, and studious,' thought she; 'but I shall make something of him yet.'

But one eye, and one ear, was yet quicker than her own. Pauline was the first to see her cousin enter. She hastily turned aside, and began to be very much interested in some Bengal roses that stood beside; but her sigh was as soft, and almost as low, as their own, and her blush was still richer and deeper. Ernest came up and asked her to dance. Her eyes were downcast, and he thought she took his arm coldly; but more than one bystander remarked how different was the animation with which the young Baroness von Lindorf waltzed with her cousin, to that with which she had danced with the handsome Prince Louis.

At length the ball ended, as all balls do—having given some delight, more discontent, and also several colds; but it had answered the Countess's purpose. All Vienna talked of the approaching marriage of the beautiful heiress with Count von Hermanstadt. Many of her young friends ventured on a little gentle raillery. Pauline blushed, smiled, sighed, and denied the charge, but was believed by none. The time soon came for her return to the Castle of Lindorf; but little of her life had been passed there. She had left it, when quite a child, for the convent, and of late she had spent much time with her aunt. Her father, a silent and reserved man, but doatingly fond of his child, came often to see her; and though Pauline could recollect nothing of the affectionate confidence which so often exists between father and daughter when left alone in the world, yet she was full of gratitude and tenderness. With the quick instinct of a loving heart, she saw that she was the Baron's first and only object—that her happiness, and even her girlish pleasures, were his constant care. There was something in his unbroken sadness, his habits of seclusion, and his gloomy deportment, that excited her youthful imagination, and gave a depth of anxious devotion to her filial attachment.

The paramount desire of the Baron appeared to be, that she should not find her home dull on returning to it. At his request the Countess von Hermanstadt had collected together a gay young party, and the old castle was for some weeks to be a scene of perpetual festival. Pauline went thither accompanied by her aunt and cousin. She at least found the journey delightful. Ernest, taken away from his books, animated by the fresh air and the rapid travelling, undisturbed by the presence of strangers, and anxious to please, now that he had no fear of either ridicule or coldness, was in high spirits. He drew their attention to every spot haunted by an association, and told its history as those tell who are steeped to the lip in poetry—rich in imagery, abounding in anecdote, he flung around all of which he spoke his own warm and fanciful feeling. Pauline fixed upon him her large blue eyes, where tenderness struggled with delight; while in the interest excited by his various details, she forgot the sweet and inward consciousness that would have fixed her eyes on the ground, or anywhere rather than on her cousin's face. The Countess was delighted to see everything going on so prosperously, and already began to plan wedding fêtes.

Night had fallen ere they approached the castle, the first view of which was singularly striking. The party had gradually sunk into silence, the road for miles had wound through a dense forest, with no other light than that flung over the road by the lamps of the carriage, and the torches which the out-riders carried before them, forming strange and fantastic outlines. The red light played over the drooping boughs of the forest trees; the flickering rays only illumined the outside, and all beyond was impenetrable obscurity: from the depths of that thick darkness came forth wild sighs and sounds; the mournful murmur of the pine leaves, the creaking of the branches as they swayed heavily in the wind; these, mingled with the hoarse cry of the night-birds. Sometimes disturbed from his gloomy perch, the dusk wings of the owl flapped across the road, and his hooting disturbed the sad low music of the night; it was neither time nor place for gay converse: the whole party felt the subduing influence, and leant back in deep thought. Suddenly they cleared the wood, and the carriage paused for a moment that they might catch the first view of the castle of Lindorf; visible for miles around,—there it stood in the centre of a vast plain, on the summit of a high hill, with not a single rise to intercept, or a single object to distract the view. It rose in bold relief against the deep blue sky, with the large round moon shining directly behind it;— even at that distance you could mark the square towers and the indented battlements, while the mass of the building itself seemed immense. The sky, of that intense purple which marks a slight frost, was covered with floating clouds, and on the further edge, sheltered in their shadow, were scattered a few pale stars; but the broadway of heaven was flooded by moonlight; no longer shut out by the thick forest,—her rays silvered whatever they touched, and the long grass of the plain looked like undulating water, so thickly did the crisped dew lie upon it, and so clearly did the moonshine glitter through the frosted moisture. Ernest gazed upon the dark and distant castle with an emotion for which he could not himself have accounted; he remembered it not—and yet it seemed strangely familiar. The moonlight clothed it like a garment, and the old towers shone like silver; but even while they gazed, the brightness was departing.—One mass of vapour flowed in after another like the dark tide coming in upon the shore; a black ridge rose above the castle; it darkened—it widened— its edges grew luminous as they approached the moon: gradually half her disk was hidden by them. 'Is it an omen?' asked Ernest of his own thoughts. Even as he asked the question, the black clouds swept over the moon, and entire darkness covered the whole scene. 'Drive on,' cried Ernest, impatiently; and the horses set off at full gallop, but even the exhilaration of rapid motion failed to drive away the weight that had fallen upon his heart. He could not divest himself of the idea that the castle was in some way connected with his destiny, —and that such destiny was ill-fated. When at length they arrived, and drove slowly up the steep ascent as the old gate creaked on its hinges to receive them, and they alighted in the hall of black carved oak, he felt a cold shudder come over him. Again he asked himself—'Is it an omen?' and the voice of his inward spirit answered 'Yes!'

A fortnight passed away, and one fête succeeded to another. At first Pauline clung to her cousin's side,—she wandered with him in the antique gardens, and would leave the dancers to gaze with him from the terrace which overlooked the vast plain below. Gradually she gave more and more into the pleasures around her; and the mornings were devoted to her young companions, and the evening saw her the gayest, as well as the loveliest of the assembled circle. This was a relief to Ernest—it left him more at liberty to indulge his own solitary pursuits, and to feed on the visionary melancholy, which was half thought—and half feeling. He was wrong, however, in the conclusion that he drew from the change in his cousin; he merely supposed that she was attracted by the amusements so natural to her age; he knew not that even that fair young brow had already learnt the bitter task of dissembling. He knew not that often did that bright young head lay down in weariness and sorrow on a pillow wet with frequent tears. Love only rightly interprets love. Pauline saw that her cousin had only for her the calm and gentle tenderness of a brother; —they had been brought up together, and there was nothing in the pretty and playful child, that had grown up beside him, to excite his imagination. But she—she loved him with all that poetry which is only to be found in a woman's first affection; it is the early colour that the rose-bud opens to the south wind,—the warmth that morning breathes upon a cloud whose blush reddens, but returns not. Pure, shy, sensitive, tender, and unreal; it is the most ethereal, yet most lasting feeling life can know. The influence of a woman's first love is felt on her whole after-existence: never can she dream such dream again. For a woman there is no second-love—youth, hope, belief, are all given to her first attachment; if unrequited, the heart becomes its own Prometheus,* creative, ideal, but with the vulture preying upon it for ever.—If deceived, the whole poetry of life is gone; the very essence of poetry is belief, and how can she, whose sweet eager credulity has once learnt the bitter truth—that its reliance was in vain, how can she ever believe again?

Pauline learnt to know Ernest's heart by her own, and she felt the difference. Night after night she left the ball-room in all the false flutter of that excitement whose fever destroys the heart which it animates. But once in her own room, the colour left her cheek, and the light, her eye; she flung herself down, with a burst of tears, long and painfully repressed, while she thought that Ernest had not entered the hall throughout the evening. He, in the meanwhile, saw her seemingly happy and amused—and gave more and more into his pursuits; he would spend days in the old forest adjoining, till the midnight stars shone through the darkling branches like the eyes of a spirit, awakening all that was most ethereal in his nature. Hours too were past on the winding and lovely river—lost in those vague but impassioned reveries which fade, and for ever, amid the sterner realities of life. The dreaming boyhood prepares for adventurous man; we first fancy, then feel, and, at last, act and think. He delighted too in rambling through the ancient castle—filled with the memory of other days: not a face in the picture gallery but he conjured up its history, and he loved to assign to each some one of the spacious chambers for the site of their adventures. Many of the rooms in the left wing were all but deserted,—and one afternoon, while wandering carelessly along, he found his way into a chamber that had apparently not been opened for years; he was struck with the beauty of some richly wrought oak panels. While leaning against one of them he chanced to touch a hidden spring; the panel flew open—and discovered a narrow flight of winding stairs. To kindle a phosphorous match, to light a small wax taper, was the work of a moment; and he began to descend the staircase:—childishly eager to discover something —he did not much care what, so long as it was a discovery. It wound to a much greater distance than he had supposed, and, at last, ended at a sort of low arch—the door of which was heavily barred inside. With great difficulty he succeeded in unfastening it; at last it yielded to his efforts, and he opened it. It opened inwards—and even then, though he perceived the open air, he could scarcely make his way through the matted ivy, and the thickly grown shrubs that extended beyond. The moment he arrived beyond their shade he found himself in a portion of the castle grounds which he had never seen before; it was a lovely little garden of small extent, girdled in by lofty walls and tall trees—but a fairy land in miniature as far as it extended. The hues of autumn were now upon the boughs—but the evergreens shone with untiring verdure; and various late flowers appeared in that gorgeous colouring which belongs to the last season of earth's fertility. He wound through a narrow path of green and purple,—for the carefully trained grapes hung in arches overhead, with fruit as rich as those of the eastern garden discovered by Aladdin. Ernest was enchanted with his discovery, and hurried on, when his attention was caught by the sound of singing; it was a female voice of the most touching sweetness. The words were inarticulate, but the air, an old German melody, was exquisitely marked. Ernest followed whither the voice led—he paused amid some laurel trees, and a scene like a picture presented itself to his astonished gaze; it was a bright open grass plot—a very rendezvous for every stray sunbeam,—and in the middle glittered and danced a little fountain which threw up its silvery jets in the air, and then fell over large shells, stones, and rugged pieces of granite, which formed a sort of basin; a number of creeping plants were around it, and one or two lilies grew as if carved in ivory. Seated on one of the huge stones scattered around—singing a low sweet air, or rather humming it, for the words were inaudible, was a female figure. Ernest could see only a very pretty back—an exquisitely shaped head bending forward, and a profusion of black hair hanging down in plaits—the ends somewhat fancifully fastened with a scarlet flower.

Ernest felt that he was an intruder, but he did—as all other young men would have done—remain rooted to the spot. He knew the melody that she was singing to the music of the plashing fountain; he had not heard it for years, but now it came freshly back to his memory haunted with a thousand vague fancies: suddenly the low sweet singing ceased; the maiden rose hastily from her seat, and, turning round, showed the exact likeness of his favourite picture—the Beatrice Cenci. There was not the peculiar head-gear,—for the hair was simply parted back; but everything else was exact in resemblance. There was the same low white forehead, the same black arched eyebrow, the same Grecian outline of face, the same small and scornful lip. She looked towards him, and there were the

same large, dark, and melancholy eyes. Surprise made Ernest
both speechless and motionless—not so the lovely stranger;
she bounded towards him with something between the spring
of the startled fawn, and the confidence of an eager child.

'I knew some one would come at last to free me from my
weary captivity,' exclaimed she, in one of those thrilling voices
which have a magic beyond even their music; 'you are not a
prisoner too?' asked she, seeing the bewildered expression of
Ernest's countenance.

'A prisoner! No,' said he, too much astonished to know
what he was saying, and taking one of the small and delicate
hands which were extended so imploringly towards him.

'You will save me—help me, will you not?' asked the girl;
'they have kept me here many years, and I long to go into
the beautiful world that lies beyond these high walls. I sometimes wish I were a bird, and then I would spread my wings
on the free air, and fly away, and be so happy. But you will
take me with you, will you not?' whispered she, looking up
in his face with the sweet and impatient look of a pleading
child. 'You look very kind—I may trust you, may I not?'

'With my life I will answer to that trust,' cried young
Hermanstadt; 'but who are you,—who keeps you here?'

'My uncle, the Baron von Lindorf,' muttered she, in a
low frightened voice. 'They tell me that there is a castle, and
vassals, and gold, that should be mine, and that is why he
keeps me here. He is very cruel!'

'Good God!' cried Ernest, 'come this moment with me—
and in his usurped place—before his own guests—I will force
him to do you right.'

'No, no,' replied the captive, her lip whitening, and the
pupils of her large eyes dilating with sudden terror. 'No, let
us fly,—you do not know how cruel he is, and how strong.
Let us only get beyond these high walls. How did you get in?'

'I found by chance a long, concealed passage.'

'And you can come again? Ah! now I shall not mind being
a prisoner. You will come and talk to me—and not tell me to
be quiet, like old Clotilde, or frown upon me like Heinrich?'

'You shall not stay here—come with me this moment. I
will protect you from them all!'

'No,' replied the captive, 'not now; you do not know my uncle's power—he would kill us both; we must escape without his knowing it. Do you think you can manage it in a few days?'

'Certainly! but the sooner the better.'

'What is your name?' interrupted the prisoner.

'Ernest von Hermanstadt.'

'They call me Minna. I used to have another name, but it is so long ago that I have forgotten it; I have grown so much since I was here. I could not reach those flowers when I came here first;—my pretty flowers, and my singing fountain—I shall be sorry to leave you! You never scold Minna; but it is a brave world yonder—you will take me into it, Ernest?' asked she; and again those sweet eyes were raised beseechingly to his.

'Come with me now—I will pledge my life for your safety!'

'No, come to-morrow—can you—without being seen? To-morrow morning, when those clouds are reddening, and the waters of the fountain are rosy with their shadows? I always come here then, I love the fresh air of the morning.'

At this moment a shrill voice in the distance was heard calling—'Minna, Minna.' Ernest would have pressed forward, when the maiden caught his arm, trembling from head to foot. 'Go, go,' whispered she, then, clasping her little hands with an air of passionate entreaty, she added:—'I expect you to-morrow at sunrise'; and before he could answer, she had darted away. Once she looked back, but it was to wave her hand in token that he should depart. Ernest lingered for a moment, and then hurried back to the hidden passage; he carefully effaced all traces of his progress—and drew the ivy after him when he entered the arched door, that he barred; and then hurriedly sought his own chamber, which he left no more that night. This was an act of too frequent occurrence, on his part, to excite the least surprise; and the supposed student was left undisturbed,—for, for him there was as little study as rest. That sweet face floated before his eyes, that low melodious voice haunted his ear—and the name of Minna lingered upon his lip. 'Now,' thought he, 'I understand the cause of my uncle's gloom and abstraction; no marvel that he has no

heart for gaiety with such a crime pressing upon it. I faintly
remember hearing that his brother had fallen in some cam-
paign that they fought together;—doubtless, with his last
breath he commended his orphan girl to one bound by blood
to protect her. How has that dying trust been violated; how
has that child been oppressed! Made a prisoner—debarred all
the social enjoyments of her age—deprived of rank and birth-
right, immured in solitude and ignorance. Great God! can
such cruelty exist among the creatures thou hast made? but
retribution, sooner or later, overtakes the guilty. Poor Pauline!
how will her gentle and affectionate nature be grieved to hear
this thing of the father she idolises; it must be kept from her.
Wealth, what a subtle tempter thou art! Even my uncle—
the man I deemed so noble, so generous, so full of high feeling, and knightly qualities; even he has for thy sake played
traitor to the dead, and broken every sacred tie of duty and
of affection! I will think no more of it.' This resolve was
easily executed; for the image of Minna excluded every other
thought. Her beauty, her grace, her childishness had captiv-
ated Ernest's imagination; fate, too, had set her stamp upon
the fiery passion to which he utterly abandoned himself. 'How
strangely,' murmured he to himself, as, thrown in the deep
window-seat, he gazed out upon the silent night—'are the
links knitted together, which time unravels! The picture my
boyhood discovered, and which so haunted my youth, has it
not now fulfilled its mission? The chance likeness has led to
the predestined result. I feel it,—Minna has been predestined
to be my bride. Fate, in filling my heart with her face, from
the earliest years kept it free from all those passing fancies
which would have detracted from the intense devotion of my
present love. How wonderfully have we met! Minna—sweet
Minna, life owes you much happiness; will it not be my delicious task to pay the debt?'

The night passed in one long, but happy reverie; and the
light sleep into which Ernest fell at last was soon broken by
the anxiety, which visited even his dreams, to catch the first
crimson break of morning. He started from his bed—and the
dark clouds in the east were beginning to redden; he hurried
to the deserted suite of rooms—down the winding staircase,

and in a few moments found himself again in the little garden. Cautiously he entered the vine-covered alley, and paused
for a moment amid the thick shelter of the laurels; with a
glance he drank in the beauty of the scene; the feeling of the
painter and the poet—and Ernest had the imagination of both
—overpowered, during an instant, the feeling of the lover.
Huge bodies of vapour—a storm in each—were hurrying over
a sky, dashed alike with the hues of the tempest and the morning; some of the vapours were of inky blackness, others spread
like a scroll of royal purple; some undulated with the light
struggling through, others were of transparent whiteness; but
those upon the east were of a deep crimson—and the round,
red sun had just mounted above an enormous old cedar. Red
hues were cast upon everything; even the lilies blushed, and
the waters of the little fountain were like melted rubies: on
the same stone which she had occupied the previous day sat
Minna, but her head was now turned towards the spot where
she had last seen Ernest. A movement amid the boughs caught
her quick ear; she started from her seat upon the granite, and
Ernest was at her feet. Shy, silent, with her long eyelashes
drooping upon her flushed cheek; there was a sweet consciousness about her—even more fascinating than her yesterday's childish confidence. Ernest led her to her place, and
knelt beside her; he had no words but those of love; he had
a thousand plans for the future ready on his tongue; he could
only speak of the present. 'Yes, Minna; may I not call you
so, though I am jealous of the very air bearing away the music
of that name? I have loved you for years: not a feature in that
beautiful face but has been long graven in my soul. I will
show you your picture, sweet one, when you come home
with me. Will you come to my home?'

And the maiden smiled and said, 'I shall be so happy.'

But the words of lovers are a language apart; their melody
is a fairy song departing with the one haunted hour; to repeat
it is to make it commonplace—cold, yet we can all remember it. Enough, that everything was planned for flight. The
following morning they were to meet again; and Minna was
only to return to the castle of Lindorf as the bride of Ernest
von Hermanstadt. None there could question his right to

protect her. The clouds gathered overhead; a vast vapour like a shroud, but black as night, came sweeping over the sky; a fierce wind shook the branches of the mighty cedar, and the slighter shrubs were bowed to the very earth; a hollow sound came from among the boughs, and a few large drops of rain disturbed the fountain, whose waters were dark as if the sunshine had never rested there.

'You must go, sweet one; this is no weather for that slight form. To-morrow, at sunset—'

'Why cannot I give you this?' exclaimed Minna, holding up one of the tresses with its scarlet flower.

'You must,' cried Ernest, kissing the plait of the black hair, which was soft and glossy as the neck of the raven.

'I have nothing,' said she, sadly, 'that I can cut it with.'

Ernest took from his pocket a little Turkish dagger—and with that Minna severed the glossy tress.

'I must go now,' said she, 'they will seek me if I stay out in the rain.'

Ernest pressed her tenderly to his heart, and they parted. He caught the last wave of the flowers in her hair—the last sound of her fairy foot, and turned mournfully away. All that day he was occupied in preparations for his departure; he rode over to the castle of Krainberg which belonged to a fellow student, whom he found on the point of departure. The young Baron, delighted with the romance, of which however he understood little more than that his grave and quiet friend was actually engaged in an elopement—agreed to remain to witness the marriage. He was also to have his chapel prepared, a priest in readiness, and then to leave his castle as a temporary residence for the bride and bridegroom. His mother had left Lindorf—or he would have trusted his secret with her, and intreated her countenance. In his own mind, Ernest was not sorry that her absence rendered this impossible; he liked the excitement, the strangeness, the adventure of his present plan, and his mother's calm and worldly temper would have interposed a thousand delays, and have arranged everything in the most proper and commonplace manner.

He was early at their rendezvous, the fountain, but early as he was, Minna was there before him; she approached him

in a hurried and agitated manner, her slight frame trembling
with emotion, her large eyes glancing from side to side like
those of the frightened deer—and he could feel every pulse
beating in the little feverish hand, which he kissed.

'Let us go at once,' whispered she, 'they will soon come to
seek me.' Ernest needed no urging to speed; he led, or almost
carried her, down the vine alley, and they reached the dark
portal without molestation. Minna drew back, terrified at the
gloomy passage—but Ernest's caresses reassured her, and she
ran up the winding stairs; in a short time they reached the
little chamber, which was his study, and that gained, they were
in comparative safety. Here they waited a short time, partly
to give the lovely fugitive time to compose herself—partly,
that it might be dusk before they attempted to leave the
castle: that, however, was matter of no difficulty. A staircase
led direct from Ernest's chamber to the garden—and he had
the key of a small wicket which led to the woods around; once
there, and escape was certain. Minna sat down in the old oak
chair, which was Ernest's usual place. With what delight did
he contemplate her charming figure bending over the table,
and examining his favourite volumes with a curiosity which
even fear and timidity could not quite dispel! what a delicious augury did the enthusiastic young student draw from her
apparent interest! How many happy hours would they pass
together over those very volumes! but there was little time
even for the most delightful anticipations of the future. The
dinner hour of the castle had now arrived—and every creature in it was busily engaged. Now then was the time to leave
it. Carefully wrapping up his precious charge in his cloak, he
led her to the little gate, where his servant was in waiting.
Placing her before him, he sprung up on his horse, a strong
and stately black steed, and a few moments more saw them
galloping rapidly along the road that led to Arnheim castle.
They needed to make all possible haste, for the storm, which
had been gathering all day, now threatened to burst over their
heads:—their way lay through a thick wood—and the elements had already commenced their strife. The creaking of
the huge pine branches, mixed with the hurried sweeping of
the leaves, of which a dry shower every now and then whirled

from the earth—from the gathered heaps of autumn, or came down in hundreds from overhead. The birds, disturbed from their usual rest, flew around, beating the air with their troubled wings, and uttering shrill cries; the thunder rolled along in the distance, and a few large drops of rain fell heavily upon the ground; there was an unnatural heat in the air, and gleams of phosphoric light streamed along the burthened sky. But Ernest heeded not the storm; he only feared for the sweet burthen that rested so trustingly in his arms—he only drank the perfumed breath of the warm lips so near his own; he only felt the beating of the heart, now and henceforth to be pillowed on his own; he only heard the low murmur of a voice which now and then whispered his name—as if that name were to her all of love and safety. He spurred his horse to its utmost speed; the sparks flew from its hoof. He cut his way through the fresh wind, and felt as if the excitement of the impassioned moment were cheaply purchased, though his life were its ransom. They reached the castle of Krainberg before the storm burst forth in all its fury. The master was in waiting to receive them, and Ernest felt all a lover's pride as he marked the astonishment and admiration with which Von Krainberg gazed on the beautiful stranger. They led her at once to the chapel; Ernest grudged himself the pleasure of even seeing her till he had a right to gaze upon her—till every look was at once homage and protection; he was impatient, in her strange and isolated situation, to call her his own—his wife. A close, damp air struck upon them as they entered the chapel; it had long been out of use, and the hastily lighted tapers burnt dim in the sepulchral atmosphere. The mouldering banners were stirred by the high wind, and the breathing was oppressed by the dust; many tombs were around, and the white effigies seemed like reluctant witnesses glaring upon the hopes of humanity, with cold and stony eyes. A monk, bowed with extreme age, pale, emaciated, and his white head tremulous with palsy, stood beside the altar—and his long, thin fingers trembled beneath the weight of the sacred volume. He began the ceremony, and his low, tremulous voice could scarcely be heard through the moaning of the wind amid the tombs. The ground beneath their feet was hollow, and sent forth a hollow echo;—the graves below had once been filled with the dead, and now only a little dust remained in their vacant places: they had perished as it were a second time. There was a mournful contrast between the place of the bridal and the bride; there she stood in that radiant loveliness, which is heaven's rarest gift to earth. Her dress was of the simplest white, gathered at the waist by a belt of her own embroidery—ornament she had none. The daughter of the noble house of Von Lindorf wedded the heir of the as noble house of Von Hermanstadt, dressed as simply as a peasant. Her black hair hung down in its long plaits, like serpents—the scarlet flower at each end; a bright colour flushed her cheek, and her eyes seemed filled with light.

The aged priest closed the holy book, and Ernest turned to salute his bride; but even he started back at the sudden clap of thunder that pealed through the chapel. The building shook beneath the crash, and a flood of lightning poured in at the windows, casting a death-like light on the stony faces of the white figures on the monuments:—it was but for a moment—and Ernest caught his trembling bride to his heart. She was pale with terror, for now the storm rushed forth in all its fury, and a sudden gust of wind and rain dashed against the painted window at the end of the chapel. The repeated flashes threw a strange radiance around, and strange noises mingled together.

'It is an awful night,' said the young baron of Krainberg, as he led the way to the hall, which, as they entered, was lit up with one livid blaze. Ernest supported the almost insensible form of his bride; he murmured a few caressing words—but even love, in all its strength, felt powerless before the war of the immortal elements.

The next morning but few traces of the tempest remained; the river that wound through the valley was somewhat swollen, and a few giant pines dashed down to earth would never again cast their long shadows before them on a summer morning; but the sky was soft, clear, and blue, and a few white clouds wandered past, light as down. The leaves glittered with the lingering rain-drops, and a fresh, sweet smell came from the herbage of the valley. Ernest was seated in a little breakfast parlour, looking to a terrace that commanded the country; he

was seated at the feet of his bride, whose small fingers were
entwined in his black hair. What a world of poetry seemed
in the depths of her large, shining eyes, which looked upon
him so tenderly—so timidly; their dream, for it was a dreamlike happiness, was broken in upon by the entrance of Ernest's
servant, who asked to speak to his master. There was something in the man's manner which commanded instant attention, and Von Hermanstadt followed him out of the room.

'Sir,' exclaimed the man, 'here is your letter to the Baron—
he died suddenly last night. The lady Pauline is in a dreadful state, and the steward intreated that you would go up
there at once.'

Ernest felt that this was a case which admitted of no delay.
Saying a few hasty words about important business to Minna,
reserving the death till he could have time to tell it sooth-
ingly, he flung himself upon his horse, and galloped to Lindorf.
Though grave and solitary, both in manners and habits, the
Baron had been much beloved by his domestics, and the voice
of weeping was heard on every side. Ernest hurried to his
uncle's chamber; there the daylight was excluded, and the ray
of the yellow tapers fell dimly upon the green velvet bed
where lay the last Baron of Lindorf. In him ended that noble
house; with his arms folded, so as to press the ebon crucifix to
his bosom—his head supported by a damask cushion, lay the
Baron. Ernest paused for a moment, awe-struck by the calm
beauty which reigned in the face of the dead; the features
were stately and calm, the brow had lost the care-worn look
it wore in life, and peace breathed from every lineament of the
sweet and hushed countenance. 'Can the dead,' thought Ernest,
'struck down with an unrepented crime—can the oppressor
of the orphan look thus?'

He had not time for further reflection, for a convulsive
motion on the other side of the bed showed him Pauline
crouched in a heap at the feet of the corpse—her face buried
in the silken counterpane. Her bright hair was knit up with
pearls, and she still wore the robe of the previous evening;
how terrible seemed its gay colours now!

'We have not been able,' whispered an old grey-headed servant, 'to get her to speak or to move.'

Ernest's heart melted with the tenderest pity. He took the passive hand, and covered it with tears and kisses. 'Pauline, dearest, look up,' said he, passing his arm round her, so as to raise her head. What his words could not effect, the movement did; she was roused from her stupor, and, giving one wild glance at the corpse, she leant her head on her cousin's shoulder, and burst into a passion of tears. Soothing her with the tenderest words, he carried her to her chamber. 'At least,' said he to himself, as he left her, 'the memory of her father shall be sacred.'

The old steward met him, and said—'There is a letter for you which my master was writing at the time of his death. I know many circumstances which it is now of the last importance that you should know too. For God's sake, Sir, go and read the letter, and I will be within call.'

The old man led the way to his master's room. He looked round it piteously for a moment, and then hurried away, hiding his face in his hands. Ernest had never been in the room before; and yet how full it seemed of the living presence of him who was no more! There was his cloak flung on a chair; —there lay open books of which he and Ernest had recently been talking. There, too, was a flask of medicine—alas! how unavailing!—and a goblet of water, half drank. But one object more than all riveted Ernest's attention;—there was the picture of Beatrice Cenci. It was a portrait as large as life: his own seemed to have been a copy of it. How well he knew that striking and lovely face! He knew not why, but he gazed upon it with a sudden terror; the large black eyes seemed to fix so mournfully upon his own. He turned away, and saw the letter on the table, addressed to himself. He seated himself, and began to read the contents; though the tears swam in his eyes as he saw the handwriting of an uncle who, whatever his faults, had always been kind, very kind, to himself. It ran thus:—

'My beloved Ernest,—For dear to me as a child of my own is the boy who has grown up at my side. I have long been desirous of communicating to you the contents of the following pages, but I have found it too painful to speak—I find that I must write. My confidence will not be misplaced, for

I have noted in you a judgment beyond your years, and a delicacy which will estimate the trust reposed in you. My health is declining rapidly, and I would fain secure protection for my darling Pauline, and another as dear and more unfortunate. I have rejoiced to see that my sister's plan for a marriage between you and my daughter is not likely to take place. You do not love your cousin—you prefer the solitary study and the lonely ramble—so would not a lover. She, too, is amused in your absence. I hear her step and song among her companions, and you are not with them. It is for the best—you will be a safe and affectionate friend. I hope she will never marry.

'Alas!—On me and mine has rested a fearful curse! I married one whose beauty let the picture now opposite to me attest, and her heart was even lovelier than her face. An Italian artist painted her as Beatrice Cenci: he said that the costume suited her so well. I have since thought it an omen that we should have chosen the semblance of one so ill-fated. For years we were most happy, but at last an unaccountable depression seized upon my wife. She became wayward and irritable. This led to the quarrel between your mother and ourselves. She knew not the fatal cause. After the birth of her third and last child, her malady took a darker turn. Ernest, it was melancholy madness, and incurable! In a paroxysm of despondency, she murdered the infant in her arms, and died a few hours afterwards in a state of raving insanity!

'I will not dwell on my after-years of misery. I was roused by fear of the headstrong and violent temper of my eldest girl, Minna—I saw in it the seeds of her mother's malady. My terror was too well founded. She was found one evening attempting to strangle her little sleeping sister, who was then six years old—Minna being just fourteen. A brain fever followed, and a report was spread of her death. Why should our family calamity be made the topic of idle curiosity? But, in reality, she has resided in this castle—her state requiring constant and often strict restraint. I have been scarcely ever absent from the castle; but, alas! my tenderness has answered but in part. With a caprice incidental to persons in her dreadful situation, she has taken an extreme dislike to me, and fancies that

I am her uncle, and imprison her to detain the vast possessions of which she fancies herself the heiress.'

The fatal paper dropped from Ernest's hand. He remained
pale, breathless, the dew starting, and the veins swelled of his
forehead. 'God of heaven, have mercy on me!—What have I
done?' Again he caught up the letter, and, with a desperate
effort, read to the close.

'My faithful Heinrich and his sister Clotilde are the only
depositories of this secret. While I live, I shall devote myself
to the care of my ill-starred Minna, who is the very image of
her mother. When I die—and the shadow of death even now
rests upon my way—I commend her to her God and to you.
You will be to her and to Pauline as a brother. I know I can
rely upon you.'

'Married to a maniac—a hopeless maniac!—What will my
mother say?'—exclaimed Ernest, as he paced the room. The
image of his beautiful bride rose before him; he felt as if his
tenderness and his devotion must avail; he would watch her
every look—anticipate her very thoughts. He started—it was
the steward who came into the room.

'I see,' said the old man, 'that you have read my master's
letter. Alas! I have dreadful news to tell. The Baroness Minna
has evaded all our precautions. She has escaped, I know not
whither. I only trust it is alone.'

'Heinrich,' said Ernest, solemnly, 'I speak to you as the
trusted and valued friend of my beloved uncle. Minna is with
me. I married her last night—deceived, alas! by a narrative
which I ought never to have credited. I at least ought to have
known my uncle too well to believe that he could be guilty
of fraud or oppression. The rest of my life will be too little
to atone for that moment's doubt. Old man, hear me swear
to devote myself to his children!'

'God bless you!' sobbed the old man, as he clasped the
hand which Ernest extended towards him.

Months passed away in unceasing watchfulness on the part
of Ernest. With trembling hope he began to rely on Minna's
complete recovery. Wild she was at times, and her fondness
for him had a strange character of fierceness; but his influence
over her was unbounded, and her passion for music was a

constant resource. By Heinrich's advice they left the castle, that no painful train of thought might be awakened; and they resided in a light, cheerful villa, amid the suburbs of Vienna. Her husband found all the plans of mutual study in which the young student lover had so delighted, were in vain. It was impossible to fix her attention long on anything. Companionship there was none between them, and the call on his attention was unceasing; but his affection became even deeper for its very fear, and it was hallowed by the feeling of how sacred it was as a duty. Gradually as he became more and more satisfied about Minna, he grew more anxious for Pauline. He saw her drooping day by day; her spirits became unequal, and her eyes were rarely without tears. Too late he discovered how she loved him. Her bodily weakness seemed to render her less capable of repressing her feelings. Her eye followed him, go where he would; she hung upon his least word, and she shrunk away from her sister. The proposed visit to his mother brought on such a passion of tears, that he had not the heart to insist upon it—especially when he looked upon her pale, sunken cheek, and watched her slow, dispirited step. Once or twice he saw Minna watching her with a wild, strange glance in her large, black eyes, as if there was an intentive feeling of jealousy.

It was now the first week in June, and the weather was unusually hot; and there was thunder in the air, which added to the oppression. The moon, too, was at its full; and Minna, always restless at that time, was now unusually so. At last, towards evening, she sank on the window-seat in a deep slumber. Pauline was walking on the terrace below; and Ernest, who saw that she was scarcely equal to the fatigue, went down to give her his assistance. She took his arm, and they walked up and down together. At last she leant over the balustrade, and her eyes filled with tears as she watched the moonlight turning the flowers to silver.

'I wish,' said she, 'I were a flower—happy in the sunshine— happy in the soft night air. No beating heart within, to make me wretched.' And she dropped her head on his arm, and wept.

Before Ernest had time to utter even a few soothing words, a bright blade glittered in the moonlight, and Pauline sunk with a faint scream on the pavement.—Minna had stabbed her sister to the heart! There she stood: her cheek flushed with the deepest crimson, and her eyes flashing the wild light of insanity—waving the weapon she had so fatally used. It was the little Indian dagger Ernest had lent her to sever the long tress of hair. She had concealed it till this moment.

'Yes,' cried she, 'I have killed her at last. They thought I did not know her, but I did. She took away my father's heart from me, and would have taken away my husband's; but I have killed her at last.'

By this time the servants came rushing from all parts. At their approach, Minna seemed seized with some vague fear, and attempted to fly. Ernest had just time to pass his arms around her, though she struggled violently. They raised Pauline, but the last spark of life had fled—the pale and lovely features were set in death!

Minna lived on for years—her insanity taking, every succeeding year, a darker colour. Ernest never left her side. Fierce or sullen, violent or desponding, he watched her through every mood. She wore herself away to a shadow, till it was a marvel how that frail form endured. For months before her death, she was almost ungovernable, and did not know him the least. She scarcely ever slept, but one night slumber overpowered her. The sun was shining brightly into the chamber, and its light fell upon the whitened hair and careworn features of her husband, who had been watching by her for hours. A sweet and meek expression was in her eyes when she awoke.

'Ernest, dearest Ernest,' said she, in a soft, low whisper. She raised her head from the pillow, and, like a child, put up her mouth to kiss him. She sank back: her last breath had passed in that kiss!

He laid her in the same tomb with her father and sister; and the next day, the noble, the wealthy, and still handsome Count von Hermanstadt entered the order of St Francis.

PASSAGE IN THE SECRET HISTORY OF AN IRISH COUNTESS

Joseph Sheridan Le Fanu

MY DEAR FRIEND—You have asked me to furnish you with a detail of the strange events which marked my early history, and I have, without hesitation, applied myself to the task, knowing that while I live, a kind consideration for my feelings will prevent your giving publicity to the statement; and conscious that, when I am no more, there will not survive one to whom the narrative can prove injurious, or even painful.

My mother died when I was quite an infant, and of her I have no recollection, even the faintest. By her death, my education and habits were left solely to the guidance of my surviving parent; and, as far as a stern attention to my religious instruction, and an active anxiety evinced by his procuring for me the best masters to perfect me in those accomplishments which my station and wealth might seem to require, could avail, he amply discharged the task. My father was what is called an oddity, and his treatment of me, though uniformly kind, flowed less from affection and tenderness, than from a sense of obligation and duty. Indeed, I seldom even spoke to him except at meal times, and then his manner was silent and abrupt; his leisure hours, which were many, were passed either in his study or in solitary walks; in short, he seemed to take no further interest in my happiness or improvement than a conscientious regard to the discharge of his own duty would seem to claim. Shortly before my birth a circumstance had occurred which had contributed much to form and to confirm my father's secluded habits—it was the fact that a suspicion of *murder* had fallen upon his younger brother, though not sufficiently definite to lead to an indictment, yet strong enough to ruin him in public opinion. This disgraceful and dreadful doubt cast upon the family name, my father felt deeply and bitterly, and not the less so that he himself was thoroughly

convinced of his brother's innocence; the sincerity and strength
of this impression he shortly afterwards proved in a manner
which produced the dark events which follow. Before, however, I enter upon the statement of them, I ought to relate the
circumstances which had awakened the suspicion; inasmuch as
they are in themselves somewhat curious, and, in their effects,
most intimately connected with my after-history.

My uncle, Sir Arthur T——n, was a gay and extravagant
man, and, among other vices, was ruinously addicted to gaming; this unfortunate propensity, even after his fortune had
suffered so severely as to render inevitable a reduction in his
expenses by no means inconsiderable, nevertheless continued
to actuate him, nearly to the exclusion of all other pursuits;
he was, however, a proud, or rather a vain man, and could
not bear to make the diminution of his income a matter of
gratulation and triumph to those with whom he had hitherto
competed, and the consequence was, that he frequented no
longer the expensive haunts of dissipation, and retired from
the gay world, leaving his coterie to discover his reasons, as
best they might. He did not, however, forego his favourite
vice, for, though he could not worship his great divinity in
the costly temples where it was formerly his wont to take his
stand, yet he found it very possible to bring about him a sufficient number of the votaries of chance to answer all his ends.
The consequence was, that Carrickleigh, which was the name
of my uncle's residence, was never without one or more of
such visitors as I have described. It happened that upon one
occasion he was visited by one Hugh Tisdall, a gentleman of
loose habits, but of considerable wealth, and who had, in early
youth, travelled with my uncle upon the continent; the period
of this visit was winter, and, consequently, the house was
nearly deserted excepting by its regular inmates; it was, therefore, highly acceptable, particularly as my uncle was aware that
his visitor's tastes accorded exactly with his own. Both parties seemed determined to avail themselves of their suitabil-
ity during the brief stay which Mr Tisdall had promised; the
consequence was, that they shut themselves up in Sir Arthur's
private room, for nearly all the day and the greater part of
the night, during the space of nearly a week, at the end of

which the servant, having one morning, as usual, knocked at
Mr Tisdall's bed-room door repeatedly, received no answer,
and, upon attempting to enter, found that it was locked; this
appeared suspicious, and the inmates of the house, having been
alarmed, the door was forced open, and, on proceeding to the
bed, they found the body of its occupant perfectly lifeless,
and hanging half way out, the head downwards, and near the
floor; one deep wound had been inflicted upon the temple,
apparently with some blunt instrument which had penetrated
the brain, and another blow, less effective, probably the first
aimed, had grazed the head, removing some of the scalp, but
leaving the skull untouched; the door had been double locked
upon the *inside*, in evidence of which the key still lay where it
had been placed in the lock. The window, though not secured
on the interior, was closed; a circumstance not a little puzz-
ling, as it afforded the only other mode of escape from the
room; it looked out, too, upon a kind of court-yard, round
which the old buildings stood, formerly accessible by a narrow door-way and passage lying in the oldest side of the
quadrangle, but which had since been built up, so as to pre-
clude all ingress or egress; the room was also upon the second
story, and the height of the window considerable; near the
bed were found a pair of razors belonging to the murdered
man, one of them upon the ground, and both of them open.
The weapon which had inflicted the mortal wound was not
to be found in the room, nor were any footsteps or other traces
of the murderer discoverable. At the suggestion of Sir Arthur
himself, a coroner was instantly summoned to attend, and an
inquest was held; nothing, however, in any degree conclusive was elicited; the walls, ceiling, and floor of the room were
carefully examined, in order to ascertain whether they contained a trap-door or other concealed mode of entrance—but
no such thing appeared. Such was the minuteness of invest-
igation employed, that, although the grate had contained a large
fire during the night, they proceeded to examine even the very
chimney, in order to discover whether escape by it was possible; but this attempt, too, was fruitless, for the chimney,
built in the old fashion, rose in a perfectly perpendicular line
from the hearth, to a height of nearly fourteen feet above the

roof, affording in its interior scarcely the possibility of ascent, the flue being smoothly plastered, and sloping towards the top, like an inverted funnel, promising, too, even if the summit were attained, owing to its great height, but a precarious descent upon the sharp and steep-ridged roof; the ashes, too, which lay in the grate, and the soot, as far as it could be seen, were undisturbed, a circumstance almost conclusive of the question. Sir Arthur was of course examined; his evidence was given with clearness and unreserve, which seemed calculated to silence all suspicion; he stated that, up to the day and night immediately preceding the catastrophe, he had lost to a heavy amount, but that, at their last sitting, he had not only won back his original loss, but upwards of four thousand pounds in addition; in evidence of which he produced an acknowledgment of debt to that amount, in the hand-writing of the deceased, and bearing the date of the fatal night; he had mentioned the circumstance to his lady, and in presence of some of the domestics; which statement was supported by *their* respective evidence. One of the jury shrewdly observed, that the circumstance of Mr Tisdall's having sustained so heavy a loss might have suggested to some ill-minded persons accidentally hearing it, the plan of robbing him, after having murdered him in such a manner as might make it appear that he had committed suicide; a supposition which was strongly supported by the razors having been found thus displaced, and removed from their case; two persons had probably been engaged in the attempt, one watching by the sleeping man, and ready to strike him in case of his awakening suddenly, while the other was procuring the razors and employed in inflicting the fatal gash, so as to make it appear to have been the act of the murdered man himself; it was said that while the juror was making this suggestion, Sir Arthur changed colour. Nothing, however, like legal evidence appeared against him, and the consequence was, that the verdict was found against a person or persons unknown, and for some time the matter was suffered to rest, until, after about five months, my father received a letter from a person signing himself Andrew Collis, and representing himself to be the cousin of the deceased; this letter stated that Sir Arthur was likely to incur not merely suspicion, but personal risk, unless he could account for certain circumstances connected with the recent murder, and contained a copy of a letter written by the deceased, and bearing date, the day of the week, and of the month, upon the night of which the deed of blood had been perpetrated. Tisdall's note ran as follows:—

'DEAR COLLIS—I have had sharp work with Sir Arthur; he tried some of his stale tricks, but soon found that *I* was Yorkshire too*—it would not do—you understand me—we went to the work like good ones, head, heart and soul; and, in fact, since I came here, I have lost no time. I am rather fagged, but I am sure to be well paid for my hardship; I never want sleep so long as I can have the music of a dice-box, and wherewithal to pay the piper. As I told you, he tried some of his queer turns, but I foiled him like a man, and, in return, gave him more than he could relish of the genuine *dead knowledge*. In short, I have plucked the old baronet, as never baronet was plucked before; I have scarce left him the stump of a quill; I have got promissory notes in his hand to the amount of —— if you like round numbers, say, thirty thousand pounds, safely deposited in my portable strong box, alias double-clasped pocket-book. I leave this ruinous old rat-hole early on to-morrow, for two reasons—first, I do not want to play with Sir Arthur deeper than I think his security, that is, his money, or his money's worth, would warrant—and, secondly, because I am safer a hundred miles from Sir Arthur, than in the house with him; look you, my worthy, I tell you this between ourselves—I may be wrong, but, by G—, I am as sure as that I am now living, that Sir A—— attempted to poison me last night; so much for old friendship on both sides. When I won the last stake, a heavy one enough, my friend leant his forehead upon his hands, and you'll laugh when I tell you, that his head literally smoked like a hot dumpling; I do not know whether his agitation was produced by the plan which he had against me, or by his having lost so heavily; though it must be allowed that he had reason to be a little funked, which-ever way his thoughts went; but he pulled the bell, and ordered two bottles of Champagne. While the fellow was bringing them he drew out a promissory note to the full amount, which he signed, and, as the man came in with the bottles and glasses, he desired him to be off; he filled out a glass for me, and, while he thought my eyes were off, for I was putting up his note at the time, he dropped something slyly into it, no doubt to sweeten it; but I saw it all, and, when he handed it to me, I said, with an emphasis which he might or might not understand, "there is some sediment in this, I'll not drink it." "Is there," said he, and at the same time snatched it from my hand and threw it into the fire. What do you think of that? have I not a tender chicken to manage? Win or lose, I will not play beyond five thousand to-night, and to-morrow sees me safe out of the reach of Sir Arthur's Champagne. So, all things considered, I think you must allow that you are not the last who have found a knowing boy in yours to command,

HUGH TISDALL.'

Of the authenticity of this document, I never heard my father express a doubt; and, I am satisfied that, owing to his strong conviction in favour of his brother, he would not have admitted it without sufficient inquiry, inasmuch as it tended to confirm the suspicions which already existed to his prejudice. Now, the only point in this letter which made strongly against my uncle, was the mention of the 'double-clasped pocket-book,' as the receptacle of the papers likely to involve him, for this pocket-book was not forthcoming, nor any where to be found, nor had any papers referring to his gaming transactions been found upon the dead man; however, whatever might have been the original intention of this Collis, neither my uncle or my father ever heard more of him; but he published the letter in Faulkner's newspaper,* which was shortly afterwards made the vehicle of a much more mysterious attack; the passage in that periodical to which I allude, occurred about four years afterwards, and while the fatal occurrence was still fresh in public recollection; it commenced by a rambling preface, stating that 'a *certain person* whom *certain* persons thought to be dead, was not so, but living, and in full possession of his memory, and moreover, ready and able to make *great* delinquents tremble'; it then went on to describe the murder, without, however mentioning names; and in doing so, it entered into minute and circumstantial particulars of which none but an *eye-witness* could have been possessed, and by implications almost too unequivocal to be regarded in the light of insinuation, to involve the '*titled gambler*' in the guilt of the transaction. My father at once urged Sir Arthur to proceed against the paper in an action of libel, but he would not hear of it, nor consent to my father's taking any legal steps whatever in the matter. My father, however, wrote in a threatening tone to Faulkner, demanding a surrender of the author of the obnoxious article; the answer to this application is still in my possession, and is penned in an apologetic tone: it states that the manuscript had been handed in, paid for, and inserted as an advertisement, without sufficient inquiry, or any knowledge as to whom it referred. No step, however, was taken to clear my uncle's character in the judgment of the public; and, as he immediately sold a small property, the application of the proceeds of which were known to none, he was said to have disposed of it to enable himself to buy off the threatened information; however the truth might have been, it is certain that no charges respecting the mysterious murder were aftcrwards publicly made against my uncle, and, as far as external disturbances were concerned, he enjoyed henceforward perfect security and quiet. A deep and lasting impression, however, had been made upon the public mind, and Sir Arthur T——n was no longer visited or noticed by the gentry and aristocracy of the county, whose attentions and courtesies he had hitherto received. He accordingly affected to despise these enjoyments which he could not procure, and shunned even that society which he might have commanded. This is all that I need recapitulate of my uncle's history, and I now recur to my own. Although my father had never, within my recollection, visited, or been visited by my uncle, each being of sedentary, procrastinating, and secluded habits, and their respective residences being very far apart—the one lying in the county of Galway, the other in that of Cork—he was strongly attached to his brother, and evinced his affection by an active correspondence, and by deeply and proudly resenting that neglect which had marked Sir Arthur as unfit to mix in society. When I was about eighteen years of age, my father, whose health had been gradually declining, died, leaving me in heart wretched and desolate, and owing to his previous seclusion, with few acquaintances, and almost no friends. The provisions of his will were curious, and when I was sufficiently come to myself to listen to, or comprehend them, surprised me not a little: all his vast property was left to me, and to the heirs of my body, for ever; and, in default of such heirs, it was to go after my death to my uncle, Sir Arthur, without any entail. At the same time, the will appointed him my guardian, desiring that I might be received within his house, and reside with his family, and under his care, during the term of my minority; and in consideration of the increased expense consequent upon such an arrangement, a handsome annuity was allotted to him during the term of my proposed residence. The object of this last provision I at once understood; my father desired, by making it the direct, apparent interest of Sir Arthur that I should die without issue, while at the same time he placed me wholly in his power, to prove to the world, how great and unshaken was his confidence in his brother's innocence and honour, and also to afford him an opportunity of showing that this mark of confidence was not unworthily bestowed. It was a strange, perhaps an idle scheme, but as I had been always brought up in the habit of considering my uncle as a deeply injured man, and had been taught almost as a part of my religion, to regard him as the very soul of honour, I felt no further uneasiness respecting the arrangement, than that likely to result to a timid girl, of secluded habits, from the immediate prospect of taking up her abode for the first time in her life among total strangers; previous to leaving my home, which I felt I should do with a heavy heart, I received a most tender and affectionate letter from my uncle, calculated, if any thing could do so, to remove the bitterness of parting from scenes familiar and dear from my earliest childhood, and in some degree to reconcile me to the measure. It was upon a fine autumn that I approached the old domain of Carrickleigh. I shall not soon forget the impression of sadness and of gloom which all that I saw produced upon my mind; the sunbeams were falling

with a rich and melancholy tint upon the fine old trees, which
stood in lordly groups, casting their long, sweeping shadows
over rock and sward; there was an air of neglect and decay
about the spot, which amounted almost to desolation; the
symptoms of this increased in number as we approached the
building itself, near which the ground had been originally
more artificially and carefully cultivated than elsewhere, and
whose neglect consequently more immediately and strikingly
betrayed itself. As we proceeded, the road wound near the
beds of what had been formerly two fish-ponds, which were
now nothing more than stagnant swamps, overgrown with
rank weeds, and here and there encroached upon by the strag-
gling underwood; the avenue itself was much broken; and in
many places the stones were almost concealed by grass and
nettles; the loose stone walls which had here and there intersected the broad park, were, in many places, broken down,
so as no longer to answer their original purpose as fences;
piers were now and then to be seen, but the gates were gone;
and, to add to the general air of dilapidation, some huge trunks
were lying scattered through the venerable old trees, either
the work of the winter storms, or perhaps the victims of some
extensive but desultory scheme of denudation, which the pro-
jector had not capital or perseverance to carry into full effect.
After the carriage had travelled a mile of this avenue, we
reached the summit of rather an abrupt eminence, one of the
many which added to the picturesqueness, if not to the
convenience of this rude passage; from the top of this ridge
the grey walls of Carrickleigh were visible, rising at a small
distance in front, and darkened by the hoary wood which
crowded around them; it was a quadrangular building of considerable extent, and the front which lay towards us, and in
which the great entrance was placed, bore unequivocal marks
of antiquity; the time-worn, solemn aspect of the old building,
the ruinous and deserted appearance of the whole place, and
the associations which connected it with a dark page in the
history of my family, combined to depress spirits already pre-
disposed for the reception of sombre and dejecting impressions.
When the carriage drew up in the grass-grown court-yard
before the hall-door, two lazy-looking men, whose appearance

well accorded with that of the place which they tenanted,
alarmed by the obstreperous barking of a great chained dog,
ran out from some half ruinous out-houses, and took charge
of the horses; the hall-door stood open, and I entered a
gloomy and imperfectly lighted apartment, and found no one
within; however, I had not long to wait in this awkward
predicament, for before my luggage had been deposited in the
house, indeed, before I had well removed my cloak and other
muffles, so as to enable me to look around, a young girl ran
lightly into the hall, and kissing me heartily, and somewhat
boisterously exclaimed, 'my dear cousin, my dear Margaret—
I am so delighted—so out of breath, we did not expect you
till ten o'clock; my father is somewhere about the place, he
must be close at hand. James—Corney—run out and tell your
master—my brother is seldom at home, at least at any reas-
onable hour—you must be so tired—so fatigued—let me show
you to your room—see that Lady Margaret's luggage is all
brought up—you must lie down and rest yourself—Deborah
bring some coffee—up these stairs; we are so delighted to see
you—you cannot think how lonely I have been—how steep
these stairs are, are not they? I am so glad you are come—I
could hardly bring myself to believe that you were really
coming—how good of you, dear Lady Margaret.' There was
real good-nature and delight in my cousin's greeting, and a
kind of constitutional confidence of manner which placed me
at once at ease, and made me feel immediately upon terms of
intimacy with her. The room into which she ushered me,
although partaking in the general air of decay which pervaded
the mansion and all about it, had, nevertheless, been fitted
up with evident attention to comfort, and even with some
dingy attempt at luxury; but what pleased me most was that
it opened, by a second door, upon a lobby which communicated with my fair cousin's apartment; a circumstance which
divested the room, in my eyes, of the air of solitude and sadness which would otherwise have characterized it, to a degree
almost painful to one so dejected in spirits as I was. After
such arrangements as I found necessary were completed, we
both went down to the parlour, a large wainscoted room,
hung round with grim old portraits, and as I was not sorry

to see, containing, in its ample grate, a large and cheerful fire. Here my cousin had leisure to talk more at her ease; and from her I learned something of the manners and the habits of the two remaining members of her family, whom I had not yet seen. On my arrival I had known nothing of the family among whom I was come to reside, except that it consisted of three individuals, my uncle, and his son and daughter, Lady T——n having been long dead; in addition to this very scanty stock of information, I shortly learned from my communicative companion, that my uncle was, as I had suspected, completely retired in his habits, and besides that, having been so far back as she could well recollect, always rather strict, as reformed rakes frequently become, he had latterly been growing more gloomily and sternly religious than heretofore. Her account of her brother was far less favourable, though she did not say any thing directly to his disadvantage. From all that I could gather from her, I was led to suppose that he was a specimen of the idle, coarse-mannered, profligate, low-minded '*squirearchy*'—a result which might naturally have flowed from the circumstance of his being, as it were, outlawed from society, and driven for companionship to grades below his own—enjoying, too, the dangerous prerogative of spending much money. However, you may easily suppose that I found nothing in my cousin's communication, fully to bear me out in so very decided a conclusion. I awaited the arrival of my uncle, which was every moment to be expected, with feelings half of alarm, half of curiosity—a sensation which I have often since experienced, though to a less degree, when upon the point of standing for the first time in the presence of one of whom I have long been in the habit of hearing or thinking with interest. It was, therefore, with some little perturbation that I heard, first a slight bustle at the outer door, then a slow step traverse the hall, and finally witnessed the door open, and my uncle enter the room. He was a striking looking man—from peculiarities both of person and of garb, the whole effect of his appearance amounted to extreme singularity. He was tall, and when young his figure must have been strikingly elegant; as it was, however, its effect was marred by a very decided stoop; his dress was of a sober colour, and in fashion anterior to any thing which I could remember. It was, however, handsome, and by no means carelessly put on; but what completed the singularity of his appearance was his uncut, white hair, which hung in long, but not at all neglected curls, even so far as his shoulders, and which, combined with his regularly classic features, and fine dark eyes, to bestow upon him an air of venerable dignity and pride, which I have never seen equalled elsewhere. I rose as he entered, and met him about the middle of the room; he kissed my cheek and both my hands, saying—

'You are most welcome, dear child, as welcome as the command of this poor place and all that it contains can make you. I am most rejoiced to see you—truly rejoiced. I trust that you are not much fatigued—pray be seated again.' He led me to my chair, and continued, 'I am glad to perceive you have made acquaintance with Emily already; I see, in your being thus brought together, the foundation of a lasting friendship. You are both innocent, and both young. God bless you— God bless you, and make you all that I could wish.'

He raised his eyes, and remained for a few moments silent, as if in secret prayer. I felt that it was impossible that this man, with feelings so quick, so warm, so tender, could be the wretch that public opinion had represented him to be. I was more than ever convinced of his innocence. His manner was, or appeared to me, most fascinating—there was a mingled kindness and courtesy in it which seemed to speak benevolence itself—it was a manner which I felt cold art could never have taught—it owed most of its charm to its appearing to emanate directly from the heart—it must be a genuine index of the owner's mind. So I thought. My uncle having given me fully to understand that I was most welcome, and might command whatever was his own, pressed me to take some refreshment; and on my refusing, he observed that previously to bidding me good night, he had one duty further to perform, one in whose observance he was convinced I would cheerfully acquiesce. He then proceeded to read a chapter from the Bible; after which he took his leave with the same affectionate kindness with which he had greeted me, having repeated his desire that I should consider every thing in his

house as altogether at my disposal. It is needless to say that
I was much pleased with my uncle—it was impossible to
avoid being so; and I could not help saying to myself, if such
a man as this is not safe from the assaults of slander, who is?
I felt much happier than I had done since my father's death,
and enjoyed that night the first refreshing sleep which had
visited me since that event. My curiosity respecting my male
cousin did not long remain unsatisfied—he appeared upon the
next day at dinner. His manners, though not so coarse as
I had expected, were exceedingly disagreeable; there was an
assurance and a forwardness for which I was not prepared;
there was less of the vulgarity of manner, and almost more
of that of the mind, than I had anticipated. I felt quite uncomfortable in his presence; there was just that confidence in his
look and tone, which would read encouragement even in mere
toleration; and I felt more disgusted and annoyed at the coarse
and extravagant compliments which he was pleased from time
to time to pay me, than perhaps the extent of the atrocity might
fully have warranted. It was, however, one consolation that
he did not often appear, being much engrossed by pursuits
about which I neither knew nor cared any thing; but when
he did appear, his attentions, either with a view to his amusement, or to some more serious advantage, were so obviously
and perseveringly directed to me, that young and inexperienced as I was, even *I* could not be ignorant of his prefer-
ence. I felt more provoked by this odious persecution than I
can express, and discouraged him with so much vigour, that
I employed even rudeness to convince him that his assiduities
were unwelcome—but all in vain.

This had gone on for nearly a twelvemonth to my infinite
annoyance, when one day as I was sitting at some needle-
work with my companion Emily, as was my habit, in the parlour, the door opened, and my cousin Edward entered the
room. There was something, I thought, odd in his manner—
a kind of struggle between shame and impudence—a kind of
flurry and ambiguity which made him appear, if possible,
more than ordinarily disagreeable.

'Your servant, ladies,' he said, seating himself at the same
time; 'sorry to spoil your *tete-a-tete*; but never mind, I'll only

take Emily's place for a minute or two, and then we part for a while, fair cousin. Emily, my father wants you in the corner turret—no shilly, shally, he's in a hurry.' She hesitated, 'be off—tramp, march,' he exclaimed, in a tone which the poor girl dared not disobey.

She left the room, and Edward followed her to the door. He stood there for a minute or two, as if reflecting what he should say, perhaps satisfying himself that no one was within hearing in the hall. At length he turned about, having closed the door as if carelessly with his foot, and advancing slowly, as if in deep thought, he took his seat at the side of the table opposite to mine. There was a brief interval of silence, after which he said—

'I imagine that you have a shrewd suspicion of the object of my early visit; but I suppose I must go into particulars. Must I?'

'I have no conception,' I replied, 'what your object may be.'

'Well, well,' said he, becoming more at his ease as he proceeded, 'it may be told in a few words. You know that it is totally impossible, quite out of the question, that an off-hand young fellow like me, and a good-looking girl like yourself, could meet continually as you and I have done, without an attachment—a liking growing up on one side or other—in short, I think I have let you know as plain as if I spoke it, that I have been in love with you, almost from the first time I saw you.' He paused, but I was too much horrified to speak. He interpreted my silence favourably. 'I can tell you,' he continued, 'I'm reckoned rather hard to please, and very hard to *hit*. I can't say when I was taken with a girl before, so you see fortune reserved me—'

Here the odious wretch wound his arm round my waist: the action at once restored me to utterance, and with the most indignant vehemence I released myself from his hold, and at the same time said—

'I have not been insensible, sir, of your most disagreeable attentions—they have long been a source of much annoyance to me; and you must be aware that I have marked my disapprobation, my disgust, as unequivocally as I possibly could, without actual indelicacy.'

I paused, almost out of breath from the rapidity with which I had spoken; and without giving him time to renew the conversation, I hastily quitted the room, leaving him in a paroxysm of rage and mortification. As I ascended the stairs, I heard him open the parlour-door with violence, and take two or three rapid strides in the direction in which I was moving. I was now much frightened, and ran the whole way until I reached my room, and having locked the door, I listened breathlessly, but heard no sound. This relieved me for the present; but so much had I been overcome by the agitation and annoyance attendant upon the scene which I had just gone through, that when my cousin Emily knocked at my door, I was weeping in strong hysterics. You will readily conceive my distress, when you reflect upon my strong dislike to my cousin Edward, combined with my youth and extreme inexperience; any proposal of such a nature must have agitated me—but that it should have come from the man whom of all others I most loathed and abhorred, and to whom I had, as clearly as manner could do it, expressed the state of my feelings, was almost too overwhelming to be borne: it was a calamity, too, in which I could not claim the sympathy of my cousin Emily, which had always been extended to me in my minor grievances. Still I hoped that it might not be unattended with good, for I thought that one inevitable and most welcome consequence would result from this painful *eclaircissement,** in the discontinuance of my cousin's odious persecution.

When I arose next morning, it was with the fervent hope that I might never again behold the face, or even hear the name of my cousin Edward; but such a consummation, though devoutly to be wished, was hardly likely to occur. The painful impressions of yesterday were too vivid to be at once erased; and I could not help feeling some dim foreboding of coming annoyance and evil. To expect on my cousin's part any thing like delicacy or consideration for me, was out of the question. I saw that he had set his heart upon my property, and that he was not likely easily to forego such an acquisition—possessing what might have been considered opportunities and facilities almost to compel my compliance. I now keenly felt the unreasonableness of my father's conduct in placing me to reside with a family of all whose members, with one exception, he was wholly ignorant, and I bitterly felt the helplessness of my situation. I determined, however, in case of my cousin's persevering in his addresses, to lay all the particulars before my uncle, although he had never in kindness or intimacy gone a step beyond our first interview, and to throw myself upon his hospitality and his sense of honour for protection against a repetition of such scenes. My cousin's conduct may appear to have been an inadequate cause for such serious uneasiness; but my alarm was caused neither by his acts nor words, but entirely by his manner, which was strange and even intimidating to excess. At the beginning of the yesterday's interview, there was a sort of bullying swagger in his air, which towards the end gave place to the brutal vehemence of an undisguised ruffian—a transition which had tempted me into a belief that he might seek even forcibly to extort from me a consent to his wishes, or by means still more horrible, of which I scarcely dared to trust myself to think, to possess himself of my property.

I was early next day summoned to attend my uncle in his private room, which lay in a corner turret of the old building; and thither I accordingly went, wondering all the way what this unusual measure might prelude. When I entered the room, he did not rise in his usual courteous way to greet me, but simply pointed to a chair opposite to his own—this boded nothing agreeable. I sat down, however, silently waiting until he should open the conversation.

'Lady Margaret,' at length he said, in a tone of greater sternness than I thought him capable of using, 'I have hitherto spoken to you as a friend, but I have not forgotten that I am also your guardian, and that my authority as such gives me a right to controul your conduct. I shall put a question to you, and I expect and will demand a plain, direct answer. Have I rightly been informed that you have contemptuously rejected the suit and hand of my son Edward?'

I stammered forth, with a good deal of trepidation—

'I believe—that is, I have, sir, rejected my cousin's proposals; and my coldness and discouragement might have convinced him that I had determined to do so.'

'Madam,' replied he, with suppressed, but, as it appeared to me, intense anger, 'I have lived long enough to know that *coldness* and discouragement, and such terms, form the common cant of a worthless coquette. You know to the full, as well as I, that *coldness and discouragement* may be so exhibited as to convince their object that he is neither distasteful or indifferent to the person who wears this manner. You know, too, none better, that an affected neglect, when skilfully managed, is amongst the most formidable of the engines which artful beauty can employ. I tell you, madam, that having without one word spoken in discouragement, permitted my son's most marked attentions for a twelvemonth or more, you have no right to dismiss him with no further explanation than demurely telling him that you had always looked coldly upon him, and neither your wealth nor your *ladyship* (there was an emphasis of scorn on the word, which would have become Sir Giles Overreach* himself) can warrant you in treating with contempt the affectionate regard of an honest heart.'

I was too much shocked at this undisguised attempt to bully me into an acquiescence in the interested and unprincipled plan for their own aggrandisement, which I now perceived my uncle and his son to have deliberately entered into, at once to find strength or collectedness to frame an answer to what he had said. At length I replied with some firmness—

'In all that you have just now said, sir, you have grossly misstated my conduct and motives—your information must have been most incorrect, as far as it regards my conduct towards my cousin; my manner towards him could have conveyed nothing but dislike; and if any thing could have added to the strong aversion which I have long felt towards him, it would be his attempting thus to trick and frighten me into a marriage which he knows to be revolting to me, and which is sought by him only as a means for securing to himself whatever property is mine.'

As I said this, I fixed my eyes upon those of my uncle, but he was too old in the *world's ways* to faulter beneath the gaze of more searching eyes than mine; he simply said—

'Are you acquainted with the provisions of your father's will?'

I answered in the affirmative; and he continued—'Then you must be aware that if my son Edward were, which God forbid, the unprincipled, reckless man, you pretend to think him'—(here he spoke very slowly, as if he intended that every word which escaped him, should be registered in my memory, while at the same time the expression of his countenance underwent a gradual but horrible change, and the eyes which he fixed upon me became so darkly vivid, that I almost lost sight of every thing else)—'if he were what you have described him, think you, girl, he could find no briefer means than wedding contracts to gain his ends—'twas but to gripe your slender neck until the breath had stopped, and lands, and lakes, and all were his.'

I stood staring at him for many minutes after he had ceased to speak, fascinated by the terrible, serpent-like gaze, until he continued with a welcome change of countenance—

'I will not speak again to you, upon this topic, until one month has passed. You shall have time to consider the relative advantages of the two courses which are open to you. I should be sorry to hurry you to a decision. I am satisfied with having stated my feelings upon the subject, and pointed out to you the path of duty. Remember this day month—not one word sooner.'

He then rose, and I left the room, much agitated and exhausted.

This interview, all the circumstances attending it, but most particularly the formidable expression of my uncle's countenance while he talked, though hypothetically, of *murder*, combined to arouse all my worst suspicions of him. I dreaded to look upon the face that had so recently worn the appalling livery of guilt and malignity. I regarded it with the mingled fear and loathing with which one looks upon an object which has tortured them in a night-mare.

In a few days after the interview, the particulars of which I have just detailed, I found a note upon my toilet-table, and on opening it I read as follows:—

'MY DEAR LADY MARGARET,—You will be, perhaps, surprised to see a strange face in your room to-day. I have dismissed your Irish maid, and secured a French one to wait upon you—a step rendered necessary by my proposing shortly to visit the continent, with all my family.—Your faithful guardian,

ARTHUR T——N.'

On inquiry, I found that my faithful attendant was actually gone, and far on her way to the town of Galway; and in her stead there appeared a tall, raw-boned, ill-looking, elderly Frenchwoman, whose sullen and presuming manners seemed to imply that her vocation had never before been that of a lady's maid. I could not help regarding her as a creature of my uncle's, and therefore to be dreaded, even had she been in no other way suspicious.

Days and weeks passed away, without any, even a momentary doubt upon my part, as to the course to be pursued by me. The allotted period had at length elapsed; the day arrived upon which I was to communicate my decision to my uncle. Although my resolution had never for a moment wavered, I could not shake off the dread of the approaching colloquy; and my heart sunk within me, as I heard the expected summons. I had not seen my cousin Edward since the occurrence of the grand *eclaircissement*; he must have studiously avoided me—I suppose from policy, it could not have been from delicacy. I was prepared for a terrific burst of fury from my uncle, as soon as I should make known my determination; and I not unreasonably feared that some act of violence or of intimidation would next be resorted to. Filled with these dreary forebodings, I fearfully opened the study door, and the next minute I stood in my uncle's presence. He received me with a politeness which I dreaded, as arguing a favourable anticipation respecting the answer which I was to give; and after some slight delay, he began by saying—

'It will be a relief to both of us, I believe, to bring this conversation as soon as possible to an issue. You will excuse me, then, my dear niece, for speaking with an abruptness which, under other circumstances, would be unpardonable. You have, I am certain, given the subject of our last interview fair and serious consideration; and I trust that you are now prepared with candour to lay your answer before me. A few words will suffice—we perfectly understand one another.'

He paused; and I, though feeling that I stood upon a mine which might in an instant explode, nevertheless answered with perfect composure, 'I must now, sir, make the same reply which I did upon the last occasion, and I reiterate the declaration which I then made, that I never can nor will, while life and reason remain, consent to a union with my cousin Edward.'

This announcement wrought no apparent change in Sir Arthur, except that he became deadly, almost lividly pale. He seemed lost in dark thought for a minute, and then with a slight effort said, 'You have answered me honestly and directly; and you say your resolution is unchangeable; well, would it had been otherwise—would it had been otherwise —but be it as it is—I am satisfied.'

He gave me his hand—it was cold and damp as death; under an assumed calmness, it was evident that he was fearfully agitated. He continued to hold my hand with an almost painful pressure, while, as if unconsciously, seeming to forget my presence, he muttered, 'strange, strange, strange, indeed! fatuity, helpless fatuity!' there was here a long pause. 'Madness *indeed* to strain a cable that is rotten to the very heart —it must break—and then—all goes.' There was again a pause of some minutes, after which, suddenly changing his voice and manner to one of wakeful alacrity, he exclaimed, 'Margaret, my son Edward shall plague you no more. He leaves this country on to-morrow for France—he shall speak no more upon this subject—never, never more—whatever events depended upon your answer must now take their own course; but as for this fruitless proposal, it has been tried enough; it can be repeated no more.' At these words he coldly suffered my hand to drop, as if to express his total abandonment of all his projected schemes of alliance; and certainly the action, with the accompanying words, produced upon my mind a more solemn and depressing effect than I believed possible to have been caused by the course which I had determined to pursue; it struck upon my heart with an awe and heaviness which *will* accompany the accomplishment of an important and irrevocable act, even though no doubt or scruple remains to make it possible that the agent should wish it undone.

'Well,' said my uncle, after a little time, 'we now cease to speak upon this topic, never to resume it again—remember you shall have no farther uneasiness from Edward; he leaves Ireland for France on to-morrow; this will be a relief to you; may I depend upon your *honour* that no word touching the subject of this interview shall ever escape you?' I gave him the desired assurance; he said, 'it is well—I am satisfied—we have nothing more, I believe, to say upon either side, and my presence must be a restraint upon you, I shall therefore bid you farewell.' I then left the apartment, scarcely knowing what to think of the strange interview which had just taken place.

On the next day my uncle took occasion to tell me that Edward had actually sailed, if his intention had not been interfered with by adverse circumstances; and two days subsequently he actually produced a letter from his son, written, as it said, *on board*, and despatched while the ship was getting under weigh. This was a great satisfaction to me, and as being likely to prove so, it was no doubt communicated to me by Sir Arthur. During all this trying period, I had found infinite consolation in the society and sympathy of my dear cousin Emily. I never in after-life formed a friendship so close, so fervent, and upon which, in all its progress, I could look back with feelings of such unalloyed pleasure, upon whose termination I must ever dwell with so deep, so yet unembittered regret. In cheerful converse with her I soon recovered my spirits considerably, and passed my time agreeably enough, although still in the utmost seclusion. Matters went on smoothly enough, although I could not help sometimes feeling a momentary, but horrible uncertainty respecting my uncle's character; which was not altogether unwarranted by the circumstances of the two trying interviews whose particulars I have just detailed. The unpleasant impression which these conferences were calculated to leave upon my mind, was fast wearing away, when there occurred a circumstance, slight indeed in itself, but calculated irresistibly to awaken all my worst suspicions, and to overwhelm me again with anxiety and terror.

I had one day left the house with my cousin Emily, in order to take a ramble of considerable length, for the purpose of sketching some favourite views, and we had walked about half a mile when I perceived that we had forgotten our drawing materials, the absence of which would have defeated the object of our walk. Laughing at our own thoughtlessness, we returned to the house, and leaving Emily without, I ran up stairs to procure the drawing books and pencils which lay in my bed-room. As I ran up the stairs, I was met by the tall, ill-looking French woman, evidently a good deal flurried; 'Que veut, Madame?' said she, with a more decided effort to be polite, than I had ever known her make before. 'No, no—no matter,' said I, hastily running by her in the direction of my room. 'Madame,' cried she, in a high key, 'restez ici si vous plaite, votre chambre n'est pas faite'—your room is not ready for your reception yet. I continued to move on without heeding her. She was some way behind me, and feeling that she could not otherwise prevent my entrance, for I was now upon the very lobby, she made a desperate attempt to seize hold of my person; she succeeded in grasping the end of my shawl, which she drew from my shoulders, but slipping at the same time upon the polished oak floor, she fell at full length upon the boards. A little frightened as well as angry at the rudeness of this strange woman, I hastily pushed open the door of my room, at which I now stood, in order to escape from her; but great was my amazement on entering to find the apartment pre-occupied. The window was open, and beside it stood two male figures; they appeared to be examining the fastenings of the casement, and their backs were turned towards the door. One of them was my uncle; they both had turned on my entrance, as if startled; the stranger was booted and cloaked, and wore a heavy broad-leafed hat over his brows; he turned but for a moment, and averted his face; but I had seen enough to convince me that he was no other than my cousin Edward. My uncle had some iron instrument in his hand, which he hastily concealed behind his back; and coming towards me, said something as if in an explanatory tone; but I was too much shocked and confounded to understand what it might be. He said something about *repairs—*

window-frames—cold, and safety.' I did not wait, however, to ask or to receive explanations, but hastily left the room. As I went down the stairs I thought I heard the voice of the French woman in all the shrill volubility of excuse, which was met, however, by suppressed but vehement imprecations, or what seemed to me to be such, in which the voice of my cousin Edward distinctly mingled.

I joined my cousin Emily quite out of breath. I need not say that my head was too full of other things to think much of drawing for that day. I imparted to her frankly the cause of my alarms, but at the same time, as gently as I could; and with tears she promised vigilance, and devotion, and love. I never had reason for a moment to repent the unreserved confidence which I then reposed in her. She was no less surprised than I, at the unexpected appearance of Edward, whose departure for France neither of us had for a moment doubted, but which was now proved by his actual presence to be nothing more than an imposture practised, I feared, for no good end. The situation in which I had found my uncle had removed completely all my doubts as to his designs, I magnified suspicions into certainties, and dreaded night after night that I should be murdered in my bed. The nervousness produced by sleepless nights and days of anxious fears increased the horrors of my situation to such a degree, that I at length wrote a letter to a Mr Jefferies, an old and faithful friend of my father's, and perfectly acquainted with all his affairs, praying him, for God's sake, to relieve me from my present terrible situation, and communicating without reserve the nature and grounds of my suspicions. This letter I kept sealed and directed for two or three days always about my person, for discovery would have been ruinous, in expectation of an opportunity which might be safely trusted, whereby to have it placed in the post-office; as neither Emily or I were permitted to pass beyond the precincts of the demesne itself, which was surrounded by high walls formed of dry stone, the difficulty of procuring such an opportunity was greatly enhanced. At this time Emily had a short conversation with her father, which she reported to me instantly. After some indifferent matter, he had asked her whether she and I were upon good terms, and whether I was unreserved in my disposition. She answered in the affirmative; and he then inquired whether I had been much surprised to find him in my chamber on the other day. She answered that I had been both surprised and amused. 'And what did she think of George Wilson's appearance?' 'Who?' inquired she. 'Oh! the architect,' he answered, 'who is to contract for the repairs of the house; he is accounted a handsome fellow.' 'She could not see his face,' said Emily, 'and she was in such a hurry to escape that she scarcely noticed him.' Sir Arthur appeared satisfied, and the conversation ended.

This slight conversation repeated accurately to me by Emily, had the effect of confirming, if indeed any thing was required to do so, all that I had before believed as to Edward's actual presence; and I naturally became, if possible, more anxious than ever to despatch the letter to Mr Jefferies. An opportunity at length occurred. As Emily and I were walking one day near the gate of the demesne, a lad from the village happened to be passing down the avenue from the house; the spot was secluded, and as this person was not connected by service with those whose observation I dreaded, I committed the letter to his keeping, with strict injunctions that he should put it without delay into the receiver of the town post-office; at the same time I added a suitable gratuity, and the man having made many protestations of punctuality, was soon out of sight. He was hardly gone when I began to doubt my discretion in having trusted this person; but I had no better or safer means of despatching the letter, and I was not warranted in suspecting him of such wanton dishonesty as an inclination to tamper with it; but I could not be quite satisfied of its safety until I received an answer, which could not arrive for a few days. Before I did, however, an event occurred which a little surprised me. I was sitting in my bed-room early in the day, reading by myself, when I heard a knock at the door. 'Come in,' said I, and my uncle entered the room. 'Will you excuse me,' said he, 'I sought you in the parlour, and thence I have come here. I desired to say a word with you. I trust that you have hitherto found my conduct to you such as that of a guardian towards his ward should be.' I dared not withhold my assent. 'And,' he continued, 'I trust that you have not found me harsh or unjust, and that you have perceived, my dear niece, that I have sought to make this poor place as agreeable to you as may be?' I assented again; and he put his hand in his pocket, whence he drew a folded paper, and dashing it upon the table with startling emphasis he said, 'did you write that letter?' The sudden and fearful alteration of his voice, manner, and face, but more than all, the unexpected production of my letter to Mr Jefferies, which I at once recognised, so confounded and terrified me, that I felt almost choking. I could not utter a word. 'Did you write that letter?' he repeated with slow and intense emphasis. 'You did, liar and hypocrite. You dared to write this foul and infamous libel; but it shall be your last. Men will universally believe you mad, if I choose to call for an inquiry. I can make you appear so. The suspicions expressed in this letter are the hallucinations and alarms of moping lunacy. I have defeated your first attempt, madam; and by the holy God, if ever you make another, chains, straw, darkness, and the keeper's whip shall be your lasting portion.' With these astounding words he left the room, leaving me almost fainting.

I was now almost reduced to despair—my last cast had failed—I had no course left, but that of eloping secretly from the castle, and placing myself under the protection of the nearest magistrate. I felt if this were not done, and speedily, that I should be *murdered*. No one, from mere description, can have an idea of the unmitigated horror of my situation—a helpless, weak, inexperienced girl, placed under the power, and wholly at the mercy of evil men, and feeling that she had it not in her power to escape for a moment from the malignant influences under which she was probably fated to fall—and with a consciousness that if violence, if murder were designed, her dying shriek would be lost in void space—no human being would be near to aid her—no human interposition could deliver her.

I had seen Edward but once during his visit, and as I did not meet with him again, I began to think that he must have taken his departure—a conviction which was to a certain degree satisfactory, as I regarded his absence as indicating the

removal of immediate danger. Emily also arrived circuitously
at the same conclusion, and not without good grounds, for
she managed indirectly to learn that Edward's black horse
had actually been for a day and part of a night in the castle
stables, just at the time of her brother's supposed visit. The
horse had gone, and as she argued, the rider must have departed with it. This point being so far settled, I felt a little
less uncomfortable; when being one day alone in my bed-
room, I happened to look out from the window, and to my
unutterable horror, I beheld peering through an opposite
casement, my cousin Edward's face. Had I seen the evil one
himself in bodily shape, I could not have experienced a more
sickening revulsion. I was too much appaled to move at once
from the window, but I did so soon enough to avoid his eye.
He was looking fixedly into the narrow quadrangle upon
which the window opened. I shrunk back unperceived, to
pass the rest of the day in terror and despair. I went to my
room early that night, but I was too miserable to sleep. At
about twelve o'clock, feeling very nervous, I determined to
call my cousin Emily, who slept, you will remember, in the
next room, which communicated with mine by a second door.
By this private entrance I found my way into her chamber,
and without difficulty persuaded her to return to my room
and sleep with me. We accordingly lay down together, she
undressed, and I with my clothes on, for I was every moment
walking up and down the room, and felt too nervous and
miserable to think of rest or comfort. Emily was soon fast
asleep, and I lay awake, fervently longing for the first pale
gleam of morning, reckoning every stroke of the old clock
with an impatience which made every hour appear like six.
It must have been about one o'clock when I thought I heard
a slight noise at the partition door between Emily's room and
mine, as if caused by somebody's turning the key in the lock.
I held my breath, and the same sound was repeated at the
second door of my room—that which opened upon the lobby
—the sound was here distinctly caused by the revolution of
the bolt in the lock, and it was followed by a slight pressure
upon the door itself, as if to ascertain the security of the lock.
The person, whoever it might be, was probably satisfied, for

I heard the old boards of the lobby creak and strain, as if under the weight of somebody moving cautiously over them. My sense of hearing became unnaturally, almost painfully acute. I suppose the imagination added distinctness to sounds vague in themselves. I thought that I could actually hear the breathing of the person who was slowly returning down the lobby; at the head of the stair-case there appeared to occur a pause; and I could distinctly hear two or three sentences hastily whispered; the steps then descended the stairs with apparently less caution. I now ventured to walk quickly and lightly to the lobby door, and attempted to open it; it was indeed fast locked upon the outside, as was also the other. I now felt that the dreadful hour was come; but one desperate expedient remained—it was to awaken Emily, and by our united strength, to attempt to force the partition door, which was slighter than the other, and through this to pass to the lower part of the house, whence it might be possible to escape to the grounds, and forth to the village. I returned to the bed-side, and shook Emily, but in vain; nothing that I could do availed to produce from her more than a few incoherent words—it was a death-like sleep. She had certainly drank of some narcotic, as had I probably also, spite of all the caution with which I had examined every thing presented to us to eat or drink. I now attempted, with as little noise as possible, to force first one door, then the other—but all in vain. I believe no strength could have effected my object, for both doors opened inwards. I therefore collected whatever moveables I could carry thither, and piled them against the doors, so as to assist me in whatever attempts I should make to resist the entrance of those without. I then returned to the bed and endeavoured again, but fruitlessly, to awaken my cousin. It was not sleep, it was torpor, lethargy, death. I knelt down and prayed with an agony of earnestness; and then seating myself upon the bed, I awaited my fate with a kind of terrible tranquility.

I heard a faint clanking sound from the narrow court which I have already mentioned, as if caused by the scraping of some iron instrument against stones or rubbish. I at first determined not to disturb the calmness which I now felt, by uselessly watching the proceedings of those who sought my life; but as

the sounds continued, the horrible curiosity which I felt overcame every other emotion, and I determined, at all hazards, to
gratify it. I, therefore, crawled upon my knees to the window, so as to let the smallest portion of my head appear above
the sill. The moon was shining with an uncertain radiance
upon the antique grey buildings, and obliquely upon the narrow court beneath, one side of which was therefore clearly
illuminated, while the other was lost in obscurity, the sharp
outlines of the old gables, with their nodding clusters of ivy,
being at first alone visible. Whoever or whatever occasioned
the noise which had excited my curiosity, was concealed under
the shadow of the dark side of the quadrangle. I placed my
hand over my eyes to shade them from the moonlight, which
was so bright as to be almost dazzling, and, peering into the
darkness, I first dimly, but afterwards gradually, almost with
full distinctness, beheld the form of a man engaged in digging
what appeared to be a rude hole close under the wall. Some
implements, probably a shovel and pickaxe, lay beside him, and
to these he every now and then applied himself as the nature
of the ground required. He pursued his task rapidly, and with
as little noise as possible. 'So,' thought I, as shovelful after
shovelful the dislodged rubbish mounted into a heap, 'they
are digging the grave in which, before two hours pass, I must
lie, a cold, mangled corpse. I am *their's*—I cannot escape.' I
felt as if my reason was leaving me. I started to my feet, and
in mere despair I applied myself again to each of the two
doors alternately. I strained every nerve and sinew, but I might
as well have attempted, with my single strength, to force the
building itself from its foundation. I threw myself madly upon
the ground, and clasped my hands over my eyes as if to shut
out the horrible images which crowded upon me. The paroxysm passed away. I prayed once more with the bitter, agonised
fervour of one who feels that the hour of death is present and
inevitable. When I arose, I went once more to the window and
looked out, just in time to see a shadowy figure glide stealthily along the wall. The task was finished. The catastrophe of
the tragedy must soon be accomplished. I determined now to
defend my life to the last; and that I might be able to do so
with some effect, I searched the room for something which

might serve as a weapon; but either through accident, or from an anticipation of such a possibility, every thing which might have been made available for such a purpose had been carefully removed. I must then die tamely and without an effort to defend myself. A thought suddenly struck me—might it not be possible to escape through the door, which the assassin must open in order to enter the room? I resolved to make the attempt. I felt assured that the door through which ingress to the room would be effected was that which opened upon the lobby. It was the more direct way, besides being, for obvious reasons, less liable to interruption than the other. I resolved, then, to place myself behind a projection of the wall, whose shadow would serve fully to conceal me, and when the door should be opened, and before they should have discovered the identity of the occupant of the bed, to creep noiselessly from the room, and then to trust to Providence for escape. In order to facilitate this scheme, I removed all the lumber which I had heaped against the door; and I had nearly completed my arrangements, when I perceived the room suddenly darkened, by the close approach of some shadowy object to the window. On turning my eyes in that direction, I observed at the top of the casement, as if suspended from above, first the feet, then the legs, then the body, and at length the whole figure of a man present itself. It was Edward T——n. He appeared to be guiding his descent so as to bring his feet upon the centre of the stone block which occupied the lower part of the window; and having secured his footing upon this, he kneeled down and began to gaze into the room. As the moon was gleaming into the chamber, and the bed curtains were drawn, he was able to distinguish the bed itself and its contents. He appeared satisfied with his scrutiny, for he looked up and made a sign with his hand, upon which the rope by which his descent had been effected was slackened from above, and he proceeded to disengage it from his waist: this accomplished, he applied his hands to the window-frame, which must have been ingeniously contrived for the purpose, for with apparently no resistance the whole frame, containing casement and all, slipped from its position in the wall, and was by him lowered into the room. The cold night wind waved the bed-curtains, and he paused for a moment—all was still again—and he stepped in upon the floor of the room. He held in his hand what appeared to be a steel instrument, shaped something like a hammer, but larger and sharper at the extremities. This he held rather behind him, while, with three long, *tip-toe* strides, he brought himself to the bedside. I felt that the discovery must now be made, and held my breath in momentary expectation of the execration in which he would vent his surprise and disappointment. I closed my eyes—there was a pause—but it was a short one. I heard two dull blows, given in rapid succession: a quivering sigh, and the long-drawn, heavy breathing of the sleeper was for ever suspended. I unclosed my eyes, and saw the murderer fling the quilt across the head of his victim: he then, with the instrument of death still in his hand, proceeded to the lobby door, upon which he tapped sharply twice or thrice—a quick step was then heard approaching, and a voice whispered something from without—Edward answered, with a kind of chuckle, 'her ladyship is past complaining; unlock the door, in the devil's name, unless you're afraid to come in, and help me to lift the body out of the window.' The key was turned in the lock —the door opened—and my uncle entered the room. I have told you already that I had placed myself under the shade of a projection of the wall, close to the door. I had instinctively shrunk down cowering towards the ground on the entrance of Edward through the window. When my uncle entered the room he and his son both stood so very close to me that his hand was every moment upon the point of touching my face. I held my breath, and remained motionless as death.

'You had no interruption from the next room?' said my uncle.

'No,' was the brief reply.

'Secure the jewels, Ned; the French harpy must not lay her claws upon them. You're a steady hand, by G—; not much blood—eh?'

'Not twenty drops,' replied his son, 'and those on the quilt.'

'I'm glad it's over,' whispered my uncle again—'we must lift the—the *thing* through the window, and lay the rubbish over it.'

They then turned to the bedside, and, winding the bed-clothes round the body, carried it between them slowly to the window, and, exchanging a few brief words with some one below, they shoved it over the window sill, and I heard it fall heavily on the ground underneath.

'I'll take the jewels,' said my uncle; 'there are two caskets in the lower drawer.'

He proceeded with an accuracy which, had I been more at ease, would have furnished me with matter of astonishment, to lay his hand upon the very spot where my jewels lay; and having possessed himself of them, he called to his son—

'Is the rope made fast above?'

'I'm not a fool—to be sure it is,' replied he.

They then lowered themselves from the window. I now rose lightly and cautiously, scarcely daring to breathe, from my place of concealment, and was creeping towards the door, when I heard my cousin's voice, in a sharp whisper, exclaim, 'Scramble up again; G—d d—n you, you've forgot to lock the room door'; and I perceived, by the straining of the rope which hung from above, that the mandate was instantly obeyed. Not a second was to be lost. I passed through the door, which was only closed, and moved as rapidly as I could, consistently with stillness, along the lobby. Before I had gone many yards, I heard the door through which I had just passed double locked on the inside. I glided down the stairs in terror, lest, at every corner, I should meet the murderer or one of his accomplices. I reached the hall, and listened for a moment to ascertain whether all was silent around; no sound was audible; the parlour windows opened on the park, and through one of them I might, I thought, easily effect my escape. Accordingly, I hastily entered; but, to my consternation, a candle was burning in the room, and by its light I saw a figure seated at the dinner table, upon which lay glasses, bottles, and the other accompaniments of a drinking party. Two or three chairs were placed about the table, irregularly, as if hastily abandoned by their occupants. A single glance satisfied me that the figure was that of my French attendant. She was fast asleep, having probably drank deeply. There was something malignant and ghastly in the calmness of this bad woman's features, dimly

illuminated as they were by the flickering blaze of the candle.
A knife lay upon the table, and the terrible thought struck
me—'Should I kill this sleeping accomplice in the guilt of
the murderer, and thus secure my retreat?' Nothing could be
easier—it was but to draw the blade across her throat—the
work of a second. An instant's pause, however, corrected
me—'No,' thought I, 'the God who has conducted me thus
far through the valley of the shadow of death, will not abandon me now. I will fall into their hands, or I will escape
hence, but it shall be free from the stain of blood—His will
be done.' I felt a confidence arising from this reflection, an
assurance of protection which I cannot describe. There was
no other means of escape, so I advanced, with a firm step and
collected mind, to the window. I noiselessly withdrew the
bars, and unclosed the shutters—I pushed open the casement,
and, without waiting to look behind me, I ran with my utmost
speed, scarcely feeling the ground under me, down the avenue,
taking care to keep upon the grass which bordered it. I did
not for a moment slack my speed, and I had now gained the
centre point between the park-gate and the mansion house—
here the avenue made a wider circuit, and in order to avoid
delay, I directed my way across the smooth sward round
which the pathway wound, intending, at the opposite side of
the flat, at a point which I distinguished by a group of old
birch trees, to enter again upon the beaten track, which was
from thence tolerably direct to the gate. I had, with my utmost
speed, got about half way across this broad flat, when the
rapid treading of a horse's hoofs struck upon my ear. My
heart swelled in my bosom, as though I would smother. The
clattering of galloping hoofs approached—I was pursued—
they were now upon the sward on which I was running—
there was not a bush or a bramble to shelter me—and, as if
to render escape altogether desperate, the moon, which had
hitherto been obscured, at this moment shone forth with a
broad clear light, which made every object distinctly visible.
The sounds were now close behind me. I felt my knees bending under me, with the sensation which torments one in
dreams. I reeled—I stumbled—I fell—and at the same instant

the cause of my alarm wheeled past me at full gallop. It was one of the young filleys which pastured loose about the park, whose frolics had thus all but maddened me with terror. I scrambled to my feet, and rushed on with weak but rapid steps, my sportive companion still galloping round and round me with many a frisk and fling, until, at length, more dead than alive, I reached the avenue-gate and crossed the stile, I scarce knew how. I ran through the village, in which all was silent as the grave, until my progress was arrested by the hoarse voice of a sentinel, who cried, 'Who goes there?' I felt that I was now safe. I turned in the direction of the voice, and fell fainting at the soldier's feet. When I came to myself, I was sitting in a miserable hovel, surrounded by strange faces, all bespeaking curiosity and compassion. Many soldiers were in it also: indeed, as I afterwards found, it was employed as a guard-room by a detachment of troops quartered for that night in the town. In a few words I informed their officer of the circumstances which had occurred, describing also the appearance of the persons engaged in the murder; and he, without loss of time, proceeded to the mansion-house of Carrickleigh, taking with him a party of his men. But the villains had discovered their mistake, and had effected their escape, before the arrival of the military.

The Frenchwoman was, however, arrested in the neighbourhood upon the next day. She was tried and condemned upon the ensuing assizes; and previous to her execution confessed that '*she had a hand in making Hugh Tisdall's bed.*' She had been a housekeeper in the castle at the time, and a kind of *chere amie* of my uncle's. She was, in reality, able to speak English like a native, but had exclusively used the French language, I suppose to facilitate her disguise. She died the same hardened wretch which she had lived, confessing her crimes only, as she alleged, that her doing so might involve Sir Arthur T——n, the great author of her guilt and misery, and whom she now regarded with unmitigated detestation.

With the particulars of Sir Arthur's and his son's escape, as far as they are known, you are acquainted. You are also in possession of their after fate—the terrible, the tremendous retribution which, after long delays of many years, finally over-took and crushed them. Wonderful and inscrutable are the dealings of God with his creatures.

Deep and fervent as must always be my gratitude to Heaven for my deliverance, effected by a chain of providential occur-rences, the failing of a single link of which must have ensured my destruction, I was long before I could look back upon it with other feelings than those of bitterness, almost of agony. The only being that had ever really loved me, my nearest and dearest friend, ever ready to sympathise, to counsel, and to assist—the gayest, the gentlest, the warmest heart—the only creature on earth that cared for me—*her* life had been the price of my deliverance; and I then uttered the wish, which no event of my long and sorrowful life has taught me to re-call, that she had been spared, and that, in her stead, *I* were mouldering in the grave, forgotten and at rest.

APPENDIX A

PRELIMINARIES FOR *THE VAMPYRE*

PUBLISHED in the April 1819 issue of the *New Monthly Magazine* (old series: 11/63, 193–6), the three sections that make up these 'Preliminaries' appeared immediately before *The Vampyre* and under the heading 'Original Communications'. The brief opening editorial statement is by the *New Monthly* sub-editor Alaric Watts, except that the last sentence belongs to the magazine's owner Henry Colburn. The 'Extract of a Letter from Geneva' has been attributed to a number of writers. W. M. Rossetti ascribes it to Madame Gatelier, and is partially endorsed by Rieger. Byron thought it belonged to Polidori, and the case for Polidori's authorship has been made again by Grudin. But, as Macdonald points out, Polidori's protests to Colburn at the time of publication, and the fact that he crossed out the 'Extract' in his own copy of *The Vampyre*, suggest he is not responsible. Macdonald proposes the minor and somewhat unscrupulous hack writer John Mitford, whose *Private Life of Lord Byron* appeared in 1828 (*The Diary of Dr John William Polidori*, ed. W. M. Rossetti (London, 1911), 13; James Rieger, 'Dr. Polidori and the Genesis of *Frankenstein*' in *Studies in English Literature*, 3 (1963), 461; *Byron's Letters and Journals*, ed. L. A. Marchand (12 vols.; London, 1973–82), vi. 125–7; Peter D. Grudin, *The Demon Lover* (New York, 1987), 74–7; Macdonald, *Poor Polidori*, 184, 276).

The final section on the history of the vampire probably belongs to either Mitford or Watts; the 'ED.' signature indicates Watts.

(We received several private letters in the course of last autumn from a friend travelling on the Continent, and among others the following, which we give to the public on account of its containing anecdotes of an Individual, concerning whom the most trifling circumstances, if they tend to mark even the minor features of his mind, cannot fail of being considered important and valuable by those who know how to appreciate his erratic but transcendent genius. The tale which accompanied the letter we have also much pleasure in presenting to our readers.—*Ed.*)

EXTRACT OF A LETTER FROM GENEVA,
WITH ANECDOTES OF LORD BYRON, &C.

'I BREATHE freely in the neighbourhood of this lake; the ground upon which I tread has been subdued from the earliest ages; the principal objects which immediately strike my eye, bring to my recollection, scenes, in which man acted the hero and was the chief object of interest. Not to look back to earlier times of battles and sieges, here is the bust of Rousseau —here is the house with an inscription denoting that the Genevan philosopher first drew breath under its roof.* A little out of the town is Ferney the residence of Voltaire; where that wonderful, though certainly in many respects contemptible, character, received, like the hermits of old, the visits of pilgrims, not only from his own nation, but from the farthest boundaries of Europe.* Here too is Bonnet's abode,* and, a few steps beyond, the house of that astonishing woman Madame de Stael,* perhaps the first of her sex, who has really proved its often claimed equality with the nobler man. We have had before, women who have written interesting novels and poems, in which their tact at observing drawing-room characters has availed them; but never since the days of Heloise have those faculties which are peculiar to man, been developed as the possible inheritance of woman. Though even here, as in the case of Heloise, our sex have not been backward in alleging the existence of an Abeilard in the person of M. Schlegel as the inspirer of her works.* But to proceed: upon the same side of the lake, Gibbon, Bonnivard, Bradshaw* and others, mark, as it were, the stages for our progress; whilst upon the other side there is one house built by Diodati, the friend of Milton,* which has contained within its walls, for several months, that poet whom we have so often read together, and who—if human passions remain the same, and human feelings, like chords, on being swept by nature's impulses shall vibrate as before—will be placed by posterity in the first rank of our English Poets. You must have heard, or the Third Canto of Childe Harold will have informed you, that Lord Byron resided many months in this neighbourhood.* I went with some friends a few days ago, after having seen Ferney, to view this mansion. I trod the floors with the same feelings of awe and respect as we did, together, those of Shakspeare's dwelling at Stratford. I sat down in a chair of the saloon, and satisfied myself that I was resting on what he had made his constant seat. I found a servant there who had lived with him; she, however, gave me but little information. She pointed out his bed-chamber upon the same level as the saloon and dining-room, and informed me that he retired to rest at three, got up at two, and employed himself a long time over his toilette; that he never went to sleep without a pair of pistols and a dagger by his side, and that he never eat animal food. He apparently spent some part of every day upon the lake in an English boat.* There is a balcony from the saloon which looks upon the lake and the mountain Jura; and, I imagine, that it must have been hence, he contemplated the storm so magnificently described in the Third Canto; for you have from here a most extensive view of all the points he has therein depicted. I can fancy him like the scathed pine, whilst all around was sunk to repose, still waking to observe, what gave but a weak image of the storms which had desolated his own breast.

> The sky is changed!—and such a change; Oh, night!
> And storm and darkness, ye are wond'rous strong,
> Yet lovely in your strength, as is the light
> Of a dark eye in woman! Far along
> From peak to peak, the rattling crags among,
> Leaps the live thunder! Not from one lone cloud,
> But every mountain now hath found a tongue,
> And Jura answers thro' her misty shroud,
> Back to the joyous Alps who call to her aloud!
>
> And this is in the night:—Most glorious night!
> Thou wer't not sent for slumber! let me be
> A sharer in thy far and fierce delight,—
> A portion of the tempest and of me!*
> How the lit lake shines a phosphoric sea,
> And the big rain comes dancing to the earth!
> And now again 'tis black,—and now the glee
> Of the loud hill shakes with its mountain mirth,
> As if they did rejoice o'er a young earthquake's birth.
>
> Now where the swift Rhine* cleaves his way between
> Heights which appear, as lovers who have parted

In haste, whose mining depths so intervene,
That they can meet no more, tho' broken hearted;
Tho' in their souls which thus each other thwarted,
Love was the very root of the fond rage
Which blighted their life's bloom, and then departed—
Itself expired, but leaving them an age
Of years all winter—war within themselves to wage.

I went down to the little port, if I may use the expression,
wherein his vessel used to lay, and conversed with the cot-
tager, who had the care of it. You may smile, but I have my
pleasure in thus helping my personification of the individual
I admire, by attaining to the knowledge of those circumstances which were daily around him. I have made numerous
enquiries in the town concerning him, but can learn nothing.
He only went into society there once, when M. Pictet took
him to the house of a lady to spend the evening. They say he
is a very singular man, and seem to think him very uncivil.
Amongst other things they relate, that having invited M. Pictet
and Bonstetten to dinner, he went on the lake to Chillon,
leaving a gentleman who travelled with him to receive them,
and make his apologies.* Another evening, being invited to
the house of Lady D—— H——,* he promised to attend,
but upon approaching the windows of her ladyship's villa,
and perceiving the room to be full of company, he put down
his friend, desiring him to plead his excuse, and immediately
returned home. This will serve as a contradiction to the report
which you tell me is current in England, of his having been
avoided by his countrymen on the continent. The case happens to be directly the reverse, as he has been generally sought
after by them, though on most occasions, apparently without
success. It is said, indeed, that upon paying his first visit at
Coppet, following the servant who had announced his name,
he was surprised to meet a lady carried out fainting; but
before he had been seated many minutes, the same lady, who
had been so affected at the sound of his name, returned and
conversed with him a considerable time—such is female curiosity and affectation! He visited Coppet frequently, and of
course associated there with several of his countrymen, who
evinced no reluctance to meet him whom his enemies alone
would represent as an outcast.*

Though I have been so unsuccessful in this town, I have
been more fortunate in my enquiries elsewhere. There is a
society three or four miles from Geneva, the centre of which
is the Countess of Breuss, a Russian lady, well acquainted
with the *agrémens de la Société*, and who has collected them
round herself at her mansion. It was chiefly here, I find, that
the gentleman who travelled with Lord Byron, as physician,
sought for society.* He used almost every day to cross the
lake by himself, in one of their flat-bottomed boats, and
return after passing the evening with his friends about eleven
or twelve at night, often whilst the storms were raging in the
circling summits of the mountains around. As he became intimate, from long acquaintance, with several of the families
in this neighbourhood, I have gathered from their accounts
some excellent traits of his lordship's character, which I will
relate to you at some future opportunity. I must, however,
free him from one imputation attached to him—of having in
his house two sisters as the partakers of his revels. This is,
like many other charges which have been brought against his
lordship, entirely destitute of truth. His only companion was
the physician I have already mentioned. The report originated
from the following circumstance: Mr Percy Bysshe Shelly, a
gentleman well known for extravagance of doctrine, and for
his daring in their profession, even to sign himself with the title
of Aθεος in the Album at Chamouny,* having taken a house
below, in which he resided with Miss M. W. Godwin and
Miss Clermont, (the daughters of the celebrated Mr Godwin*)
they were frequently visitors at Diodati, and were often seen
upon the lake with his Lordship, which gave rise to the
report, the truth of which is here positively denied.

Among other things which the lady, from whom I procured
these anecdotes, related to me, she mentioned the outline of
a ghost story by Lord Byron. It appears that one evening Lord
B., Mr P. B. Shelly, the two ladies and the gentleman before
alluded to, after having perused a German work, which was
entitled Phantasmagoriana,* began relating ghost stories; when
his lordship having recited the beginning of Christabel, then
unpublished, the whole took so strong a hold of Mr Shelly's
mind, that he suddenly started up and ran out of the room.
The physician and Lord Byron followed, and discovered him

leaning against a mantle-piece, with cold drops of perspiration trickling down his face. After having given him something to refresh him, upon enquiring into the cause of his alarm, they found that his wild imagination having pictured to him the bosom of one of the ladies with eyes (which was reported of a lady in the neighbourhood where he lived) he was obliged to leave the room in order to destroy the impression.* It was afterwards proposed, in the course of conversation, that each of the company present should write a tale depending upon some supernatural agency, which was undertaken by Lord B., the physician, and Miss M. W. Godwin. My friend, the lady above referred to, had in her possession the outline of each of these stories; I obtained them as a great favour, and herewith forward them to you, as I was assured you would feel as much curiosity as myself, to peruse the *ebauches** of so great a genius, and those immediately under his influence.'†

(The superstition upon which this tale is founded is very general in the East. Among the Arabians it appears to be common: it did not, however, extend itself to the Greeks until after the establishment of Christianity; and it has only assumed its present form since the division of the Latin and Greek churches; at which time, the idea becoming prevalent, that a Latin body could not corrupt if buried in their territory, it gradually increased, and formed the subject of many wonderful stories, still extant, of the dead rising from their graves, and feeding upon the blood of the young and beautiful. In the West it spread, with some slight variation, all over Hungary, Poland, Austria, and Lorraine, where the belief existed, that vampyres nightly imbibed a certain portion of the blood of their victims, who became emaciated, lost their strength, and speedily died of consumptions; whilst these human bloodsuckers fattened—and their veins became distended to such a state of repletion as to cause the blood to flow from all the

---

† We have in our possession the Tale of Dr ——, as well as the outline of that of Miss Godwin. The latter has already appeared under the title of 'Frankenstein, or the modern Prometheus'; the former, however, upon consulting with its author, we may, probably, hereafter give to our readers.—ED.*

passages of their bodies, and even from the very pores of their skins.

In the London Journal of March, 1732, is a curious, and of course *credible* account of a particular case of vampyrism, which is stated to have occurred at Madreyga, in Hungary.* It appears, that upon an examination of the commander in chief and magistrates of the place, they positively and unanimously affirmed that, about five years before, a certain Heyduke, named Arnold Paul, had been heard to say, that, at Cassovia, on the frontiers of the Turkish Servia, he had been tormented by a vampyre, but had found a way to rid himself of the evil, by eating some of the earth out of the vampyre's grave, and rubbing himself with his blood. This precaution, however, did not prevent him from becoming a vampyre[†] himself; for, about twenty or thirty days after his death and burial, many persons complained of having been tormented by him, and a deposition was made, that four persons had been deprived of life by his attacks. To prevent further mischief, the inhabitants having consulted their Hadagni,[‡] took up the body, and found it (as is supposed to be usual in cases of vampyrism) fresh, and entirely free from corruption, and emitting at the mouth, nose, and ears, pure and florid blood. Proof having been thus obtained, they resorted to the accustomed remedy. A stake was driven entirely through the heart and body of Arnold Paul, at which he is reported to have cried out as dreadfully as if he had been alive. This done, they cut off his head, burned his body, and threw the ashes into his grave. The same measures were adopted with the corses of those persons who had previously died from vampyrism, lest they should, in their turn, become agents upon others who survived them.

We have related this monstrous rodomontade, because it seems better adapted to illustrate the subject of the present observations than any other instance we could adduce. In many parts of Greece it is considered as a sort of punishment after death, for some heinous crime committed whilst in existence,

---

[†] The universal belief is, that a person sucked by a vampyre becomes a vampyre himself, and sucks in his turn.
[‡] Chief bailiff.

that the deceased is doomed to vampyrise, but be compelled to confine his infernal visitations solely to those beings he loved most while upon earth—those to whom he was bound by ties of kindred and affection. This supposition is, we imagine, alluded to in the following fearfully sublime and prophetic curse from the 'Giaour.'*

> But first on earth, as Vampyre sent,
> Thy corse shall from its tomb be rent;
> Then ghastly haunt thy native place,
> And suck the blood of all thy race;
> There from thy *daughter, sister, wife,*
> At midnight drain the stream of life;
> *Yet loathe the banquet, which perforce*
> Must feed thy livid living corse.
> Thy victims, ere they yet expire,
> Shall know the demon for their sire;
> As cursing thee, thou cursing them,
> Thy flowers are withered on the stem.
> But one that for *thy crime* must fall,
> The youngest, best beloved of all,
> Shall bless thee with a *father's* name—
> That word shall wrap thy heart in flame!
> Yet thou must end thy task and mark
> Her cheek's last tinge—her eye's last spark,
> And the last glassy glance must view
> Which freezes o'er its lifeless blue;
> Then with unhallowed hand shall tear
> The tresses of her yellow hair,
> Of which, in life a lock when shorn
> Affection's fondest pledge was worn—
> But now is borne away by thee
> Memorial of thine agony!
> Yet with thine own best blood shall drip
> Thy gnashing tooth, and haggard lip;
> Then stalking to thy sullen grave,
> Go—and with Gouls and Afrits rave,
> Till these in horror shrink away
> From spectre more accursed than they.

Mr Southey has also introduced in his wild but beautiful poem of 'Thalaba', the vampyre corse of the Arabian maid Oneiza, who is represented as having returned from the grave for the purpose of tormenting him she best loved whilst in existence.* But this cannot be supposed to have resulted from the sinfulness of her life, she being pourtrayed throughout the whole of the tale as a complete type of purity and innocence. The veracious Tournefort gives a long account in his travels of several astonishing cases of vampyrism, to which he pretends to have been an eye-witness; and Calmet,* in his great work upon this subject, besides a variety of anecdotes, and traditionary narratives illustrative of its effects, has put forth some learned dissertations, tending to prove it to be a classical, as well as barbarian error.

We could add many curious and interesting notices on this singularly horrible superstition, and we may, perhaps, resume our observations upon it at some future opportunity; for the present, we feel that we have very far exceeded the limits of a note, necessarily devoted to the explanation of the strange production to which we now invite the attention of our readers; and we shall therefore conclude by merely remarking, that though the term Vampyre is the one in most general acceptation, there are several others synonimous with it, which are made use of in various parts of the world, namely, Vroucolocha, Vardoulacha, Goul, Broucoloka, &c.—ED.)

APPENDIX B
NOTE ON *THE VAMPYRE*

John Polidori

THIS note by John Polidori was published as part of the Introduction to his only full-length novel, *Ernestus Berchtold*, which appeared, like *The Vampyre*, in 1819. The note is appended to the opening sentence, which reads: 'The tale here presented to the public is the one I began at Coligny, when Frankenstein was planned, and when a noble author having determined to descend from his lofty range, gave up a few hours to a tale of terror, and wrote the fragment published at the end of Mazeppa.'

THE tale which lately appeared, and to which his lordship's name was wrongfully attached, was founded upon the groundwork upon which this fragment was to have been continued. Two friends were to travel from England into Greece; while there, one of them should die, but before his death, should obtain from his friend an oath of secrecy with regard to his decease. Some short time after, the remaining traveller returning to his native country, should be startled at perceiving his former companion moving about in society, and should be horrified at finding that he made love to his former friend's sister. Upon this foundation I built the Vampyre, at the request of a lady, who denied the possibility of such a ground-work forming the outline of a tale which should bear the slightest appearance of probability. In the course of three mornings, I produced that tale, and left it with her. From thence it appears to have fallen into the hands of some person, who sent it to the Editor in such a way, as to leave it so doubtful from his words, whether it was his lordship's or not, that I found some difficulty in vindicating it to myself. These circumstances were stated in a letter sent to the Morning Chronicle three days after the publication of the tale, but in consequence of the publishers representing to me that they were compromised as well as myself, and that immediately they were certain it was mine, that they themselves would wish to make the *amende honorable* to the public, I allowed them to recall the letter which had lain some days at that paper's office.

APPENDIX C
AUGUSTUS DARVELL

Lord Byron

THIS tale by Lord Byron is his contribution to the ghost story competition of 1816, and was first published at the end of his *Mazeppa*
(1819), where it was entitled 'A FRAGMENT' and dated '*June* 17, 1816'.
Byron sent the tale to his publisher John Murray shortly after *The
Vampyre* appeared, in order to demonstrate 'how far it resembles
Mr. Colburn's publication'. He instructed Murray: 'If you choose to
publish it in the Edinburgh Magazine (*Wilsons & Blackwoods*) you
may—*stating why*, & with such explanatory proem as you please.'
Murray apparently decided not to publish it in *Blackwood's*, and instead appended it to *Mazeppa*, though without a 'proem' or Byron's
permission, a decision that clearly irked Byron even a year later: 'I
shall not allow you to play the tricks you did last year with the prose
you *post*scribed to Mazeppa—which I sent to you *not* to be published if not in a periodical paper, & there you tacked it without a
word of explanation and be damned to you' (Byron, *Letters*, vi. 126;
vii. 58).

IN THE year 17—, having for some time determined on a
journey through countries not hitherto much frequented by
travellers, I set out, accompanied by a friend, whom I shall
designate by the name of Augustus Darvell. He was a few
years my elder, and a man of considerable fortune and ancient
family—advantages which an extensive capacity prevented him
alike from undervaluing or overrating. Some peculiar circumstances in his private history had rendered him to me an object
of attention, of interest, and even of regard, which neither the
reserve of his manners, nor occasional indications of an inqui-
etude at times nearly approaching to alienation of mind, could
extinguish.

I was yet young in life, which I had begun early; but my
intimacy with him was of a recent date: we had been educated
at the same schools and university; but his progress through

these had preceded mine, and he had been deeply initiated into what is called the world, while I was yet in my noviciate. While thus engaged, I had heard much both of his past and present life; and although in these accounts there were many and irreconcileable contradictions, I could still gather from the whole that he was a being of no common order, and one who, whatever pains he might take to avoid remark, would still be remarkable. I had cultivated his acquaintance subsequently, and endeavoured to obtain his friendship, but this last appeared to be unattainable; whatever affections he might have possessed seemed now, some to have been extinguished, and others to be concentred: that his feelings were acute, I had sufficient opportunities of observing; for, although he could control, he could not altogether disguise them: still he had a power of giving to one passion the appearance of another in such a manner that it was difficult to define the nature of what was working within him; and the expressions of his features would vary so rapidly, though slightly, that it was useless to trace them to their sources. It was evident that he was a prey to some cureless disquiet; but whether it arose from ambition, love, remorse, grief, from one or all of these, or merely from a morbid temperament akin to disease, I could not discover: there were circumstances alleged, which might have justified the application to each of these causes; but, as I have before said, these were so contradictory and contradicted, that none could be fixed upon with accuracy. Where there is mystery, it is generally supposed that there must also be evil: I know not how this may be, but in him there certainly was the one, though I could not ascertain the extent of the other—and felt loth, as far as regarded himself, to believe in its existence. My advances were received with sufficient coldness; but I was young, and not easily discouraged, and at length succeeded in obtaining, to a certain degree, that common-place intercourse and moderate confidence of common and every day concerns, created and cemented by similarity of pursuit and frequency of meeting, which is called intimacy, or friendship, according to the ideas of him who uses those words to express them.

Darvell had already travelled extensively; and to him I had applied for information with regard to the conduct of my intended journey. It was my secret wish that he might be prevailed on to accompany me: it was also a probable hope, founded upon the shadowy restlessness which I had observed in him, and to which the animation which he appeared to feel on such subjects, and his apparent indifference to all by which he was more immediately surrounded, gave fresh strength. This wish I first hinted, and then expressed: his answer, though I had partly expected it, gave me all the pleasure of surprise —he consented; and, after the requisite arrangements, we commenced our voyages. After journeying through various countries of the south of Europe, our attention was turned towards the East, according to our original destination; and it was in my progress through those regions that the incident occurred upon which will turn what I may have to relate.

The constitution of Darvell, which must from his appearance have been in early life more than usually robust, had been for some time gradually giving way, without the intervention of any apparent disease: he had neither cough nor hectic,* yet he became daily more enfeebled: his habits were temperate, and he neither declined nor complained of fatigue, yet he was evidently wasting away: he became more and more silent and sleepless, and at length so seriously altered, that my alarm grew proportionate to what I conceived to be his danger.

We had determined, on our arrival at Smyrna, on an excursion to the ruins of Ephesus and Sardis,* from which I endeavoured to dissuade him in his present state of indisposition —but in vain: there appeared to be an oppression on his mind, and a solemnity in his manner, which ill corresponded with his eagerness to proceed on what I regarded as a mere party of pleasure, little suited to a valetudinarian; but I opposed him no longer—and in a few days we set off together, accompanied only by a serrugee and a single janizary.*

We had passed halfway towards the remains of Ephesus, leaving behind us the more fertile environs of Smyrna, and were entering upon that wild and tenantless track through the marshes and defiles which lead to the few huts yet lingering over the broken columns of Diana—the roofless walls of expelled Christianity, and the still more recent but complete

desolation of abandoned mosques—when the sudden and
rapid illness of my companion obliged us to halt at a Turkish
cemetery, the turbaned tombstones of which were the sole
indication that human life had ever been a sojourner in this
wilderness. The only caravansera* we had seen was left some
hours behind us, not a vestige of a town or even cottage was
within sight or hope, and this 'city of the dead' appeared to
be the sole refuge for my unfortunate friend, who seemed on
the verge of becoming the last of its inhabitants.

In this situation, I looked round for a place where he might
most conveniently repose:—contrary to the usual aspect of
Mahometan burial-grounds, the cypresses were in this few in
number, and these thinly scattered over its extent: the tombstones were mostly fallen, and worn with age:—upon one of
the most considerable of these, and beneath one of the most
spreading trees, Darvell supported himself, in a half-reclining
posture, with great difficulty. He asked for water. I had some
doubts of our being able to find any, and prepared to go in
search of it with hesitating despondency—but he desired me
to remain; and turning to Suleiman, our janizary, who stood
by us smoking with great tranquillity, he said, 'Suleiman,
verbana su,' (i.e. bring some water,) and went on describing
the spot where it was to be found with great minuteness, at
a small well for camels, a few hundred yards to the right: the
janizary obeyed. I said to Darvell, 'How did you know this?'
—He replied, 'From our situation; you must perceive that this
place was once inhabited, and could not have been so without springs: I have also been here before.'

'You have been here before!—How came you never to
mention this to me? and what could you be doing in a place
where no one would remain a moment longer than they could
help it?'

To this question I received no answer. In the mean time
Suleiman returned with the water, leaving the serrugee and
the horses at the fountain. The quenching of his thirst had
the appearance of reviving him for a moment; and I conceived
hopes of his being able to proceed, or at least to return, and
I urged the attempt. He was silent—and appeared to be col-
lecting his spirits for an effort to speak. He began.

'This is the end of my journey, and of my life—I came here to die: but I have a request to make, a command—for such my last words must be—You will observe it?'

'Most certainly; but have better hopes.'

'I have no hopes, nor wishes, but this—conceal my death from every human being.'

'I hope there will be no occasion; that you will recover, and—'

'Peace!—it must be so: promise this.'

'I do.'

'Swear it, by all that'—He here dictated an oath of great solemnity.

'There is no occasion for this—I will observe your request; and to doubt me is—'

'It cannot be helped,—you must swear.'

I took the oath: it appeared to relieve him. He removed a seal ring from his finger, on which were some Arabic characters, and presented it to me. He proceeded—

'On the ninth day of the month, at noon precisely (what month you please, but this must be the day), you must fling this ring into the salt springs which run into the Bay of Eleusis: the day after, at the same hour, you must repair to the ruins of the temple of Ceres, and wait one hour.'

'Why?'

'You will see.'

'The ninth day of the month, you say?'

'The ninth.'

As I observed that the present was the ninth day of the month, his countenance changed, and he paused. As he sate, evidently becoming more feeble, a stork, with a snake in her beak,* perched upon a tombstone near us; and, without devouring her prey, appeared to be stedfastly regarding us. I know not what impelled me to drive it away, but the attempt was useless; she made a few circles in the air, and returned exactly to the same spot. Darvell pointed to it, and smiled: he spoke—I know not whether to himself or to me—but the words were only, ''Tis well!'

'What is well? what do you mean?'

'No matter: you must bury me here this evening, and exactly where that bird is now perched. You know the rest of my injunctions.'

He then proceeded to give me several directions as to the manner in which his death might be best concealed. After these were finished, he exclaimed, 'You perceive that bird?'

'Certainly.'

'And the serpent writhing in her beak?'

'Doubtless: there is nothing uncommon in it; it is her natural prey. But it is odd that she does not devour it.'

He smiled in a ghastly manner, and said, faintly, 'It is not yet time!' As he spoke, the stork flew away. My eyes followed it for a moment, it could hardly be longer than ten might be counted. I felt Darvell's weight, as it were, increase upon my shoulder, and, turning to look upon his face, perceived that he was dead.

I was shocked with the sudden certainty which could not be mistaken—his countenance in a few minutes became nearly black. I should have attributed so rapid a change to poison, had I not been aware that he had no opportunity of receiving it unperceived. The day was declining, the body was rapidly altering, and nothing remained but to fulfil his request. With the aid of Suleiman's ataghan* and my own sabre, we scooped a shallow grave upon the spot which Darvell had indicated: the earth easily gave way, having already received some Mahometan tenant. We dug as deeply as the time permitted us, and throwing the dry earth upon all that remained of the singular being so lately departed, we cut a few sods of greener turf from the less withered soil around us, and laid them upon his sepulchre.

Between astonishment and grief, I was tearless.

BIOGRAPHICAL NOTES

Edward Bulwer (1803–73) was born in London and educated at Cambridge. He entered Parliament as a Radical in 1831, and later as a Tory in 1852, becoming Secretary for the Colonies in 1858. Upon inheriting his family's Knebworth estate in 1843, he adopted his mother's surname, becoming Edward Bulwer Lytton. He was one of the most popular novelists of the day, and published with great success in a number of different genres: historical romances like *The Last Days of Pompeii* (1834), silver-fork novels of high society like *Pelham* (1828), works of science fiction like *A Strange Story* (1862) and *The Coming Race* (1871), Newgate novels like *Paul Clifford* (1830) and *Eugene Aram* (1832), and novels of middle-class domestic life, including *The Caxtons* (1849) and *What Will He Do With It?* (1858). He also wrote eleven volumes of poetry, hugely successful plays, and a pioneering sociological study, *England and the English* (1833). Bulwer was editor of the *New Monthly Magazine* from 1831 to 1833; later, some of his best fiction was serialized in *Blackwood's*. See James Campbell, *Edward Bulwer-Lytton* (Boston, 1986).

William Carleton (1794–1869), a native of County Tyrone, Northern Ireland, received little formal education and spent a good deal of his youth wandering the Irish countryside. At 17 he prepared for the Catholic priesthood, but converted to the Church of Ireland some time before 1830. His keen observation of rural life is evident in his two series of *Traits and Stories of the Irish Peasantry* (1830 and 1833), and in *Tales of Ireland* (1834). He wrote several novels, including *Fardorougha the Miser* (1839), *Rody the Rover; or, the Ribbonman* (1845), and *The Evil Eye* (1860), as well as more than seventy tales, poems, and essays for a dozen Irish periodicals, including *The Christian Examiner*, *The Dublin Literary Gazette*, and *The Dublin University Magazine*. See Eileen A. Sullivan, *William Carleton* (Boston, 1983).

Allan Cunningham (1784–1842) was born in Keir, Dumfriesshire, and as a boy idolized Scott and walked in the funeral procession of Burns. He was apprenticed at 11 as a stonemason, and the trade supported him for the rest of his life. After 1810 he lived almost exclusively in London. He is best known for *Remains of Nithsdale and Galloway Song* (1810), the historical novel *Paul Jones* (1826), an edition of *The Works of Robert Burns* (1834), and a handful of ballads, especially 'A Wet Sheet and a Flowing Sea' (1825). His first magazine fiction was commissioned by *Blackwood's* in 1819, but he later contributed to the *London* and the *New Monthly*. See David Hogg, *The Life of Allan Cunningham* (London, 1875).

Catherine Gore (1800–61) was born Catherine Moody and married an officer, Charles Gore, in 1823. They had ten children together. Gore's first novel, *Theresa Marchmont*, appeared in 1824, and over the next thirty-five years she produced nearly seventy volumes of drama, poetry, and fiction. *Women as They Are, or Manners of the Day* (1830), *Mothers and Daughters* (1831), and *Cecil: or the Adventures of a Coxcomb* (1841) established her as the leading practitioner of the silver-fork novels of high society, though other novels such as *The Hamiltons, or the New Era* (1834) and *Mrs Armytage, or Female Domination* (1836) deal with weightier issues. Her tales and verses appeared frequently in a number of leading magazines, including *Bentley's*, the *New Monthly*, and *Tait's*. See Bonnie Anderson, 'The Writings of Catherine Gore' in *Journal of Popular Culture*, 10 (1976), 404–23.

James Hogg (1770–1835) was born in Ettrick Forest, and spent some of his youth as a shepherd before joining the literary life of Edinburgh in 1810. He settled as a farmer at Yarrow from 1816. His principal works include *Confessions of a Justified Sinner* (1824), *Songs by the Ettrick Shepherd* (1831), and *The Domestic Manners and Private Life of Sir Walter Scott* (1834). Hogg published most of his magazine fiction in *Blackwood's*, but other pieces appeared in *Fraser's*, the *Metropolitan*, the *New Monthly*, and the *Dublin University*. See Lewis Simpson, *James Hogg: A Critical Study* (Edinburgh, 1962).

Letitia E. Landon (1802–38), better known as 'L. E. L.', was an immensely popular author of the 1820s and 1830s. She published six volumes of poetry, including *The Fate of Adelaide* (1821), *The Improvisatrice* (1824), and *The Vow of the Peacock* (1835), as well as four novels, most notably *Ethel Churchill* (1837). Landon also contributed voluminously to annuals like *Friendship's Offering*, and to magazines like *Fraser's* and the *New Monthly*. In the mid-1820s scandal began to circulate about her personal life, particularly her liaisons with her mentor William Jerdan and the magazinist William Maginn, and though the rumours gradually died down, their revival in 1834 led her fiancé John Forster to break off their engagement. After a period of depression and ill-health, Landon accepted the marriage proposal of George Maclean, Governor of Cape Coast, West Africa, but within four months of her marriage and emigration to

Africa, she was dead, apparently from an accidental overdose of prussic acid. See Glennis Stephenson, *Letitia Landon: The Woman behind L. E. L.* (Manchester, 1995).

Joseph Sheridan Le Fanu (1814–73) was born in Dublin into an old and well-established Huguenot family. The playwright Richard Brinsley Sheridan had married his great-aunt. Le Fanu was educated at Trinity College and was called to the Irish Bar in 1839, though he never practised. He wrote poetry, essays, political commentary, and historical romances, but he is best known for his skilfully constructed tales of terror and mystery, particularly *The House by the Churchyard* (1863), *Wylder's Hand* (1864), *Uncle Silas* (1864), and *Guy Deverell* (1865). Le Fanu also published collections of short fiction, most notably *In a Glass Darkly* (1872), which features the terrifying vampire story 'Carmilla'. He was a key contributor to the *Dublin University Magazine* for over thirty years, and its owner and editor from 1861 to 1869. See W. J. McCormack, *Sheridan Le Fanu and Victorian Ireland* (Oxford, 1980).

Charles Lever (1806–72) was a native of Dublin, and grew up a member of the Anglo-Irish class. He trained in medicine at Trinity College, but was unable to establish himself as a physician, and turned to writing. After 1845 he lived in Italy, becoming British Consul at Trieste in 1867. His many novels include *The Confessions of Harry Lorrequer* (1837), *Charles O'Malley, the Irish Dragoon* (1840), *Roland Cashel* (1850), and *Lord Kilgobbin: A Tale of Ireland in Our Own Time* (1872). Lever's work appeared in several important periodicals, including *Blackwood's*, *The Cornhill*, and the *Dublin University Magazine*, which he edited from 1842 to 1845. See Lionel Stevenson, *Doctor Quicksilver: The Life of Charles Lever* (London, 1939).

John Polidori (1795–1821) was the son of a distinguished Italian scholar and translator. He received his medical degree from Edinburgh in 1815 at the unusually early age of 19, and displayed his fascination with the stranger aspects of science in his thesis on somnambulism. In 1816 he became Lord Byron's personal physician and travelling companion, and was present at the famous ghost story competition at the Villa Diodati that was the genesis of Mary Shelley's *Frankenstein* (1818) and his own *The Vampyre* (1819). Polidori returned to England in 1817 but he failed to establish himself as a writer or a physician. He committed suicide in his father's house in 1821. His other works include *Ernestus Berchtold; or, The Modern Oedipus* (1819), *Ximenes, the Wreath, and Other Poems* (1819), and

The Fall of the Angels: A Sacred Poem (1821). *The Vampyre* was his only contribution to the magazines. See D. L. Macdonald, *Poor Polidori: A Critical Biography of the Author of The Vampyre* (Toronto, 1991).

Horace Smith (1779–1849) made his fortune as a merchant and insurance broker, before becoming a stockbroker in 1812. With his brother James, a solicitor, he published *Rejected Addresses* (1812), an enormously successful collection of poetic parodies. In 1816 Smith became a member of the London literary circle that included Shelley, Hunt, and Keats, and he followed Shelley to the Continent in 1821. After 1825 he produced a series of pseudo-Waverley novels, the best known of which are *Brambletye House* (1826), *Reuben Apsley* (1827), and *Arthur Arundel* (1844). Smith's finest magazine work appeared in the *London* and the *New Monthly*. See Arthur H. Beavan, *James and Horace Smith* (London, 1899).

N. P. Willis (1806–67) was born in Portland, Maine, and educated at Yale. He was a member of the so-called Knickerbocker group of New York writers, but travelled extensively in Europe, and made his national and international reputation with a collection of travel sketches, *Pencillings by the Way* (1835), and three collections of short tales, most notably *Inklings of Adventure* (1836). He was one of the pre-eminent magazine editors and writers of his age, and most of his work first appeared in leading journals like *Graham's* and *Godey's* in America, and the *Metropolitan* and the *New Monthly* in Britain. See Courtland P. Auser, *Nathaniel Parker Willis* (New York, 1969).

EXPLANATORY NOTES

Attribution of *The Vampyre* is based on *The Vampyre and Ernestus Berchtold*, eds. D. L. Macdonald and Kathleen Scherf (Toronto, 1994), 21–6; attributions of all other tales from the *New Monthly Magazine* are based on the *Wellesley Index to Victorian Periodicals*, eds. W. Houghton *et al.* (5 vols.; Toronto, 1966–89), iii. 182–234. Attribution of Carleton's 'Confessions of a Reformed Ribbonman' is based on his *Traits and Stories of the Irish Peasantry*, second series (Dublin, 1833), where the tale appeared, with minor alterations, as 'Wildgoose Lodge'; attribution of Hogg's 'Some Terrible Letters from Scotland' is based on the *Metropolitan Magazine*, 3 (1832), 422; attributions of tales from the *Dublin University Magazine* are based on the *Wellesley*, iv. 228, 238; attribution of the tale from *Fraser's* is based on the *Wellesley*, ii. 335.

The Vampyre

Published in the April 1819 issue of the *New Monthly Magazine* (old series: 11/63, 195–206) as 'A TALE BY LORD BYRON', *The Vampyre* is actually the work of Byron's personal physician, John Polidori. Twitchell asserts that this tale 'set off a chain reaction that has carried the myth both to heights of artistic psychomachia and to depths of sadistic vulgarity, making the vampire, along with the Frankenstein monster, the most compelling and complex figure to be produced by the gothic imagination'. Frayling observes that *The Vampyre* is 'probably the most influential horror story of all time'. For details of the genesis and reception of Polidori's tale, see the Introduction, vii–xiii (James Twitchell, *The Living Dead: A Study of the Vampire in Romantic Literature* (Durham, NC, 1981), 103; *Vampyres: Lord Byron to Count Dracula*, ed. Christopher Frayling (London, 1991), 107).

The annotation that follows draws on the scholarship of previous editions of *The Vampyre*, particularly that of Macdonald and Scherf (Toronto, 1994).

3 *ton*: fashionable world.

Lady Mercer ... left the field: an unflattering portrait of Lady Caroline Lamb (1785–1828), who married William Lamb in 1805, and who had a brief but tempestuous affair with Byron in 1812, the most famous episode of which occurred in July of that year when she dressed in a page's uniform in order to gain access to his rooms after his interest in her had begun to wane. In May 1816 Lamb published her highly successful novel *Glenarvon*, an extravagant *roman-à-clef* which featured Byron as the villainous hero Clarence de Ruthven, Lord Glenarvon. Less than five months later, when Polidori wrote *The Vampyre*, he borrowed the Ruthven name, thus ensuring that readers of his tale would immediately associate Byron and the vampyre. In the revised version, Polidori changed Ruthven's name to Strongmore, possibly because there actually was a Lord Ruthven at the time, more probably because by 1819 he wished to claim the tale as his own, and to make its connection with Byron less obvious.

5 *Lord Ruthven's affairs . . . to travel*: Byron's financial affairs had grown increasingly straitened during the opening months of 1816. He left England for good on 25 April of that year.

6 *faro table*: faro is one of the oldest of all gambling games played with cards, and apparently named from the picture of a pharaoh on a French deck of cards. The game was a favourite of high-born gamblers throughout Europe in the late eighteenth and early nineteenth centuries.

8 *Mahomet's paradise . . . had no souls*: cf. a note to *The Giaour*, in which Byron explains that 'the Koran allots at least a third of Paradise to well-behaved women; but by far the greater number of Mussulmans interpret the text their own way, and exclude their moieties from heaven' (*Lord Byron: The Complete Poetical Works*, ed. Jerome McGann (Oxford, 1980–93), iii. 419).

9 *Pausanias*: (*fl.* AD 143–76); a Greek traveller and geographer, whose *Description of Greece* is an invaluable guide to ancient ruins.

16 *Smyrna*: now Izmir, a port in western Turkey.

ataghans: in a note to *The Giaour*, Byron describes an ataghan as 'a long dagger worn with pistols in the belt, in a metal scabbard, generally of silver; and, among the wealthier, gilt, or of gold' (Byron, *Complete Poetical Works*, iii. 418).

17 *drawing room*: formal reception.

'*busy scene*': the phrase is a common one. It appears in the same context immediately following 'The Editor's Introduction' in Frances Sheridan's *Memoirs of Miss Sidney Bidulph* (1761); see also Byron, 'I Would I were a Careless Child', 'This busy scene of splendid Woe' (Byron, *Complete Poetical Works*, i. 122).

Sir Guy Eveling's Dream

Published in the January 1823 issue of the *New Monthly Magazine*
(7/25, 59–64), this tale by Horace Smith purports to be '*Extracted
from an old Manuscript*' which 'appears to have been an Essay upon
Sleep'. Smith was a voluminous contributor to the *New Monthly*
in the first half of the 1820s. In a letter of July 1824 Charles Lamb
stated that 'the best' of the *New Monthly* was by Smith (*The Letters
of Charles and Mary Lamb*, ed. E. V. Lucas (3 vols.; London, 1935),
ii. 432).

25 *bruited*: spoke.

   Fountains Abbey: the Cistercian monastery founded in the
   twelfth century near Ripon, Yorkshire.

   maugre . . . not agnize: despite . . . of a proud, haughty temperament . . . recognize.

26 *ribalds . . . giglots*: knaves, revellers, swashbucklers . . . harlots.

   ronyons and bonarobas: strumpets and wenches.

   tristful ostent: sad appearance.

   incontinent: immediately.

27 *cautelously*: cautiously or craftily.

   Nathless . . . amort: nevertheless . . . dispirited.

   happy man be my dole: my destiny must be fortunate.

28 *our late King Edward*: presumably Edward VI, who acceded
   to the throne in 1547 and died six years later at the age of 15.

   St Mary Woolnoth Church: a church in the City of London.
   The reference here is to the second church on this site, built
   in the fifteenth century and subsequently replaced (after being
   damaged in the Great Fire of 1666) by Hawksmoor's church
   from 1716. There is no record of the tower of the second
   church having been damaged by lightning.

   within the Bar: within Temple Bar, the old gate of the City of
   London.

29 *facete entertainment and argute compassment*: elegant entertainment and subtle contrivance.

   the dulcimer of Miriam: a confused allusion, presumably to the
   biblical Miriam, sister of Moses and Aaron, who celebrates the
   crossing of the Red Sea by playing a timbrel, not a dulcimer
   (Exodus 15: 20).

29 *likelihood of sphere*: promising circumstances.

  applejohns ... sack-posset: long-preserved apples; marzipan; sugar-plums; delicacies; a sherry in hot milk.

30 *tirevolant*: the word is not found elsewhere, but must refer to some form of headdress or possibly cape.

31 *intenerated*: softened.

  a Bezonian and a lozel: a vagabond and a scoundrel.

  gimmal rings ... braveries: rings composed of two or three parts; jewelled necklaces; pieces of finery; adornments.

32 *writhled*: withered or wrinkled.

  Spittal for the crazed: lunatic asylum.

Confessions of a Reformed Ribbonman

Published in the 23 January and 30 January 1830 issues of the *Dublin Literary Gazette* (1/4, 49–51; 1/5, 66–8), this tale by William Carleton is based on historical fact. In the first instalment, a bracketed subtitle describes it as '*An owre true tale*', and an editorial note explains that 'had the following story been a pure fiction, it would not have gained a place in our pages, but ... it is unfortunately "a true record"', and 'afford[s] an insight into the habits and secret actions of a very extraordinary set of wretches, some of whom are said even yet to disgrace the wilder parts of the country'.

The incidents described in the tale took place on 30 October 1816, near Reaghstown, in County Louth. The Ribbonmen were a secret organization of Irish nationalists founded in about 1808 to combat the Orangemen of the northern counties; they soon became notorious for their sectarian outrages. The name derives from the green ribbon worn as a badge by members. Events leading up to the atrocities described in Carleton's tale began on 10 April 1816, when Michael Tiernan, Patrick Stanley, and Philip Conlon broke into a huntsman's lodge occupied by Edward Lynch. The three men demanded guns and assaulted Lynch and members of his family before being driven off. At the trial Lynch and his son-in-law Thomas Rooney identified the invaders and, in the face of strong public sympathy, all three men were convicted and hanged, most probably on 21 August. In the early hours of 30 October, the Ribbonmen meted out their revenge. Led by Paddy Devaun, a weaver and parish clerk at Stonetown Chapel, they massacred Lynch and seven others, including his daughter and grandchild. In the aftermath, Devaun and seventeen other Ribbonmen were executed. In summing up, Judge Fletcher noted that 'religious bigotry had no part in producing these monstrous crimes. There were not here two conflicting parties arrayed under the colours of orange and green; not Protestant against Catholic, nor Catholic against Protestant—no, it was Catholic against Catholic' (Daniel J. Casey, 'Wildgoose Lodge: The Evidence and the Lore' in *County Louth Archaeological and Historical Journal*, 18 (1974), 140–64; Barbara Hayley, *Carleton's Traits and Stories and the 19th Century Anglo-Irish Tradition* (Gerrards Cross, Bucks., 1983), 124).

In about 1814 Carleton himself became a Ribbonman but, in his *Autobiography*, he insisted he was 'seduced into this senseless but most mischievous system' by an 'adroit scoundrel', as 'in like manner were hundreds, nay thousands, of unreflecting youths'. Later Carleton described the first time he heard 'a brief outline of the inhuman and hellish tragedy' of the Lynch massacre, and called 'the effect upon me . . . the most painful I ever felt from any narrative. It clung to me until I went to bed that night—it clung to me through my sleep with such vivid horror that sleep was anything but a relief to me.' Carleton also claimed that he had seen the gibbeted tar sack which contained Devaun's body, and explained how the body had decomposed and begun to ooze out the bottom of the sack in 'long ropes of slime shining in the light' (*The Autobiography of William Carleton*, preface by Patrick Kavanagh (London, 1968), 77–8, 114–17).

When Carleton's tale appeared in the *Literary Gazette*, its chief rival, the *Dublin Monthly Magazine*, labelled it 'offensive' and claimed it was best 'to avoid controversial discussion', but by 1852 the *Edinburgh Review* noted that it was in Carleton's works, 'and in his alone, that future generations must look for the truest and fullest—though still far from complete—picture of those, who will ere long have passed away from that troubled land, from the records of history, and from the memory of man for ever'. W. B. Yeats chose this tale as one of five for inclusion in his *Stories from Carleton*, and remarked that 'the whole matter made a deep impression on the mind of Carleton, and again and again in his books he returns to the subject of the secret societies and their corruption of the popular conscience'. More recently, critics have commented on the effectiveness of the tale's first-person narrative, and Hayley explores the 'psychological inertia that holds the narrator passive in a wild dreamlike hell—'he describes scenes, movements and expressions as hell-like or Satanic time and time again, as he is carried along towards actions from which his mind revolts and of which the memory "sickens" him' (*Dublin Monthly Magazine*, 1 (1830), 174; *Edinburgh Review*, 96 (1852), 389; W. B. Yeats, *Stories from Carleton* (London, 1889), xiii; Hayley, *Carleton's Traits and Stories*, 125).

In 1833 Carleton revised the 'Confessions' as 'Wildgoose Lodge' for inclusion in his *Traits and Stories of the Irish Peasantry*, second series. He made dozens of minor alterations in wording and punctuation, but only one important change. In the magazine text, Carleton writes 'we directed our steps to the house in which this man (the only Protestant in the parish) resided'. In revision, he changed this to the harmless 'in which this devoted man resided', and thus removed the incorrect implication that the massacre of the Lynches was due to sectarian hostility (Hayley, *Carleton's Traits and Stories*, 124–5, 133).

36 *ghud dhemur tha thu*: may be translated approximately as 'how are you?'

37 *ma bouchal . . . gosther*: my boy . . . my son . . . chatter.

Monos and Daimonos

Published in the May 1830 issue of the *New Monthly Magazine* (28/112, 387–92). This tale by Edward Bulwer was subtitled '*A Legend*' and published over the signature '𝕲𝕷𝖄𝕹𝕯𝕺𝕮𝕳', which appeared in 'Old English' font as here. 'Monos' means single and 'Daimonos' is taken from 'daimon', which in ancient Greek refers to a lesser divinity, not necessarily malevolent. In an 1835 letter to the editor of the *Southern Literary Messenger*, Poe listed 'Monos and Daimonos' as one of those tales that was 'invariably' popular with readers because it displayed 'the ludicrous heightened into the grotesque: the fearful coloured into the horrible: the witty exaggerated into the burlesque: the singular wrought out into the strange and mystical'. A year later Poe cited 'Monos and Daimonos' to support his claim that, in Bulwer's writings, 'all is richly, and glowing intellectual—all is energetic, or astute, or brilliant, or profound'. Poe's 'Silence—A Fable' (1838) is heavily indebted to 'Monos and Daimonos', to the point where, as Mabbott points out, some sentences are taken 'almost verbatim'. Bulwer reprinted a slightly revised version of 'Monos and Daimonos' in *The Student* (1835), where he observed that the tales in this collection 'belong rather to the poetical than the logical philosophy . . . they utter in prose, what are the ordinary didactics of poetry' (*The Letters of Edgar Allan Poe*, ed. John Ward Ostrom (2 vols.; New York, 1966), i. 57–8; *The Complete Works of Edgar Allan Poe*, ed. James A. Harrison (17 vols.; New York, 1902), viii. 222; *Collected Works of Edgar Allan Poe*, ed. T. O. Mabbott (3 vols.; Cambridge, Mass., 1978), ii. 193; Edward Bulwer, *The Student* (2 vols.; London, 1835), i. pp. viii–ix).

55 *Dædal*: variously adorned.

The Master of Logan

Published in the April 1831 issue of the *New Monthly Magazine* (31/124, 321–36). This tale, like many of Cunningham's finest, is set in Nithsdale and draws on his extensive knowledge of Scottish superstition and sectarian feeling. In 1840 Thomas De Quincey praised Cunningham for 'those many excellent, sometimes brilliant, pages, by which he has delighted so many thousands of readers, and won for himself a lasting name in the fine literature of modern England' (*The Collected Writings of Thomas De Quincey*, ed. David Masson (14 vols.; London, 1897–8), iii. 159).

63 *Gray*: slightly misquoted from Thomas Gray's 'Elegy Written in a Country Church-yard', 92.

Nith: river in south-western Scotland.

64 *last year . . . James Stuart*: James VII of Scotland, James II of England (1633–1701); his three-year reign ended in late 1688.

thunder-plump: a sudden, heavy thundershower.

douce: sedate, respectable.

Montrose and David Lesley: James Graham, 5th Earl and 1st Marquis of Montrose (1612–50), was appointed King's Lieutenant in Scotland in 1644, and won many victories in the following year. David Leslie, Lord Newark (?–1682), commander of the Covenanters' army, defeated Montrose at Philiphaugh, near Selkirk, in 1645.

65 *chambering*: sexual indulgence or lewdness.

Turkey shoe: most probably a shoe made of 'Turkey leather'; that is, 'leather tawed with oil, the hair side not being removed until after the tawing' (*OED*). Cf. Walter Scott's *Kenilworth*, ch. 5: 'a small dagger of exquisite workmanship . . . hung in his Turkey-leather sword-belt'.

66 *Godly Covenant . . . southern crest*: the National Covenant of 1638 was a public petition eventually signed by nearly 300,000. It asserted that the Scottish church had a direct relationship with God, without requiring the king's interposition, and provided an excuse for condemning Charles I's attempts to anglicize the Church of Scotland. Oliver Cromwell invaded Scotland and defeated Leslie at the battle of Dunbar in 1650.

unsonsie: luckless or unfortunate.

67 *Proud Preston*: town in Lancashire, 'called, by way of distinction from other towns of that name, *Proud* Preston' (Masson,

De Quincey, xiii. 308). The Scots were soundly defeated by Cromwell at the battle of Preston in 1648.

69 *fashed*: vexed or disturbed.

70 *chanting the Gallant Graemes*: a traditional ballad included by Walter Scott in his *Minstrelsy of the Scottish Border* (1802–3), and described by him as a 'lamentation' for the 'final discomfiture and cruel death' of James Graham, 5th Earl and 1st Marquis of Montrose (see note to p. 64 above).

coup: tumble or overturn.

71 *gowans*: wild flowers, usually daisies.

Queen of Sheba: see 1 Kings 10: 1–13 and 2 Chronicles 9: 1–12.

73 *falderols . . . tires*: falderols are vagaries; tires is an obsolete form of attires, and here refers most probably to a headdress.

75 *gilpin*: a sturdy young person.

wynted: spoiled or sour.

coost the cauld of: recovered from.

76 *her favourite Church*: Lady Anne is a member of the Scottish Episcopal Church, structurally similar to the established Church of England, and governed by bishops. The preacher is a member of the Presbyterian Church of Scotland, founded on the model established by John Calvin in Geneva in the mid-sixteenth century, and governed without bishops.

78 *In the blinded . . . native darkness*: in 1560 the Scottish parliament abolished papal supremacy and adopted John Knox's *Confession of Faith*.

79 *General Assembly*: ruling body of the Church of Scotland.

80 *cittern*: more commonly cithern, an instrument like a guitar, but strung with wire and played with a quill.

pellock: porpoise.

81 *darg*: day's work.

slarg: dirty, besmirched.

Green Criffel: prominent hill near Dumfries.

83 *lugs*: ears.

streeket: stretched out or composed for burial.

84 *the Witch of Endor*: see 1 Samuel 28.

bonds of iniquity . . . the land: after the Restoration in 1660, Charles II reintroduced episcopacy, but the move was violently resisted by many of the people and the Church of Scotland was re-established in 1690.

accession of the Stuarts: the Stuarts acceded to the Scottish throne in 1371, and united the Scottish and English thrones in 1603.

Calvin: see note to p. 76 above.

86 *glozing*: specious.

The Victim

Published in the December 1831 issue of the *New Monthly Magazine* (32/132, 571–6). This anonymous tale appeared as 'A TRUE STORY. BY A MEDICAL STUDENT', and clearly exploits contemporary fear over the infamous murders committed by Burke and Hare, who in 1828 smothered sixteen people in Edinburgh and then delivered the corpses to the back door of the celebrated anatomist Robert Knox, where they received payment. At their trial in 1829, Hare turned King's evidence, and Burke was hanged (and dissected). Copycat 'burkings' occurred in London throughout 1831. Bulwer's editorial note to 'The Victim' emphasizes that the tale was inserted 'in the hope that any little impression it may create, will serve to swell the general desire for immediate reform in a system which most urgently and fearfully demands it'. Less than a year later the first Anatomy Act was passed, which gave anatomists legal access to unclaimed pauper bodies from the workhouses. For the best discussion of 'Burkophobia', 'the dead body business', and 'the doctor/scientist as a figure of threat', see Tim Marshall, *Murdering to Dissect: Grave-robbing, Frankenstein and the Anatomy Literature* (Manchester, 1995).

87 *Dawlish*: a small town on the south Devonshire coast below the Exe estuary. It was fashionable in the nineteenth century, and appears in Austen's *Sense and Sensibility* (1811), and in Dickens's *Nicholas Nickleby* (1839).

88 *Abercrombie... diseases of the brain*: John Abercrombie (1780–1844) was a graduate of Edinburgh and the author of books on pathology, morality, and the intellect. He made his name with *Pathological and Practical Researches on Diseases of the Brain and Spinal Cord* (1828), a detailed and influential compilation based on his own case studies.

91 *Rembrandt... loved to paint*: Rembrandt van Rijn (1606–69), Dutch painter and etcher, and master of the chiaroscuro effect, a style which exploits strong contrasts between the light and dark areas of the composition.

92 *'Before Decay's ... beauty lingers ... wanting there'*: slightly misquoted from Byron's *The Giaour* (Byron, *Complete Poetical Works*, iii. 42).

95 *'if thy right hand ... cut it off?'*: Matthew 5: 30.

96 *rhino*: money.

suffocated ... cutting up: the gang's choice of suffocation to murder its victims, and the subsequent sale of those victims to doctors, would have been recognized by contemporary readers as a direct reference to the murderous practices of Burke and Hare (see headnote above).

Some Terrible Letters from Scotland

Published in the April 1832 issue of the *Metropolitan Magazine* (3/12, 422–31) as 'COMMUNICATED BY THE ETTRICK SHEPHERD', this tale by James Hogg both reflects and exploits the immense public anxiety over the cholera epidemic. Cholera killed over 32,000 people in Britain in 1831–2, including nearly 10,000 in Scotland. 'Of external news', wrote Thomas Carlyle from Craigenputtoch in October 1832, 'greatly the most momentous is that *Cholera* has been at Dumfries for some three weeks; but seems now to be rapidly abating. It was rather beyond the average in violence, and the terror of the whole region has been immeasurable.' The scourge received intense coverage in several magazines, including the *Metropolitan*, where the actions of the government were frequently defended, and where it was noted that 'the small, close, damp, and confined habitations of the poor and destitute are the chief abodes of the cholera; and the drunken and the profligate, the weak and unhealthy, the ill-fed and ill-clothed, are the miserable victims of this malady, having not sufficient constitutional stamina to resist the invasion'. Such rhetoric did little to counteract the widespread conviction that the government was using the epidemic to reduce surplus populations, and that doctors approved because it provided them with a steady supply of corpses for the anatomy table (*The Collected Letters of Thomas and Jane Welsh Carlyle*, ed. C. R. Sanders (21 vols.: Durham, NC, 1970–), vi. 249; 'Is the Epidemic Cholera in London?' in the *Metropolitan Magazine*, 3 (1832), 319–26; R. J. Morris, 'Class, Power and Cholera' in *Cholera 1832* (New York, 1976), 95–128).

99 *summer that Burke was hanged*: the summer of 1829. See headnote to 'The Victim' above.

Troughlin: an imaginary location; Dalkeith and Musselburgh are real towns to the east of Edinburgh.

shilpit: pale.

saur: odour.

106 *the Lammermuirs*: a range of hills lying between Berwick-upon-Tweed and Edinburgh.

Teviotdale: the valley of the River Teviot, lying to the south of Hogg's native Ettrick Forest. The village of Roxburgh lies further north-east, towards Kelso.

Campbell or Galt: Thomas Campbell (1777–1844) and John Galt (1779–1839), noted Scottish writers both resident in London at this time.

107 *Glauber's salts*: sulphate of sodium, used as a purgative.

Oh, she pe tat tam bhaist te Collara Mòr: 'Oh, it be that damn beast the Great Cholera.'

108 *peen raiter . . . pot-hato*: 'been rather too heavy on the herring and potato'.

Fisherrow: a small port just to the east of Edinburgh.

109 *crap*: crept.

110 *gars a' ane's heart grue*: makes all one's heart shudder.

112 *burked*: suffocated. See headnote to 'The Victim' above.

The Curse

Published anonymously in the November 1832 issue of *Fraser's Magazine* (6/34, 559–66). Though *Fraser's* published a good deal of sensation fiction in its early years, little of it reached the extremes of madness and remorse found in 'The Curse'. The epigraph to the tale has not been identified. Astolpho is a paladin in Ariosto's *Orlando Furioso*, but the quotation does not appear in any of the standard translations.

114 *'even from my boyish days'*: *Othello*, I. iii. 132.

'were still in the flesh': Romans 7: 5: 'For when we were in the flesh.'

'For never having dream'd . . . of constancy': slightly misquoted from Byron's *Don Juan*, Canto II (Byron, *Complete Poetical Works*, v. 148).

115 *'dry bones'*: Ezekiel 37: 4: 'O ye dry bones, hear the word of the Lord.'

116 *'Blessed are the dead . . . Lord'*: Revelations 14: 13.

'he may flourish . . . for ever': adapted from Psalm 37: 35–6.

116 *'For why?... be overthrown'*: Psalm 1: 6 of the metrical version of the Scottish Psalter.

   They who sleep... hand of God: this sentence combines parts of, respectively, Hebrews 11: 38, Matthew 5: 13, Hebrews 11: 37, Revelations 7: 14, and Acts 7: 55.

117 *It was in those days... might devour*: in 1650 Charles II signed the National Covenant of Scotland (see note to p. 66 above), but after the Restoration in 1660 he reneged and reintroduced episcopacy. It then became a criminal offence to attend a presbyterian sermon.

118 *James Sharp*: Sharp (1613–79), one of the negotiators sent by the Scottish presbyterians to legitimate their Church, changed sides, and was rewarded by Charles II with the Archbishopric of St Andrews. He became a ruthless supporter of imposed episcopacy, and was murdered by Fife Covenanters in 1679.

120 *Scots Worthies*: a book by John Howie (1735–93) first published in 1774. It contains biographical sketches of Scottish reformers and martyrs from the Reformation to the English Revolution.

121 *the holy Stephen... an angel*: Acts 6: 15: 'And all... looking steadfastly on him, saw his face as it had been the face of an Angel.' St Stephen was the first Christian martyr.

Life in Death

Published anonymously in the March 1833 issue of the *New Monthly Magazine* (37/147, 302–7). A parenthetical statement inserted immediately below the title states that 'the ground-work of this tale will be recognized by the reader', a reference to Mary Shelley's *Frankenstein* (1818), another tale in which an obsessive scientist pursues the secrets of life with disastrous consequences. The epigraph to the tale has not been identified.

130 *'They may rail at this earth...'*: misquoted from the song 'They may rail at this life' by Thomas Moore (1779–1852).

My Hobby,—Rather

Published in the October 1834 issue of the *New Monthly Magazine* (42/166, 203–4), this tale by N. P. Willis appeared over the initial 'H', and is one of three tales that made up the 'My Hobby,—Rather' series. The tale was given the title 'The Disturbed Vigil' when it was reprinted as part of the 'Scenes of Fear' chapter in Willis's *Inklings of Adventure* (1836). Poe wrote of Willis: 'If called on to designate

him by any general literary title, I might term him a magazinist—
for his compositions have invariably the species of *effect*, with the
brevity which the magazine demands' (Harrison, *Complete Works*,
xv. 11).

139 *Old Play*: Charles Villier's version of *The Chances, A Comedy*
(1682), III. v. 15–16.

festival of Dian: the Roman goddess Diana, here aptly introduced for her associations with the moon and the hunt.

famed university of Connecticut: Yale, founded in New Haven
in 1701.

141 *horrible appetite . . . incredulously*: a domestic cat preying on a
corpse is a part of folklore and fact. See George L. Kittredge,
Witchcraft in Old and New England (Cambridge, Mass., 1929),
178–9; and M. L. Rossi, A. W. Shahrom, R. C. Chapman, and
P. Vanezis, 'Postmortem Injuries by Indoor Pets' in *The American Journal of Forensic Medicine and Pathology*, 15 (1994),
105–9.

The Red Man

Published in the June 1835 issue of the *New Monthly Magazine*
(44/174, 194–207). Catherine Gore had taken up residence in Paris
in 1832, and this tale shows her exploiting local materials to powerful effect, drawing both on recent incidents of crime and punishment
in that city, and on the older lore of pre-Revolutionary cruelties.

143 *Béranger*: Pierre-Jean de Béranger (1780–1857), popular French
poet, strongly associated with the republicanism of 1830. The
lines quoted here, slightly adapted from his poem 'Le petit
homme rouge' (1826), translate as: 'A devil dressed in scarlet,
hunchbacked, cross-eyed, and red-haired, a snake serves as his
tie; he has a hooked nose, he has a cloven hoof.'

Zamiel . . . Feuergeist: in Weber's opera *Der Freischütz* (1821),
Zamiel or Samiel the Black Hunter is a devil. A *Feuergeist* is
a fire-spirit.

145 *since the Place de la Grève . . . heroes*: the Place de la Grève,
renamed as the Place de l'Hôtel de Ville in 1806, had been the
principal site of executions in Paris since the fourteenth
century, and had therefore witnessed many of the deaths of
'heroes' and others in the Revolution; but the place of execution had recently been transferred to the Barrière St Jacques
on the Left Bank in 1830.

145 '*Monsieur de Paris*' ... *hand*: customary title given to a Parisian
    executioner, a post that was passed from father to son in the
    family of Sanson (here Anglicized by Gore, perhaps for the
    sake of biblical resonance) for several generations. The incum-
    bent referred to here is Henri Sanson (1767–1840), the fifth
    executioner of that name, who took over from his father, the
    more infamous Charles-Henri, in 1795.

    the judicial assassination ... adduced: a confused reference to
    a real miscarriage of justice in 1833 involving the Dupuytren
    household. The former cook, Gillard, was in fact the victim not
    of the murder but of a false accusation of complicity in the
    murder of the chambermaid Idate by his friend Lemoine. It
    was Lemoine who was (justly) executed by Sanson in Septem-
    ber 1833, while Gillard, originally sentenced to ten years' hard
    labour, was pardoned upon appeal a few weeks later (Pierre
    Bouchardon, *Le Cuisinier de la baronne Dupuytren* (Paris,
    1930)).

    priest of a new sect: Lemoine (see note above) was accom-
    panied to the scaffold by the self-styled 'Primate of the Gauls',
    a former army chaplain named Ferdinand-François Châtel who
    had founded in 1830 a sect calling itself the New French
    Catholic Church, of which he made himself bishop.

147 *the monomaniac Papavoine*: Louis-Auguste Papavoine, executed
    in 1825 for stabbing to death two young children in the Bois
    de Vincennes.

    Tyburn ... Surgeons'-hall!: Tyburn, near what is now Marble
    Arch, was the site of most public executions in London until
    1783, and Newgate was the city's principal prison; Jack Ketch
    was a notorious hangman of the later seventeenth century,
    whose name came to be applied to hangmen of later periods
    as a generic title; Surgeons' Hall was part of the Old Bailey
    site in central London, where the bodies of recently executed
    criminals were dissected and exhibited.

    Thurtell: John Thurtell was hanged in 1824 for the murder of
    a Mr Weare, a gambling partner to whom he owed money; at
    Gill's Hill, Hertfordshire, he shot Weare in the face and
    clubbed him to death with the pistol.

    fascis: tied bundle.

148 *Cuvier*: Georges Cuvier (1769–1832), French anatomist, noted
    for his method of reconstructing whole bodies from partial
    remains.

149 *The times of the Frédégondes and Brunéhauts*: the period of violent feuding among the Merovingian royal houses of the late sixth century, provoked by Frédégond or Fredegund, the mistress of Chilperic I, King of Soissons. Fredegund first persuaded Chilperic to murder his queen, Galswinthe, and went on to arrange the assassination of Chilperic's half-brother Sigebert I, husband to her arch-enemy Brunéhaut or Brunhild. Frédégonde is thus one of the most notorious figures of medieval French history, a byword for murderous cruelty.

150 *Parvis de Nôtre Dame!*: the square in front of the cathedral.

the first revolution: the Revolution of 1789–94, here distinguished from the more recent insurrection of July 1830.

massacre at the prison of L'Abbaye: one of the most notorious massacres of September 1792, in which suspected counter-revolutionary prisoners were killed by mobs who feared that Paris was under imminent military attack.

159 *the Lauzuns and Polignacs*: powerful families of French nobles from what is now Lot-et-Garonne and the Haute Loire.

161 *a hired berline*: a four-wheeled covered carriage.

Post-Mortem Recollections of a Medical Lecturer

Published in the June 1836 issue of the *Dublin University Magazine* (7/42, 623–8). This tale by Charles Lever was renamed 'The "Dream of Death"' and inserted into his high-spirited novel *Arthur O'Leary* (1844), apparently at the request of Lever's close friend Samuel Hayman, who described 'Post-Mortem Recollections' as 'powerfully written' and *O'Leary* as 'one of [Lever's] very best books'. When Maria Edgeworth praised 'Post-Mortem Recollections', Lever described them to her as 'little else than a transcript of my own feeling during recovery from the only severe illness I ever had. [They] have so much of truth about them that they were actually present to my mind day after day' (W. J. Fitzpatrick, *The Life of Charles Lever* (2 vols.; London, 1879), i. 198; Edmund Downey, *Charles Lever: His Life in His Letters* (2 vols.; Edinburgh, 1906), i. 249–50).

165 *Hamlet*: III. i. 64–5 (slightly misquoted).

171 *the awful punishment... compared to this*: the Etruscan king Mezentius meted out this punishment to his enemies (see Virgil's *Aeneid*, viii. 482 ff.).

172 *I had heard... at his own bosom*: Lever visited North America in 1829, and stayed several months with an Indian tribe, during which time he undoubtedly 'heard' this legend. His friend

Samuel Hayman notes that Lever 'easily found the red man's haunts, and . . . got so thoroughly in accord with them, that the Indian sachem formally admitted him into tribal privileges, and initiated him into membership'. The legend of the male suckling the child is also found in ch. 23 of the Icelandic Flóamanna saga (Fitzpatrick, *The Life of Charles Lever*, i. 53).

The Bride of Lindorf

Published in the August 1836 issue of the *New Monthly Magazine* (47/188, 449–65). While most of Landon's prose work is highly sentimental historical fiction, this tale is unusual as an exercise in the Gothic vein, complete with themes of madness and incest.

176 *'something more exquisite still'*: quoted from Thomas Moore's poem 'The Meeting of the Waters'.

177 *Salvator Rosa*: the Neapolitan painter (1615–73) much admired in England by such Gothic novelists as Horace Walpole and Ann Radcliffe for the 'sublime' quality of his gloomy landscapes.

178 *Velasquez . . . '. . . vexation of spirit'*: Diego Rodríguez de Silva y Velázquez (1599–1660), Spanish painter best known for his portraits. The biblical phrase 'all is vanity and vexation of spirit' is repeated several times in Ecclesiastes.

Beatrice Cenci: a young Roman noblewoman (1577–99) who was, with her brother and stepmother, tried and executed in 1599 for the murder of her father, Count Francesco Cenci. Her case aroused much sympathy, as Francesco had subjected his daughter to imprisonment, brutality, and (it was widely understood) incestuous assault. Percy Bysshe Shelley made Beatrice the heroine of his unperformed verse drama *The Cenci* (1819), and claimed inspiration from the portrait of Beatrice attributed to the Bolognese painter Guido Reni. The portrait has since then been re-assessed as neither a representation of Beatrice Cenci, nor by Guido Reni.

184 *Prometheus*: in Greek myth, the Titan who rebels against the gods by giving fire to Man; Zeus punishes him by chaining him to a rock while a vulture eats his liver.

Passage in the Secret History of an Irish Countess

Published in the November 1838 issue of the *Dublin University Magazine* (12/82, 502–19). This tale by Joseph Sheridan Le Fanu is the fifth of twelve 'extracts' that make up 'The Purcell Papers', a series of tales that Le Fanu published in the *Dublin* between January 1838 and October 1840, and that were all purported to have been written or discovered by 'the Reverend Francis Purcell of Drumcoolagh'. In a prefatory note to 'Passage in the Secret History', Purcell observes that 'the following paper is written in a female hand, and was no doubt communicated to my much regretted friend, by the lady whose early history it serves to illustrate, the Countess D——. She is no more—she long since died, a childless and a widowed wife.... Strange! two powerful and wealthy families, *that* in which she was born, and that into which she had married, have ceased to be—they are utterly extinct. To those who know any thing of the history of Irish famil- ies, as they were less than a century ago, the facts contained in this paper will at once suggest *the names* of the principal actors; and to others their publication would be useless; to us, possibly, if not prob- ably, injurious.'

Sullivan points out that Le Fanu borrows part of the plot of 'Passage in the Secret History' from the first Gothic novel, Horace Walpole's *Castle of Otranto* (1764): 'Sir Arthur T—— and his son Edward plot their kinswoman's death in order to inherit her con- siderable property, but as in *Otranto* mistake the daughter of the house, Emily T——, for their intended victim and bludgeon her to death.' Le Fanu reprinted 'Passages in the Secret History' as 'The Murdered Cousin' in his collection of *Ghost Stories and Tales of Mystery* (1851), and then expanded the tale into one of his finest full- length novels, *Uncle Silas* (1864) (Kevin Sullivan, 'Sheridan Le Fanu: The Purcell Papers, 1838–40' in *Irish University Review*, 2 (1972), 5–19).

205 *I was Yorkshire too*: 'Yorkshire' here means cunning or full of trickery.

206 *Faulkner's newspaper*: *The Dublin Journal*, published and edited by George Faulkner (1699?–1775) from 1728 until his death; the paper survived until 1825.

215 *eclaircissement*: moment of clarification.

217 *Sir Giles Overreach*: a character in Philip Massinger's comic play *A New Way to Pay Old Debts* (1633). He swindles his own nephew out of his property, but is eventually driven mad when tricked out of it in turn.

Appendix A: Preliminaries for *The Vampyre*

236 *Rousseau . . . under its roof*: Jean-Jacques Rousseau (1712–78), philosopher and writer, was born at 40 Grand' Rue, Geneva. His bust and memorial are located at the Plainpalais, just south of Geneva, where Byron, Polidori, and the Shelleys visited in

late May 1816. Rousseau's major works include *La Nouvelle Héloise* (1761), *Émile: ou De l'éducation* (1762), *Du Contrat Social* (1762), and *Les Confessions* (1782).

236 *Ferney the residence of Voltaire... Europe*: born François-Marie Arouet (1694–1778), French philosopher, scientist, moralist, and man of letters. From 1758 until 1777 Voltaire lived on his estate at Ferney, just north-east of Geneva, where his crusades against tyranny and cruelty made him one of the most famous men in Europe. His writings include *Lettres Philosophiques* (1734), *Candide* (1759), and *Dictionnaire Philosophique* (1764).

Bonnet's abode: Charles Bonnet (1720–93), Swiss naturalist and philosopher, noted for his discovery of parthenogenesis (reproduction without fertilization) and his development of the catastrophe theory of evolution.

Madame de Stael: Anne-Louise-Germaine Necker (1766–1817) was the daughter of Jacques Necker, Louis XVI's minister of finance, and the author of two novels and several important works of political and literary theory, including *De l'Influence des passions sur le bonheur des individus et des nations* (1796), *De la Littérature considérée dans ses rapports avec les institutions sociales* (1800), and *De l'Allemagne* (1810). Her family estate was at Coppet, near Geneva.

days of Heloise... her works: Pierre Abélard (*c.*1079–*c.*1142), French philosopher and theologian, fell passionately in love with his pupil Héloise (*c.*1098–*c.*1164), and though their secret marriage caused Héloise's father to have Abélard brutally castrated, they continued a passionate correspondence until his death. Héloise was known for her learning, and for her effectiveness and piety as a monastic administrator. August Wilhelm Schlegel (1767–1845), in addition to his work as a translator of Shakespeare, was one of the most influential disseminators of the ideas of German Romanticism, notably in works such as *Ueber dramatische Kunst und Litteratur* (1809–11). After studying Schlegel's writings for a number of years, Madame de Staël met him in 1804, after which he became her frequent companion and counsellor, as well as one of the most brilliant members of her salon at Coppet.

Gibbon, Bonnivard, Bradshaw: Edward Gibbon (1737–94), English scholar and historian best known for his *The History of the Decline and Fall of the Roman Empire* (1776–88); from

1783 to 1793 he lived at Lausanne, where he finished the *Decline and Fall* in 1787. François Bonivard (1493–1570), Genevan patriot and the hero of Byron's 'The Prisoner of Chillon' (1816); Bradshaw has not been identified.

Diodati, the friend of Milton: the poet John Milton (1608–74) did not in fact stay at the Villa Diodati during his visit to Geneva in June 1639, though he did spend a good deal of time with the distinguished theologian Giovanni Diodati, whose residence seems to have been in the centre of Geneva's old city. Giovanni was the uncle of Milton's closest friend Charles Diodati, whom Milton had met at St Paul's School, and whose death he memorializes in 'Epitaphium Damonis' (1645). The Villa Diodati was built over a period of several years in the first half of the seventeenth century by Gabriel Diodati, a distant relative of Giovanni's, and is located just outside Geneva, at Cologny, on the south side of the lake. Byron and Polidori moved into the Villa on 10 June 1816.

many months in this neighbourhood: in fact, Byron spent only about four and a half months in Switzerland, from May to October 1816. He composed the Third Canto of *Childe Harold* in May and June.

237 *I found a servant . . . English boat*: for Byron's routine and behaviour during the summer of 1816, see L. A. Marchand, *Byron: A Biography* (3 vols.; New York, 1957), ii. 609–59.

and of me!: misprint: Byron's text reads 'and of thee!' (Byron, *Complete Poetical Works*, ii. 111).

the swift Rhine: misprint: Byron's text reads 'the swift Rhone' (ibid.).

238 *M. Pictet and Bonstetten . . . his apologies*: Marc-Auguste Pictet (1752–1825) was a leading member of the Genevan Société des Arts and the Société de Physique et d'Histoire Naturelles, and with his younger brother Charles helped to found the *Bibliothèque britannique* (1796); Charles Victor von Bonstetten (1745–1832) wrote a number of works in philosophy but is best known for his comparative study of national characteristics, *L'Homme du midi et l'homme du nord, ou l'influence des climats* (1824), and for his collection of autobiographical sketches, *Souvenirs* (1832). Polidori records that on 26 May 'Pictet called, but L[ord] B[yron] said "not at home".' Byron later defended his actions by explaining that Polidori had not consulted him about the invitation: '*He* asked Pictet &c. to dinner—and of

course was left to entertain them.' Byron did not visit the Château de Chillon until nearly a month after this episode, when he and Shelley were touring Lake Geneva (Rossetti, *Diary*, 98; Byron, *Letters*, vi. 127).

238 *Lady D—— H——*: Lady Dalrymple Hamilton (1779–1852) was the eldest daughter of the first Viscount Duncan of Camperdown; she married Sir Hew Dalrymple Hamilton in 1800.

as an outcast: Byron later remarked that the incidents at the Hamiltons' and at Coppet were 'true'. He added: 'I never gave "the English" an opportunity of "avoiding" me—but I trust that if ever I do, they will seize it' (Byron, *Letters*, vi. 127).

239 *Countess of Breuss . . . sought for society*: Countess Catherine Bruce, who in 1815–22 lived near Geneva in the splendid Maison D'Abraham Gallatin, where Polidori frequently enjoyed the 'pleasures of society' (see Viets, 'Polidori's *The Vampyre*', 87–8).

Αθεος in the Album at Chamouny: in July 1816, under the 'Occupation' column in the hotel register at Chamonix, Shelley signed himself 'Δημοκρατικος, Φιλάνθρωποτατος, κάι 'αθεος' —Democrat, Philanthropist, and Atheist. The scandalous entry was quickly seized upon by Shelley's enemies in England, particularly Robert Southey.

Miss M. W. Godwin and Miss Clermont . . . Mr Godwin: Mary Wollstonecraft Godwin, who began *Frankenstein* as her contribution to the ghost story contest of June 1816; she married Shelley in December of that same year. Claire Clairmont became Byron's mistress immediately before he left England in April 1816; their daughter Allegra was born in January 1817. William Godwin, best known for his *An Enquiry Concerning Political Justice* (1793) and the terror novel *Caleb Williams* (1794), was Mary's father and Claire's step-father. In early June 1816, Mary, Claire, and Shelley lived in a little cottage called the Maison Chappuis, about an eight-minute walk up a hill to Byron's Villa Diodati.

German work . . . Phantasmagoriana: according to Mary Shelley in her 1831 Introduction to *Frankenstein*, the party read 'some volumes of ghost stories, translated from the German into French'. The work in question is *Fantasmagoriana, ou recueil d'histoires d'apparitions de spectres, revenans, fantômes, etc.; traduit de l'allemand, par un amateur* (Paris, 1812) translated by Jean-Baptiste-Benoît Eyriès from the first two volumes of the five-volume *Gespensterbuch* (1811–15), edited by Friedrich

Schulze and Johann Apel (Mary Shelley, *Frankenstein*, ed. Marilyn Butler (Oxford, 1994), 194).

240 *Christabel... destroy the impression*: Samuel Taylor Coleridge's 'Christabel', composed between 1798 and 1801, and first published, with Byron's help, in May 1816. The lines which terrified Shelley read as follows:

> Beneath the lamp the lady bow'd,
> And slowly roll'd her eyes around;
> Then drawing in her breath aloud,
> Like one that shudder'd, she unbound
> The cincture from beneath her breast:
> Her silken robe, and inner vest,
> Dropt to her feet, and full in view,
> Behold! her bosom and half her side—
> A sight to dream of, not to tell!
> And she is to sleep by Christabel.

In his *Diary*, Polidori gives a more lurid eyewitness account of the same incident (S. T. Coleridge, *Christabel* (London, 1816), 17–18; Rossetti, *Diary*, 128).

ebauches: rough sketches.

Tale of Dr ——... *our readers.*—*ED.*: this seems to announce Colburn's intention to publish Polidori's only full-length novel *Ernestus Berchtold, or The Modern Oedipus* (1819), which, like *The Vampyre*, had its origins in the ghost story competition of June 1816. In the event, *Berchtold* was published by another firm.

241 *London Journal... Hungary*: this account of Arnold Paul appeared in the *London Journal* for 11 March 1732. Paul was the most famous vampire of the eighteenth century, and details of his case were endlessly reprinted.

242 *the 'Giaour'*: see Byron, *Complete Poetical Works*, iii. 64–5.

243 *Mr Southey... whilst in existence*: Robert Southey's *Thalaba the Destroyer* (1801) introduced the vampire into English literature. In the opening stanzas of book VIII, Oneiza, daughter of Moath and lover of Thalaba, is discovered to be demonically possessed, and when Thalaba hesitates to strike her,

> Moath firm of heart,
> Performed the bidding; thro' the vampire corpse
> He thrust his lance; it fell,

> And howling with the wound,
>   Its demon tenant fled.
> A sapphire light fell on them,
> And garmented with glory, in their sight
>   Oneiza's Spirit stood.

243 *Tournefort . . . and Calmet*: French botanist Joseph Pitton de Tournefort, whose *Relation d'un Voyage du Levant* (1702) was the eighteenth century's first account of vampirism, and contains an extended eyewitness description of the dissection of a Greek *vrykolakas*. Dom Augustin Calmet was one of the most famous biblical scholars of his day, as well as the leading eighteenth-century authority on vampires; his *Dissertations sur les apparitions des anges, des démons & des esprits, et sur les revenans et vampires de Hongrie, de Boheme, de Moravie & de Silesie* (1746) cites more than five hundred 'documented' cases of vampirism.

Appendix C: Augustus Darvell

248 *hectic*: a consumptive fever.

Ephesus and Sardis: like Smyrna (see note to p. 16 above), ancient cities of Asia Minor, now Turkey.

serrugee and a single janizary: serrugee: a driver in charge of the post-horses; janizary: a Turkish soldier, often used as an armed escort for tourists.

249 *caravansera*: inn or travellers' hostel.

250 *a stork, with a snake in her beak*: this image is an ancient one, and possibly of Jewish origin. Cf. Nietzsche in *Daybreak* (1881): 'the Christian of the Middle Ages . . . *supposes* he is no longer going to escape "eternal torment." Dreadful portents appear to him: perhaps a stork holding a snake in its beak but *hesitating* to swallow it' (*Daybreak*, trans. R. J. Hollingdale (Cambridge, 1982), 46).

251 *ataghan*: see note to p. 16 above.

THE OXFORD SHERLOCK HOLMES

ARTHUR CONAN DOYLE   **The Adventures of Sherlock Holmes**
The Case-Book of Sherlock Holmes
His Last Bow
The Hound of the Baskervilles
The Memoirs of Sherlock Holmes
The Return of Sherlock Holmes
The Valley of Fear
Sherlock Holmes Stories
The Sign of the Four
A Study in Scarlet

The Oxford World's Classics Website

www.worldsclassics.co.uk

- Information about new titles
- Explore the full range of Oxford World's Classics
- Links to other literary sites and the main OUP webpage
- Imaginative competitions, with bookish prizes
- Peruse *Compass*, the Oxford World's Classics magazine
- Articles by editors
- Extracts from Introductions
- A forum for discussion and feedback on the series
- Special information for teachers and lecturers

www.worldsclassics.co.uk

American Literature

British and Irish Literature

Children's Literature

Classics and Ancient Literature

Colonial Literature

Eastern Literature

European Literature

History

Medieval Literature

Oxford English Drama

Poetry

Philosophy

Politics

Religion

The Oxford Shakespeare

A complete list of Oxford Paperbacks, including Oxford World's Classics, OPUS, Past Masters, Oxford Authors, Oxford Shakespeare, Oxford Drama, and Oxford Paperback Reference, is available in the UK from the Academic Division Publicity Department, Oxford University Press, Great Clarendon Street, Oxford OX2 6DP.

In the USA, complete lists are available from the Paperbacks Marketing Manager, Oxford University Press, 198 Madison Avenue, New York, NY 10016.

Oxford Paperbacks are available from all good bookshops. In case of difficulty, customers in the UK can order direct from Oxford University Press Bookshop, Freepost, 116 High Street, Oxford OX1 4BR, enclosing full payment. Please add 10 per cent of published price for postage and packing.